Marrying Mozart

STEPHANIE COWELL

Marrying Mozart

A NOVEL

VIKING

VIKING

Published by the Penguin Group

Penguin Group (USA) Inc., 375 Hudson Street,
New York, New York, 10014, U.S.A.
Penguin Books Ltd, 80 Strand, London WC2R oRL, England
Penguin Books Australia Ltd, 250 Camberwell Road, Camberwell, Victoria 3124, Australia
Penguin Books Canada Ltd, 10 Alcorn Avenue, Toronto, Ontario, Canada M4V 3B2
Penguin Books India (P) Ltd, 11 Community Centre, Panchsheel Park,
New Delhi - 110 017, India
Penguin Books (N.Z.) Ltd, Cnr Rosedale and Airborne Roads, Albany,
Auckland, New Zealand
Penguin Books (South Africa) (Pty) Ltd, 24 Sturdee Avenue,
Rosebank, Johannesburg 2196, South Africa

Penguin Books Ltd, Registered Offices:
80 Strand, London WC2R oRL, England

First published in 2004 by Viking Penguin,
a member of Penguin Group (USA) Inc.

1   3   5   7   9   10   8   6   4   2

Publisher's Note: This is a work of fiction. Names, characters, places, and incidents either are
the product of the author's imagination or are used fictitiously, and any resemblance to actual
persons, living or dead, business establishments, events, or locales is entirely coincidental.

LIBRARY OF CONGRESS CATALOGING-IN-PUBLICATION DATA
Cowell, Stephanie.
Marrying Mozart : a novel / by Stephanie Cowell.
p.   cm.
ISBN 0-670-03268-9 (alk. paper)
1. Mozart, Wolfgang Amadeus, 1756–1791—Fiction.   2. Mozart, Constanze, 1763–1842—
Fiction.   3. Mannheim (Germany)—Fiction.   4. Composers' spouses—Fiction.
5. Weber family—Fiction.   6. Composers—Fiction.   7. Sisters—Fiction.   I. Title.
PS3553.O898M37 2003
813'.54—dc21   2003052546

This book is printed on acid-free paper. ∞

Printed in the United States of America
Set in Adobe Garamond   Designed by Francesca Belanger

for Russell,
in a time
of joy

*"Questo giorno di tormenti, di capricci e di follia,
in contenti e in allegria solo amor può terminar."*

"This day of difficulties, impulse, and silliness
 can only conclude in happy contentment through love."

from Mozart's *Le Nozze di Figaro,* Finale Act Four
first performance, Vienna 1786

ACKNOWLEDGMENTS

Thanks to my husband, Russell Clay, for his love, encouragement, literary advice, and companionship during the writing of this book; to my agent, Emma Sweeney; and to my editor, Carole DeSanti, for her understanding of my artistic vision and her sensitive editing, which helped to shape the manuscript; also to associate editor Karen Murphy and the whole Viking team. Special thanks to my younger son, filmmaker/editor Jesse Cowell, who named the novel in a moment of inspiration.

Others who read through drafts and made the novel richer by their historical and artistic comments include Katherine Kirkpatrick, Sally Lowe Whitehead, Elsa Okon Rael, Christine Emmert, Judith Ackerman, Ellen Beschler, and Richard Somerset Ward. Dr. Jean Houston came into my life in time to read a partial early draft, and gave me an irreplaceable spiritual gift from the generosity of her heart. Thanks to my father and stepmother, Jimmy and Viraja Mathieu, who first took me to Salzburg. It was Viraja who introduced me to the Mozart family letters.

Others who extended me their help in the particular

journey of this book are Sandra Scofield, Mary Cunnane, Sebastian Ritscher, Madeleine L'Engle, John Kavanaugh, Lori Lettieri, Alice Tufel, Phil Milito, Renee Cafiero, and Bob Blumenfeld. My love to my older son, James Nordstrom, his wife, Jessica, and my granddaughters; my sister Jennie, her husband, Jerry, and son, David; and my husband's large and warm family, particularly Eugenia Head. I am enriched by the support of my colleagues at work; the clergy, parishioners, staff, and musicians of my church, St. Thomas Church Fifth Avenue; and all the sisters of the Community of the Holy Spirit.

The genesis of this novel occurred in my adolescence when I fell in love with Mozart's operas and spent many a cold winter's afternoon waiting on line for tickets to the old Metropolitan Opera House. Those years, and my years as an opera singer, include friends with whom I sang a great deal of Mozart. They are too many to list, but I do thank them for what we shared.

Marrying Mozart

Sophie Weber, February 1842, Salzburg

IFOUND MY SISTER'S WEDDING HAT TODAY IN A ROUND box of thin wood at the bottom of my wardrobe. The white velvet had discolored, but there were the flowers I myself had fastened, now as fragile as old paper. Sixty years ago I had pinned the hat on her soft hair when she married the young Mozart.

There were letters as well under the hat when I lifted it, but I didn't read them, only sat with the hat on my wide skirts for a time. The afternoon passed; I can't say how. It was a short winter afternoon such as we have in Austria, light dulled and curtains half drawn against the noise of carriages and horses in the street below. My landlady's little girl brought candles early. The child looks in on me often, as does her mother, because I'm old and heavy, walk short distances with great effort, and need someone to bring meals and take away the chamber pot.

Though I have not been away from my rooms in many years, I'm not alone. Visitors come. A few days ago an Englishman came. He knocked hopefully at the door, gazing curiously at me, addressing me with respect, wanting to know what I remember of my sisters and what we were to that then obscure young composer who came into our lives.

"You are one of the four Weber sisters," he said quietly.

"Yes, monsieur, I am."

"The ones for whom he wrote music and whom he knew so intimately? Madame, I'm so moved. I plan to stay a time in Austria and would like to visit at your convenience. Would you speak with me? Would you be so very kind?"

He said he was a biographer. He has not yet returned, but he will.

Not yet, not yet, but in a little time I will put the box away, and perhaps tomorrow, when I am not so tired, I will look at the letters. Some are from her, most from him. What do I remember? Oh, very much. But I am trembling a little. I will have to use my cane.

I rise slowly. For a moment I close my eyes, and my dusty, small, darkish room fades from me, as does my heavy body, and I am again with my sisters tumbled together with our mother and father in the fifth-floor rooms we rented on a side street in Mannheim. I can hear music, laughter, the pouring of wine. It is Thursday evening, musicians are coming to play, and there is our Mozart as he climbed the stairs for the first time. It was on a Thursday; it must have been on a Thursday. I was eleven years old, wearing a white pinafore over my dark dress, the youngest of the household. . . .

PART ONE

Mannheim and the Webers,

1777

*U*p five flights of cracking wood steps of a modest town house in the city of Mannheim, Fridolin Weber stood peering over his candle, which cast a dim light down the rounded banister below. "Mind the broken step," he called convivially to his visitors. "Come this way, come this way."

Of middle years, he was a lean man but for a small round stomach under his vest, and he wore a long coat to his knees and mended white cotton hose to his breech buckles. His lank graying hair was caught with a frayed black ribbon at his neck and hung limply down his back. He craned his long neck to see down the stairs.

Behind him, the front parlor of the cramped apartment had been dusted, polished, and abundantly lit with eight candles. There, near the clavier, his four daughters, age eleven to nineteen, stood dressed in their best ordinary gowns, hair glistening with curls that one hour before had been tightly wrapped in rags. It was Thursday. Things somehow always turned out well on Thursday evenings when friends came.

The rest of the rooms were dark, except for the fire in the kitchen, for all the candles were in here. The parlor had been tidied, and a shawl draped over the clavier; all the music had been sorted in neat heaps on the floor. Weber's corpulent wife, Maria Caecilia, emerged from the kitchen as if she had not been baking there for hours, and stood by his side, murmuring the words he knew she would speak. "There won't be enough wine. Your cousin Alfonso drinks like a fish."

"Pour small glasses," he said, squeezing her arm, and then, turning to the dark stair again, called down happily, "Yes, come up, come up, dear friends—I've been waiting for you."

From the darkness of the stair emerged Heinemann, a violinist from court, extending his always damp hands, and balding Cousin Alfonso, who wore his wig only for his cello performances. The four girls stood nudging one another, whispering, curtseying. Their hands were a little worn and pricked from washing and sewing. There was about them the scent of youth, youth that, with a little soap and a clean petticoat, was as fresh as flowers.

Wine was poured in small glasses, and two more musicians arrived. Every now and then Fridolin Weber peered through the window down to the street. He knew everybody, everything. He knew the world of music especially, because he copied it page after page for a small fee. In addition, he was a versatile musician. For what occasion had he not played his half-dozen instruments at which he was adequately proficient, or poured forth his meager, congenial, slightly hoarse singing voice? But he was modest, his narrow shoulders rounded.

"Who else do you expect this Thursday, Weber?" asked Alfonso, already enjoying his third glass of wine. "You seem to be waiting. Is it Grossmeyer, the choirmaster? He had rehearsal this night, I thought."

"Some new friends, recommended to me—a matron from Salzburg and her twenty-one-year-old son, who has composed a great deal already." He leaned against the window frame to look down, and then drew in his breath with pleasure. "Perhaps that . . . yes, that must be them. They're making their way to the door below." Negotiating among chairs, music stands, and guests, he crossed the room and opened the door to the landing once again. The cold breeze whisked into the room, and the candles fluttered. "Come up, come up," he cried.

An ample-busted woman with a long mournful face under her piled hair appeared panting on the top step. Behind her, trying to slow his climb in consideration, was her son, a pale young man with large eyes and a large nose, somewhat below middle height but neatly made with supple hands beneath his lace cuffs.

"Frau Mozart, a pleasure, and Herr Mozart, I presume?"

"You're most gracious to invite us," replied Frau Mozart.

In a flurry of consultation the four girls disappeared into another room and returned with two more chairs that they offered, and Weber himself brought more wine. Introductions were made, and bows exchanged. Frau Mozart balanced her wine cautiously on her knee. She wore no rouge, and she gathered her dark skirts closely, as if wanting to leave as little of them as possible flowing about her; her mouth was compressed like a tightly drawn purse. She looked into every corner of the room, taking in the piles of music and the few sconces without candles.

Weber rubbed his hands and rocked back and forth in his

pleasure. "Do I understand you've arrived from Salzburg just two weeks ago? And that your husband is employed there as musician by the Archbishop's court?"

"Indeed, sir; we've come here looking for greater opportunities for my son."

"Why, there are opportunities enough here, Alfonso will tell you. I copy, I compose a little, I play several instruments. If music is wanted, I'm there to make it." All this time Herr Mozart said nothing, but looked about the room seriously, bowing when he caught someone's eye.

Cakes and coffee came; the wondrous fragrance of the hot beverage stirred with cinnamon and cream filled the rooms. Weber would not stint on his Thursday evenings, not even if they had nothing but porridge for three days following, thick and lumpy, with no sugar and only third-quality milk.

"Now we'll have music," Fridolin Weber cried when the cake lay in crumbs on coat fronts and across the parlor floor. "What's an evening without music? Alfonso, have you brought parts for your new trio? Come, come."

At once the four girls clustered against the wall to make room, while Weber, with a sweep of his coattails, sat down at the clavier and candles were moved to illuminate the music. The sound of strings and clavier soared through the small chamber, Fridolin Weber playing deftly, nodding, exclaiming at passages that pleased him. They finished the last movement with a great sweep of Heinemann's bow, after which he lay his violin on his knee, perspiring and wearing a great smile. Some other brief pieces followed, and then Weber stood and called, "And will you play something as well, Herr Mozart?"

The young man leapt up to the clavier; he pushed back his cuffs and began a sonata andante with variations. Each successive variation gathered in depth. Weber leaned forward. There was a rare delicacy to the young man's playing, and an unusual strength in his left hand, which made the musicians look at one another. Heinemann grinned, showing small, darkened teeth. He sat breathing through his mouth, fingers drumming on his breeches above the buckle.

Maria Caecilia Weber maneuvered her full skirts through the crowded room, refilling the coffee cups. She glanced briefly at the man with little white hands who played with such concentrated intimacy, noting that when a spoon she carried clattered to the floor, his shoulders stiffened slightly, and he did not lower them again for a few minutes.

The music ended as abruptly as it had begun, and both Alfonso and Heinemann rose to their feet clapping firmly. The young man's face was still absorbed, as if he barely noticed the small parlor with its shadowy gathering. He said in his light tenor voice, "A fine instrument, Herr Weber. It reminds me of one I knew in London when I was there years ago as a boy. The Tschudi clavier. My sister and I played a duet on it; it had a remarkable mechanism for color and volume."

"Sir, I thank you," replied Fridolin, rubbing his hands. "If an instrument could have a soul, mine does. Yes, yes, whatever you all may say, we know it. We all know it. You're a gifted player! With what piece have you favored us? One of your own, I trust?"

Mozart's large eyes were now almost playful, and he kept a few fingers on the raised clavier lid as if unwilling to leave it. "The last movement of a sonata I wrote in Munich a few years back. I've some themes for another sonata for the daughter of Herr Cannabich, your orchestral director here. Though young, she's gifted."

"But you know Cannabich? We all play with him from time to time," Fridolin said, while Alfonso poured another glass of wine and hooted loudly. Now by a sudden waver of candlelight Fridolin could see that the young man's face was faintly scarred with smallpox, old marks likely from childhood. Fridolin glanced at Frau Mozart's stolid expression, thinking how she must have worried and suffered! It was God's mercy, he thought, that his own lovely girls had not been afflicted.

He cried, "Another cup of coffee, come!"

The last drop of coffee was sipped; the last piece of chamber music ended. Then the two older sisters, Josefa and Aloysia, wound their arms about each other's waist and began a duet. Both voices were very high, but Josefa's had darker tones. From the corner the two younger girls watched the rise and fall of their sisters' full breasts, heard the quick fioritura, sighed at the higher notes that rang round and round the little room.

Heinemann shook his head with pleasure. "In such parlors all over Europe, young girls are singing," he said. "It's an art every cultivated woman learns, yet none I believe can do so with more grace than your daughters, dear Weber."

"Sir, I thank you," replied Weber in a low voice.

The chiming of a clock some streets away announced that the hour of eleven had come. The guests thanked their host several times and descended; Fridolin Weber, easily made gay with a little wine, held the stub of the candle for them. "Good night, good night!" he called as they went forth onto the streets of Mannheim.

Husband and wife cleared away the glasses and retreated, yawning, to their bedchamber, which was furnished with a large iron bedstead, some trunks, a wardrobe, and a dark portrait of Christ as a child. Maria Caecilia Weber sank down on the mattress edge, which sagged beneath her; she had already removed her corset and pulled on her wool sleeping gown. She was now winding her hair in rags, her swollen fingers deftly dipping each rag first in the warm, milky broth of a cracked cup. "You and your old friends," she muttered. "Alfonso never returns the invitations; we never eat at his expense."

"What does that matter?" replied Fridolin as he undressed. The last small candle flickered in the mirror, revealing his thin legs as he sighed a little to pull off his stockings.

"As far as the young man and his mother are concerned, they haven't any money, that's clear. 'What else does he compose?' I asked the good woman, and she puffed out her bosom and murmured, 'Everything!'—as if we should welcome another composer when there are two to be found under every market stall. Did you notice how much cake and wine they consumed, as if they made their dinner from it? Can't you find any better people to invite? Is this how you look out for the future of your poor girls? What will happen to them? How will they find husbands without dowries? Do you ever plan for the future? How can you provide for four girls on the salary of a music copyist and second tenor in the chapel choir?" Having finished her hair, she flopped heavily into a reclining position on the feather mattress that had been part of her own dowry long ago.

"Soft, soft," her husband said. "You see, pigeon, it's not all that bad; what does it matter if we're poor? We have music and friendship. And they sing beautifully."

"What will that gain them?" came her voice from the pillow. She raised her head and looked at her husband intensely. "Fridolin, listen to me. You know what happened to my own two sisters, my beautiful sisters! Little Gretchen. You remember the story."

"I can't forget it; it means so much to you."

"Youth doesn't last forever; they must understand it. And the older two are certainly of an age to be betrothed."

"Yes, yes, my love," he said, pulling on his nightcap and stretching out next to her. "That's wise and true. He plays well, that young man; I believe he has plans for an opera."

Maria Caecilia had fallen silent, only vaguely aware of her husband's callused fingertips on her breast and his yawns. She thought of the beauty of her four daughters as they stood by candlelight in the parlor. "Fridolin," she whispered. "They aren't ordinary girls; there is nothing ordinary about them. I have my plans for them. I have my plans."

But her husband was asleep.

*I*n the Webers' apartment on the fifth story of the old stone house in Mannheim, there were, other than the tiny parlor and dining room, a kitchen and two sleeping chambers, each also small. In the second stood two more iron bed stands with torn hangings, each narrow enough for one girl yet, out of necessity, sleeping two. A print of Caecilia, the patron saint of music, eyes raised to heaven and delicately playing a viola, was hung on one wall, while chemises and petticoats dangled everywhere from hooks. To get to the door of the room, you had to climb over one of the beds.

Dawn was coming, creeping through the window over the four lovely girls, still in dreams, none yet twenty, half naked: nightdresses fallen from plump, clear shoulders, pulled up high on downy thighs. The warm scent of perspiration, of old gowns, of sensuality blossoming like a garden. Four girls trying to be beautiful on a few yards of good cloth, two pendants from their late, mourned grandmother, and an insufficient number of much mended white hose.

With the first light the eldest, Josefa, sat up, her brown hair in tangled curls. She climbed over Aloysia, making the bed groan with her plumpness, her bare thighs as soft as warm bread beneath her old nightdress, and then climbed even less carefully over the feet of the smaller girls. Six o'clock by the church clock, and they had not gone to bed until one. She stretched to her full height, which made her head nearly touch the sloping ceiling, arching back her full shoulders. Oh, why was it her turn to begin the day? The first clavier pupil came at seven, and father must have his coffee and an ironed shirt.

In the kitchen she coaxed a fire and put the heavy iron on the grate to heat. Outside the small window she could see the milk wagon. Little Sophie was to run down and make sure they had fresh milk for the day; if Sophie didn't, Josefa wouldn't for certain. Nothing woke her Sophie, the sloth. Well, they would have dry bread and no milk; it was not her concern. And it was the turn of Aloysia, who thought herself above such things, to trudge down to the common cistern to empty the chamber pots for the refuse collector.

Beyond the church spires, the sky was growing light.

Josefa spat on the iron to test its readiness, sprinkled the shirt with water from a bowl, and began to iron fiercely, the muscles in her firm arm working. What a life, she thought. Always having to pretend you have money when you don't; isn't that the way it is? How to bring them from their precarious existence where they were always late with the rent? It had concerned her the past few years since she had begun to understand that none of her darling father's musical endeavors had yet lifted them from the edge of poverty.

She pressed the iron's nose firmly into the rough linen of the sleeve where it was set into the body, beginning to hum an aria from one of Piccinni's popular operas, and then to sing more fully, her rich tones ringing through the small rooms.

From the half-open door of the bedroom came Aloysia's more silvery voice. "Oh shut up, shut up, shut up. I need sleep."

"*You* need sleep! You took up more than half of the bed last night; you always do. You're always squeezing me out, and this morning there wasn't any room, and I couldn't move you, you lump, you cow."

"No decent person should have to sleep with you, Josefa, the way you toss and turn and shout things in your dreams! I want a bed of my own."

"Well, you'll never have one. You'll be married soon enough to some brute who'll *never* let you sleep."

Josefa put down the iron and ran to the bedroom door, where now both Aloysia and Constanze had raised their heads from their pillows, and were looking bewildered at their angry eldest sister. Sitting up, arms half covering her naked little breast where her gown had slipped away, the delicate Aloysia declared, "I'd rather sleep with Constanze; let's change. She'll come to me; you sleep with Sophie."

The iron sizzled, and Josefa rushed back, but it was only the cloth of the board. She began to iron again while Aloysia entered the kitchen and opened the cupboard for bread, her feet bare and her hair tumbled down her back. By this time only Sophie was still in bed, for she was seldom disturbed by anything.

Aloysia began to grind the coffee beans.

"I know something you don't," she said airily. "We're singing this evening. Father told me last night after the guests left. We're singing at the Countess's, two duets and then a solo each. Constanze must let me have her lace."

"Are you sure we're engaged to sing?" asked Josefa, at once practical. "How much will they pay us?"

"The saints alone know. If they think you're pretty, maybe they'll give extra. Don't let any of the men feel you. Mama says they will try for sure in those places, so you must be careful, for you don't want to be damaged."

The remainder of the household began to stir. Fridolin came out with moderately hairy legs showing under his shirt and said he was so weary he could die. The last up was Maria Caecilia, the bed creaking as she rose to her hasty breakfast. At seven the pupil, an impoverished lawyer in a threadbare coat, arrived, and as the sound of his excruciating mistakes echoed through the fifth-story rooms, the four sisters disappeared to their bedchamber to discuss what the eldest two could wear that night.

Somewhat before the hour of nine, fourteen-year-old Constanze, having lent her lace and pearl pin, leaned out the parlor window to watch her father and older sisters rattle down the dark street in a hired carriage. The excitement rose from the dust of the wheels and floated up and through her. It was her sisters' third time to sing before good Mannheim society; on the last occasion a kind butler had sent them home with napkins full of sweet cakes and oranges, and Aloysia and Josefa had sat up by candlelight until past two describing the chandeliers, the livery of footmen, the rich wide gowns of the women, and all the faces staring stupidly at them.

Constanze looked about the room, which smelled of burned candles.

Papa had given them all lessons. As early as she could recall, he had lined them up by the clavier according to age, his sharp, stubbly chin nodding, the worn white lacing of his shirt trembling, his fragile veined left hand conducting the air while his right hand played the ivory keys, which were tuned regularly and almost always in perfect pitch. They sang in Italian, the language in which almost all fashionable songs were written. When Fridolin was drunk, however, he sang bawdy songs in German, gathered her squealing to his lap, and told her she was his cabbage, his dumpling.

She remembered standing there all little and chubby, barely reaching the clavier, while her two older sisters, still little girls themselves, pushed and shoved each other under the portrait of the Virgin and Child near high dusty windows that overlooked the street. Sophie was then only a mewling infant; but Josefa had put forth her voice boldly, and Aloysia sang like a lark. Aloysia never had to work at singing, whereas Constanze always struggled. Her notes came tentatively as she gazed from under her lashes at her beloved Papa. She didn't want to sing; she wanted to please him.

Recently, Josefa and Aloysia had sung without her.

Something rustled, and she heard bare feet on the squeaking floorboards. Turning, she could see Sophie, who at nearly twelve was still quite shapeless, heading toward her across the room past the many chairs and piles of music. The edges of the girl's nose were red, and her eyes watery, but her face bore the same freckled, unperturbed look she had worn since the age of two. Even now as always Constanze could hear the homey click of Sophie's wood rosary beads, which the girl kept in her pocket. Sophie was devout. She had at least ten saints to whom she lisped prayers in a litany at bedtime, lulling the others to sleep; she had the hierarchy of saints and angels and cherubim in her head, and could draw you a picture (the figures blurred and clumsy) on the back of a discarded sheet of music of the throne of God if you wanted to know exactly what it looked like.

She was also nearsighted; yesterday, returning from the candle and soap shop, she had mistook a tall nun for a priest, curtseying and murmuring, "Good day, Father," to the suppressed laughter of her three older sisters. Plans to purchase her spectacles had been discussed.

"Are you waiting up?" she whispered to Constanze. "The bed's cold without you." She slid her arm around her sister. "I'm glad I don't have to go sing; I sound like a sick frog. But you don't mind not going, Stanzi?"

"No, I don't like strange people staring at me."

They huddled closer, peering down at the dark street, Sophie rubbing her bare feet against each other for warmth, for the fire had long gone out.

Sophie said, "It's so cold for October! I heard Papa say it's going to be a snowy winter; I love snow falling. It makes me feel safe to be here when it falls. The butcher told Aloysia we'd have our first snow long before Christmas."

"He's always telling her things as he wraps the sausages. He can't keep his eyes from her. I think I saw her reading a note this morning on the scrap paper; maybe it was from him."

"Perhaps it wasn't a love note," said Sophie. "Perhaps it was a list of the dresses she'd like; she's always making those. She looks in shop windows and writes them down."

"No, I'm certain it was a love note, but we don't have to worry. Aly won't marry a butcher: never. She just likes to flirt." Constanze peered out into the night at a single horse trotting by. "You know Mama doesn't want us to marry anyone in trade and live a plain life, as she puts it, with only one good dress for church and that not trimmed. She wants us to marry as high as we can, or at least she hopes Aly will. She hopes she'll marry someone who is at least asked to dine in the Elector's palace, maybe even a baron. I heard her and Father in the kitchen earlier today, speaking about it the way they do. She says such a marriage could be made even if the girl has no dowry, if she has charm and beauty."

Sophie propped her elbows on the windowsill, her face serious. "Yes, and she was also quarreling with Papa earlier about Aloysia and Josefa's going out to sing at all. She says it cheapens a woman to sing in public. You know, of course, what Papa answered! Serious and sad, looking off as he does when he's crossing her. He said that it's only until our fortunes increase, that they are safe as holy sisters and no man dares come within ten feet of them!"

Constanze stroked the long window draperies reflectively. As long as she could remember, she had lived in a house full of girls who loved to chatter and bicker. Her mother held opinions about everything, whether she knew that subject or not; and her father's philosophical friends weekly settled the world's problems over a few bottles of wine, shouting and waving their hands. In the midst of all this she seldom offered an opinion but to Sophie, who had been placed in her arms smelling of milk when she was but a day old, and to whom, even then, she told everything.

Now they snuggled close, rubbing their feet together. Constanze knew every angle of Sophie's little body, having slept with her since the age of five. They shared secrets; she never told her mother about the mangy neighborhood cats and dogs Sophie fed, hiding food in her apron and slipping down the stairs.

Staring out into the street, along which only an old sentry walked, swinging his lantern, she said thoughtfully, "I suppose Aloysia might end up marrying a prince; she's so beautiful. Even Uncle Thorwart, who's been in and out of the best houses, says it."

"Beauty's a temporal gift," replied Sophie, "whereas the real treasures are of the soul."

"Beauty's more useful in the world. I wish I had it, and I know Josefa does."

"Josefa's soul is beautiful." Sophie raised her freckled face, her nearsighted expression making her look as if she had a clear insight into life. An old soul, her paternal grandmother had once called her.

Constanze sighed. "You're right, but our Josy stands inches over almost every man, and she doesn't keep quiet; she blurts things out. She loves books, not people, and she breaks all the nice things she has. The fan she holds when she sings tonight will be in splinters because she'll twist it and twist it during the hard parts of the songs. I hope not, because Cousin Alfonso's wife gave it to Aloysia last New Year's. There will be a fight again, and they'll be at each other's throats. I hate that, and it kills Papa."

"Mama's family were farmers before they became very prosperous, and she says Josefa takes after them," Sophie replied, "and that she wishes Josefa had stopped growing but of course she couldn't help that. How can anyone help growing?" The two girls rubbed feet again. "Mama could have been a lady if she hadn't fallen in love with Papa; she says that every time they quarrel. They still had their family fortune then before most of it was lost. But you *do* have beauty, Stanzi; your eyes are beautiful, and your face has a lovely heart shape."

"No man ever died of love for a woman's eyes."

"Well, then, your soul's beautiful just like Josefa's, and that's worth having."

"How would you know? You're not twelve yet; you've hardly been in the world! You can hardly know what's worth having and what's not."

"I see things. I know things. I sit in a corner making dumplings and observe. I've observed you all forever."

Constanze smiled suddenly, her dark eyes soft; it was a sweet, reflective young smile. In the dark parlor surrounded by the closed clavier, the piles of music, and the many books, she felt very comfortable. The heavy book on the lives of great dead composers was sliding off the others and any moment might fall to the floor. It's best that Aloysia and Josefa keep singing, she thought. Perhaps then we'll have more money so Mama won't worry as much and then we'll have hot creamy chocolate every single morning. But why do they want things to be another way? Aren't we happy the way we are now when we gather about the table and all talk at once about music pupils, mother's family's silver before they lost it, court gossip, and what's new at the small theater? Or the way we are on

Thursdays, when all the people I love best come up the stairs? Don't they know that the only important thing is that all of us remain together forever? Papa holds us together, and Mama, and I will, as well. This is my place. I'll hold us together by my love.

Her hand tightened on the windowsill; she breathed deeply once and held on as if she suddenly understood the depth of the promise she had just made.

But the next moment she was a child again, looking up at her mother who had just appeared at the parlor door in her huge white nightdress. "Why are you up? Come to bed, my little fleas," Maria Caecilia said.

"We couldn't sleep! Just a time longer. We want to wait up for them."

Their mother's contralto was benevolent. "Drape your quilt around you then. Stanzi, I will never forget how ill you were when you were a little girl. Every time you cough I shudder." The voice dropped to the low warning she used to tell one of her fearful stories. "My dearest friend as a girl always stood by windows. My saintly friend Therese. It was when our family still had our best silver. And she caught a consumption, and died young."

"I thought you said she recovered."

"Nothing could save her. You are lucky to be so healthy, whereas my sisters, my poor sisters!" She sighed. Constanze squirmed a little, hoping that the story would not be related once again this evening. It was hard to pay attention to stories that had interested you in the first telling, but grew unbearably dull after time.

But their mother demurred. "Fetch your quilts." She yawned,

and her voice trailed back at them as she moved heavily down the hall. "Ah, why do they always stay away so long when they sing? But perhaps if the Blessed Virgin wills it, someone will notice their beauty this evening."

As their mother departed, Sophie stared down at the floor, the corner of her mouth beginning to twitch. "Our aunts," she whispered. "I forgot to tell you before! A letter came today. They're coming for Christmas."

Constanze covered her own mouth with both hands. "Oh Sophie, when have they not come for Christmas? The ridiculous old things huffing up the stairs panting, 'Blessed Saint Elizabeth!' 'Blessed Virgin Mary!' 'Blessed Saint Joseph!' "

They began to giggle, flinging themselves on the sofa and stuffing their faces against the pillows to smother the sound. Their mother's sisters were old, had always been old; when the world was created they were old. There was Elizabeth with her contradictory stories, who kept holy relics in her purse and pressed them against her nieces' foreheads. And Gretchen, who was simpleminded, though no one admitted it; they claimed it was merely bad memory brought on by some obscure sorrow. Both ate a great deal and were so fat that they did indeed have increasing difficulty in climbing the stairs, taking longer each year. Constanze had kept a record for the last three Christmastides.

Now from the depths of the pillow cushion Constanze gasped, "Oh what will they bring us this time! Dresses six years too small for us, moth-eaten shawls that stink of mildew! And they think bathing's unhealthy so they never do it! Thank God we never have to go to their house."

Sophie raised her shiny face and whispered, "No, they always come here; it's been years since we went to Zell, where Mama and Papa lived and where they met. But it's not nice to laugh at others. I'll have to tell it in confession. I try not to, but you know, they're . . . so . . ."

". . . stupid . . . and Papa says . . ."

". . . they smell like . . ."

Now they were shrieking, and only their mother's sharp call from down the hall made them stifle their laughter; but tears ran down their cheeks, and they careened into the pile of books, which finally tumbled onto the floor. Poking each other, they marched with contorted faces to fetch their quilts. When they could stop laughing but for a hiccup now and then, they knelt by the window, still not daring to look at each other, and shared a cup of cold, grainy coffee between them. The street wavered before Constanze's eyes, and she lost track of how many times the sentry passed.

Hours later they were awoken as the two older sisters burst into the room and opened the wicker basket they carried. Fruits and little creamy chocolates rolled across the top of the music table by the ink pot, and their father happily cried, "A triumph, a triumph!"

igh among the roofs, chimneys, and church spires of Mannheim that very same evening, Wolfgang Mozart, the

Webers' guest from the night before, sat in the smaller of the two garret rooms he and his mother had rented, writing the closing rondeau of a flute concerto. Chewing his lip, he hunched forward, the edges of his fingers inky, humming, now and then tapping his feet. He was so utterly engrossed, he knew nothing but the rapid dancing of the solo flute that flowed out from his mind through his fingers. The solitary candle sloped from the draft. Quickly his pen moved up and down the lines of music, filling in all the instrumental parts. Though the room was cool, he was hot as he worked, and had thrown off his coat. His old shirt was open down his delicate neck.

"Wolfgang," came the murmur from the other room. "Wolferl?"

He grasped the pen, the small black marks on the page rushing forth, ink seeping onto his fingertips and into the crevices of his nails. His mother's voice called again. "Wolfgang, do you hear? Are you still working on that Dutchman's commission?"

He flung the words over his shoulder: "I'm well into the last movement."

His mother coughed; and then, "You won't make the flute part too difficult, will you, dear? He *is* an amateur, remember, and he does have pride."

Mozart glanced down at the plethora of rapid notes. "Oh, he'll manage to breathe somewhere," he muttered, and for a moment he wondered where and how.

"For Christ's sake, don't catch a chill," Frau Mozart called.

The rapid movement that had been inside his head was now

slowly fading; it had flowed from his mind and now lay in cramped, rapid penmanship on the music staves before him. How many hours had he worked? He never remembered. *If only I could finish it all tonight,* he thought. The whole commission, second quartet, both concerti. If only my hand and eyes weren't tired. He slumped slightly, one hand on the side of the newly dried ink markings, listening to the sound of late carriages and merrymakers rising up from the street.

After a time he drank some ale and began to gather the music pages. In the rooms below a girl was laughing. He recognized the strange quiet inside himself that always came after working for some hours.

In the next room, also by one candle, Frau Mozart sat up in bed with a portable desk across her knees; she looked up from her writing, her small eyes blinking. Then she closed her eyes for a moment, lips moving in relief, and returned to her letter home to Salzburg.

Dear Husband,

Last evening we went on your recommendation to that music copyist. Listen. Weber is a good man but hasn't two pennies, and I can't trust his wife; she is interested only in her own opportunities. The two older girls sing not badly. Our evening there was not unpleasant, but I suppose there must be more important people in Mannheim to know than this. There was certainly no one there last night to further our son's career. Strangely, here as in Augsburg, everyone seems to have forgotten the prodigy he was, how all of Europe clustered about him. It is as if that never happened.

I wish you had come with us and did not have to remain in your wretched work for the Archbishop.

Wolferl worked several hours tonight on the Dutchman's commission, after two days of complaining how he dislikes writing for flute, particularly when it will be destroyed by the playing of an amateur like DeJean. However, three days ago he completed the first quartet and has promised to make a copy to send you; he wishes me to mention particularly the middle movement with the flute set against pizzicato strings. Two hundred silver florins for the commission when complete, husband! I thank God for our good fortune; this will pay for much.

Tomorrow we go to a private gathering of the best people, where Wolferl is to play for the dancing. We do not know if we will be paid. I still believe something will occur here to forward his talents. I hope he will get a commission for an opera, for a successful opera of all things will truly establish his name, or, if not, at least obtain the position of vice kapellmeister at the court. (The present one, they say, is not long for this world.) Meanwhile, we try to save money and dine out at others' expense when we possibly can, and only have a fire while dressing.

Above all things I intend to keep him away from Augsburg. I still feel half sick to think of what might have occurred if I had not come suddenly upon your son and that wicked girl, her petticoats entirely raised above her thighs . . .

The rest of the sentence she wrote with the page half covered by her free hand, so that for a few days following her little finger was edged with ink. She finished the letter then and signed it,

Your loving and devoted Wife, who trusts in God's mercy.

Maria Anna Mozart

*M*any feet below the houses of the city lay one of the city's beer cellars, which offered the local beer and plenty of it, in addition to plates of greasy chops so thick you could just fit your jaws around them, a sort of porridge, rich veined cheeses, large hocks of ham with knives stuck deeply in them to encourage the appetite, dishes of mustard and cabbage, and so on. It was a place where the hour and day were forgotten, for no light penetrated the vaulted, subterranean chambers that were inadequately lit by too few candles, enough to make a shapely buxom shadow of the hostess, and a lean knifelike shadow of the host. These shadows, and that of the resentful beer house boy, dipped and danced with their trays against the stone walls. The smell of beer was so great that one could imagine it rising in a flood beneath the flagstones, then seeping and leaking through the whole city, street by street, until it found its way to the river.

To enter this establishment you opened a heavy door in an alley behind a group of stables and made your way at your peril down the steep, worn, centuries-old steps. Women were here, shrieking in laughter, sometimes suddenly throwing up their skirts to their knees, and in the dim light their white hose glimmered. Law students came, as did actors and poor musicians. Here Mozart came with his friend, the horn player Leutgeb, one week following the completion of the first flute concerto.

They had taken possession of part of a long table in the rear, where the air was thick with pipe smoke. Mozart's shirt was open, and Leutgeb was pouring more beer. Leutgeb was also a native of Salzburg, where he played horn for the chapel orchestra; he was twenty-five, pleasantly fat and big, with a booming, raucous laugh that shook his whole body. His face was fleshy and never well shaven, as if to say to the world, See what an easygoing fellow I am!

"So you had your cousin with her drawers half down, you dog," he cried above the noise of music and voices. "My God, Mozart, I'll make you drunk until you tell me all of it. How much did you have of her?"

"Near to all, by heaven."

"You were on the sofa at your uncle's, and her hand was . . ."

"Where I'd have it, friend, where I'd have it; but the story ends ridiculously. We heard the door open, and I raised my head over the sofa back; standing there was *my own blessed mother.* The high sofa back was between us; I'm sure she didn't know how close we'd come. I thought she was out having her hat trimmed, by God, but there she stood."

Leutgeb roared. "Devil take it, my cock would have fallen off like the handle of a cracked china cup if my mother had stumbled on such a thing."

Mozart closed his small hands slowly, as if the girl's flesh was within them, and leaned back like a prince leisurely surveying his domain. He said, "I won't mince words with you; I won't tell you anything but the truth. I could have had her all, I know I could have had her all, but my mother and I were leaving within the hour to come here, so I can't sleep contemplating it." He gazed intensely into the smoky air. "If letter writing were copulating, my cousin and I would have done it a dozen times. I tell you it was the best part of our stay in Augsberg! The orchestra there, my friend, could bring on cramps."

Now he turned his head to study a few noisy students, and slowly leaned forward, arms on the table. "I mustn't think about her," he said seriously. "You led me on, you dog. I can't become involved with a woman for a long time. They don't want me to marry until I'm thirty. I must secure a decent income for my father, for without my earnings they'll live wretchedly. I have to make good on the promise of my childhood." He selected a bone with some meat left on it, and resumed eating.

"What promise?" the horn player asked, wiping his greasy mouth with a large white handkerchief. He thrust back his fair hair, which was already receding slightly.

"You know, you crazed shit! Here I am at one and twenty trying to live up to what I was as a little boy. My good, honorable father thought to make a future with me and my sister by taking us on tour all over Europe." Mozart took Leutgeb's handkerchief and wiped his own mouth broadly. "I was five years old when we began to tour, the protégé in a little white wig. Let me have that vinegar."

Leutgeb slid the bottle adroitly down the table.

Mozart sprinkled it on the bone. "I'm told Empress Maria Theresa in Vienna took me on her knee and kissed me; I don't much remember. Now my sister's grown, and my father is back once more in Salzburg licking the arse of the Archbishop, in whose dismal employment he has earned his bread as church musician these many years. He hints I must return there and play organ for his Arch Grossness's chapel for a pitiful stipend and eat at table with the cooks if I can't do well here. What a fate; hang me first for a bastard thief."

Leutgeb offered a bowl of onions. "We won't have to hang you. I've found some work here; you will as well."

Mozart shook his head. "Some work, but not enough. I've this flute commission, and maybe a mass for the court chapel. Unfortunately, I've grown up, and people still expect the darling prodigy. They don't know what to do with a man below middle height whose nose is too big. I'm to play at the Elector's palace in a week. God willing, he won't present me with another gold watch, as Princes are inclined to do. I speak lightly, but I tell you, old friend, there's a sense of urgency in me."

Mozart began piling up the bones, absorbed, for a moment, as if it were a complicated game of chess he was playing for some great wager. Delicately balancing the top one, he drew in his breath as they all fell to a heap beside the onions, then turned away from them to face his old friend with a wry smile. "I'm much afraid if I don't make enough money, my father will insist I return to Salzburg where I was born and beg the Archbishop to employ me as His Holiness employs him, when the truth is His

Holiness loathes the sight of me and knows I despise that mangy, provincial town. I may go to Paris; I may remain here. In any case, I must succeed for my family. My parents and sister have always given their lives for me. Leutgeb, old friend, what a thing to have to repay."

Leutgeb whistled for the boy to bring beer. Leaning on the table, he patted the young composer's hand. "Come!" he said happily. "We're young, why worry? Look, if music fails us, we can both retreat to my grandfather's cheese shop in Vienna, and live on great mounds of the stuff, then invite the cousin and both share her. She seems to have enough to go round. Vienna is the most marvelous place in the world; this town is dung compared to it." He thrust his arm around Mozart's shoulders, and shook him lightly. "Does your family really expect you to live like a monk for the best years of your life? At least enjoy the society of women if you must keep your breeches buttoned for nine more years. I know some sweet girls here. I believe you said you've been to the Webers for one of their musical Thursdays. Two are little girls, but I tell you, Aloysia, the second eldest, is the loveliest apple cake with cream you ever saw; you could eat her in two bites and lick your fingers. But of course they're good girls, and a decent man wouldn't—" Leutgeb stood up suddenly. "By God, look!" he said, peering through the smoky room. "There's a couple of pretty tarts coming this way. Don't go home with them; they'll make you sick (by God! I knew a fellow who lost his nose to syphilis!). Still, let's buy them beer."

And the girls rushed shrieking at them, feathers in their tangled hair, moist sweat beneath clustered powder on the skin visible above their low-cut dresses, one showing the edge of a hard, brown nipple. Beneath the smoke the two musicians and the girls in their faded dresses caught fingers. It was a dark, hot, secret world here, Mozart thought. One could be another man.

Twenty or thirty feet up in the street the constables walked, and some men and women made their way home from a lecture about freedom of thought and free love.

That very moment in her narrow bedroom in the garret rooms in Mannheim, with the portrait of Christ on the dresser as well as a miniature of her husband and daughter, Mozart's mother sat in her dressing gown and evening cap, blowing her inflamed nose now and then, her feet resting on a stool, rereading for the third time the letter that had come that day from her husband.

My dear Wife,

I have on your suspicion gotten the whole truth from my brother and his daughter, and I have begged him to lock her up on bread and water before she inveigles any more good young men. They still, I fear, will find ways to write to each other. Intercept any letters you can. He must not involve himself for many years, and I fear for the warmth of his blood. He is more emotional than prudent, though he won't hear it from me. We have put our whole lives into him, and he must not permit distractions from his work.

Yes, the flute quartet is exceptional, as is the little piano-violin duet he sent to Nannerl. His gifts blossom rapidly, so the amount of time we must be content to have you both remain in Mannheim must be carefully considered. If they do not recognize Wolfgang's genius soon, I must suggest you travel even farther with him. I have enclosed what money I can spare, though things are dear. Our daughter wears herself out giving clavier lessons; she is a saint of God. The enclosed longer letter you will give to him: my thoughts on the flute quartet's excellent middle movement and news of the latest musical intrigue as it will affect us, written in code. The world is a terrible place, one can get through it only being as somber a Catholic as one can and trusting in no man but those dearest to us.

I am your devoted Husband,

Leopold Mozart

Maria Anna Mozart glanced at the enclosed letter with its code. Wise, she thought, nodding. Who could trust anything in the world indeed, and in Salzburg the Archbishop had his spies everywhere.

Taking a new sheet of paper, she replied,

My dear Husband,

Yes, thank God he is far away from Augsburg. As for young women though, Husband, there is nothing as ubiquitous as young women. They are everywhere, and we must be very vigilant. If he does keep his wretched cousin in his heart (forgive me for speaking unkindly of a member of your family), his heart will at least be safe and he will not notice any other girl. Therefore, I find it best not to intercept these letters, as long as we remain so many fortunate miles away, for what harm can be done between a young man and woman with so many miles between them?

I take care of my health as well as I can.

She dusted the letter with sand to dry the ink, and folded it. Her long face, with its look of concern, was tired. She folded her hands, coughed several times, and began her evening prayers.

Wolfgang Amadeus Mozart sat before the looking glass in his garret room on a cold November twilight a week after the meeting with Leutgeb in the beer cellar. He was dressing for his first and long-hoped-for appearance at the palace at a gala celebrating the Elector's name day, the Feast of Saint Carlo Borromeo.

Mozart was already several men, perhaps more than he realized, but the ones he knew well he kept strictly divided. The man who caroused in the cellar and closed his fingers around the whore's brown nipple was worlds away from the serious young musician who meticulously put the finishing touches on his dress. As carelessly as he had eaten the beer hall chops, he now just as carefully buttoned on his shirt with the great lace, and his embroidered coat and breeches, each item of clothing un-wrapped from under the more common cloth that protected it from the smut of the parlor fire and dust of the street. On his cheeks he dabbed the smallest amount of rouge. The white peri-wig had been newly brushed that afternoon. On top of that he placed his three-cornered hat, then descended the many dark flights of stairs to set off by foot for the palace, his low-heeled shoes tapping rapidly on the cobbles. A few flakes of snow were beginning to fall.

At the palace gates he made his way through the many arriv-ing guests until a footman took him to a little room that was without any manner of fire. After a time he began to walk up and down, rubbing his hands together to keep them flexible enough to play. When he pushed back the heavy draperies, he could see the snow drifting outside the window and resting on the tops of the gates.

Rooms away he heard bright laughter; one servant rushed by with a basket of pale candles, and another wheeled a cart full of wines. Over the halls came the smell of hot food. By this time his hands were so cold he could hardly feel them. Then another footman poked his head about the corner and gave an exclama-tion of disgust. "Are you the music maker?" he snapped. "What are you doing here? Don't you have the sense to go where the others wait?"

And you wait the very first in the line of the worse fools, Mozart thought. He clasped his icy hands behind him and fol-lowed the footman, who flung open a door to another small antechamber.

It was already occupied. An unusually tall young woman clutching a fan was striding up and down in a wide blue dress that she kicked out of her way as she went. In spite of her powdered-white hair, which was mounted over pads on her head, he recognized her as one of the Weber daughters who had sung duets a few weeks before in the little parlor. Below the low bodice, her waist was tightly corseted, and every now and then she took a deep furious breath, as if she could not get enough air.

He remembered how after his evening at her house she had run down the steps two at a time to return his mother's purse, which she had left behind, then bolted up the same way. Tonight she seemed a great, wild creature imprisoned in whalebone and satin. Her powdered hair smelled of lavender and orange blossoms.

He bowed formally, and she curtseyed, keeping her head erect so as not to topple her hair. "I've forgotten which Weber sister you are," he said.

"I'm the eldest, Josefa. My younger sister Aloysia and I are singing tonight. She's talking to someone with our father in another room now. It's our first time here . . . and you?"

"My first time in many years." He lowered his voice and inclined his head to the sound of chatter from the nearby assembly hall and the scrape of chairs over the music of a string trio. "Tell me, did they listen when you sang, or did they talk the whole while?"

"Ah, you know how it is!" she whispered. "They ignore me, and I ignore them. There's a great deal of food in there, and we haven't been offered any. We left the house in such a hurry we forgot the basket my youngest sister packed for us. But this is only our fourth concert. They always talk, says my father, and they hardly ever consider that we might like to have a sip of wine or a bite of chicken." They both became aware of the footman who stood by the door like a wax figure, wearing his shiny white wig and the trimmed livery of the Elector, and they lowered their voices.

When Josefa was called again, Mozart stationed himself by the crack of the door and looked over the brilliantly lit room filled with people seated on gilded chairs. The sisters stood as close together as their great skirts allowed. The candlelight shining through the few loose strands of powder-dusted hair made those tendrils look like white fire. At the clavier he could also see their father, the copyist Weber, bobbing up and down as he accompanied them in an Italian love duet. Their voices rose higher and higher. Aloysia moved her tiny hands; Josefa clutched her closed fan tightly. One voice was brighter and took the highest notes, which rang small and pure over the heads of the audience. Aloysia. *Aloysia, Aloysia,* the mother had called her, lovingly, chiding. He recalled the warmth and laughter of the large family.

He was the last to play.

He heard his name murmured, and then the sound of his heeled shoes on the floor. There were candles everywhere, and the smell of perfumed clothing and hair powder, and under it always the stink of perspiration. How accustomed he was to this walk, having entered such palace rooms all over Europe when he was so small he had to be lifted to the chair before the keyboard to play, legs clad in white silk stockings dangling.

They were looking at him now as they had then, quieter than

they had been for the Weber sisters. Some remembered who he was, perhaps. And there in the center, in two high-back armchairs cushioned in red velvet, were the somber Elector of Mannheim, Carl Theodor, with his long, middle-aged face heavy from years of good eating, and his wife, Electress Maria Elizabeth, leaning her head on her hand slightly so as not to disturb her high cascade of powdered hair. Hand over his heart, he bowed. The major-domo stared straight ahead of him. "Herr Wolfgang Amadeus Mozart from Salzburg," he intoned.

Mozart bowed again. *"Si son Excellence daigne le permettre!"* If his Excellence deigns to permit it! "Graciously begging your indulgence, I am most honored to present you with my new composition, a sonata in four movements in C major."

A few more who had been speaking turned to gaze curiously at him. He seated himself at the clavier keyboard, gazing at the familiar length of black naturals and the white accidentals. Candles glittered in the wood sconces carved with roses. What was the instrument like? You never knew until you tried it; then, if keys stuck, or the action was slow, it seemed like your fault. Fridolin Weber's playing had been stiff, and he had not been able to judge.

He rubbed his hands to warm them, then began.

Under his hands the instrument was responsive, and during the andante he could feel the two sisters watching him from the crack in the door. Someone was talking; he bit his lip and finished the last movement a little more quickly than he would have liked, then stood, bowing.

Elector Carl Theodor and his wife beckoned to him, and at

once he went forward, kissing their perfumed, limp hands in turn. "Has it been truly fifteen years since you were here, Mozart?" the Elector said. "I recall you as a child with your ceremonial sword and your elegant court dress, hardly to my wife's knee! Don't you recall the little fellow, my dear?"

From a chair near them the Elector's daughter stammered, *"On ne peut pas jouer mieux!"* No one is able to play better. She then added, "You told me of him, Papa!" Mozart smiled at her good nature, and kissed her freckled hand.

"Do you play yourself, my lady?"

"*Un peu.* Perhaps if you were remaining a time in Mannheim, you could give me lessons."

That will get me closer to an appointment, he thought, and kissed her hand again between the jeweled rings. "That would be a great honor, Gracious Princess!" Then the majordomo pressed a small velvet bag in his hands, and he bowed again, hand to his heart.

Just as a great silver tray of cakes was carried into the room he was shown out, his mind filled with the possibility of the lessons and the certainty of moving closer to a position. Still deep in thought, he saw the Weber sisters and their father had not yet left but were just now fastening their cloaks.

"Ah, young Mozart!" Fridolin Weber cried. "A pleasure to see you again. A fine piece, beautifully played. The guests seemed suitably impressed, as they should have been. Now, have you a carriage? No? We hired one to save my daughters' dresses from the weather. Let us take you to your lodging. Where's your music?"

"In my head, Herr Weber." Through the window he could

see how the snow was piling in the yard. "I gratefully accept your offer."

"Come, my dears."

The four of them ran through the snow and climbed into the carriage, squeezing together on the facing cushioned seats, for the width of the dresses took up a great amount of room. Both girls had to struggle to keep their heads erect. Slowly the small carriage, drawn by a weary horse, began to nudge its way through the many grander ones of departing guests; the air was filled with cries of "Make way, make way, make way for the Bishop, for the Countess!" A few hot bricks, surrounded by bundles of straw, lay on the coach floor to warm their feet.

Josefa reached behind her, tugged, and then sighed. "I hate and despise tight corsets," she exclaimed. "If it were up to me, I'd sing in my dressing gown. Stupid, pretentious people! One man kept gaping at me until I thought his wooden teeth would fall in his wineglass. Hasn't he ever seen a tall woman before? Now I'm truly starving—where's the basket they gave us, Papa? If they hadn't, I swear I would have slipped half a dozen chicken legs in with my music."

"They have paid us, dear; we can't ask for more."

"Yes, darling Papa, and you played so well for us. Now, be the table chamberlain and serve us food."

Fridolin Weber removed the linen covering from the basket and, holding it in the air like a waiter at the finest table, said, "We can't eat if you won't join us, Mozart. Will you? Good. Yes, when people make music, they must eat soon after. Come, reach in; there's no ceremony here."

Hurled against one another with every jerk of the carriage, the four of them pulled forth fowl, fish, and cakes, and sat back to eat as neatly as they could, sharing the linen basket covering as a napkin. The horses clopped slowly, and the road was crowded, rumors circulated of a carriage broken down a little ahead. Fridolin reached below the food and pulled out a few bottles of wine that they passed about, having no cups; outside the snow fell softly over the city and drifted in through the slightly open window to their laps.

Mozart glanced at Josefa as he passed her the bread. Her eyes were warm in her long, thoughtful face, and she laughed as robustly as she ate. Her nails were bitten to the quick, and she had a space between her front teeth.

Between mouthfuls, she demanded curiously, "Do you play in such houses often, Herr Mozart? The sort with twenty or fifty servants all looking as if they had died and been stuffed and then sewn dead into their livery?"

"More than I can begin to count, Mademoiselle Weber. Unfortunately, they have paid me as I expected they would." Wryly, he extracted a gold watch from the velvet bag and let it dangle back and forth with the movement of the carriage. Now he was smiling. "I felt the shape of it when they presented it and withheld my groans. Can it be gold ducats, I asked myself. Ah no, said I."

Aloysia had chosen only sweets, and she was now taking cautious bites from a piece of chocolate almond cake. Her blue shoe was half off her heel, showing her white stocking, slightly discolored with blue dye. Mozart looked at her curiously; so this was the one who was driving his friend Leutgeb from his senses. How little she was! Rather like a porcelain doll he had seen once in an empty anteroom on one of his childhood tours, sitting all alone in a large velvet-covered chair, her legs stuck out before her, her head to one side. He wondered if, should he ever pass that way again, he would find it sitting there still.

Her voice was light. "Herr Mozart," she said.

"Mademoiselle Weber."

"You mentioned when we met a few weeks ago that you had been in London as a boy to play the clavier. (I also play excellently; we all do but for our smallest sister, who wants to be a nun.) Father says you've traveled all about the world, to Vienna and Munich and Paris. But oh, Paris! Were you truly at Versailles?"

"I was indeed, mademoiselle."

"Oh to see it! I think I should faint at even approaching such an exquisite court, the most civilized court in the world—walls trimmed with gold, porphyry, women in hair like sailing ships, or set with bird's feathers, or with flowers! I've seen drawings in a book, and a dressmaker we know was once there. Is it true you played for the King himself?" Her lips were almost trembling. "And that, more, you've even seen Venice and the Grand Canal, the palazzo of the Doge? Does he truly walk under a golden umbrella? Can there be no streets but only water and bridges and gondolas gliding in the night? *Mon Dieu,* you have lived a wonderful life."

"Some of it was wonderful, and some not," he replied, his hand over the top of the wine bottle so it would not splash about. "I can't be myself much of the time in such places, and most of the people I play to don't listen or don't understand my music. I'd rather make music with friends; if I didn't have to earn a living, that's all I'd do. I enjoyed playing at your house last month."

"Sir, I thank you," cried their father, his voice bright with wine.

Aloysia leaned forward, as if with the jolting she might fall toward him. She lowered her eyes as she spoke. "May I suggest, Herr Mozart, that you can afford to dismiss such things because you have them in abundance."

"But sometimes these things are cold and unwelcoming, mademoiselle."

"Do you think so? If you say so, it must be so, and certainly I wouldn't know because, as a woman, I stay mostly at home. But even if we do, we're highly educated in music. We've hardly ever been to school; we've lived just the four of us, with Mother and Father. Papa taught reading and writing at home, and of course we speak Italian and French, as any educated person does, but all this was secondary to music, wasn't it, Papa? *Mon Dieu,* sometimes we have games to see who can play or sing the most difficult things at sight." She wriggled the blue shoe so that it fell from her foot. Now she was laughing openly, joyfully. He could see her bare throat quiver under the opened cloak. It was unadorned: no pearl on a gold chain, nothing. "I always win."

"You don't always," said Josefa.

But Aloysia's thoughts returned to the previous subject. "I'm certain you're mistaken, Herr Mozart! I'm certain I wouldn't find living in such a beautiful palace as Versailles cold! I'd be lost at first in the thousands of rooms, but that would be for only a short time. Some kind nobleman would graciously show me the way. Imagine having servants to do everything for you, even dress you. Imagine having twenty dresses, and a personal chambermaid to wash your silk hose and brush your hair two hundred strokes every night."

Josefa's reply was sudden and severe. "Oh, there you go with your fantasies and great plans!" she said. "Tomorrow none of them will take down the family chamber pots and start the fire in the cold, but we will." Her deep brown eyes darkened. She put one hand on her father's arm, as if to comfort him, to say none of these wants were his fault. She sank back in the carriage shadows, drawing her cloak over her dress.

But Weber cried cheerfully, "There, there, who can say what tomorrow may bring? I repeat the maxim often; my daughters hear it daily, to their boredom! Here's your street, Herr Mozart. Yes, tomorrow, we would much enjoy the pleasure of your company. May I expect you at seven? Very good, very good."

The young composer climbed from the carriage and heard their voices as they drove away, "Good night, Mozart, good night, dear Mozart," and then their laughter.

Clocks striking over the city, rich, sonorous, the echo drifting over the houses, the roofs, the church spires. The good priests turned over on thick linen sheets in their beds; the merchants pulled their sleeping caps down over their ears. Musicians were snoring lightly: singers and flautists embraced their feather pillows. Outside the modest provincial theater the hand-lettered posters announcing the new performances were slightly stained with wet snow. The street cobbles smelled of horse dung, the alleys of sewage and old cooking. Later, before dawn, the maids would rise and light the fires and prepare the strong coffee and hot chocolate, then run into the street for fresh, warm bread from the baker's boy. But now it was late, and the clocks each struck at a slightly different time, so that midnight in one street arrived some minutes before midnight several streets away.

Mozart walked alone after the carriage had rolled away, a little tipsy, whistling to himself. He opened the door of the house and took off his shoes, mounted the creaking steps, unlocked the upper door, and passed into his ugly garret room, which served as parlor, dressing room, and bedchamber. There, waiting for him, was his narrow bed. The room was very cold, but at least he could feel the small fire from where his mother slept, paid for with money from home on the strength of what the flute commission and other work would bring. He took off his wig and set it on the table. He also took out the watch, grimacing slightly. He might sell it in another city, not here. Yes, he would sell it in a faraway city, where the prince's valet would never come across it hanging in a jeweler's window at a reduced price.

"Wolfgang, is that you?" came his mother's sleepy voice from the other room; she coughed once or twice. "Why did you come so late?"

"They made me wait forever before they called me in to play. Are you better?" he asked, joining her in her room.

"My chest aches; the landlady brought me a mustard plaster and a hot stone wrapped in flannel for under my feet. The fire's such a comfort. But you have a clavier lesson for Mademoiselle Cannabich in the morning. Oh, what a shame they made you wait so long. Did you have the opportunity of speaking to His Highness about composing a new opera for Mannheim?"

"There was no time; I'll have to find another opportunity."

"Your father wrote that your old friend Padre Martini from Italy sends you his love and prayers; he wishes you'd write and tell him how you're getting on."

Mozart listened somewhat anxiously to her coughing, and then heated some wine on her low fire and sat on her bed as she drank it, stroking her hand. A few more age spots had appeared there since last he had looked. After a time she fell asleep, and he kissed her cheek, then returned to his own room.

There he lay on his bed in only his shirt, his arm beneath his head, thinking of the rolling ride home in the carriage, and the two girls' hair powder, which flecked onto their dark cloaks. He thought of Josefa's bitten nails and how she had retreated to the shadows of the carriage quite suddenly, and of Aloysia's eyes as she spoke of Venice.

Two of the clock. A song for soprano and keyboard had almost finished itself in his head. When dawn came into the room high above the houses, he would write it down from memory, and sign it W. A. Mozart, with his usual flourish. It was yet many hours before seven in the evening when he was expected at the Webers.

*T*he bottles of wine had arrived from the vintner by late Thursday afternoon; the scent of apple cake was rising from the kitchen; and the hour was just a little past six, which meant the guests would not climb the five flights of steep stairs for another hour. Aloysia Weber had shut herself in the narrow chamber that she shared with her three sisters, its two beds chastely hidden behind cheap white cotton hangings, its wardrobe, its dozens of hooks full of dresses, its scattered shoes, and its large jewelry box whose contents were mostly imitation. When Sophie was six years old, she had emptied the box to make it into a house for her pet white mice. ("They have feelings, too, you know. How would you like to live in a nasty hole in the wall?") It had been restored, though it was never quite the same; it now always held a strange scent, and one corner of the dark velvet lining had been nibbled.

Aloysia had just finished unwinding the rags from her hair, and one never knew just how they would hang until that was done. Would the thick curls at the back of the neck be crooked? No, they were perfect, much better than last night. But she had been lovely enough then; her father and others had said it. "Such a delicious girl," she could hear one of the men murmuring after she had concluded her aria at the palace. The way one or two of them looked at her! Not that they interested her very much, but they were, as her mother said, possibilities, their names to be added to a list in a little book, discussed over many hours of coffee. It was a leather-bound book tooled in flowers that her mother kept hidden in secret places (lastly behind the flour canister), which none of them had ever been allowed to look in or touch. Last night, however, Aloysia had been given permission for the first time to come to the kitchen and list a few men who had heard her sing. Most she could only describe; she did not exactly know their names. She also did not know if they were already married.

Some years ago, when Josefa had first started to have a shape beneath her chemise, her mother had gathered her two older daughters together and had begun to discuss the subject of marriage with them. To be an old maid was a terrible thing: no fate could be worse than that. To be unchosen was horrid! Was not even death preferable? They could not begin, their mother said, to think of their futures too soon. Now and then a girl trained to music could eke out a precarious existence. The occasional woman wrote for her bread, or was a clever dressmaker, but even with these things her true goal was to marry as well as she could. Aloysia remembered that evening in the kitchen, both girls sitting close to their mother, listening to her every word.

At first the names of suitors were modest prospects: printers, a furniture upholsterer with a small workshop, a schoolmaster. Then two years later Frau Caecilia Weber had looked at her newly blooming second child and, smacking her lips gently, observed, "An old school friend of mine has a daughter without dowry who has just married a Count, and she is not nearly as beautiful as you. Oh no, my sweet, not nearly as lovely. If such a blessing could occur, you could have all the pretty things you

deserve, my Aloysia, my own little flea." That was the day everything changed. It was a spring day, and she had run up the steps
with her nose buried in sprigs of linden blossoms. She could
hear her mother's voice. "I know how you long for fine things,
my Aloysia."

Today on her way back from delivering a pile of copied music, she stood for a long time in front of a French dressmaker's
shop window, where she could make out, behind the small
panes, a length of pale pink brocade. Pressing her forehead
against the cold glass, Aloysia almost felt her soul leave her body
and wind itself in the cloth. She so wanted first a dress from that
cloth, and then another in milkmaid style made of the finest
white muslin, with a wide, pale pink silk sash that would tie
around her waist and bow so extravagantly at the small of her
back that the ends would flutter down the skirt. She had seen a
drawing of such a dress worn in the court of France.

"Aloysia, are you coming? Have you polished the candle
sconces? It is Thursday, you know!"

Why must the world stop for Thursdays? Must they all be ral-
lied weekly to this running about so, tidying the parlor, finding
enough candles, always making sacrifices when no one in particular ever came, whereas last night at the Elector's palace there
had been the women with little dark beauty marks shaped like
stars or moons. How could Josefa laugh at it? They had fought
about it this morning while studying a new duet. And didn't it
matter to Josefa that she was nineteen and not yet betrothed?
Just like the younger ones, who never gave it a thought.

"Aloysia!" called her sisters and mother.

At least she could wear her pink silk hose, embroidered at the ankle with small scarlet flowers, which her father had bought her the first time she sang in public. If by chance her skirt pulled up an inch or so above her shoes, Leutgeb would notice. The blustering horn player was in love with her, and, though his name had never been mentioned by her mother, she found that when he looked at her, her body grew warm all over.

But now, rummaging through boxes and under the bed, she could not find the embroidered hose. Dropping to her knees, she searched the bottom of the wardrobe, hurling things out. "Someone borrowed them, likely," she muttered. "Will I *ever* have anything not borrowed, remade, or lent?"

Blessed saints, could it be true? There, stuffed under the shoes, wrapped in canvas, was the fan cousin Alfonso's wife had given her, which Josefa had begged to borrow again last night, because she said she could not sing without a fan. Obviously, after they had finished singing, Josefa had hidden it somewhere because it was broken. From under it, Aloysia pulled out the hose with the flowers, splattered with street muck.

She leapt up in her shift and petticoat and rushed into the hall where she collided with Josefa, who was carrying table draping. "You farmer's daughter—you ruined it, you mauled it, look!" She opened the fan with its silk portrait of Venice, gesturing at the few cracked slats. "You ruin everything, everything! There's a split in the Grand Canal. I don't know who brought you into this family, Josefa Weber, what ugly gypsy brought you in his cart and sold you for two kreuzers, but you're here to ruin my life, and I wish to the Blessed Virgin we could sell you back again."

"I never broke the fan; you stuffed it away yourself," cried Josefa, throwing down the linen. "You hid it under the shoes so you wouldn't have to share it anymore, and that broke it. What's a fan supposed to do under twenty shoes?"

Aloysia slapped her, and Josefa took her by the hair and pulled her a few feet down the hall. The harder Aloysia tried to shake her off, the more her elder sister continued to drag her toward the parlor by the curls. Aloysia shrieked, her piercing, light voice ringing from room to room, and was about to dig her teeth into her sister's arm when their father, half shaven, his bare chest dusted with gray hair, rushed toward them shouting, "Josy, let go!"

Thrown off suddenly, Aloysia stumbled against a parlor chair and a pile of music. "You did take it; you did!" she sobbed. "And now you made me scream, and I've hurt my voice, you ugly bitch. You can't wait for me to hurt my voice, can you?" Her hands flew to her ragged hair and aching head, and tears spilled from her blue eyes. Her voice was shaking. "And you've ruined the curl. I won't come out of our room tonight; that's it. I have no voice; it's gone, it's gone."

Sophie, who had heard the shouting from the kitchen, bolted out like a weed driven by wind; seeing her father already held the girls apart, she retrieved the fan from under the table. "Oh, Aly," she murmured, stammering a little as she did when there was a quarrel, "look, it's only two slats that need replacing. Why must you go into such passions for things that can be mended, things that are inconsequential?" She fished for her wrinkled handkerchief and wiped Aloysia's face.

Aloysia sobbed, "There's a tiny tear in the silk; it goes all the way from the canal to the base of San Marco."

"I'll take it to the second floor to Hoffman; he repairs fans and umbrellas. He'll do us a favor since I found his lost dog. Don't cry. Hush, hush, darling," pleaded Sophie, just as Constanze also rushed from the kitchen holding her father's ironed shirt like a banner, its arms floating behind.

"Girls!" she commanded. "Mama says you must all be quiet or she'll come with her wooden spoon and then the cakes will never be finished! Look at the mantel clock; it's nearly seven, and people will be arriving in ten minutes. Not one of us is dressed. Papa, here's your shirt. You have soap on your nose. What will people think of us? It will be all over Mannheim."

But Aloysia stood stubbornly by the chair. "The fan isn't *inconsequential*," she sobbed, the balled handkerchief in her hand. "It's inconsequential to all of *you* because you don't care. Some of us might *care*, some of us might want to be at our *best*. *Mon Dieu, c'est terrible!* And the stockings are filthy; Stanzi, you promised to wash them after I wore them last time when I gave you ten kreuzers of my singing money. None of you care about me, and I haven't any hose. I couldn't find any."

"There's some in the kitchen. Be still: Mama says."

"Oh, her spoon, of course!" Aloysia cried. "Does she think we are children to threaten with a spoon? I earned fifteen silver florins last night and pay for the bread on the table, and she thinks I'm no more than a child!" And she rushed off without a glance at Josefa, who, with an angry shrug, marched off to retrieve the table linen from the hall floor.

Now alone for the moment, Sophie stood by the window, untying her apron and looking down at the approaching evening. Her heart still beat fast from the quarrel. Few carriages passed. Squinting hard, she saw the shapes of what looked like two men walking toward the street door of their house; it was all she could make out with her nearsightedness, but when they opened the front door below, she cried, "Someone's come early; Stanzi, help me!"

From the kitchen her mother called out threats, prayers, and directions. The gingerbread was not ready. Constanze hurried out with her dress half fastened, her fingers lacing as fast as they could, and began to light the candles. Aloysia emerged fully dressed. I have never belonged in this family, she thought severely, suppressing her last sob.

Still, she felt simultaneously the old pride that had brought them all through much. They were the daughters of the musician Fridolin Weber, from a family of Webers. It was Thursday, and, as her father once told her, tickling her and rubbing his unshaven face against hers, on this night in this house, no one is unhappy. So she moved closer to her sisters, and they all stood as one, hands touching, smelling of clean brushed clothes perfumed with lavender, hair drawn plainly back for two younger girls, still curled for Aloysia, and pushed under a cap for Josefa, who had stayed too late at the book shop and had not had time to fuss.

Constanze in her plain dark dress looked at the door.

Sophie unlatched it.

Leutgeb strode forward to kiss the hands of the girls; by his side was the smaller Mozart, large, kind eyes looking about at all of them. In his bass voice, Leutgeb boomed, "We're too early, but perhaps we'll be forgiven when you see the nice cakes and wine we have for you."

Sophie rushed forward to look at the basket placed on the table. "Oh, chocolate cake with cherries," she cried, jumping up and down a little. "And sweet wine . . . Father loves sweet wine." Her freckled face brimmed with gratitude as she squinted at both musicians.

From her parents' bedchamber, she heard her father curse in the name of Saint Elizabeth as he dropped something on the floor. He would bend, groaning, to pick it up, his back curving. Her mother was still in the kitchen banging pots, wiping off dishes.

Mozart held a narrow paper portfolio in both his arms. "I've brought something as well," he said.

"What, more cakes?" asked Sophie.

"No, not cakes. A challenge. I am come to set a challenge for Mademoiselle Aloysia."

"What? What?" cried the girls all at once, clamoring about him, but he shook his head. Suddenly he was not shy at all; instead, his face was full of mischief. "But you'll have to wait a time until all the guests come."

Within the half hour the room was crowded, a pupil of their father's had arrived, and a church musician, then a few members of a horn band, followed by dear Heinemann and Alfonso with violin and cello, as always, by their sides. The younger girls ran back to find extra wineglasses and plates, and the cake was set among the music, the glazed cherries nestled among the chocolate thick as fine velvet. Sophie gazed at all with relief as the guests consumed the cake and her father grew visibly merrier. And at last there was their parents' oldest friend, honest Uncle Thorwart, whom they had known from childhood; this heavy man who panted from the stairs winked at them. He had brought from the best chocolatier in town a painted wood box of chocolates, likely filled with sweet nuts, drops of blackberry liqueur, and marzipan, whose sugared-almond taste lingered for hours on the tongue. It was a generous box of at least four layers. If the guests mostly addressed themselves to their mother's gingerbread with cream and the several additional bottles of wine that remained, there would be enough chocolate to enjoy in secret later on.

Thorwart, meticulously dressed, placed his ringed hand over his heart. "Those stairs! My breath! Girls, come kiss your old uncle."

The room's configuration changed: chairs were rearranged, people moved about. Mozart had taken his place at the clavier and drew several pages of music from his portfolio. Fridolin demanded quiet, and the parlor became so still that the only sounds were the crackling fire in the fireplace and the rousing November wind outside the window.

"Now," Mozart said, "I present a challenge to Mademoiselle Aloysia in the presence of her family. Mademoiselle, I heard you say last night in the carriage that you can read all music at sight. Very well! I've written this song for you from a text by Metastasio, and if you can read it straight off without an error, you may have it. If not, I tear it up."

A flurry of voices rose up, a few hands drawing her closer. "Amusing; he's likely made it difficult. Aloysia, stand behind him to see the notes clearly. The light's poor; who'll hold the candle?"

For a moment Aloysia could not remember the boast she had made coming home in the carriage, expansive with her success and the quickly drunk wine, and flush with the odd sensuality of sitting almost knee to knee with this intense young man who had ridden in the gondolas of the Venetian canals. Whatever it had been, now she had to make good on it, or be shamed that she had not been taught music well enough.

Mozart adjusted the music so she could see it better, then he beckoned for Sophie, who held a candle for her sister, to step closer.

He played the first bars.

Aloysia sang the opening line of the recitative in a small, tremulous voice, as if she had never sung before anyone, but by the tender melodic line of the andante sostenuto, encouraged by the nods of the others, who saw she had made no mistakes so far, she began to gain courage.

> *"Non so d'onde viene quel tenero affetto*
> *Quel moto, che ignoto mi nasce nel petto"*

She knew music; she had heard it as she was curled within the womb and after she lay swaddled in her cradle. By the first gentle spill of sixteenth notes and the sustained high Bb that followed shortly after, she felt those about her stir with admiration, and her voice took on an authority of its own. Forgetting everything but the music before her, she sprang into the allegro agitato. Her voice opened like a heart in love, and she became one with the notes. Dresses, cake, muddy hose fell away as insignificant. She sang as if she had never sung before. She stood erect, one hand at her side almost imperceptibly beating time. The song returned to the first tempo, and her silvery voice rose in glittering scale to the high Eb. Mozart's hands on the keys flashed, lifting her up. She was not reading the song; she became it.

When the last trill rang out to the dark corners of the room, beyond the piles of old music and the empty wineglasses, she stood poised, startled and motionless. "The purity of that voice," someone said. For a moment she had been in another world. Vaguely, she felt her hand taken and someone's dry kiss above it. She withdrew it distractedly, as if someone had mistakenly taken up something that belonged to her. There was a strange desire to cry. Could the song be over? Could it have ended and left her?

Everyone was clapping; Sophie's arm was about her waist.

The words with their melody repeated themselves in her mind; she moved her lips, drawing a little close to the clavier as if she would begin again.

"Non so d'onde viene quel tenero affetto . . ."
(I don't know from whence comes this tender affection . . .)

Mozart stood up clapping as well, but she looked at him as if he were a stranger. What had he to do with this moment? What was she thinking? The notes were his. Still, without her voice, weren't they but dry marks? Yet how could it be? She stood confused. Was it his song? Or was it hers?

"Mademoiselle," he said, "you've won the wager. The song's yours. I'll orchestrate it so that you can sing it in concert, and all who hear it will be as amazed as we are here today."

She felt a moment's fierce tenderness for him. He looked at her. For a moment nothing was ordinary, and she reached for his warm hand. Oh, she thought, come with me. Yet they were pressed in on all sides, and there was her father being the dear fool, calling in a loud voice for the best three remaining bottles of wine to be dusted off and brought at once. How could he think of wine at this moment?

With that the music stopped within her, and she knew herself to be only a sixteen-year-old girl in a stuffy parlor. Could she have so quickly lost the mystery of those moments and the happiness of the singer when she becomes the song and touches eternity? But family and guests were all pressing about them, candles tilted and dripping wax. "Mind the candle," Josefa cried, receiving the wine bottles from her father.

Now she was being hugged by all, aware of how intensely a few of the men looked at her, even Thorwart, who was called uncle by the girls even though he wasn't really a blood relative. There was the self-contained composer, his left hand still resting soundlessly on the keys, also looking steadily at her. If she embraced him, she would regain the moment. *Slip away,* her eyes said; slip away and come with me. *Come with me, dear Wolfgang Mozart.* Her heart was beating very fast.

She left the room as a string trio began, escaping to the unmade beds and scattered clothing of her shared bedroom, even closing the door a little, but not all, so that she might hear the composer's footsteps following her down the hall. The door from the parlor creaked softly, and she opened hers. In the shadow she saw a man walking softly under the portraits of long-dead Weber ancestors posing in their horrible dull garments.

She lightly ran forward the few steps and felt her hands caught by another's; they were not Mozart's supple hands, but wider, meaty ones. It was Leutgeb who had followed her. "Do you know what happens to kisses not given?" he said softly, looming above her. "They become sorrow, like words never spoken. You are the most beautiful girl in the world, and your voice is like that of an angel."

Lifting her face, she allowed him to kiss her mouth. And as he kissed her, she felt all the magnificence of the song return.

Some minutes later she straightened her dress and slipped back into the parlor, where the second movement of the string trio had just begun. She could see her father's good head nodding as he played his violin.

Sometime after the song had been sung and acclaim was yet ringing about the parlor for Aloysia, Josefa Weber slipped from the room to hide on the cold hall steps. She had observed her sister's departure, and shortly after it Leutgeb's; now Josefa sat with her arms hugging her chest. Why had she made up with her before? Here in their very own parlor Aloysia had taken the prize of admiration, while Josefa's own voice was larger and more passionate, able to make the very pictures on the wall tremble and the candle flames waver. She could have sung equally well at sight, but, not having been asked to enter the competition, she was vanquished. Oh, it was always this way, always since Aloysia's birth.

Josefa remembered peering over the cradle at the very tiny fragile child who, anxious relatives muttered, hovered between life and death. For weeks following Aloysia's birth Josefa had stumbled over kneeling aunts whispering over their rosary beads. The child lived, and, from shortly after that time, everything changed.

Josefa had been the darling of her parents for three and a half brief years of life as an only child. Later, even after it seemed Aloysia would live, it was Josefa who was the first to read, the first to have a music lesson, the first to sing to aunts and grand-mothers as she stood on a chair and was held steady by her ador-ing mother, and then, dressed in her childish best, the first to sing to her father's musical friends on Thursdays. Suddenly, though, there was another songbird, a higher, lighter, purer voice, yanking at her dress as she sang, almost pulling her from the chair. At the age of seven Josefa had had enough; she pushed her sister down ten minutes before guests arrived, and had then been slapped for it. Friends who had first lifted Josefa into their arms now exclaimed playfully at her weight, and they lifted tiny Aloysia instead. The younger girl darted like a sparrow; she was more appealing. And yet Josefa loved her small sister as some-thing finer and sweeter than she could ever be. Hadn't there been that day at the menagerie so long ago to prove it forever?

The tiger, behind the slats of its wood, wheeled cage, was old and lethargic. Josefa and Aloysia had approached the cage hand in hand, each drawn by the other's courage to go forward. Were they six and nearly three? Aloysia wore a little crushed bonnet, and the few feet to the heavy wood cage seemed very long as they pulled each other closer. Then the beast roared. He rose, glaring at them, and swiped one paw through the bars. Aloysia stood petrified, some inches away from the great curving claws; someone was shouting, but before the large keeper could reach them, Josefa yanked her baby sister's limp arm and pulled her away so fast that Aloysia tumbled in the dust. Josefa was shaking so hard she had to lean against the wall. Still trembling, she picked up her sobbing sister and dusted her off. Was it minutes, hours, before their parents found them? "Why didn't you protect your little sister?" her mother had cried later. "You know you have to take care of her; how could you let her go so close?" Her father's voice had replied angrily, "It's not the girl's fault, Caecilia; she saved her." Josefa still recalled the sensation of his mustache against her cheek as he knelt and held her close.

Now, years later, she sat on the landing outside her family's apartment, trying to keep her tears within. She could hear that the trio was done, that now someone accompanied a violin. Then everyone called for a duet, and the cry went up, "But where's Josefa? Where's our Josefa?" That was her father's voice calling, "Where's my girl?"

The door creaked open, and Sophie emerged, blinking, onto the landing. "Josy?" she murmured.

From the shadows the eldest sister held her breath. The love in the smallest sister's voice sounded again. Josefa could not bear to hear Sophie's questioning plea and leapt to her feet. "I was too warm inside," she said. "That's why I left."

Inside she crossed, smiling, to Aloysia. The sisters each wound an arm about the other's waist and, lifting their faces, sang purely and truly as if nothing had occurred at all: as if one had not been fondled in a dark hall under the small dour portraits of their ancestors, and the other had not fled to the stairs to confront her unhappiness. Their voices rose in thirds to the top notes, glistening off the low flames of the candles and echoing about the empty wine bottles. Then another magical evening came to a close, and the guests reluctantly began to depart.

The parlor was empty, the music of Mozart's song lay on top of a pile of other musical scores, and the four sisters gathered close on the two iron bedsteads. Wooly, worn nightgowns pulled down over their drawn-up knees, their faces scrubbed free of rouge, the girls climbed bare-legged from bed to bed and shared a cup of cold coffee while Sophie foraged through the remaining one and a half layers of chocolates in the painted wood box. She had just finished a marzipan enclosed in dark bitter chocolate and flavored with a hint of boysenberry.

"Don't eat them all."

"I only had six."

"Oh, how can you all be such pigs!" Aloysia said. "You'll be fat and won't have fashionable figures, no matter how tightly you lace your corsets!"

Laughter burst out, quickly followed by a sharp admonition

from their mother in the next room. Father had a headache; Mother was taking care of him. Then Constanze turned to her smaller sister and whispered, "They're almost asleep; don't wake them. Sophie, did you manage to steal it?"

Wiping her fingers on the quilt, Sophie reached under the bed and, with a crooked smile, drew out from under her pile of clothes the leather-tooled book of suitors.

Aloysia sat straight up in horror. "You shouldn't have taken that," she whispered sharply. "You know Mother doesn't want us to touch it." She put the coffee cup carefully on the dresser and reached for the book, but Sophie rolled away.

Constanze said, "Why shouldn't she touch it? You did the other night. I saw you."

"It was the first time she said I could enter possibilities, and I looked at only the one page. Where did you find it tonight? She moved it; I looked. Well, I did look."

"Why, to enter that horn blower's name?" whispered Josefa. "Sophie found it under the flour barrel."

"You're not supposed to open it! There are things in it that are private! It's Mother's."

"I *am* going to open it!" Sophie said. "Shh! Be quiet! We'll just look at it tonight, and I'll tiptoe and put it back. It's her plans for our futures, and we have a right to know her plans."

Sophie, Constanze, and Aloysia gathered closer, Aloysia with some confusion in her face, the same expression she had been wearing ever since disappearing down the hall earlier that evening. Her lower lip, thrust forward, gave her a look between childish and arrogance, and she cast a resentful look at Josefa, who sat with arms folded.

Sophie turned the pages carefully, holding the candle close. A bit of glowing wick flew off and landed on a page, and she pressed it out with her fingers and rubbed at the mark. It had been several days since Constanze and Sophie made plans to steal the book this very evening. "It is our futures," Constanze had said. Josefa had sworn to have nothing to do with the plan, and even now she sat a little apart, rubbing her big bare feet with their large toes and looking disapproving. Her dark hair fell uncurled down her back to her waist, making her inquisitive face seem even longer.

The early pages were crammed with sketches of dresses that had been fashionable twenty years before, and a number of old family recipes. A curious printed invitation to a ball fell out, along with some bit of fabric. They turned the pages more rapidly now, past family accounts meticulously kept and then abandoned, until they reached the names of possible suitors; then they looked mischievously at one another. The first of these pages listed the names of tradesmen, the names of their fathers, and their approximate yearly income.

"Oh, these are from some time ago," Constanze whispered. "Look, the ink's faded. Will you all be still? Look, here's Weidman. I remember him, but he's married now and has three sons. Here's Lorenz Holsbauer: something odd happened to him. I think they made him go for a soldier; he was in some kind of scandal."

"How do you know?" Josefa asked, moving closer to look over her sister's shoulder.

"I notice things. You don't. You're always reading philosophy or Rousseau."

"I notice what's important, not nonsense. Don't let the wax drip! When were these written? I wasn't even twelve years old. Matthias Aldgasser. Oh, dear God, Matthias! He became a priest, had to, because he preferred . . . don't listen, Sophie. He preferred—"

"What did he prefer?" the youngest girl cried, bouncing on the mattress.

"Hush, or we'll stuff a pillow over your face. He was . . . there was a scandal. Never mind; it would corrupt you to know."

"I'm already corrupted having stolen the book," Sophie said. "I'll have to make my confession and do penance, say at least a full rosary on my knees on the stone church floor. Don't push, Aloysia."

"I'm not," Aloysia whispered. "I don't think we should be looking at this at all. You could bunch a shawl under your knees, Sophie. And since when are you interested, Mademoiselle Maria Josefa?"

Still they turned more pages. "Ah, this list is more recent," Josefa said. The rest of their small room was now in shadow, with the shapes of their hanging dresses and hats like the ghosts of their lives watching over them. Josefa glanced toward the mirror, where she could see only the reflections of their dark faces and the sputtering light of the candle.

Constanze pulled the quilt over her knees. "Even if they are more recent, half these men are married already. The decent ones are snatched from the shelves as fast as fresh bread in the market, and the ones left we wouldn't want to rub bare feet with under a quilt."

"They'd be rubbing something more than that!" Josefa whispered with a smile. "Sophie, did you eat the very last marzipan chocolate?"

"Will you be still?" Constanze ran her finger down a few more pages. "Why, now it becomes fantastical!" she murmured seriously. "Look here. Here're her plans for you, Aloysia; your name's on the top of the page. Here's the name of a Swedish baron. She can't be serious. Where does she get such ideas? Sweden's very cold in winter, and they say the days are only a few hours long. You wouldn't be able to borrow things from us, Aly, if you lived so far away."

Aloysia wound her curls around her fingers. "I wouldn't need to borrow anything if I married a baron. And it's not as if she got the name from a book she read. The Baron visited here some months ago; he may have been at the court concert last night as well, but I couldn't see everyone's face when I was concentrating on the sixteenth notes in the duet. And Mama described him only once, rather vaguely. Did you steal this book just to tease me? Perhaps you don't care what you do, but I care very much! I'd have all the dresses I wanted then, all of them!"

"And what about Monsieur Horn Player Leutgeb, Mademoiselle Go-Hide-in-the-Dark?"

Aloysia pulled the book away so suddenly they heard the page tear, and all four looked down at it in horror. Constanze rummaged in a box under the bed until she found some paste, and they mended it as neatly as they could, heads together, fingers smoothing the page as if it were a holy relic.

Aloysia's eyes shone with tears again even as they finished. "Never mind," she said. "I'll tell her I ripped it accidentally. Or maybe she won't notice. Put it back under the barrel carefully. Leutgeb's nothing to me. I don't like everyone knowing my thoughts; you can't know them anyway. You couldn't understand them. You're not me. You haven't my reasons. And I will marry well, and you'll be fortunate if I let you visit me!"

She withdrew under her quilt, turning away from them a little, and did not look up when Constanze came back from returning the book to the kitchen. Though she closed the door as quietly as possible, her bare feet creaked the boards.

"Safely back?" one girl whispered.

Constanze nodded grimly. "Is there a chocolate with sweet chestnut paste?" she asked, her long loose hair falling over the box like a benediction. "The candle won't last but a minute more."

"There it goes!"

They all watched as it sputtered once; the wick slowly fell over into the last puddle of wax, glowed briefly, and died. The room smelled of waxy smoke and sweet chestnuts. In the smoky darkness, the paper in the candy box rustled as the girls rummaged.

"Papa says Herr Heinemann's teeth are blackened from too much sugar," Sophie whispered with her mouth full. "And Uncle Thorwart ate the whole top layer. He's getting awfully fat; he wears those English coats and will have to have a larger one made. Ah, it's cold outside. Can you feel the wind creeping under the sill?"

Constanze pulled her quilt closer. "Listen," she whispered even more softly. "Don't go to sleep yet. I almost forgot. This is terrible and sad! When I ran down the stairs before to say goodnight to Cousin Alfonso, I saw the tailor's daughter, whom we haven't seen in weeks, and now I know why. She's with child for certain. She couldn't hide it."

Aloysia now crawled closer to the others. "What? Without the blessing of the Church and the sacrament of marriage? We must thank God we were not brought up to do such things and bring terrible shame on our family."

Now they could see a little by the moonlight through the curtainless window. Huddled together, their wool nightgowns pulled down to cover their toes, they grew serious over the plight of the tailor's daughter. What a terrible thing! Every good girl knew that she must *withhold* until certain conditions, financial and social, were met. Flirtation was allowed, of course, even a passionate kiss on the lips on rare occasions. (The others felt Aloysia stiffen.) In empty alleys, in cloakrooms of great houses, near any room with a soft, inviting bed, however, vigilance *must* be upheld.

There were stories of too many glasses of good wine drunk, girls half dazed, an unremembered night but for a petticoat stained with blood that would not wash out. (The first spilled blood of unmarried virgins did not wash out. Their mother had always assured them of that, and their aunts had nodded solemnly and sworn it by heaven.)

Sophie blew her nose and wound her rosary in her fingers.

"How did Papa meet Mama exactly?" she asked eagerly. "Both our aunts have a different story. It was a love match though, Mama said. I think they ran away. Aunt Elizabeth says her parents were against it. They were rich, and Papa was poor but full of prospects."

"I thought Mama's family lost their money when she was ten."

"No indeed, seventeen."

"I'll ask her."

"She'll tell you something different every time."

"Oh, shut up! We were speaking of marriages in general."

With voices even lower, the conversation turned to sanctified marriage, and they sat more erect in the darkness. They told one another the stories of courtships and marriages: marriages of wealthy women and the elegance of their dresses, marriages of scrub girls, marriages betrayed and reconciled; of fidelity and infidelity, great dowries, large settlements, and true love, which was the rarest thing of all. Exhausted by so many marriages, they fell asleep one by one, until only Sophie and Josefa remained awake, now lying in heaps under blankets on their two close beds, faces almost touching, whispering.

Sophie said, "You could have sung that song at sight, Josy."

"Yes; when he writes another, I will."

"I like Mozart; he has a nice smile. I thought he would follow Aly down the hall, but he didn't. I wonder why he didn't. Maybe he's in love with someone else. Maybe it's you. Does she love Leutgeb, do you think? He and she were behind the hall door for the whole first movement of the trio, so perhaps she does. And what will Mama say to that?"

"Oh, really, I don't care. Such nonsense."

"I noticed something about the book. The first several pages have been cut out—the early writing."

"More nonsense. Good night."

Sophie lay awake for a time. She turned her head slightly to look at her sisters, sleeping this way and that, embracing pillows, curling in lumps under quilts, a hand with bitten fingernails dangling near the iron headboard. What was it like to be in love?

But the future was too complicated. There were things to be done in the morning: hose to be hung to dry, shirts to be ironed, and that all to one purpose. Under her breath she said her nightly prayer, which she and Constanze shared, that they might all remain together and that nothing would ever divide them. The pink flowered hose would be washed; the fan would be mended. She looked about the shadowy room at their garments thrown this way and that, their petticoats flung across the one chair, everything hazy in her nearsightedness. She put out her hand to touch her sisters, reassuring herself of their presence, protecting them.

In the marital bedroom, breeches and shirt draped also where they could find space, Fridolin Weber and his wife lay in bed, still talking softly. He wore a wet cold cloth over his forehead to remedy another of his frequent headaches. "Ah, your Thursdays," Caecilia Weber said affectionately, for their old friend Thorwart had come with many bottles of wine to replace the ones they had drunk, and Aloysia had sung like an angel from heaven.

Still, she added sternly, "I must speak to Aloysia tomorrow. I saw Leutgeb follow her. I have my plans for her. Don't smile, Fridolin. Thorwart moves in high circles and will help us. He'll find some good prospects. I swear before a year more turns, someone with an old family name will marry our girl. One can't have these matters arranged too soon before some other more unworthy girl gets the best opportunity."

"You're not thinking of the Prince of England, I hope?"

"You jest with me, Fridolin."

"You fill her head with too many things, my dear. I want only her happiness. She's very gifted, but rash." Fridolin handed her the wet cloth, which she again dipped in water and wrung out. "Perhaps one of our girls will marry Mozart. I like that young man, my wife. I like him very much indeed."

"Yes, he has a kind nature," answered Caecilia. "But he doesn't know how to get on in the world. Thorwart doubts he'll do well in Mannheim; he's hoping to be commissioned for an opera, but the wrong people are against him, and he wants to have the position of vice kapellmeister for the court but may not. He has enemies."

"Why does he have enemies?"

"Because he doesn't know how to manage people; people don't know what to think of him. He doesn't fit in. Thorwart tells me that. But we can't consider him as a suitor. He has promised not to think of marriage until he succeeds. I heard him say so."

"Let's hope that won't be a long time, for his sake. I know how eager young men are! But my love, Josefa left us for a time tonight. I thought the quarrel was made up, and then she left us. Do you know why?"

"Oh, she falls into dark moods and sulks! You know she never listens to me. Yes, she despises me for all I've done for her. She's my eldest, the most dependable but the least to be trusted. She distorts stories to suit herself, then changes them the next day. The same unfortunate characteristic of my dearest sister Elizabeth. I don't know if she herself knows truth from lies, and she's so tall and ungainly. I dare not tell anyone the size of her feet. I have begged our shoemaker not to reveal it. Perhaps she will have to sing for a living, for it's unlikely she'll find a husband at all."

"God will provide, as He always has. Will you pinch out the candle, dear? I'm quite tired, and have lessons to give in the morning." He kissed his wife's fragrant cheek, touched her full breast under the wool nightdress, then, with much tenderness, took her in his arms.

hree days before Christmas, Maria Caecilia was baking alone in her kitchen, the apron that sloped down from her ample breasts covered with flour and egg. No one else was home.

Their Thursdays had been canceled for a few weeks because of the great many performances all musicians played in Mannheim during this brief season. Sophie was at her Latin lesson, and Constanze was copying music at the house of a friend. The two older girls had sung several times in private houses, as they were doing today, and Maria Caecilia was grateful she did not have to go. If truth be told, she was not musical. She liked a few old country tunes, but to anything more complicated, she was quite deaf.

All morning she had combined eggs, flour, and spices, grinding ginger and nutmeg, whisking brandy with sugar. Now she had already baked a great deal, and the water was boiling. She listened once, and then again, wiping the eggshells and the sharply odorous gingerroot away from the table. The first batches of cakes lay cooling on trays by the window.

She had just brewed coffee in the iron pot when Johann Franz Thorwart knocked on the door.

He came into the kitchen in his customary high, gleaming English boots with their clanking spurs, and removed his hat. He was a well-built man of medium height, his graying hair in two rolls on either side of his head and the rest in a neat pigtail down his back. Carefully he placed the sword by the cupboard of dishes. "Ah, the scent of coffee and baking!" he said, kissing her cheek. "Sometimes great dinners (and, my dear, I have sat at some great dinners these years!) can disappear, for all I care, when one can have coffee and cake. No, don't think of removing us to the parlor! This warm kitchen is the finest place in the city! Better than a palace! Yes, I am cheerful! Business is good; business is very good."

Maria Caecilia took down two of her best small plates and wiped them on her apron.

Both she and Fridolin knew Johann Franz Thorwart from their hometown of Zell; his family had lived across the courtyard from hers, and it was Thorwart who had introduced her to Fridolin when she was seventeen. She found him entirely admirable. From humble beginnings, he had risen steadily. He was a factotum, secretary, and bookkeeper; served wealthy men in private matters; and discreetly moved money from this pocket to that. When he walked down the street, he hummed buoyantly, and wore an English-style frock coat that was all the rage, and those boots with spurs. His waistcoat pocket was filled with neatly folded papers, any of which he could find at once. His hands were wide and very clean. He was a man of business, and she trusted business far more than music. Two years ago he had appeared in Mannheim, and the Webers had taken him happily into their family circle.

She said, "You will have extra cream with your coffee as always?"

"As always, Maria Caecilia."

She dusted the best cushioned chair for him, and he seated himself, laying his hat on his knee and taking up a book that he saw on the table. "This can belong to no one but Josefa, for only she would be reading Rousseau," he said, frowning at the title, then reaching carefully into his pocket for his reading spectacles. "Dangerous stuff," he said. "Here the writer goes on and on about the rights of the poor. The poor, as Christ said, are always with you! They crowd the streets of Paris like vermin. I saw them on one of my journeys and prayed for them. It's obvious they are wasteful and spend their earnings in drink." He tapped the book. "Rousseau is wrong. If we're wise, we will not consider pulling down those above us who sustain us. The ancient order sustains us. God preserve the health of our Elector and our Emperor. No pauper lines my pockets and pays my rent!"

With the edge of his hand he pushed the book away and into a little dusting of flour. "I tell you, I don't know what is happening to the world. The New World colonies simply rebelling and trying to make themselves a new country, turning their back on England last year. The United States, indeed! Mark my word, even if they succeed they will come crawling back after some time. I have full trust we'll never see such a revolution on our beloved European shores."

Maria Caecilia shook her head as she filled the plates. "My little Sophie now reads these things as well."

"Take it from her. Mad, foolish young people."

"Hopefully, they'll soon grow out of them. You and your wife will come for Christmas dinner? My sisters will be here for some weeks; I expect they'll arrive any hour. You will have a cake with your coffee? Do take some home. I remember as a boy you loved cakes."

"And you loved them as well, still do. Ah, your *lebkuchen.*"

He sat for a moment inhaling the steam from his coffee cup, then ate a bite of the cake. "My dear Caecilia," he said, "how clever you are, managing all these years on I don't know what. But you know, I've admired you since we first met. The girl you were! So pretty, so virtuous, so devout! I can still see you leaning from the window early one morning in a chemise with pink ribbons. You didn't know I saw you; the light was gray, and there you were. You blush."

She brought her floury hand to her cheek. "My dear Johann, you're kind to remember all these years."

"Do you recall how I took you for pastry in Zell with your sisters just before you met Fridolin? But time is passing, and I'm expected at the palace on business within the hour. Let me come quickly to the heart of my visit. We were to speak of Aloysia, and this Swedish Baron. I have found more concerning him."

"Ah, have you?" she said, sinking down to a chair opposite him and beginning to breathe more rapidly. "Is there a chance of this occurring?"

"A rather good one, my dear."

"Johann, for the love of Saint Anne, tell me! This is my dearest hope! I'll make six novenas to the Blessed Saint for any good news."

"He's a widower and quite taken, I hear, with virtuous German girls who are musical. He was there indeed last month when our Aloysia sang with her sister in the Elector's palace. When I begin my negotiations, I will at once make clear that only through holy matrimony may he have her, with some added provision, of course, to her parents for the loss of her daily company."

"My friend! So he heard her sing?"

"Indeed, he both heard and saw her." Thorwart patted his lips with his handkerchief, and drank again, then sat back expansively. "And was, I am told by some acquaintances, much taken with her. I do not have the pleasure of his personal acquaintance, of course, but I know those who do. I shall make discreet inquiries. I assure you, my dear, this is neither the first nor the last marriage I have helped to arrange."

She was too moved to touch her coffee. "How can we ever thank you?"

"I am repaid in honor, in doing the best for my old friend Fridolin's daughter."

They spoke of other things for a time then. His wife was well, his daughter well, though they could not join the Webers for Christmas dinner. Opportunities of a financial nature were opening to him in the Mannheim court, for which he thanked God; still, he might not be there much longer. The Elector of Munich was ill, and if he died, Mannheim's Elector Carl Theodor would move to Munich with his court, succeeding to the Munich princeship, and Thorwart would follow. Musicians would follow as well.

He ate cake and gossiped pleasantly, crossing his legs at the knee, playing with the polished wood buckle of his breeches. Then he stood, pleading business. She curtseyed; he bowed, took his hat, sword, and cloak, and went away into the snowy streets.

Long after the sound of his footsteps had died away, Maria Caecilia stood by the warm bake oven gazing at his empty coffee cup and the crumbs on his plate. He had recalled her at seventeen; he had recalled her as she once was. Reflectively, she began to move across the rough wide floorboards of her kitchen where she had cooked so many hundreds of meals. Though she was now middle-aged, with graying hair hidden under her cap, she felt her old beauty and opportunities as if they pressed inside her, wanting to grow again. Even when she turned to a bit of

She wiped her hands on her apron. She had forgotten where she had hidden the book of suitors and, after some minutes of searching on her knees, located it on the lowest cupboard shelf under the clean sheets. Impatiently she skimmed the pages of household budgets and home herbal remedies until she came to the one she sought. Strange, it looked as if it had been ripped and mended. That puzzled her, but she was too taken with the words written there to dwell on it, with the almost holy feeling that filled her. There was the name of the Swedish Baron. Taking a pen and the ink bottle, she pushed aside her baking and carefully added the new information she had learned: forty years of age, widower, loves music, has house of forty rooms in Gothenburg; pack very warm clothes for Aloysia. A muff, she must have a fur muff. Warm petticoats; it was by the sea after all. Weekly letters to her, yearly extended visits. To marry her beautiful child well, and then the others. Maria Caecilia felt calmer now.

But she heard her own sisters' voices on the stair, the panting and complaining as they ascended. As she slipped the book under the clean sheets again, her memory flew back in time to twenty or more years earlier in Zell at the guild hall dance. There was her younger sister Gretchen, fresh as spring with yellow braids tumbling down her back and much sought after by the officers, and Elizabeth, as lovely as a Madonna, modest, tall, devout, dipping her knees to the music, turning to smile at Caecilia over the sound of the wind band. Then the three of them were going home laughing, arms linked. Now as she opened the door she saw only two ungainly, shapeless women straggling up the stairs in their crushed, lopsided hats, dragging several baskets from which dangled pairs of wool hose. A slipper tumbled out from one basket, and the neighboring boy who helped them muttered, "Jesus Christus!" as he fled to retrieve it. Maria Caecilia felt her smile stiffen on her lips. What had happened to them all? Youth must not be wasted; it must be made to last forever. Aloysia would be a Swedish baroness by the sea.

She went forward with her arms out, tears in her eyes.

hree weeks passed.

The voices of the choirs singing masses had risen up as usual in the churches that Christmas, accompanied at home by the baking of cookies and pastry and the roasting of geese until golden brown. Then the worst of winter set in. Cold wind blew through the streets; there were no fresh vegetables or fruit to be had; gingerbread stands were closed; and fires, no matter how hearty, seldom warmed rooms sufficiently. The only sensible thing was to go to bed with a hot brick wrapped in flannel to keep one warm. Snow fell, and fewer travelers came through. Many people had departed before this time to winter in more lively cities. And now Maria Caecilia's two sisters were also leaving to return to Zell.

They passed Aloysia, who was sitting on the cold landing before the door. Bumping into her drawn-up knees, they cast morose glances toward the rooms they had just left and the sound of bitter shouting.

Aunt Elizabeth stood upright to her full height, her crooked hat with the ancient bowed feather almost touching the ceiling. "I find it lacking in charity that your parents should argue so loudly, niece! Where are the consoling joys of man and wife?"

Gretchen added in her stuttering, vague way, "I have my theories on such things. Darling Aly, have I mentioned them to you?" Her face, which was plain as lumpy pudding, looked hopeful.

"I think so, Auntie," replied Aloysia dully.

Elizabeth sniffed. "Have you wrapped your feet well, Gretchen? It will be cold in the carriage."

Both aunts bent down and planted sticky kisses on Aloysia's pale cheek. "Good-bye, dear Aloysia," they said, blessing her. "Don't sit here too long; we had a dear friend who died of sitting on cold stairs. There was nothing that could be done for her, though physicians came. She was laid out in the parlor with candles. We'll return for your marriage. Your mother has hinted of fine things. You will wear the black petticoats we sewed for you girls? Black is a practical color—doesn't show dirt, needs less washing."

"Oh yes, Auntie, of course. Good-bye, dear Aunties."

After the aunts had managed to get down the stairs, yelling all the while at the boy who helped them, Aloysia remained outside her family's cluttered rooms, clasping her knees and shivering. It was the very spot to which Josefa had retreated two months before, but then that landing had always been the place of retreat when one of the four sisters wanted to be alone. Still written on the wall from years before in Josefa's tiny, bold print was a list of ten things that would make life perfect. (A bed all to myself,

never having to recite my French verbs, being loved best . . .)
One had to bend down low to see it. It could only have been
written by a lanky, grubby child stretched low on a creaking
step. Tiresome! Josefa never could speak good French, though
she read Rousseau.

*Your mother hinted of fine things; we will return for your mar-
riage.* Aloysia played with a lock of her hair. The Swedish Baron
had departed for his own country; Uncle Thorwart had been
apologetic. There were other fish in the sea, he had said. If the
court moved to Munich, there would be more opportunities.

Aloysia rubbed her hands, sticking them deep in her skirts to
warm them. The name of the Baron had been angrily crossed
out in the book. The enchanting handful of singing engagements in houses lit by hundreds of candles were over as well, and
all the money the family had earned had been spent on entertainment and food. Yesterday Sophie had trudged to the pawn
shop again with their mother's jewelry.

Even now Sophie slipped grimly out of the family's rooms;
her new, gold-framed spectacles made her look like some young
university boy. She was followed by Constanze, who sank to the
steps and began to sew.

"How can you hold the needle? It's so cold!" Aloysia murmured. "And how can you have the patience?"

"I must do something." The small face bent over her work.

"I hope the neighbors don't see us sitting here."

"Why? They've heard everything already. Mother has broken
two plates and thrown a pile of music at Father. I saved the blue
serving bowl and hid it in our wardrobe with the wineglasses."

"Don't squint at the stitches, Stanzi; it will make you look older earlier."

"I'm older already," Sophie said. "Troubles age one, but what can be done? We live in a fallen world. If we were still in the Garden of Eden, there would be no need for money. May I share Mama's shawl, Aloysia? We'll be here an hour or two, maybe more, and I'm freezing."

"Sit closer. There's a little coal left in the parlor, but I can't bear to be there. I thought you were good at making them stop quarreling, Sophie! Can't you make them?"

The youngest girl shook her head and wiped her nose. "You go," she muttered. "Mama melts for you."

"I tried, but they didn't pay any attention to me. I even cried. I won't go in, though I'll catch a wretched cold here and won't be able to sing even if anyone asked me, which they haven't since Christmas."

Sophie said, "It always gets worse in winter. Have you noticed it's always this time of year it happens? We must just somehow hold out until spring comes and there's more work. I suppose other people's parents quarrel also." She sighed, looking about her as if astounded to be able to see the world so clearly with her spectacles. "Uncle Thorwart doesn't quarrel with his wife."

Aloysia answered sharply, "He doesn't speak to his wife; he's had a mistress for years. How can Mother and Father forgive him so easily about setting my hopes up for a Swedish marriage and then dashing them again? He should have known the Baron was already married. Don't you dare laugh at me, any of you!"

The shouts arose even louder from the depths of the rooms

within, with their father's defensive, breaking voice, followed by their mother's accusations. Aloysia pressed her hands over her ears.

At that moment Josefa came up the steps, her market basket swinging from one hand and an open book in the other. She was always reading, sprawled on the bed, hidden on the roof, finding a better world. Now she read so intensely that she bumped a little into one wall, then glanced at it in disgust. Her face filled with more disgust on seeing her three sisters huddled there and hearing the shouting from within. "Oh saints above," she cried. "Everyone on the street will be talking about us now; I guess we'll have no dinner. Why must she always berate Papa? He does the best he can."

Constanze clutched the sewing against her dress. "It makes Mama sad having always to make do. Still, I think that man and wife should never turn on each other, even in the worst of times. It's providing for all of us that does it. If they married us off, they wouldn't have to feed and clothe us."

Sophie stood up. Since Christmas her tiny chest had developed some roundness, but not enough to make her sisters hope she would ever have any real curves, not that she minded in the least. "I refuse to see us as merely mouths to feed," she said. "We each have our own sacred purpose."

Josefa closed her book with a snap. "Marriage? No, thank you, I've seen enough of marriage not to want it. This is how it ends up; you hear the quarrels down the street. Ugh! And Mama's no saint; do open your eyes, Constanze Weber. Papa is what he is, and never promised more. If she wanted wealth, she shouldn't have married him. But likely he's the only one who asked her; that's what Aunt Gretchen said."

"That's not true! Dozens asked her!" Aloysia cried.

"Again, the differences of story."

"Earth doesn't promise happiness," said Sophie. "I was reading Josefa's Rousseau. 'Mankind is crushed by a handful of oppressors, a famished crowd vanquished by sorrow and hunger, a multitude whose blood and tears the rich drink peacefully . . . ' Oh, never mind. Josy, tell us what to do."

Josefa glanced toward their rooms. "I'll do what I must, and God help me," she said. "Constanze, take this food inside; Sophie, you tell them we've gone out. Aloysia and I are going to see Father's brother, our Uncle Joseph. It's time I brought out my plans."

Joseph Weber's office was on the second floor of his large house in a more elegant neighborhood of Mannheim. It was filled with heavy antique German furniture, large portraits of severe strangers, and a few shelves of well-thumbed ledger books tucked near others of theology and law. On the mantel above the fire stood an engraved silver cup given years before by his merchants' guild. *Nothing has changed since the last time we were here*, Josefa thought. *Even the wine decanter and the plate of small pork pies.*

"The Frauleins Weber," droned the servant as he closed the door behind them.

"Good day, dear Uncle," said the girls, making their curtseys.

The man in the tasseled wool cap who had been working behind the desk looked up. He was Fridolin's elder brother by some ten years, and he had Fridolin's spryness, except that he was almost entirely bald. "Well, nieces!" he said abruptly. "You find me at a very busy time. You might have sent word. Are you here to inquire about my health? Unlikely. There's so little commerce between my brother and myself since our quarrel, I can't recall when he's last come. He's sent you perhaps. No? You're well? Good. Have a pork pie. How much do you want to borrow today?"

Josefa smiled, curtseying again deeply. "Dearest Uncle," she said in her singer's voice, which reverberated under her cloak. "You speak abruptly only because we've surprised you at your work, for which we are so very sorry. Still, you can't conceal the goodness of your heart, for even now, every Sunday at dinner, our Papa tells us of how kind you were to him as a boy, and how much he admires and loves you. Surely you understand that all men are not equally fortunate in all areas of life's endeavors. I recall you bought me a hat once. Unfortunately, it is long outgrown."

Once more she made the smallest curtsey. "Yes, I confess it," she said, looking aside modestly. "We are in need of funds. Dearest Uncle, I would not ask you to part with any of your money unwisely. I would not dream of asking you for any if I could not offer sound collateral and a note of terms of repayment."

Assuming a queenly manner, she gazed at him.

Her uncle stared at them. "Repayment?" he croaked when he found his voice. "Collateral? What can you offer me that any money put into your hand will ever see the inside of my cash box again, eh? Tell me." Uncle Joseph put down his scratchy pen and narrowed his small eyes. "I could have timed your arrival by the season," he said. "Was it not this time last year that the two of you appeared just as abruptly at my door? And, in the name of sweet Saint Elizabeth, what collateral?"

Josefa faced him with chin upraised. "My work," she said clearly. "I have been planning this for some time. I intend to open a music shop with Papa to advise us. We will sell printed music, clavier strings, violins, and violoncellos."

"And where will you find the money to begin this venture?"

"From you, dear Uncle, with a little extra added on so that we can subsist until we succeed and Papa's work increases. Now you can certainly see I am not asking for a mere loan, but capital for my shop. Here, if you will, look at this paper. The costs and profits are clear; I have been calculating them for weeks. The payments, interest added on, of course, will begin within a year. Our friends Heinemann and Alfonso will help us."

Joseph Weber rose a little, leaning on his desk. "What, what? How?" he stammered. "Does my brother know of this? What do you know of the world? From books, which I am told you buy incessantly with your little musical earnings? Blessed Savior, you're cut from your family's cloth! Of course my brother can't sustain such a large family with their longings for books, French hats, chocolates, and wine! I told him two years ago to leave Mannheim to find more work elsewhere. Would he go? No. Will he do anything practical for you girls? Engage you as ladies' companions? No. Apprentice you as seamstresses or milliners? Send you out into service with some good family? Never. He has mad, ambitious ideas for you and himself, none of which will ever come true, and now you have inherited them."

The clerk hid his scrawny face by busying himself with a pile of papers, while Uncle Joseph rose a little more, fixing his cold eyes upon them. "Music, music, music," he cried. "And now, on my hope of salvation, more music! You all do nothing but starve on it, and still you persist. Loans last year, and the one before, and nothing repaid. Here I am selling cloth and have made a fine living, while he grows poorer and pretends it doesn't matter. Will he join me in my work? No. Will he cease his ridiculous and expensive entertaining? No. He could have at least remained single; indeed, he should have joined the priesthood before he married that mother of yours."

Josefa had drawn herself up now so much she seemed twice her height. "You can say what you may against our mother, though it's unjust, unjust, but you won't speak of our darling papa," she shouted. "Can't you see I'm sincere? You don't; you don't believe me."

"Sincerity does not buy firewood; I certainly do not believe you."

"It's futile to come to you; you have no heart. Papa's a saint. We'll get on without you. I'll make my way in the world, I swear, and won't turn my back on my family. Aloysia will become a great singer and make an advantageous marriage, as will my younger sisters. She will make one soon; see how beautiful she is!"

Uncle Joseph smiled crookedly and sadly. "A great singer?" he murmured. "An advantageous marriage? You'll starve on music as your father's done, and where is the splendid suitor to climb all those flights of stairs to marry one of you? Men of good fortune want modest women; modest women don't sing in public. Heinrich, pack the pork pies for them."

"Stuff the pies up your arse!"

"Fine words, young woman! Get out! Good day to you."

Josefa rushed out of the house and down the street, with Aloysia running behind her. After some streets, she managed to pull her older sister to a stop. "I'm cold, so cold," Aloysia panted. "My legs aren't as long as yours; I can't run so fast. Let's have a coffee. It's not real coffee, only roasted barley with syrup, but they also give you a crescent roll. Did you have breakfast? I didn't. I have two kreuzers. It's all I have left from the last time we sang."

Shivering, they drank their bowls of coffee in the wood shack while the old vendor spoke to some workmen who had also come in. Aloysia ate her roll slowly, pulling off fragments bit by bit. "We should have taken Uncle Joseph's pork pies," she said sadly.

"Let him choke on them!"

"Josefa, you scared him. You scared me."

"I *hate* him. It would have been a wonderful music shop. I was going to call it Weber and Daughters—Music, Instruments, and Sundries. I *will* call it that. I'll find someone else to sponsor it."

"Josy, we can't go back there again to ask. You're too horrible to have told our uncle to stuff the pork pies up his . . ." She glanced at the workmen and ate the last crumb of her roll. "*Que tu es horrible de dire à notre oncle de s'enculer avec sa tourte au porc!*

C'est terrible, c'est très impoli! It was very impolite." Aloysia suddenly burst into giggles and then struggled for poise.

"I'd die before going back. He's a turd."

"Still, thank you for saying I'm beautiful."

"You are, you know," said Josefa angrily, then she squeezed her sister's arm warmly. "Though between you and Mother you'll make something wretched out of it. Come on. We can't go home to the others without some shred of good news. Let's try to think something up."

The sisters linked arms and hurried on, their cloaks whipping out behind them, until they found themselves before the Christuskirche with its statue of the Archangel Michael blowing his horn to the heavens high above the dome. Their father had played violin there often for choral masses.

Catching her breath, Josefa still nursed her anger. "How dare our uncle speak badly of Papa? He works so hard for us; he buys us hose when his are in tatters, he watches up for us all night when we're sick and then goes to his work. No one understands how much he does, but I do. I've seen it as long as I can remember."

She folded her arms and stared up at the trumpeting archangel. Her eyes narrowed. "Still, Uncle's right in one thing," she muttered. "What chance do we have of making things better at home? Perhaps the music shop would cost too much. There's not even much work singing in churches; the priests prefer the singing of the old castrati. Come, let's go in. At least we'll be out of the wind."

They pushed open the heavy doors and curtseyed slightly to

a few elderly priests in narrow black cassocks. One of the wizened castrati, with his throat wrapped in an enormous gray scarf wound several times around, sniffed suspiciously at them, as if he had heard Josefa's scathing words. Candles flickered before statues here and there, but the air was not still. Cold as it was, it reverberated from the sounds of the organ that someone was playing from the loft high above, with the great clunk clunk of the working bellows.

They took seats toward the back, holding hands. The castrato, a man of nearly seventy with his face like an old wrinkled apple, again glared at them. Beggars huddled in corners, making themselves as small as possible. By the back door behind the gold altar a small line of poor people gathered, waiting for alms. "We could have given them our uncle's pork pies," Josefa said almost to herself. "That is, if you wouldn't have eaten them all at once like the piggy you are."

They hardly noticed when the organ ceased, leaving a great hum in the air for a moment, and when footsteps sounded on the steps descending from the loft; they did not know their father's friend Mozart was approaching them until he touched their shoulders and bowed.

They had seldom seen him since he had come that Thursday night with the song Aloysia sang at sight. They had heard he was visiting great houses outside the city to play. Once they had noticed him in the market, and he had waved to them. Now he looked as he did when he had ceased playing the clavier that first night at their house, half in another world, small and neat, with his natural light brown hair uncurled and fastened with ribbons at the back of his head. He said, "Mesdemoiselles Weber, what is it? Why are you huddled here? You look as though something has troubled you. May I sit with you?" With that he took a place courteously beside them.

Aloysia's eyes filled with tears. Her life, which she felt ready to spring out to magnificence, had retreated since that magical night when she had stood among a pressing, admiring group of friends and family and sung his lyrical song on first sight. The music now lay under some other things, and she could not bear to look at it. It reminded her of how, in the openness of her heart that evening, she had agreed to secret meetings with Leutgeb, and how, during them, she had allowed him to put his hand where no good woman should. She should never have given so much; the faithless horn player had abruptly returned to Salzburg and, in spite of his heated promises, had never written a word to her. She had said nothing of this to anyone, of course, because she was ashamed, but now with her unhappiness over that and the lost Swedish opportunity combined with the rejection of Uncle Joseph, she blurted the story of her family's misfortunes. She said more than she would have otherwise as she tore at her handkerchief and wiped the corners of her eyes.

Josefa only nodded grimly. This young composer from Salzburg for all his kindness and her father's favor toward him was not one of them, and she had her mother's horror of showing their dirty linen to a stranger. Her mouth compressed tightly, and she felt as she had in the carriage when she had tried to hide in the shadows. Once she nudged her sister sharply to stop the flow of her grieved, high voice.

As Aloysia spoke, Mozart looked at the shivering girls as intensely as he had looked inside himself in the loft the hour before, searching for a fugue by the lamented Bach, which he had heard once years before. His eyes filled with compassion at their faces reddened by the wind, their wind-loosened hair that fell in strands down their necks, their chapped lips, and their pale clasped hands. He thought of his mother's neat gloves. The smaller girl shivered spasmodically, and flung her arms about her chest.

"Mesdemoiselles Weber," he murmured. "You honor me to trust me with these confidences. Believe me, I won't betray them. There's little work for musicians here but for the orchestra. My mother and I are thinking of leaving when she returns from her visit to my father and sister in Salzburg. Still, there must be some way to take your family from its difficulties. You sing charmingly, beautifully. You yourselves are charming and beautiful." He caught at their hands in both of his, chafing them, rubbing his supple fingers over them. "Go home now; you're cold. I know some people, and I have some influence. Perhaps I can do something to help you."

ozart took his midday meal of large veal chops and soup a few hours later in a smoky eating house with the orchestra director, Cannabich, and other musician friends who were passing through the city. They spoke of symphonies, of chamber music, of masses, of where work was; they spoke of good livings to be made that someone else always seemed just to have taken. They gathered around the table looking out at the muddy street that, in the dim light, retained the history of those who had passed this hour: the surly indentation of wheels left for a time until swept over by a beggar's broom or the trailing, ragged skirts of a half-drunken whore.

Mozart had managed some weeks before to move with his mother to the comfortable house of the privy counselor, where she was warm and happy, and coughing less. She was treated as a family member, gossiping at table, and was altogether less (he arched his shoulders to think of it) of a burden on him. Still, they needed money, and, as he had not yet completed the second concerto and flute quartets of the Dutchman's commission, he had not received any payment. In his pocket even now was a letter from his father that had arrived yesterday. "My dressing gown is in tatters. If someone had told me two years ago that I would have to wear woolen stockings and your old felt shoes over my old ones to warm myself . . ." And he had written back rapidly just that morning: "But you know, my dearest Papa, this is not my fault." Was it? It haunted him.

The clavier player and violinist who had played in a corner of the eating house had left, and Mozart scraped back his chair to go sit down at the instrument. Yesterday afternoon he had gone with friends to hear Holsbauer's opera *Günther von Schwarzburg*, and now he began to play some of the beautiful music from memory. Cannabich listened for a time, and then came to stand beside him. His hair, pulled simply back in a ribbon, here and there showed traces of white, lavender-scented powder from his recent performance. He was a family man, with three gifted children.

"Enough of that opera!" he cried stoutly. "Let's have a better tune." Leaning over the small composer, he began to play with his right hand, clenching his pipe between his teeth. *"La finta giardiniera,"* he said, words and smoke rising with the music. "You wrote it three years ago for a Munich performance. I recall parts from memory. How old were you then, you gray beard? Eighteen? And how old when you penned that gorgeous little singspiel *Bastien*? Twelve in God's name?"

Mozart said, "Nothing's better than opera for me—music, drama, poetry. Play that bit again. Use both hands; I'll sing it."

Cannabich drew up another chair and they played competitively, crossing hands. "Here come the strings. Ah, that's a nice tenor! What is happening, Wolfgang? No word on the position here?"

"Nothing, and more of nothing. I managed to corner the Elector himself on his way from chapel in a hall of the palace and asked him again about the position. 'I am sorry, my dear child,' he said solemnly, 'but there is no position.' *My dear child*—those words." Mozart played more intensely, leaning forward, and began to sing again.

"That's the girl's aria. You'll rival the women the way you sing! I met Joseph Haydn last year, you know; he has the patronage of Esterházy in Hungary. He much admires your work. Didn't his sister-in-law sing in *Finta*? "

"Yes, and his brother is *konzertmeister* at Salzburg. I've never met Joseph Haydn. Here's the tempo change."

"You know his quartets?"

"I admire them deeply. The tempo's slower here. I can't sing and play at once! What do you think opera should be, Canna-bich, eh? Comic and serious, common and heavenly?"

In the early winter dusk Mozart returned to his new rooms in the comfortable house of the privy counselor. He looked at the score of another of his unfinished operas; then, putting it aside with a sigh, he began to work again on the second flute quartet. When he put down his pen, he did not know if the church bells were signaling the last service of the night or the first of the new morning.

Mozart stood up, stretched his aching back, and began to walk up and down the room. Then he noticed another letter to him standing by the washing bowl; the writer was his cousin in Augsburg. Their hosts must have brought it in. He felt the old stirring in his breeches and laughter rising in his chest. Tearing open the seal, he stood reading it with his hand over his mouth. By God, she was witty, sexy, and priceless, and next time he would have all of her. He would travel there somehow, and tear off her petticoats and her lace-trimmed drawers. Why not? She was willing.

And then what? They should both be compromised. He would have her to support as well, and perhaps a baby, and he could not even manage his mother, father, and sister, who always waited patiently for him. No, he could not manage it all. Then, turning to some words written small in the margin, he frowned, swore, and threw down the letter. What, had she . . . he was breathless, and read it again. "I have a lover now," it read. "So very sorry it wasn't you, Wolferl. Waiting's awful. Don't worry, I'll be careful. My dull old father knows nothing; he's never felt these things. Old people never could. You don't mind so much, do you, old cousin? We're best of friends."

Mozart stood, staring straight ahead of him. Fury filled him, not only jealousy that someone he had thought of so much had not had time to wait, but that she had gone on to experience this thing and left him behind. He put the letter facedown on his flute quartet and continued his walk back and forth in his narrow bedroom. Why had he ever taken any pleasure with his cousin? Even if they had made love fully, she would have turned her attention elsewhere the moment he left the city. If he were to love someone, it should be a good girl. He stood quietly for a moment, remembering the voices of the Weber sisters as they sat together in the church confiding in him, and then their excellent singing, the one soprano darker and more sensual, the other high as an angel. They were good: nothing but virtuous and self-less thoughts passed their minds.

Josefa was too tall; he did not want a woman to tower over him—but there was Aloysia. He saw her, the line of her neck to her breast under the heavy cloak, the pretty open hand that floated on the air as she spoke, her beautiful eyes. That boor Leutgeb had played about with her feelings. Just last week Mozart had had a letter written from Salzburg from him.

Dear Mozart, dear idiot,

It's over between Mademoiselle A. and me. I'm uncertain I want to pledge my future to a singer, even such a delicious little one. Not that I compromised her: only a kiss and a touch in the dark, and what is that? But mainly, old friend, my reluctance lies with the family. They have a huge pull on her. If I marry her, I'll have the lot of them on my hands, and my grandfather's shop in Vienna doesn't sell that much cheese. They're a heavy lot, particularly that mother of hers. The father's a sort of crooked saint, kindliness himself, but with more goodwill than sense. I advise you, old friend, fall in love with some merchant's wealthy widow. We don't have much money, either of us. I have cheese, and you have genius. Forget love and look after money. Frau Weber does, believe me.

Mozart did not move. The words of the letter repeated themselves in his head until they faded before his memory of the two sisters in the church, their breath in the cold air, Aloysia's chapped, pale lips, the elder sister's bitten fingernails. Was not the world full of hopeful women, untouched, waiting? But what had it to do with him?

Yet what had happened in that room between the two of them when she had sung his song? What had happened and what had not? Mozart remained still but for his hands drumming on his music, thinking of her. What had been created between song maker and singer in that little parlor that night? Should he have followed her when she left the room? Had she intended it? No, of course not; she was simply too beautiful and good. Such women were to walk about shyly, and to be dreamed about. And besides, he knew her mother wanted a titled man of old family for the girl, and with her grace and charm she could likely have one. What had he to offer? And yet he was not half bad. He could have had his love affairs if he had wanted them, and yet he always drew back.

There was that confidential, drunken hour with Leutgeb in the beer cellar when the girls had come, and the hour after when he and the horn player had spoken so frankly of their hopes. Why hadn't he told Leutgeb, whom he trusted, that he had never taken a woman to bed? "By Christ," he murmured aloud in the room, "I couldn't say that." He was flushed even to think that the painted wallpaper of this pleasant room, the books, his coat thrown over a chair could have heard him.

He fell into his bed late that night, tossing his bedclothes to the floor. In the morning he sprang up naked from bed and stood shivering in the cold room; he threw on a dressing gown, un-corked the ink, and wrote hastily. "Mademoiselle Aloysia Weber, in all friendship, will you meet me at the Confectionery at three? Your servant in all respect, W.A.M." and sent it over by a boy.

She won't come, he thought.

But she did.

Aloysia Weber floated across the Confectionery under the gold-and-white ceiling. In the mirrors around him, he saw her approaching in her dark cloak with the muddy hem, past the small marble tables and the sideboard heaped with cakes. She was so perfectly made he could have taken her under his arm and swept her away. By the time she reached him and made her curtsey, he was not sure who he had been before she entered the doors.

He bowed, and again she curtseyed; he seated her. Then he

said as calmly as he had intended, "I have come up with a plan to solve your difficulties."

"Tell me," she said. "My father will be so grateful. No one helps us, no one, and here you are, yet a stranger to our family." She leaned forward on the chair. In her throat, the unblemished flesh of an innocent girl not quite seventeen, was a hollow where her breath quivered. He could not take his eyes from it.

"We'll give concerts together; we'll tour all Europe."

"Oh, could we? What are you saying? All Europe? With me singing and you playing as we did that evening in our rooms? Would we go to Paris? Oh Herr Mozart, would we give a concert even in Paris?" She could hardly speak the words; her white throat quivered. A loose thread from her dress lay against her collarbone.

"Yes," he said, "Paris, of course. Why not? I've just begun to plan it in my mind. I'll write many songs that show your voice off to the best effect. First we'll tour Austria, and give a concert in Vienna; I have friends there who would help us. We would go to Venice, to Florence, to Rome, and then we would go to Versailles."

"Versailles," she murmured. The loose thread moved as she breathed. He could see her reflection in every mirror over the silver cake plates.

"Versailles," he repeated. "Mademoiselle, I assure you on my honor that wherever you lift your voice in song, strangers will beg for tickets. I can do this, for my name's known. I'll take your father and Mademoiselle Josefa as well. We'll return with so much gold your family will never have to worry again." He spoke with deep assurance, though his heart beat strongly and he leaned so close across the table that he could see a few faint freckles across her cheeks. "And then, both the Viennese opera houses will want you to sing once they have heard you. There's never been such a voice, they'll say."

"Paris," she murmured. "Vienna. Can it be?"

"Without a doubt. Give me a few days, and I'll come to lay plans more clearly."

Aloysia could hardly find her voice, and when she did she put her hand on his. "We'll all be so very glad," she stammered. "My sister and I particularly. I will need a new concert dress, perhaps of pink brocade. Don't you think a dress of that fabric and color would suit me particularly, Herr Mozart?"

After a few hours they emerged from the Confectionery, hands almost touching. She kissed his cheek and, in her dark cloak and little flat shoes, disappeared around the corner of a church, while he remained gazing after her, his hand to his face where her lips had touched it.

Frau Mozart always unpacked her bags at once when she came from traveling, but this time she had gone to bed upon her return, and now morning had come with the cold day pressing outside the iron bars of the window. She had dreamed of her house plants, which she had left once more on the windowsills of her Salzburg home; she alone trimmed the dead leaves from them so lovingly, murmuring to them old Austrian endearments. But it was not in her own home where she awoke, rather in their hosts' house in Mannheim, in which she now found no charm.

Her son had gone out.

Rising and pulling on her dressing gown, she began to walk up and down her room past the still-buckled traveling bags, starting to make the bed and then forgetting it, until at last she sank into the chair and began to write.

Dear Husband,

I have returned from my two weeks' stay with you to a catastrophe. What else can it be? Your son. He did not wait for me to take off my cloak yesterday before presenting me with what he assumed I would take as good news: that he intends to go on concert tour with the impoverished Webers, particularly Mademoiselle Aloysia, with whom he is beginning to fall in love, but of course he denies that. Instead of finishing the Dutchman's flute compositions, which will bring us money, or the piano/violin duets in honor of the Electress to win her goodwill, he does little but write songs for the mademoiselle. Indeed, he performed a concert with her at some estate, and gave her and her family *half the fee!* Now what will occur with our plans to leave soon for Paris, where he will surely find the great success he deserves? He cannot quite recall we planned it; he waves it off with a dismissing hand and goes back to explaining his new idea. The Webers! He hopes to create their fortune, but what, I ask you, of our fortunes? We will all end paupers, begging on the corners of Salzburg.

She looked up, hearing footsteps, quickly blew on the letter to dry it, and turned it facedown. There was her son at the door, hair ruffled wildly as if the wind had once more gotten the best of him. Once more, as he often did when not in concert attire, he looked like an unmade bed. What was she to do with him?

She said coldly, "Wolfgang, I didn't close my eyes all night. I can only presume that you have come to your senses and thought better of the ridiculous proposition you set before me last evening."

"What, Mother, how can you call it that," he cried, coming close to her with his face full of affection. "I've arranged it all. The tour with the Webers will bring a great deal of money, enough for all of us."

"You still intend to do that? Your own father will be beside himself when he receives my letter. Do you think just to post word that this unknown chit of a girl and her farmwife sister will be singing will be enough to fill hundreds of seats? You're the only one whose name is known at all, and you yourself struggle for enough concerts and patronage. Your father goes about in such shabby garments he can barely show his face to the Archbishop (I couldn't believe the state of his shirts, truly past mending) and now you propose to divide what you earn between us and them." She turned to finish making the bed, threw up her hands, and covered her face.

Between her fingers, she said, "You haven't the power to uplift them, and it will drag us further down."

He pulled her hands away from her face. "Mother, I know voices," he said. "Aloysia has the makings of a great singer. She could be one of the finest prima donnas in Europe."

"What do I care about her abilities? She only wants what she can get from you, and I wouldn't trust her, nor any of them. I knew it from the first moment I mounted those many flights of steps."

"You say that about someone I esteem so highly? You say that? Well, I'm going, I don't know if I will be back. You've slandered her and wounded me."

He ran out and walked the cold, windy streets for a long time, until he had lessons to give. By the time they were done, and his pupils had noticed his distraction, darkness had come. Going home was an impossibility. If only Leutgeb were here. All his friends had left the city for one reason or another; even Cannabich was traveling. It was likely the court would be moving to Munich.

A wet snow had begun, and he found refuge in a familiar eating place. He bought paper and borrowed pen and ink, then began to work on a piano/violin sonata.

"Master, we must close," said the host, and Mozart looked around, startled to see everyone had gone but him, and the exhausted boy who was mopping the floor, leaning half asleep on the mop. He rushed out into the wet snow with his cloak open, and the host ran after him, crying, "Master, master," and gave him the flopping, forgotten pages. Two slipped from the man's hand and went blowing down the street. Mozart retrieved them where they had caught about a horse post, a little wet and blotted, and stood gazing at the melody under the gaslight. He wished that the eating house had not evicted him, or that he could have gone to some other quiet place where he could write more and forget his mother's blanched face, the mournful eyes that accused him and spoke against his proud and imaginative plans.

He leaned against the door of a house.

So much had happened since his promise in the Confectionery. He had written two more songs for Aloysia, recalling the rare range and timbre of her voice, which extended from a few notes below middle C to the very highest range far above the treble staff, the E, the F, and the untouchable flicker of the G, which only the rarest of voices could reach. He was a musician, and he knew the quality of her voice: even in his love he knew the voices of both the older Weber sisters were rich and enviable.

And how the whole casual, warm family had welcomed him, but more than that, much more, had been Aloysia's arms flung about him on those steps smelling of other people's cooking, and her soft lips against his, and her little breasts pressed against his chest, and her tears of relief and joy at their sudden strange blurting of love for each other. *I didn't see at first, Mozart, I didn't know. . . .* My God, she loved him. The most beautiful girl he had ever seen, and she loved him. It was as if she had been waiting for him all his life. Then she had drawn him upstairs to her family, into the room with the clavier, the burning fire, and a bottle of wine and a polished glass. He felt suddenly the contrast between the heaviness and bleakness of his dutiful life and the bright gaiety of the girls and their family, the clothes and music all thrown about, and good, kind Fridolin Weber's welcome. He had been accepted as her suitor then; he had been accepted as her betrothed.

He drew his cloak closer; a watchman passing by inspected

him for drunkenness but, seeing him sober, said, "Go home, young man." And Mozart straightened and began to walk very slowly toward the house where he and his mother were guests.

Would his plans to tour with the sisters lift the family from their obscurity and difficulties? Could he do it? Did he not owe his own family everything? Had they not given all for him? Perhaps his mother was right. He ought to make better fortune himself, and then raise her up. Within a few months of being in Paris, he should be wanted everywhere, and then could simply send for her and help make her career. Yes, then he could help lift her sweet and agile voice to fame.

By now he had reached the house; admitted by a weary maid servant, he mounted the stairs to their rooms. His mother was already in bed in her nightcap, but he could tell she was not asleep. "We are going to Paris," he said. "I have decided."

Without turning, she spoke, the voice a murmur against the blue bed hangings. "Then say you'll also forget her."

He stood quietly with his wet sonata under his coat. "I can never forget her; she's my muse. I'll go with you and make our fortune and then come back for her. She'll be more than muse then; she'll be my wife."

There was nothing Sophie loved to do more than sleep, carefully plumping the pillow just so, slipping one arm under it, drawing her knees up under her wool nightgown, so nested in the old quilting that the world disappeared. In her dreams she heard voices, raised her head, and looked about. The early morning air was still dark, and an icy rain beat at the windows. The light snow of last night had turned to rain in the unpredictable weather of the world.

Surely it was not time to rise yet, and where were her sisters? Their bedclothes were thrown back, and only the impressions of their bodies remained on the lumpy mattresses. Outside there was only rain, not even the bells of the ancient bread cart horse. She sat up, rubbing her eyes, and trundled to the door. Last night had been her twelfth birthday, and she had been given new wool slippers, but she now had no idea where they were. Perhaps, she thought sleepily, some sister had already borrowed them.

Where were Constanze and Josefa? She wound her bed quilt about her and shuffled down the hall barefoot, following the voices that came from the parlor. Who was there at this hour? It could surely not be time for pupils. Creaking open the door, she looked about bewildered, wondering at first if she had mistook morning for evening. All the family members sat or stood about the room in their night clothes, their expressions grave. Constanze was wrapped in her quilt, huddled on the sofa, with her feet drawn under her for warmth, Aloysia leaning against her; Josefa and her father stared out the window while her mother sat close mouthed in the best chair, a cap pulled over her curling rags. The fireplace was cold and dark, and the clavier still huddled under its wool shawl. Standing in the middle of them all was Wolfgang Mozart in his cloak and hat, unshaven and wet, his shoes leaving moist spots on the floor.

There was no sign of her new wool slippers.

"Why, what's happened?" she murmured, feeling for her handkerchief; her nose was already beginning to run.

Her mother turned to her, face long with sadness. "Mozart's come early with bad news. He must go away for a time to Paris. The tour with your two sisters must be temporarily postponed."

"To Paris, away from here? But if you must, you must. It's not your fault," Sophie said at once, going to him and taking his hand.

Mozart said, "We leave in an hour by coach, or I wouldn't have come so early. I had to come myself, and not merely send word. I'll send my address as soon as I arrive, the very day, and write to all of you." Words failed him then. He kissed all their cheeks, even Maria Caecilia's, who turned away a little; he embraced Fridolin Weber with both arms. Then he took Aloysia's hand and left the family's rooms with her, closing the door behind him. The others heard their voices for some time, though the words were indistinguishable, and then his footsteps going rapidly down the stairs.

When she came back, her face was wet with tears. "He promised me," she said, her mouth very tight. "He promised me and now he asks me to wait. It will be at least a year before we can be married. Now it's all settled, but the question is when? He's going to Paris without me. Oh, will I always have to wait, all my life? Will I be twenty before anything happens to me?" and she walked down the hall into the communal bedchamber, closing the door. Soon they heard her soft weeping, and Constanze, with a look of misery, ran off to comfort her. Maria Caecilia said nothing more but turned heavily to her bedchamber, followed sadly by her husband. That door, too, was closed.

Now alone in the parlor, Josefa and Sophie snuggled under one quilt, the eldest girl rubbing the feet of her little sister. Josefa did not speak at first. After a time she said, looking straight ahead, "He'll come back. He's honorable, he'll come back and try to keep his promises to us if he can, but I feel sorry for him because he loves her and she has no heart. God forgive me for saying it, for I'd do anything I could for her, but it's true. It's true, Sophie, don't protest, you kind child—but she's also weary of Mother's fantasies and her own. He at least is real. Now I'm going to make a fire and coffee. Surprisingly, Father's brother did send over some money yesterday, though it probably shortened his life to do so. Thorwart's also promised some. We'll manage for a time."

Sophie nodded. "It will all come out for the best," she said.

"Perhaps, but which way is that, darling? How do we know what's best? How do any of us know?"

Below, through the rain, Sophie heard the sound of the bread wagon's bells, and there, under the music table, as if they had been contently waiting for her, were her new wool slippers. Gratefully wriggling her feet into them, and borrowing a dressing gown that someone had left draped over the clavier, she hurried down the stairs. In the gray rain the wretched dripping horse stood waiting, water glistening on its brass bells, which were tied with bright, soaking ribbons. The street was slowly coming to life. As the girl took the two warm loaves and ran upstairs, to be greeted by the smell of newly ground coffee beans, she wished that the events of this early morning had been nothing but a dream, and that she were still asleep, warm and dry in her lumpy bed.

Sophie Weber, March 1842

YESTERDAY MONSIEUR NOVELLO CLIMBED THE STAIRS of my Salzburg rooms once more to gather stories for his biography of Mozart. I had only just enough time before he knocked to reach for the cluster of curls that I pin on my hair. I don't put my hair in rags anymore; I haven't in years. Then I sat back, cane near my hand, looking at this genial, balding musicologist who had come so far to meet me and who always brought me chocolates. I suppose the happy eating of them over many years has brought me to my considerable weight, but as a girl I was thin as a twig.

"So you and your wife live in London, monsieur?"

"We do, and gather many musicians for concerts there."

"I hear the city is damp."

"It is indeed."

He looked about at the clutter of books, garments, letters, a violin without strings, piles of papers—some tied, some loose. Sometimes I feel all the lives of my sisters and I, which went such different ways, have come home together here. There are my grandmother's oval cameo, Mother's black silk bonnet, the handwritten manuscript of Mozart's first song for Aloysia, and, of course, in the bottom of the wardrobe, the hatbox with its letters tied by a lavender ribbon.

Monsieur Novello took out a bound notebook, and his small, portable writing desk, which he balanced on his narrow knees. "Last time," he said, "you had stopped when Mozart had pledged himself to your sister Aloysia and was rushing off to triumph in Paris."

I turned my face. "I was indiscreet; I said too much."

"My dear madame, how could you say too much?"

But my conscience had nagged me on and off since his last visit. "Mama urged us not to speak too much of ourselves to others," I said sternly, looking at him over my spectacles and smoothing my capacious skirt. "She would not have liked me to reveal certain things. Alas, Monsieur Novello! Perhaps we ought to put aside the personal stories, and I'll tell you of his music instead, about how he composed. He created it all in his head, then wrote it near perfectly on paper. It's true; I saw it."

Monsieur Novello tried to conceal his distress. "Yes, madame," he said carefully, "but that is known; others have told me a great deal about that. What you can tell me I can find nowhere else in the world, nowhere. It's truly extraordinary the depth and subtlety he has put into the female characters in his operas; no one could do it half as well as he. From where did he draw them? They're so human, so fallible, and yet so playful and sensual. I believe understanding how his life entwined with yours and your sisters' while he was in his early twenties, when he was so impressionable, can shed some light on this."

"Mama would be unhappy that I've spoken."

"But I beg you, I beg you! You must tell me what you know. You must tell me about his life with all of you in the years leading to his marriage."

He even put his hand respectfully on my knee.

"On the other hand," I said, "Papa always told us to be open-hearted, and that there was nothing we should ever want to hide." I smiled in my old way. Strange, after all these years, and even in my old age, I can still smile in a way that can mean so many different things, something I learned quite young. I suppose I never seriously intended to stop my stories; I am ashamed to believe that I wanted to know once more how much he longed to hear them.

I said, "What lovely chocolates you brought today! Did I tell you how much my sisters and I loved chocolates? We would have given our souls for a box."

"Then you will continue?"

"As memory allows me."

"I thank you from the bottom of my heart!" he cried.

I ate two pieces and wiped my fingers on the monogrammed linen handkerchief he offered, though if I had been alone, I would have licked them clean. It irked me a little to see the morsels folded in the linen and tucked away.

"Your mother," he urged gently.

"Ah, yes. Nothing would have turned out as it did if it weren't for our mama. She pushed us firmly one way, and we went firmly in the other. No, if it weren't for her, everything would have been different."

I raised my cane and pointed to the wall. "Look: there's her silhouette to the right of the fireplace. A family friend made it one night when he finally got her from her baking and planning. She was a big woman, but her arms were delicate and her skin very fresh, very sweet-smelling."

"She had a complicated nature."

"From what you have heard of her elsewhere or from my stories?"

"Both indeed, madame."

He studied the picture for some time, then returned to his writing, his pen scratching the page. After a few moments, he looked up at me. "So, all that occurred was much from her influence?"

I opened my eyes wide and brought up my hands. "In one way or another. Everything was of the greatest seriousness to her. She believed in signs, as do I, and she knew in her heart at least one of her daughters was destined for greatness. That is how we lived our ordinary days, expecting something far more wonderful would fling open the door. . . ."

PART TWO

Munich and Aloysia,
1778

Late spring came, and the sisters hurried about Mannheim, saying good-bye to old friends, exchanging locks of hair and trinkets, and promising to write. The Webers were moving to Munich. The Elector there had died, and Mannheim's Elector Carl Theodor and his court had already moved to the palatial *Residenz* there. Alfonso and Heinemann had gone with them. They expected there would be even more opportunities for music in Munich.

At the last hour Sophie walked through the empty rooms looking for things they might have left behind. How odd! What life was left here when every chair and wardrobe was gone, when the hooks were empty of clothing, when not one pot in the kitchen remained? There was the dark stain on the kitchen wall where Josefa, at the age of twelve, had bled copiously after slicing her thumb while cutting apples. The floorboards of the bedroom bore the gouged marks of the iron bed feet.

She noticed a pen and some ink left on a windowsill and, finding a paper scrap, leaned over to write a note. "Dear friends, we have gone to Munich by God's grace for a more prosperous life. Come see us there. We are as always altogether, and altogether we wait for you." This she stuck on a nail on their door, hoping the new residents would not take it down right away. She was about to run down the stairs to where her family was waiting when she remembered the book of suitors, but her mother had taken it from its latest hiding place. Would that she had left it there, Sophie thought with a grimace, for she had secretly looked into it some days before and had not been pleased with what she had seen. What could she do about it now, though? Later, surely, she could do something.

She blessed the empty rooms, and hurried down to the street.

And then within weeks it was as if they had never lived anyplace else but beautiful Munich. Their new rooms, on a floor one story lower than their Mannheim residence, made it slightly easier to bring up firewood and bring down chamber pots. They were also fairly close to the great church, the Frauenkirche, with its two tall round towers rising over other buildings against the bright sky. They settled in their old careless way, everything scattered about, musicians coming on Thursdays to play and often on other nights dropping by for supper, wine, or talk. For the first time in their lives, they had almost enough money to live on, and the two older sisters began to sing here and there to some success.

Letters came regularly from their friends in Mannheim, and every week or more, a thick one from France, which Aloysia took away to the girls' communal bedroom, giving orders that no one was allowed to enter for some time. From behind the closed door they could just hear the scratch of her pen as she wrote her reply; when finished, she walked directly to Father's desk, sealing her response with white melted wax and his crest of a lyre. Do not come near, do not ask, her pursed mouth seemed to say.

In spite of the move, the family members shortly became themselves again: their quarrels, their secrets, their gregarious love of company, their father's weariness, their mother's desires to have her girls well settled. The book with the tooled-leather cover and the list of potential suitors written carefully within had indeed moved with them; it was hidden now in some new spot, which no one could find, though Sophie had looked for an hour, until her skirt was dusty. Their mother had been quiet concerning it for some months after the move, and for a time they all thought she might have forgotten about it.

She had not. In the heat of summer, as they sat about the new parlor (which looked just like the old one except the floor slanted a little and they had to stuff a wad of paper under one of the clavier legs to stabilize it), the Weber sisters heard their mother huffing slowly up the stairs. "Girls," she said, reaching up to unpin her hat, for she never went down to the street, even to buy matches or cooked fish, without it. "My girls, my little fleas, I have plans."

"Ah, not *plans*," murmured Josefa. She had an intense look in her eyes; she had been reading *Hamlet* in German for the fourth time, and had just come again to the appearance of the ghost.

"And what good mother doesn't have them? Listen!" Maria Caecilia laid her hat carefully down on the table. "I met Elisa Hoffman in the thread shop; you'll recall, my doves, she went to school with me. She asked if you were all betrothed or married

yet, and I said no, indeed, though my eldest is already twenty."
Maria Caecilia sighed and continued, "Then my kind former
schoolmate replied, 'Dear Maria Caecilia, don't be concerned! I
have a prospect. I know a man here but briefly who has planta-
tions in the West Indies, a widower of thirty with two children.' "

Maria Caecilia sat down, breathless and triumphant, and
fanned herself with a thin news journal that she had brought for
her husband.

"Which one of us will be bid for?" Josefa said, shifting on the
sofa as she prepared to return to her book. "When does the auc-
tion begin, or do we each share as we always do, getting a quar-
ter apiece of the young man? Is that by polygamy or dissection?
Please count me out. The West Indies are hot and too far.
Thirty's old. Money doesn't make one happy."

"That's true, Mama," Sophie cried. "The saintliest people are
poor." She blinked behind her spectacles. "We can't dissect him,
or we'll be hanged for murder to the beat of a soldier's drum, and
we can't share him whole. Some savages have ten wives, and Ara-
bian pashas have sixty, but we wouldn't like that. Constanze
wants to marry for love, and I'm only twelve years old and want
a life of good works. Aloysia is pledged to Mozart, and Josefa is
going to join the gypsies or run off with a theater troupe if she
can't be an entrepreneur and have her music shop. She told us.
So the idea is utterly impractical."

"What I want," said Constanze, "is to keep us all together. So
if he's not willing to have us all working in his fields, perhaps he
could live here and help bring down the chamber pots."

"Ah, what am I to do with you all?" their mother cried, sailing into the kitchen while the three younger girls followed. From her basket, Maria Caecilia pulled forth a great lettuce, the dirt still clinging to the drooping green leaves. "What do you know of life, with what words can I tell you?" She peeled back the wrapping from a large, yellow, creamy slab of butter, biting her full lip. "It's as easy to love a rich man as a poor one," she said. "Rich men are also worth loving."

"Don't you love Papa?"

"Impudence! Bad girl, Constanze Weber! Of course I do."

Sophie pinched Constanze's arm, gazing sadly at her mother's wet eyelashes. "You could ask him on a Thursday, Mama; we could look him over."

Aloysia slipped the butter away into the cupboard in the blue covered dish that had traveled from Mannhem with them, and then neatly shut the door. From the parlor came Josefa's voice: "Let me know which evening he's coming, and I'll go to the lecture at the philosophical society."

The plantation owner arrived the following Thursday with Frau Hoffman for the Webers' evening, but he complained that music gave him a headache and left early. The girls laughed so hard they had to leave the room. Only Josefa did not have her customary fun with it, for she had seldom seen her father so profoundly tired; the next day, when she vowed to scold him about it, it seemed to have left him. And Sophie at last confided in Constanze what she had seen in the book of suitors when she had stolen it some months before: under Aloysia's name were several new possibilities, all of them sons of wealthy fathers in good Munich society. Nowhere was Mozart's name. The two younger sisters linked their little fingers, swearing secrecy, but they looked with some skepticism at their mother for a time after.

Autumn came, bringing no suitors worth mentioning, rather damp and rain. Fridolin Weber rushed from lesson to lesson under his enormous black umbrella. On his face was that wild, uncomfortable look he wore when they were not quite making ends meet, and again the girls heard quarrels from behind their parents' bedchamber door. Then one morning their father came late from his rooms, his thin naked legs visible under his short nightshirt, one hand against the wall for support, and a cough shaking his body. "I'm not quite well," he said. "Josefa, my love, you will kindly take my clavier lessons? Don't shout at the young women if they're stupid; they'll go elsewhere."

That Thursday evening the usual handful of guests arrived; they were shown into the bedchamber where Fridolin lay, a hot water bottle on his chest and his throat wrapped in flannel. "We'll have our musicale here," he said. The friends looked at one another, but obliged. Five or six musicians crowded in the room between wardrobe and table, squeezing chairs where they could. Heinemann's bow caught on the bed hangings. Glasses of wine were set among the powders, pins, and health tonics cluttering Caecilia Weber's dressing table.

"What does the doctor say?"

"He bled me and ordered me to rest."

After the friends had left, Weber leaned back on his pillow, listening to the whispers of his girls, who were quietly returning the chairs and clearing away the cake plates and glasses. When he looked up, he saw Josefa standing in the doorway holding his beer, which she had heated for him, clutching it against her as if to shield its warmth. He called, "Come, sit on the bed's edge, but first close the door a little."

He took her hand in his once she was settled. "Listen to me," he said. "I'll be ready to go back to my work tomorrow, but tonight, dearest girl, while the andante was playing, I looked at all of you as if standing at a distance, and it was a strange thing. It was as if I wasn't here anymore. I shouldn't tell you this, perhaps, but I feel I must speak of it. You know there are certain things I can't tell your mother; she worries so."

Fridolin Weber leaned back on the flattened pillow, and Josefa thought, He looks older, like his own father now. Her heart skipped a beat.

"You work too hard," she said sternly. "I don't know why some people have to work so hard in life, while for others it's easier."

"I don't mind it. I have all of you and your dear mother to keep."

"Everyone wants too much of you; it's not fair."

"I didn't want to speak about me, Josy, but you. I really didn't mean to speak of me at all. We haven't had our walks lately, those times just you and I walked together. I miss them very much. I sometimes look at you over the candles at supper. You're my girl.

It's not easy being the eldest, and you're not happy. I don't know what to do to make you happy, Josy. I wish it could be done with something bought, like a hat or chocolates. That I could manage. I've had a lot of time to think today. You want things you don't know you want. Do you know any of them? Josy, with your huge and gorgeous voice, my true musician. Yes, you are a true musician. What will happen with your voice? Will it bring you happiness?"

"I'm not loved, Papa, that's it." She sat leaning forward, one hand on his foot, feeling his sharp toenails even through the covers. "The others are loved so easily. I have no patience with stupidity. I shouted at your pupil today, and I think her mother won't have us teaching her anymore. I want to be loved so much, but I don't know how to go about it. Sometimes I wish it were a long time ago when the others weren't born and there was just us." She looked up mournfully, reddening. "I'm so sorry about your pupil."

He patted her hand. "I'll go tomorrow and placate her."

In the morning they heard him dressing to go out, whistling a little. Some hours later he returned to wait for another pupil in the parlor.

Josefa, in the kitchen by the simmering soup, was engrossed in the sleepwalking scene from *Macbeth* when she heard something fall. She jumped up and rushed toward the parlor. Her father lay on the floor by the clavier. "Oh, my darling," she cried, dropping to her knees beside him. He looked at her as if puzzled to find himself there. Then his breath stopped, and the light went from his eyes.

She held his hand, her fingers caressing the hairs above his knuckles and then feeling down to the supple, hardened fingertips. A sob shook her chest. "Wake up, Papa," she whispered.

She bent down to whisper into his ear. His soft graying hair stirred. She crouched on the floor, trying to keep her growing sobs inside her, hoping no one else would come. But where is the music? she thought. Where has the music gone? And where has *he* gone, lying here, almost as if asleep from some great weariness, and not yet fifty years old? When would he stir, and rise up, and rush through the room, scattering music, saying, "The pupil's coming!" Perhaps you had only so much of yourself to give, and when you had given it all, it was over. He had given of himself for his four girls, to buy them dresses and warm sheets, firewood and veal. Yes, he had spent himself.

He's mine, she thought. I'm his. The rest of them don't matter, never did, not even Mama, who drove him on so. I was his first girl; I was here first. He said it last night; he almost said it. Oh Papa, you're so handsome, not dull like your brother. Inside there's music, music. It's still there. It's not all come out; it's here in your chest. We haven't had many walks here. The others took them away, the others who have never really loved you properly. Neither of us has ever been loved the right way; we both know it. You taught me to sing, and I don't sing, not much, but one day I will, and then each note will be for you.

The tears fell down her cheeks, and she sat back on her heels. Breathing deeply several times, she found the low center of her voice. Then tremulously she began to sing. The rich voice staggered from note to note, and as she breathed more deeply, her voice steadied and flowed forth. She sang part of a mass for the dead, for which he had played first violin so many times in Mannheim churches. "The souls of the righteous are in the hands of God." Her voice rose and rose, until it filled every corner of the room and made the windows tremble. Perhaps it would enter his body and fill it, too.

She hardly knew when the others came in and began to cry aloud, hardly felt it when her mother shook her by the shoulders and shrieked, "Stop singing, stop singing, you stupid girl; why are you singing? Christ have mercy, Christ have mercy!" But she heard her mother's heavy knees fall to the floor, and then Josefa's song ended.

There were mourners, of course, climbing the many flights of stairs. Everyone came. She played his favorite music on the clavier hour after hour, her mouth compressed, her eyes vague and watery from weeping. Tears would stop and start; then her face became hard and determined. She stared at the grief expressed by her sisters and mother as if it were something she could not quite understand. First was the requiem, and then the procession, following the coffin as it rocked in the black carriage, to the graveyard.

Wake up, Papa, Josefa thought. It will soon be Thursday again.

They rode back from the graveyard in a hired carriage because they did not have the strength to walk. Maria Caecilia could not stop weeping. "How could you sing when you found him? How could you, Josefa Weber?" she repeated again and again. "You have no heart. Tell me."

Sophie said, "She was right to sing; what else could she do?

He gave us music; she gave it back. He was her papa, and she loved him."

Maria Caecilia leaned forward, her face a cross between tenderness and fury. "She hasn't got a right to mourn like this; he's not her papa," she cried over the sound of the carriage wheels. "He never was." Then she sat back with her hand covering her mouth and her eyes closed. Josefa stared at her. She had gone so pale that Sophie thought she would fall off the seat in a faint.

"What do you mean?" Josefa whispered. "What are you saying?" she said, her voice rising in all its richness. Aloysia and Sophie put their hands over their ears, and Josefa suddenly leaned forward as if she would slap her mother, or close her large hands about her throat.

Constanze shouted, "Josy, don't! And you, Mama, do you hear me, stop it! We've all got to stay together now, we have to!"

Their mother looked up, her face wet with tears, and reached out to touch her oldest daughter's knee. "I didn't mean that," she croaked. Words failed her, and she broke down in harsh sobbing. "I don't know what I'm saying. You don't know all that was between him and me. He'd call me his little cabbage. Fat as I am, I was his little cabbage. He made me a better woman. His soul was golden; he was all the world. I was never, never worthy of him, and now he's gone."

The winter wind blew across Europe as it would, driving icy rivers before it, circling mountains, beckoning the frost. In the Munich parlor the dark leaves that were draped around the portrait of Fridolin Weber had dried in the few months since his death. Near it, one late afternoon, Sophie Weber was at the desk writing a letter to her mother's sisters, bending close over the paper and biting her lip.

Dearest Aunts Elizabeth and Gretchen,

I pray God that this finds you well and happy. It seems a very long year since my last birthday when you sent me new slippers and my family was in Mannheim.

Mother has asked me to write to say how we are doing. As she would not wish me to conceal the difficulties of our circumstances to you, I shall be honest.

Sophie chewed on the pen's edge for a moment to think straight . . . those words: *I shall be honest.* What was honest anyway? Who told the utter truth, and, besides that, what was truth? She sat upright, recalling once more her mother's words to Josefa as they all rode back from the funeral. It had taken months of soothing to lay those words to rest, apologies, late-night kitchen conversations, tears.

But now, to tell the truth to her aunts. Was not the reality too bitter to put into ink? Dare she write that their hearts and lives were in disarray, that they each struggled to discover the path that would lead them back to their former life, but they found that the way had been washed out, much like on that woodlands walk they had all taken years before. Though her father had remembered the way, and they had set out on their adventure, they soon found the bridge across the stream was gone. Such was now the truth of their lives.

Mother could do so little these days. And the others wouldn't write, or endlessly put it off.

> Father did not leave money, and his brother sent some, which has gone for firewood and food. Constanze is copying music, and Aloysia and Josefa are singing in churches and private concerts, wherever they can. Our uncle Thorwart, who has moved to Vienna, is trying to procure a small pension for Mother from the court because of Papa's service for so many years as musician under Elector Carl Theodor. By law we women must have a male guardian, and Thorwart has been appointed, though he interferes rather a lot. I can't like him as much as I did, though I must pretend it. Constanze says he brushes against her breasts all the time, and then says, "Pardon, pardon!" We have not yet told Mother.

Sophie studied the last few sentences, then carefully inked them out (certain truths must be withheld for a time for prudency), blinked back her tears, and continued:

> We go bravely forward as Papa would have wished. I am certain that God will see us through.

She put aside the paper then, because she was crying and didn't want her tears to splotch her words, and because, to her horror, for the first time in her life she was not at all certain that God *would* help them through.

e came slowly down their Munich street that same blustery day, papers and dry leaves blowing about his feet, and began to climb their stairs, resting his heavy luggage full of music once, staring unseeingly at the grooves the bag handles had worn into his palm. Tentatively, he knocked on the wrong door, and a tipsy unshaven man grumbled at him and pointed upward to "where the ladies live." His legs, under black breeches buckled at the knee, ached as he climbed the last flight, walking toward the paper sign posted on the door: THE MESDEMOISELLES WEBER: LESSONS IN CLAVIER AND SINGING AVAILABLE. PLEASE KNOCK.

The door was unlocked, and when he pushed it open, he saw Sophie at the table, looking thin and pale. The room was strange to him. It was not the one he had known in Mannheim, but here was the clavier, which he so admired, and the music, and the youngest of the Weber girls.

She turned. "Oh, Mozart," she gasped, balling her hand-kerchief in her hands. "Oh, it's you, it's you!" She leapt up and then hesitated, holding on to the edge of the desk. But she could not restrain herself for long; she ran across the room and jumped into his arms.

"Sophie," he said.

She clung to him, her too-large gray frock showing evidence that a moth had had its way. There was an ink spot on her nose where she had rubbed it. "But what are you doing here?" she said, wiping more ink on her face. "We thought you were in Paris. You didn't send word you were coming. Let me call Aloysia. You'll want to see her right away. How many days was the journey? Was it awful? You must be hungry and thirsty. Are you staying in Munich? She'll be so glad. Why don't you answer me? Do hug me. You make me miss Father, and that makes me cry. What are you doing here? Not that I'm not very glad."

Because he could not trust his voice, he only held her close, looking over the wild loose bits of her hair to the doorway, through which he heard voices and then footsteps. With a blur of dark dresses, the other three sisters rushed into the room. They were all about him; he felt their warmth and sweetness.

And there was his Aloysia, his beautiful Aloysia.

They pressed against him, hands on his sleeves and coat, stroking his arm. It was Josefa who took over her late father's role as host. Lowering her voice, she said, "Oh, Mozart, welcome! We're so glad you've come. But you look very tired. The journey must have exhausted you; they say it's ten days at least. I'm not certain we have wine, but I can make coffee. But dear saints, are you ill?"

He lifted his gaze from the recollected worn spot on the rug to the blur of their faces. "I'm not sick, no," he said, "but I have news as dark as yours. My own beloved mother fell ill when we were in Paris; the physicians could do nothing, and she passed from the earth. My journey was long; I couldn't wait to come here to those who care for me. I've lost her; I've lost her."

He stared ahead, his shapely mouth fixed. He saw his mother

lying in death, the nose now very sharp, the waxen long hands clasped about her rosary. He saw the emptiness of their rooms after his return from the graveyard, how the floor had creaked as he walked across it. She who had nursed him, and fretted for him, and waited for him to come home was gone; he would not see her again in this world. And what assurance had he been able to give her in her last hours that he would do better, he who was now left in life for better or worse; what assurance had he been able to provide of how deeply he had loved her?

The sisters drew closer, bringing him back to the present; they murmured, "Mozart, Mozart," slipping their arms about him, but he did not move. Someone stroked his cheek, prickly with pale brown stubble. They were all one to him in that moment, but he couldn't answer them. Words were impossible; only music might speak, and there was no music now.

He looked down and saw that Sophie's fingers had moved within his. "They're both in heaven," she said, raising her pointed face to his. "Your mother and our father. They're angels."

"Yes," echoed Constance. "They're angels."

He burst out, looking from one to another of them, "Your good father! I couldn't believe the letter when I received it; I can't believe he's not here. I still remember saying good-bye to him that cold morning last winter. 'Soon we'll drink wine again, Mozart!' he said. He insisted I borrow his brown music portfolio. But your poor mother! How does she do?"

Constanze replied, "She stays in her room a great deal and weeps. Maybe she'll come out for you." The four sisters looked at one another, and then Sophie ran down the hall. After a time her bedchamber door opened, and they could hear shuffling. Frau Weber emerged, holding on to the wall. Mozart was weeping himself now, and he embraced her fiercely.

He looked over Frau Weber's cap to Josefa, who stood stiffly, as if she were the sentinel of the house. Her face was pale and severe; her weight had dropped, her laced dress loose. She slipped from the room and returned shortly with a tray containing coffeepot, cups, cake plates, forks, and cake. There was already something of the spinster about her. Mozart remembered how when Aloysia had first sung his song the year before, Josefa had escaped to the hall and remained there a long time.

"Mozart, come have cake!"

They ate until the plates held only small crumbs, and their words fell away. Then, quietly, three of the sisters and their mother rose and retired from the room, bearing the coffeepot, the plates, and the forks, and letting fall the heavy curtains that pulled over the doors to keep drafts away, leaving Mozart and Aloysia alone.

The curtain had not yet fallen completely when he leapt at her, kissing her wrist, then up her woolen sleeve to her neck, her perfect ear, her slightly chapped lips. He drew her beside him on the red sofa, holding her so closely against him that he could feel her corset stiffening, and her breasts hidden beneath it. Her flesh smelled of apples and cinnamon.

"I thought of you always these months, Aloysia," he murmured. "I reread every one of your letters ten, no, twelve times, and kissed them. A hundred times I wanted to throw the whole thing over and come back to you. Your letters . . . I wish there had been more of you in them. I kept trying to find you in them.

They seemed reserved, and I know you're not reserved. I read between the lines to find you." He kissed her face as he spoke, his mouth against her lips. "Sometimes, Christ help me, I couldn't seem to touch you."

She turned her face abruptly so that his lips missed her mouth. "What did you want me to write?" she said, wrinkling bits of her skirt in her hands and staring ahead of her at the desk, where Sophie's pen was left to drip ink on her unfinished letter. "I told you about the music I was learning and about our days. If our days were dull, can you fault me for it? I have never been good at writing."

Pulling her closer, he murmured, "But there was no passion in them. I know you're passionate. Why don't you kiss me? Didn't you miss me, my love? Not at all? I was so alone."

She brushed her lips across his, then jumped up to the desk, glancing at the letter. "I know, I know, and so were we alone, though we had one another. Still, Papa's gone, and Mother has collapsed; for days she doesn't come from her bed." She turned from the desk to him, tears in her eyes, the letter now folded in her hand. Then, distractedly, she slipped it in the desk drawer. "Of course I missed you!" she said. "I have deep, deep feelings. I do love you."

She began to walk up and down the room. "But you're the one who went away," she said. "You went away. Can you know what it is just to wait? I admit my letters were a little reserved after a time. Very well, I'll tell you why. I suppose you ought to know." She paused by the window. "Early on you wrote (do you remember?) . . . you wrote that you could likely send for me to sing in Paris in the Concert Spirituel or the Concert des Amateurs, but then you wrote that it wasn't possible. Do you know how disappointed I was?"

Her words stammered over one another, and then she ran from the window to sit beside him, her voice rising. "You said you'd help me. And then, and then. Then you wrote that you were offered the position of organist at Versailles. Oh, Mozart, *Versailles!* You could have sent for me. . . . We would have been married, and I would have sung there and curtseyed daily to Marie Antoinette, the most regal Queen, a true Viennese princess, the daughter of the late Emperor of Austria. Can you imagine what I felt, stuck here in my grief without Papa, without prospects, with my dreary sisters and my mother's weeping, and knowing I might have a chance to live at Versailles itself, in Paris, the center of fashion and good taste. Yet instead I was to remain in provincial Munich, while my gifts and youth fade unseen, obscure, unwanted . . . and *you refused the position.*"

He stared at her, bewildered, not touching her, though she sat so close. "But don't you understand, the very last thing I want is to be a French court organist?" he said. "And the salary wasn't so great. I couldn't afford to dress you as you like, and they'd have put me in livery. The household musicians are lucky to eat at table below the lackeys and before the cooks. That's my father's life; I grew up with it. Do you think I want that? Is it the life I'm meant to have? No Aloysia, dearest. I wanted an opera commission. You mustn't want me to settle on something less than I could be. I would write great roles for you—just for you. That's a much better life."

"But now you have nothing."

His voice rose to the garland of dry, fragile leaves around the portrait of her late father. "It's true I have nothing now," he cried, "but that won't always be so. I need you to have faith in me. My father writes one angry letter after another. I'm not the darling little boy anymore, and I can't be obsequious. Dearest, my composing deepened while there. I'll show you the symphony I wrote in Paris, and the concerto for harp and flute."

She clenched her hands on her knees. "But you could have had the protection of the Queen."

"Yes, but I don't want to be a household organist, so I came back to my own country. You idolize the French; I can't and won't. At the opera the Italian composer Cambini stood in my way, jealous. I waited weeks for appointments that brought promises which were not kept. Could you really expect me to stay?"

She was flushed and imperious. "And do you expect me to be pleased that you return empty-handed? I've waited faithfully for you. You must succeed for me. You owe it to me. Your influence could open my voice to the world. You know, you know how well I sing and play. It *is* your fault that you didn't, that you turned down Versailles! You threw away our happiness! How can I forgive you?"

She was sobbing, and jerked her shawl closer around her sharp shoulders. Her delicate face was in profile to him; even without any rouge or curls, she was beautiful, her lower lip extended ruefully and tears rushing down her face to her chin. He gently took her by the shoulders and kissed the tears away, kissed the wet, resentful lips that still protested. "I could have had hats made by the Queen's woman, at least a modest one. Then you would truly love me!"

He seized her more firmly then, kissing her wherever his lips could reach. He could feel her little nipples, and her tiny body, which he could not hold close enough, seemed worth all the riches of the courts of Europe.

"I don't want to quarrel with you," he said into her neck. "Don't cry, don't cry, I beg you. I'll become a great success for you. Aloysia, what do I have but you? I've disappointed my father and my sister; I've lost my beloved mother; and I've failed you. Isn't this enough? Dearest, you must believe in me. You must believe that there's reason for what I do. Aloysia, what do I have without you? Every hope I had was swept away, but I thought of your family and you, and it was my whole comfort."

"You must understand why I was angry with you."

"You won't have further cause." He wiped her tears with his handkerchief; he was trembling so his hands shook. "Listen, listen, dearest," he said. "But I come with good news, too, not only terrible. Very good news. How oddly the best things come hand in hand with tragedy. I have an opera commission for the Residenztheater. His Excellency has sponsored it."

"What? Here in Munich? For our exquisite theater?"

"I thought about writing you but decided to wait to tell you in person. So you see, I have not come back empty-handed. It's an opera *seria,* my best work to date. It's called *Idomeneo.* I have a chance to succeed and begin to make a great deal of money, and then we can marry at once, my Aloysia, and never be parted again. Don't cry anymore, my beloved. Trust me."

She stroked his face gently, looking at him; she had become suddenly very still. "You are very tired," she said. "You are very tired, my love."

For three days he slept and slept in the small room behind their kitchen. He would awake startled, thinking himself in Paris or in some inn, overwhelmed with sadness when he recalled his loss and theirs. Sometimes he felt he could hardly stand. Still, outside that room there was life; he heard the sisters' chatter as they drank their morning coffee. Even in their recent grief they chattered. A knock would come at his door; a cup would be handed to him through the crack. They were there in their dressing gowns, he just behind the door in his shirt. Once, coming from his small room unexpectedly, he saw them all flee down the hall, laughing in their white smocks and bare feet, leaving behind them a drip of washing water on the floor and the smell of lavender. They surrounded him every hour of the day; they were in every corner of the rooms, asking him questions and telling him stories. In between them, Maria Caecilia moved languidly, always smiling at him when he entered the room. Sensuality hung so heavily in the air that he felt he could not breathe. Not only Aloysia but all the sisters. Even Josefa's bare long legs, visible when her dressing gown opened, haunted him. Even Sophie's chapped lips, her flat little body. He was drunk and distracted and could not compose a note.

He moved to the Cannabich house, for the famous Mannheim orchestra was now in Munich. There he wrote until his eyes could no longer focus; then he jumped up and, along with a few orchestra musicians, rushed over to the Weber rooms. With their arms full of cheeses and sausages wrapped in old news journals, the musicians bolted up the steps three at a time.

In the rooms he whirled Aloysia in his arms. "A whole day without the sight of you!" he cried. "This is more than heaven should ask of me."

After supper they all played games, dancing and chasing one another around the furniture. The sisters fled from him and he caught them, leaping over the furniture and growling. Shrieking, they ran from room to room. When he was panting too hard to run anymore, he sat down at the clavier and cried, "One of you cover my eyes with your hands, and I'll play any song you know backward."

Fluttering his covered eyelids for a moment, he saw little fingers with dry skin and guessed it was one of the younger sisters whose hands were pressed against his face. He played faster, rocking more violently as he did so, to all their shrieks. Finally, he tipped himself entirely off the chair, dragging the girl with him. "Constanze," he cried, opening his eyes. "I never thought it was you! Come, tell me what you like; I'll make a nonsense song out of it for you. Tell me or I'll tickle you!" At his tugging, Constanze rolled on top of him. Her fingernails were bitten, and there was a cut on her hand. "I'll tickle you," he said, edging his hand so that he could feel the place where her corset ended and her under petticoat tied in a knot.

She shrieked and squirmed. "Ah no, don't, don't!"

"She likes puppies," cried Sophie, jumping up and down on the sofa. "Tickle her, tickle her! She likes puppies."

"Puppies!" he cried. "Of course! I'll write a concerto for mutt and orchestra in D major with a strong wind section. I'll begin auditions for the best dog all over Munich at once."

Constanze struggled away, her hair losing its large ivory pins. He handed one to her as she stood up and tried to catch her breath. "It's like our old Thursdays," she said. "It's like Papa's Thursdays when everyone came to play." Tears filled her eyes, and it moved him. He looked about the room at all of them and breathed deeply, amazed, happy. The sensuality of all the sisters melded, blended into a single blurred sensation of youth and white cotton.

The date for the first rehearsals grew near, and he ceased to come to the Webers. Instead he sent effusive notes written on the back of music paper, filled with grotesque little drawings scratched from his fierce pen. He wrote apologetically that the opera was cast already and there were no roles for them; the light soprano had once been mistress of the Elector. She was a good singer and must remain; the other soprano role was also taken. He was working intensely, he wrote, trying to please those many men who could push the opera on the boards of the Residenztheater or jerk it away.

Cannabich brought him more music paper and also meat and soup, which often went untouched until the fat had congealed in white blobs. He wrote, ceasing only when he had to. He wrote at a desk by the window, hearing the music in his head, the words and feelings forming under his rapidly moving hand: regret; jealousy; fate; the father, Idomeneo, who for his rescue from danger at sea promised Neptune, the god of the sea, to sacrifice the first person he met when his ship returned home. The work grew on the pages with its arias and ensembles, its military marches and shipwrecks, its storms and coronation, its monster arising from the depths of seawaters.

Cannabich stood by, one hand on the hip of his silk breeches, turning over the pages. "It's longer than they expected," he said, "but the Elector heard us at rehearsal and said the music was so very moving."

Mozart pulled the pages toward him. "Good, then he will want to keep me! Did he once again call me his 'dear child'? Let the fool say what he will. My friend, if he's pleased, he'll surely grant me a position in his court, and then I can bring my father and sister here and marry."

"The little Weber girl?"

"Indeed."

Applause broke out as he stepped into the orchestra pit of the Residenztheater, surely a jewel, set around with rows of boxes, all of the most brilliant red and heavily embellished with gold. Cannabich had given over the premiere for him to conduct from the clavier.

In the back of the hall he could see the four Weber sisters. Oh, the winds: the flute, the oboe, the bassoon, and the horn riding over the stringed instruments. Onstage the monster would shortly rise from the deep to destroy the people because the King had broken his vow to sacrifice the first to greet him on land, his son, the Prince Idamante. The choruses echoed, and the old tenor sang of the sea now within him, more unrelenting than that sea that had sought to drag him to its depths.

Four singers stood together on the stage and began the great quartet. *"Andrò ramingo, e solo"*—I'll wander forth and alone. He marked the tempo. The strings played exquisitely. His soul left his body.

Aloysia sat embroidering by the window of her home a week later at dusk, green silk thread in a soft neat roll on the table beside her. Mozart stood quietly in the doorway, studying the slope of her white neck down to the slight swell of her breasts. She was humming a bit of his opera.

He thought, I must memorize her perfectly as she is now, with the strand of silk about her finger, and her embroidery of French court children held on her lap near her stomach where our real children, hers and mine, will one day grow. He had been walking about the city for some hours, starting for the house, then turning back again.

She sensed him then, and, jumping up at once, came toward him with open arms. "Is it true?" she murmured, looking at his bowed head. *"C'est terrible! Mon Dieu!* It can't be; it can't be."

"But it is," he said. "*Idomeneo*'s been withdrawn after three performances, and I'm told it won't travel; it's too difficult to perform with its orchestration and staging. And old-fashioned, not likely to catch on. 'Too deep, too dark, too difficult. Too good,' Cannabich said, 'dear Mozart, you are too good.' Can that be my fate, Aloysia, to be too good? To never quite be what people want?"

He gazed at Fridolin's clavier, his fingers moving against his breeches; sighing, he hung his head. One of his side curls was badly rolled. He sagged against the doorjamb. "My love, I can't hold any longer," he said at last. "I can't borrow any more money from home, and the opera fee must go to repay what I have already borrowed. I must return for a time to the Archbishop's service in Salzburg. I would marry you now and take you with me, but you'd be as unhappy there as I will be. Stay here with your sisters."

Her voice rose passionately. "I want to go with you!"

"Hush, I know. Oh God, to be an hour without you, my love!"

She lay her head against his shoulder, slowly stroking his ear. Once she shuddered; he felt it down her back. Her voice was unsteady as she put her words together. "It won't be forever, Wolfgang. You'll find a better position with an opera house where I can sing."

"Yes, I will find it; I must. Within several months I'll have obtained something else; all my friends are looking for me. Then we'll be together as man and wife, and I'll write great music for you. This I swear on my mother's soul."

"Don't be uneasy on my behalf, Wolfgang! I'll wait forever.

Per sempre," she repeated in Italian, standing up straight. Her small breasts heaved. For always . . . *mio tesoro, amore mio!* My treasure, my love. He could hardly break away from her kisses then. He thought to take her on the sofa amid the dusty, soft, worn cushions; he thought to lock the doors and take her, pushing up her skirts. At least there was this simple thing between man and woman, so achievable and immediate. Desire rushed through him; he jerked his head back, grasping her hand so hard it whitened. She would allow it (every part of her body cried yes), but if she swelled with child before he had a good position, what would they do?

"Good-bye," he said, kissing her many times.

"Wolfgang, don't go."

He ran down the stairs, but voices called from the window. He looked up to see Aloysia, Josefa, Sophie, and Constanze standing at the window, the curtains pushed back. The younger sisters were weeping; they likely had also heard about the opera's cancellation and felt bad for him. *Per sempre,* she had said, and there had been tears in her eyes as well. *Wolfgang, don't go.* He would never forget it.

His earliest memories were of his father lifting him into bed during some fever, and his father's spare frame, bones hardy under his blue wool coat, holding him so that they almost melded. For years they had been inseparable as they journeyed from city to city all over Europe. His father placing him before

harpsichords to play, watching from a short distance as he performed, carrying him away again—a little boy who was sometimes eager, sometimes curious, sometimes quiet. His father,
leaning over him as he wrote his first childish compositions,
later holding the splotched music paper to the light, breathing a
sharp sigh. His father standing by a window in Vienna, combing
his son's small white wig, which caught the sunlight.

And now Leopold Mozart was waiting for him again, as he always had.

The rooms were not the ones where Mozart had been born—
some years ago the family had moved across the river—but the
furnishings were arranged in the same way. He's near sixty,
Mozart thought as he pressed his lips to the stark cheek. Still, his
father was not much changed.

Mozart glanced about. On the wall was the portrait of himself
and his sister; his legs dangled from the clavier bench. He was very
young, very charming with his silky wig. On the windowsill, best
placed to catch the sun, were his mother's plants. The edges of
some of the leaves had turned brown. He drew in his breath hard.

"God bless you, my son—a safe journey?"

"Nothing unexpected; we did not overturn."

His father groaned, "My God, your mother—even after this
time I hope it is not true, that surely she must come up the steps
after you. I have had masses said."

Mozart looked about uncomfortably, then murmured, "Father, father."

For a moment Leopold Mozart covered his face with his
hands.

Mozart said, "Lord give us patience, Father, to bow to His will; she's in His hands now, having gone to her just reward. But Father, you're well? God grant it you are well, and my darling sister?"

"As well as can be expected."

Mozart put down his bags. On a shelf were the very same six porcelain plates with pictures in blue of milkmaids frolicking in some field; one showed a crack where it had been carefully mended. His father had pushed it off the table in a fit of anger years before . . . or had it been himself? He could never recall for certain which one had done it, perhaps both; then he saw his mother's reproachful shoulders as she knelt to gather the pieces and he heard his sister's weeping. Nannerl wept easily. They were careful not to make her cry. Where was she this day?

"Ah, my son, here's the letter from your great uncle. Here, where it says, 'Your wife's among the angels,' etc., etc. He sends his love to you. He asked if you were eighteen yet. He forgets things. He loved your dear mother, the angel. And another one here of condolence from your old friend Padre Martini from Bologna, that great musician and man of God, who taught you when you were fourteen."

The delicate, almost translucent, slightly wrinkled hands sifted through the papers until Mozart thought him like an old monk. Well, now he would sleep in a celibate bed.

"I wanted to show you—"

"But there's time for that, Father."

". . . the letter announcing—"

"But there's time, there's time!"

The apartment door opened, and Mozart's older sister, Nannerl, rushed toward him with her market basket on her arm, crying, "Oh, Amadé!"

He murmured, "I'm so sorry, my love. What can I bring you but myself?"

She clung to him for some moments, and then broke away, wiping her face. "I'll put away the cheese," she said.

He heard her in the kitchen. When he thought of Nannerl, as he did almost daily wherever he was, he recalled both the patient, tender older sister of their childhood tours, waiting with clasped hands until he had finished playing his music, as if content to stand there always, and the woman she was now, sitting by the window copying music. It was not that she had no beauty, but that she had no light. She would take care of their father, of course; but without her mother she felt utterly weakened. She had written that to him. She's put aside her youth entirely now, he thought as he heard her opening the kitchen cupboards. She's put it away as something too extravagant for her own use, wrapped it carefully in tissue paper and laid it away. And that was Mother's old gray-flocked dress she was wearing, the one Mother always wore to church.

They ate the familiar dishes at supper, and, when the sweets appeared at the end, Leopold leaned forward and spoke the words he had been keeping back throughout the whole meal. "Wolfgang."

"Father."

"Are you listening?"

"I am, yes."

"I've smoothed the path for your reconciliation with the Archbishop; he expects you tomorrow."

"I'll go speak with him."

"I trust you have left your affections for Mademoiselle Weber in Munich."

"Indeed not, Father; I intend to marry her."

The next day he dressed in his best coat and walked over the bridge to Getreidegasse, the street where he had been born, then with the river Salzach on his left, turned up Goldgasse until it opened to the Domplatz and the Archbishop's stately *Residenz*. Mozart's father had been a church musician in Salzburg for some thirty-five years, serving the late kindly Archbishop and, more recently, this one. Mozart thought suddenly, My father knows many aspects of music: the toil, the diligence, the exactitude. But the ecstatic love of it eludes him; he does not trust it. And what is it to trust music and the deep feelings it pulls from you?

The tapping of shoes on the marble floor announced Count Carl Arco, the chamberlain, a thin, fussy young man with a bad complexion and much lace at his throat. "We expected you earlier, Mozart," he said. "His Holiness is at dinner. Never mind, come in; you've already put him off by being late." He dropped his voice to a low warning. "Your absence this year and a half has not sat well with him. I speak in friendship, of course. My aunt sends her condolences on your loss."

He opened the door and whispered to the footman, who sang out the visitor's name.

At the end of a very long, polished table that could have easily dined twenty and was loaded with platters of meat and noodles,

Hieronymus Colloredo, Archbishop of Salzburg, was eating alone. His Grace looked up, fork in his hand, and grunted, then began to cut a smallish piece of meat into even smaller bits. He drank two or three thoughtful sips of wine, and the footman hurried forward and refilled the glass. The mouth was small, rosy, feminine.

Mozart said, "Your Princely Grace, it is my joy to greet you."

"As you say it I will take it, but I am surprised you did not come these twelve months sooner. So the prodigy has soon discovered how difficult the world can be, eh? Full of false promises, dangled hopes that you ran after in your youth. I'm happy though to see you return. I bear no grudge."

Mozart bowed again. "Your Grace," he said, his voice echoing across the plates of food. He stood, having been offered no chair. "You know how I and my family have honored you, and how much I honor you for all these years my father has been happy in your service."

"Your father is a good man."

"If I might know the duties expected of me . . ."

"Why, much the same as your father's: to train the choir of men and boys, to write church music and whatever other small pieces I may need, to play violin in the orchestra during church masses as you did when you were in my service before. I am in need of a violinist."

"I beg you, Your Grace, to be released from that duty. I am but a tolerable violinist. I assure you that my talents could be better used elsewhere."

"As I have specified, but what have you in mind?"

As some servants came to clear away the meats and bring the stewed fruit, Mozart braced his hands on the far end of the table where he stood. His voice was clear if respectful. "Your Grace," he said, "it would be to the honor of Your Grace to improve the music of this court. I am thinking first of a full and first-rate orchestra, not the small one we have at present. If we could perhaps have an orchestra here to your honor, and, with it, to make an opera house, renowned singers would come. I could compose for you in the Italian or German school. I have brought my music portfolio to show you some examples."

"What? But I do not like opera," said the Archbishop without raising his head from his fruit. "I've no use for these things. I need a violinist in my small chamber orchestra for masses and a composer for brief liturgical music, and it is that for which I engage you, perhaps later to promote you to the post of court organist. An opera, pah! What, to have my court flooded with licentious Italians all shrieking away?" All the time he spoke, he lifted spoonful after spoonful of the fruit to his mouth.

"Do you understand how lenient I and my predecessor have been with you and your father?" the Archbishop continued. "Allowing you both in the old days, and more recently, to spend years away from my service trying your skill in the world? But the world is a rougher place than you can know, and you return here to the protection of my court. I will have you, but I will not permit any more wanderings. Be content. Do not look higher than God has meant you to look." He paused for a moment. "Will you serve me?"

"I shall, Your Highness."

"Your voice is faint. I have not quite heard you."

"I shall serve you, Your Highness."

With that, Mozart left as quickly as he could; once away from the palace, he began to walk more rapidly, and then almost to run toward the river, past carriages. All the time he repeated hotly, and in half voice: "I am Mozart. I am Mozart!" He wanted to cry it to the trees . . . and where is all my music? Now people looked at him as if he were crazy. He ran past the slow procession of wagons, carriages, suppliants, priests, and visitors moving toward the Residenz, muttering, "I am Mozart, and someday all will know it. No, I am not crazy. I am Mozart." By the time he crossed the bridge he was shouting. Two priests passing him, followed by a bevy of choirboys, shook their heads. Flushing, he went on his way, swinging his music portfolio, through the city that was his birthplace.

now fell again over Munich that first day of December, gradually filling the crevices of the houses, and piling high where cold pigeons huddled above the doors of the Residenztheater in which Mozart's opera had been given so briefly. It clung to the hems of the somber cassocks of priests who hurried to mass, and it weighed down the black skirt of Sophie Weber as she mounted the creaking wood stairs of her family's building, heavy basket on her arm.

The little parlor, with its portrait of Fridolin, still draped with a sagging and long-dried garland of dark leaves, was deserted; music was piled on the table nearly a foot high. When one of the sisters wanted to find a certain piece to give a clavier lesson or to sing at a wedding, she would scatter the pile across the table and then gather the pieces together carelessly. The deep red sofa still had a tear from their move from Mannheim a year and a half before; no one had bothered to mend it. It had been spring when Mozart had departed for his work in Salzburg, and with the dissolution of the Thursday musicales, the house was devoid of any masculine presence. I'll be back for your fourteenth birthday, he had promised Sophie, but that would come within two months, and his letters to them made it seem unlikely. What his letters to Aloysia said, Sophie did not know. There was no further mention of suitors, and their mother's book was no longer anywhere to be found, though one day the girls had torn the house apart looking for it. Still there were letters back and forth from Thorwart, who was now in Vienna, and the four sisters dreaded that their mother still had her plans. The two younger girls had long decided that whoever their mother chose would be quite dreadful, no matter what his lineage, and that anything that divided them as much as a city would be unthinkable.

Sophie heard her sisters' voices from the kitchen. "Where's that girl? Didn't she come in with the bread? Sophie, where are you?"

Aloysia, Josefa, and Constanze were sitting as close to the fire as they could without singeing their long skirts. Josefa's long, thick back bent slightly as her needles roughly poked the hose she was knitting. Aloysia raised her face from embroidering a purse. "Is anything happening outside?" she asked.

Sophie put down her basket, wiped her nose, and cleaned off the moisture that had formed on her spectacles. "It's three weeks to Christmas. And they captured a thief; I saw it posted." She began to unpack the meat, which was wrapped in an old bit of music for a mass.

"*Mon Dieu*, you think the strangest things are newsworthy. You're concerned the poor man left a needy family. What else?"

"I saw a poor little kitten crying in the snow. I should have taken it home with me. Maybe I'll go back and see if it's still there."

Aloysia dropped her embroidery to her lap and turned toward her youngest sister, her face flushed with the fire. "You'll do nothing of the sort; you know cats make me sneeze. Anyway, it's time you're back; we've been waiting for you for our morning coffee. Mother's gone out."

They were drinking their coffee when they heard the jangle of the house bell below. Aloysia pushed away her cup and ran to the parlor window, from which she could see the snowy hats of two men standing by the house door, one heavy and of medium height, the other somewhat scrawny even under his coat. "It's Uncle Thorwart," she quietly called back to the kitchen. "He's come from Vienna; Mama said he might." Thorwart's appointment by the court to be their male guardian had worn further on them; he had at first made detailed budgets for them, limiting sweets, firewood, chemises, and rouge. It was only when he found none of the girls would speak to him that he relented, but he still looked at them, breathing heavily through his mouth, as if to say, Mark my words, it will turn out badly for you! (Constanze had confided to Sophie that perhaps she had been mistaken about his brushing against her breasts; the hall was narrow, their parents' friend a big man. She had stood gazing at Sophie, blinking and doubtful.)

Now Aloysia called back in a much brighter voice. "Our cousin Alfonso's with him! What could they want? Any news will be welcome."

The three other girls thrust chairs back from the kitchen fire, flung off their aprons, ran to open the door. In a moment Alfonso's shining bald head came into view on the steep stairs, followed by the heavy Thorwart in his English coat and boots, the spurs jangling. He wiped his brow. "One day," he groaned, "the family Weber will not live on the highest floor they can find. I need a plate of noodles and cheese to replenish me after my climb. Girls, come and kiss your uncle," and he kissed the three younger girls as he could, though they turned their lips away, and the younger two exchanged glances as if to say, Are we mistaken or not?

He did not approach Josefa, who stood apart.

For warmth, they all returned to the kitchen. Taking the best chair, Thorwart sat back with his heavy hands on his breeches. "Our visit's with a purpose that will interest you very much for it concerns music." He looked at them all with satisfaction, his presence seeming to fill the kitchen, while Alfonso regarded them with melting eyes, his large ears tucked beneath his hat.

"Music, Uncle?"

"Music, my dears! Ah, you don't know! My move to Vienna

has been most profitable to me, for I've found work there as general factotum to the director of one of the two opera companies. Such an incomparable city, my girls, the very center of the Austrian Empire! Why, we see the Emperor himself riding many days in the park, though not in inclement weather. We wouldn't want the Imperial Majesty to suffer from a chill. On my hope of salvation, now that I have lived in Vienna, I wouldn't dream of living anyplace else."

Thorwart's expression became businesslike, and he leaned forward. He made a quick gesture, as if straightening a pile of papers on the table before him, then cleared his throat. "My news will be of the greatest interest to you," he said solemnly, "for it's news I bring indeed. There's a position open in the opera for a soprano, a young prima donna. Alfonso and I heard of it just eight days ago, and of course we marched to the director's office and spoke of the beauty, the elegance, the range and expression of the singing voices of the two Weber daughters, the majestical Mademoiselle Josefa, who is one and twenty, and our enchanting Mademoiselle Aloysia, who is, I believe, just past eighteen."

Alfonso smiled as broadly as he always had when coming up the steps for the Thursday musicales. "And he's eager to hear you both. I'm returning to Vienna in a few days and will happily take you with me. The position pays well, very well indeed, far more than your dear father ever made. It would keep your whole family. If God wills it, one of you will have the place, and your troubles will be over."

· · ·

The two older girls threw everything out of trunks to find trimmings and feathers. They rampaged through the piles of music, leaving it all over the red velvet sofa. They missed the lessons they were to give on the clavier, so intent were they on their packing. Their mother hovered above them, crying, "Your curling rags, your false curls, your rosaries . . ." Josefa still wore an engraved silver locket that had appeared the previous summer; she had not taken it off all those months. It glittered slightly as she closed her cloak over it and prepared to bring the bags down the steps into the cold morning. She said little, though Aloysia had never stopped talking the whole three days since the news had come. Aloysia had broken her necklace and thought it was a bad omen and cried heartbreakingly.

Constanze, Sophie, and their mother waved as the older girls boarded the hulking carriage near the house, then watched it wobble away through the cobbled streets in the soft gray light, all the trunks and leather luggage tied with ropes to the top, including the little wood box their great grandfather had once taken to war. Augustin Weber it had said, the paint long faded. The carriage wobbled past notices of public hangings and signs for health tonics, which were pasted to lampposts and to the sides of houses.

That night the two younger sisters brought out their father's maps and traced with their fingers the route from Munich to the capital. They estimated how far the coach could have gotten that day, and what sort of inn would house their older sisters that night. "Their dresses will be wrinkled," Constanze said. "They stuffed too much inside the trunk."

"They're staying with Thorwart and his wife; they'll help them."

"His wife mightn't speak to them; she doesn't speak to anyone. She's given up on mankind. I heard Mama say it once."

By now they had taken down another book of engravings of Vienna, and turned the pages slowly, holding up the candle. From the other room they heard their mother rolling over in bed. They were always aware of her loneliness.

Constanze looked more closely at the picture on which a fat blob of white wax had dropped. She blew on it and scraped it off with her fingernail. "I think it must be the most beautiful city in the world," she said at last and smiled. "Oh Sophie, may it be! I think truly we'd be happy there, even Mama."

Aloysia returned three days before Christmas, appearing suddenly on the street, pulling her heavy bag after her. She abandoned it halfway up the stairs and ran the rest of the way up to their rooms. She had about her that smell of old leather and horses that clings to the garments of those who take long coach rides. And stuck to the bottom of her thick traveling shoes and along her dress's hemline was straw from the innyards. Constanze and their mother, who had been making meat dumplings, met her at the door. "What? For the love of heaven, tell us, what news, what news?" Maria Caecilia cried. For days they had been running down at any sign of the post.

Sophie, hearing their voices, hurried to the door with a cry, then stopped in amazement at the sight of her sister. Aloysia looked as she had the day long ago when she was twelve years old and had just heard her closest friend had died of scarlet fever. "Blessed Mary, what has happened?" Sophie cried. "What's the matter? We've been holding our breath since you left." She made the sign of the Cross. "Oh what's the matter?"

Maria Caecilia cried, "What news?"

"They heard four arias," Aloysia said breathlessly.

"And?"

"They kept looking at me when I sang."

"Yes, but then . . . tell us."

"They made me an offer to begin rehearsals on my first role just after the first of the year. "

"Praise God, praise Christ," their mother gasped. "But is there a contract? Is it secure? You don't know how we've been waiting for you." They pulled Aloysia inside by her cold hands. "Where are your gloves? How was the journey back? What did you wear to sing?"

"The green wool."

They pulled her to the warm kitchen still talking, one voice louder than the next. "Which arias did you sing?"

"Did you show your full range?"

"Did you show your triplets and ornamentation?"

"Who accompanied you? Alfonso . . . he's middling on the clavier. Or did they have a fortepiano?"

"They had a beautiful fortepiano, and yes, he played—"

"Did you curl your hair in back and put it up?"

"I hadn't time to do those things; one of the carriage horses was sick, and we got there hours late. Frau Thorwart came flying out at us, saying we were expected at once, that very hour. Uncle Thorwart had gone the day before and said we were coming, you see." She was panting as if she had just run for miles. "And we went at once, and they were waiting."

Sophie turned and looked toward the door, then back again to her sister. "But Aly," she said, "where's Josefa?" Then the only sounds in the kitchen were those of the water boiling in the black pot and the crinkling flames beneath it.

Aloysia closed her eyes for a moment, then looked toward the black kettle. She dropped wearily to a chair by the table. It never ceased to amaze Sophie that beautiful faces could at times be absolutely plain. Swallowing before she spoke, Aloysia whispered, "It was terrible, terrible. I didn't want her to lose to me. I wanted to win, but I didn't want her to lose. She sang after me, and her voice just rang out; it's so big and rich and dark and high, but then they had me sing two more songs. Cousin Alfonso said later they wanted a small soprano with a lighter voice. She sang very well; Father would have been so proud."

She leaned against the table. "I tried to console her, but she wouldn't allow it. This morning since the inn she would hardly speak to me, and just before when we came to Munich she insisted on getting down from the coach. She walked off I don't know where. She says she won't move to Vienna and I can go to the devil. And it's not my fault; it isn't my fault!" She dropped her head onto her arm, which rested on the table.

Maria Caecilia now sat down as well, so heavily the chair creaked. "The best joys come with difficulties," she murmured.

"What can we say to her when she comes in?" She looked about, her blue eyes bewildered. They all were silent. There was very little their mother could say to her oldest daughter these past months. Since their father's funeral, Sophie felt she had been holding together by sheer will the last of the love between Josefa and their mother, smoothing differences, telling each one varying versions of the same story until she felt exhausted. Now, perhaps, she couldn't do it anymore. She polished her spectacles, then excused herself to stand by the parlor window and watch over the cold winter street.

Josefa arrived home after dark and went at once to her bed in the farthest place by the wall, her shoulders turned to them. If they tried to reach out to her, she seemed to move even farther away. Exhausted, they all slept late the next morning. As they woke one by one and tiptoed to the kitchen in their dressing gowns, Josefa slept on, her long reddish brown hair loose on the pillow. Sophie touched the warm shoulder before she went, and then posted a notice on their apartment door that they were not well and no copied music would be ready today. The traveling bags of both sisters stood, still packed, just inside their door.

In the kitchen Aloysia, arms bare and dressed only in her smock, was bent over a bowl of warm water, washing her hair. As quietly as they could they opened cupboard doors to take out dishes and cheese and bread. Someone had lain Aloysia's new letters from Salzburg by the ale pitcher. Their mother entered; she rolled her eyes when they shook their heads at her silent question. Aloysia knelt by the fire to dry her hair.

They had gathered around the table when they heard the bed creak from their room. Then the door opened, and bare feet approached them. Josefa appeared at the kitchen door. There was a sense of voluptuousness about her—her large breasts and shoulders under the half-closed dressing gown, her hair tumbled about her shoulders—though her face was sullen and withdrawn. Sophie hardly breathed, but she nudged Constanze's knee with her own. "Where're your slippers, Josy?" she said tenderly. "You'll catch cold."

Josefa nodded, and returned a few moments later with their father's old slippers on her feet, shuffling across the floor. She sat down moodily, reached for the bread; then, feeling them all looking quietly at her, she crumbled a bit of crust and said, "I suppose Aloysia has told you what I said yesterday. Well, I meant it. I'm not going to Vienna." She tipped her head to one side, her full lower lip extended, one shoulder raised slightly under the nappy blue wool gown.

She added, "I suppose I should tell you why. It's not just disappointment. Cousin Alfonso said he'd help me find singing work there. There's another opera house, and concerts given all the time, ten times more than there are here. So it's not just that." She crumbled the crust smaller and smaller. They sensed her emotion pressing and pressing until it would burst forth. "I might not have been able to go even if I had won the place."

She looked up. "I don't always tell the truth; I'll admit it. I like to keep people guessing, and I haven't told you the truth about myself, none of you. The real reason I don't want to leave Munich is because I have a lover here."

Her three sisters and mother all looked at one another; Maria Caecilia, her dull gold wedding ring still on her finger, covered her mouth with her hand.

Constanze leaned forward, blinking. "You can't mean what you've said, Josefa," she said practically. "You don't know what you're saying . . . you've said a terrible thing. It's wrong for a girl to speak that way and make people think badly of her reputation; you shouldn't joke about such things."

"I have no reputation; I have a lover, Stanzi."

"You mean there is some man here in Munich whom you went to bed with? You can't mean that. That's not possible. I know you. You're my sister. Good women don't go to bed with men until they're married. You can tell. We would have known. What you say isn't possible."

Josefa suddenly slammed both her hands on the table; Sophie jumped. "Is it so impossible for you all to believe that someone loves me?" she cried. "Why do you all stare at me? It's true, it's true. I met him at the bookstall. We've been lovers since the summer. He's twice my age and has all the money he needs." She stood up, her large hands opening and closing rapidly as the words poured out, and stared at them all scathingly. "Where do you think I got the silver locket I always wear? It was his present to me. Yes, if you must know, he's married. His wife's sickly and is always away taking the baths, and when she dies he's promised to marry me. He will marry me; he keeps his word. So you see, I'm not going to Vienna to help my sister curl her hair for her performances. No, I'm not following you anymore, Aloysia Weber; I'm not picking up your scraps and crumbs. Someone loves me. Mother, you have never believed it could be true, and I hate you for that. Have any of you thought it? Now I've proven it's possible."

Only then did Maria Caecilia manage to rise to her feet. "How dare you stand there," she gasped, "in my very kitchen . . . and say that you have given all honor away, thrown away your good name? How *dare* you boast of it? Who is this person? I'll have the law on him. What, have you made yourself a hussy and a whore? I'll beat you with my wooden spoon. Your father would die if he had not passed already from this earth; yes, he would die of shame. What, a lover? Are you with child? Are you with child?"

"Indeed not," said Josefa scornfully, putting her chair between them. "Don't you think I have enough sense not to get with child?"

Sophie was balling up her apron as she fought tears, her throat contracting as if she were trying to swallow something large and bitter. "What are you saying, Josy?" she stammered. "Oh, what have you done? What will people say of us? And even if you do have a lover, we can't go without you. No, Mother, leave her alone; you're always saying cruel things to her. Oh, Josefa, married lovers *never* marry the girls they lie with. Even you told us that once."

By that time Maria Caecilia had found her wooden spoon, but Josefa dodged her, knocking over the bowl of milk, which splashed down her father's blue dressing gown, and ran from the kitchen. Their shouts and cries echoed through the rooms, and the girls could hear the voices of their neighbors leaning out the windows in the house next door, trying to discover what the noise was about. Sophie was now crying openly as she knelt to mop up the spilled milk. "It's not true; it can't be true," she repeated again and again.

Josefa disappeared that afternoon, and they searched the city for her, running up stairs to ask friends, inquiring at the three bookstalls they knew she liked. The third seller, scratching his head, said he did recall an unusually tall young woman talking for a long time with a man, but he did not know their names. The man bought a great many books, he said. He had no idea if the young woman had been wearing a silver locket. He said he had seen the couple a few times since the summer.

It was the worst Christmas of their lives. For the first time no one baked the festive *weihnachtsgebäck,* the honey pastry made with ginger and spices, or the *springerle,* the rectangular hard cookies with dancing figures or holy pictures stamped on them. The goose burned, and everyone cried throughout the meal, at which Josefa did not even appear. She stayed away from the rooms for two days; when she returned, she refused to say a word. When they tried to follow her the next time, they lost sight of her. Constanze looked at her curiously and with some awe. Was there a difference? It was said that you could tell when a woman fell; you could know when a bride had come through her wedding night. But they could tell nothing. If this great truth was not so, then what was true? Still Josefa declared she would not go to Vienna.

By this time it was the new year, and Aloysia's contract was to begin. They had either to send her on alone, or leave quickly with her, arranging for most of their things to be sent after. Still Josefa came and went as she pleased, with such hard, screaming words between her and their mother that the others were sick with fear. The night before they were to leave, she came home alone after midnight and dropped, fully dressed, across the bed. "Never ask me," she murmured. "I'll come," and for an hour they heard her weeping in short, furious sobs. Slowly they moved closer to her.

Aloysia clung to her. "Please don't be angry with me. You'll find singing work as well, and look, sometimes I'll pretend I'm sick and send you in my place. Promise me you'll forget this horrid person. Life's nothing to me if you don't speak with me; I love you with all my heart."

*M*y dearest dear Aloysia,

I rejoice at your incredible news and good fortune to go to Vienna. Dearest love, you see I was right from the start about the value of your voice. The only thing that hurts me is that this move will take you still farther from me. It's been too long since I've held you in my arms. God willing it will be soon that I can hold you in my arms forever.

My sister didn't bake for Christmas either; she was too sad. I found her by the open flour bin with gingerroot on her lap, still mourning our mother.

I serve daily here with discouragement for the works I want to write, and the places I want to play are so far away from me. I've been inquiring about a good post elsewhere, but every time I hear of one, someone else has been given it first. Leutgeb has returned to Vienna and writes that the Emperor is promoting opera in German, which I could compose with joy, and also that they may be looking for a kapellmeister. I have written at once to a few old acquaintances who are in His Majesty's circle, but with discretion, for if my Archbishop knew of it, he would throw me from his service. I swear faithfulness with one hand and hold the other behind my back.

Oh my love! They think because I am small and young there can't be anything great and old within me. They shall, however, find out soon.

A thousand kisses; no, more . . .

Mozart

The four sisters and their mother packed a hamper of food for the coach journey, then rattled off toward Vienna with trunks of refurbished clothing and an opera contract, their household goods to follow shortly.

Sophie Weber, April 1842

A RAINY APRIL, AND YET IT DID NOT DETER MY FRE-
quent visitor, Monsieur Novello, from coming, sheltered
by an enormous black umbrella; his large wet feet, which he
wiped on the mat, left faint tracks on the floor. After presenting
me with chocolates as he always did, he took out his pen and
journal from that folding desk. "You've been well, madame?"
he asked.

"As well as old age allows."

"I will venture to ask more questions then, and to listen."

"I've been waiting for you to send for coffee. No, it never
keeps me from sleep; I can drink it as late as I like."

He looked at me in a kind and interested way. "So Aloysia
won the contract," he said.

"Yes, she did; I think everyone knew she would. You've seen
her portrait made a few years later in the role of Zémire, haven't
you? The half turban on the hair, which was twined around
gold beads, the delicate hands, the smile. Oh, if you only knew
how very beautiful she was. It took the breath away of all who
saw her; it bewitched them. Even in those days she didn't truly
understand it."

"Tell me about your journey to Vienna."

"Dreadful. The roads were snowy, and I was feverish. Josefa was stony and wouldn't say a word the whole way."

He leaned forward, the tip of his pen glistening with blue ink. "Josefa. My father heard her sing once. Did Mozart ever write anything for her?"

"Yes, some songs and a great opera role years after."

"Of course, now I recall. His German singspiel, *Die Zauberflöte* (*The Magic Flute*, we call it in England), full of dark and good forces. She sang the evil Queen. That's what my father heard her sing when he was a student in Vienna for a time, and he never forgot it. He said she had such passion."

"You may want to see something," I said. "Bring me that box there. Be careful. I have always meant to have the lining replaced. In it you'll find a silver locket; you see I am telling you true things. Yes, you may touch it."

My guest had wiped his fingers on his handkerchief before taking up the locket. "So this was hers!" he exclaimed, weighing it in the palm of his hand. "And what curious engraving." He looked at it more closely, turning to the window. "Quite worn. I can't make out the initials. May I?" I nodded, and he opened the clasp and bent over two strands of hair, touching them with the tip of one finger. "So this is her hair and . . ."

"It's her hair, yes."

"But the other strand is her lover's, of course. The man by the bookstall."

"Perhaps not."

His eyes widened. "Then whose is it, pray?"

I lifted my hand a little to indicate the bell on the table beside him. "Ring for my landlady to bring us coffee," I said. "I think I'd like to have a large sweet cup now, Monsieur Novello. Do ring the bell."

He had been listening so carefully to my words that he had forgotten, and now he apologized and rang the bell several times.

As the last tone ceased to reverberate, I said, "You know, when we were girls still at home together, we supposed we knew everything there was to know about one another. Now that I'm old and alone, I wonder at times about the things I didn't know. Here's my landlady's step in the hall. There are so many stories to be told, and if we meet enough hours, you shall hear most of them, and perhaps understand a little more of what you have come to find."

magnificent stone houses with their sloped roofs and mansard windows all about them, Aloysia rushed into the arms of her sisters and mother. Constanze had brought her one pink silk rose. Alfonso took them all to an elegant supper café, where he predicted the rise of a great prima donna.

Returning home late, the sisters pulled on their white wool sleeping gowns in the large, empty, creaking old house they had rented, and shut themselves in the capacious bedroom on the fourth floor; they had slept together for so long they had not yet decided to sleep apart. Their mother took a room two floors below them. Aloysia lay among her sisters, her soft arm curled over her head, while the portrait of Saint Caecilia gazed down on them and the fantastical blue dress lay spread, as if resting, on the one large chair. She was so tired she fell asleep at once.

For the first few weeks they ran up and down the stairs, unable to believe the house was all theirs. It stood near St. Peter's Church, Peterskirche, in the very center of the city, where a fair amount of Vienna's citizens passed every day; you needed only to kneel by the window with your elbows on the sill to see the procession of nobility, priests, organ grinders, children with hoops. There in a corner of Petersplatz was the lemonade stall, now closed for the colder months, and there was also a bookshop with deep bins outside into which you could plunge your hand and come up with thick novels in English, and worn, gilded volumes of the great playwrights of France, Molière and Racine. Below the window was a procession of exquisite hats. Aloysia could tell the newest ones at a glance. She claimed she could distinguish on closer examination which ones had actually been made in Paris, and which copied here in the gorgeous shops in the Graben, where the most fashionable women bought their clothes. Most people spoke some French, the only truly civilized language.

Within a few weeks, all the sisters considered themselves Viennese. No one who lived here could ever wish to live any other place. It was an attitude that you could, in a brief stroll through the streets, touch everything worth having in the whole world, and see the Emperor riding in his carriage. You could speak with a shrug of all else in the country, farms through provincial towns, as if all those who lived there were simply too stupid or unworthy to be here. You could drop a spattering of French and Italian, and at once be understood by everyone.

There was only one problem: The house was not to be just their own.

All the girls were sitting around the kitchen table one morning, gossiping about neighbors and sharing news from their old city, when they became aware that their mother was stacking many new plates and cups in their capacious cupboard, among them an enormous white soup tureen.

Maria Caecilia turned to them, her hands clasped in a matronly way at her waist. "Oh my fleas," she said tenderly, gazing from one to the next with the greatest satisfaction. "My treasures! I have asked myself since cousin Alfonso found us this house, what shall we do with all the rooms? And what shall I do about our income, for though, alas, Aloysia is earning nicely, more is always needed. I prayed to be lifted from the financial constraints under which we have so often suffered since your earliest days. My Fridolin, who is now an angel, is looking after me, for the answer came. I was at once so grateful I rose from bed and said a whole rosary on my knees. What do I like to do best? What is my greatest gift? Why to cook and bake! And so, with the many extra rooms, I have decided to make our fortune and take in boarders."

Aloysia opened her eyes wide. "Boarders, Mama? Boarders?" Her lyrical voice rose. "This is how I'm to begin my life as a coveted soprano, living in a house of common boarders?"

"I have my reasons," their mother replied serenely, wiping a spot off the soup tureen. "It will bring me a comfortable old age if, by any terrible chance, you all do not marry well." But Aloysia repeated her words incredulously, then leapt up. She rushed into the larger parlor and began to play the clavier. Josefa and the younger girls followed at once, so close together they almost stepped on one anothers' skirts.

Josefa sank down into the sofa cushions, biting the edge of one finger. "She's losing her mind," she said over the fast notes of a Clementi sonata. "We're led by a madwoman."

Sophie curled close to her. "But Mama's a terrible housekeeper; all she does well is cook. Who would take care of boarders?"

"Sophie," said Constanze quietly as she stood before them, "I think *we* would. Girls, let's not talk about it; let's not argue. Maybe she'll forget about it by tomorrow."

No one brought up the subject at dinner that night.

The following afternoon, shortly after the four sisters had closeted themselves away in an empty room to pin a pattern to a length of pink brocade for a dress for Aloysia's new role, they heard the sound of a man's feet mounting the stairs. They listened as the footsteps passed the room in which they worked. Josefa stood up abruptly, put down the pins she was holding, and started for the door. "I won't stand for it," she said. "What would Papa say?"

First came the furniture movers, banging secondhand beds and wardrobes up the stairs; they brought tables, chairs, and hat stands. Two fat women who dealt in used sheets, pillows, and bed curtains followed, negotiating loudly with Frau Weber about the price; at one point they almost left in fury, carrying a dozen pillows in their arms. By the end of the week, the large house was stuffed with scratched furniture and mismatched linens.

The first three boarders moved in the next day: Hans Haussman, a silk merchant who at once complained about the meals; the cellist Giovanni Forza, who practiced scales in his room from four in the morning and stank of raw garlic; and a tall portraitist in his twenties, called Joseph Lange, who kept to himself. There were those sheets to change, shaving water to bring. Constanze was right in her assessment, for she and Sophie were pressed into service to help at meals, supplying knives, more ale, another helping of veal. Reluctantly, they became used to the despised strangers, lowering their eyes when near them, waiting to emerge from their own room when they heard one of the boarders in the hall.

Aloysia and Josefa would have nothing to do with the whole matter.

The men's laundry was piled in a small stone room and

attended to by a laundress who came twice weekly. Aloysia passed the dark room each day that early spring as she slipped into the still barren garden behind the house to study her music.

Once, she almost walked into the portraitist, Lange. "Ah, the air," he said. "I can almost smell the linden blossoms already. Mademoiselle, there's nothing more beautiful than Vienna in the spring." He bowed to her slightly and she nodded curtly. As he went, she imagined she could detect the scent of linden blossoms in the air, until the linseed oil and paint smell that clung to the man's coat erased it. Her father had tried painting for a time, Aloysia remembered. His easel was set up in the parlor when he decided he would paint portraits to supplement their income; only a total lack of ability had deterred him.

"Wolfgang Mozart is a genius, young woman." Those had been the Munich conductor Cannabich's words to her when they met in the street after Mozart had returned to Salzburg. "A genius, and a good kind man, loves you; never forget that." The conductor's face had been serious, and he had looked tired. The two of them stood by a bakery talking for a time, before he bowed to her and walked away.

Aloysia thought about their encounter that spring day as she sat on a bench in the garden behind their new house, writing a letter to her fiancé.

Mozart's own rich and charming letters came regularly to Vienna. How many plans, schemes, determinations he had; how clever he was. But more than that, they gave her advice on the style and technique of her singing. She studied them. In the first weeks at the opera, when other sopranos had snarled at her and tried to edge her offstage or drown her delicate voice with their larger ones, she had despaired and he had understood; he pointed out her gifts and how she could use them to her best advantage. She had depended on her father's teaching more than she knew, and now she depended on the young composer.

Wolfgang, send me all styles of cadenzas you've heard on your travels. And come to me quickly, for I'm longing for you. I'm longing for our marriage. Why don't you come and turn the city upside down with your music, and take me away from this wretched boardinghouse to live in splendid rooms?

Two strangers have sent me flowers. Last night after the performance, several of us were invited by the director to a fine supper. You don't know how I felt having to return home after all the laughter. Mother expects a large portion of my earnings. I want some pearls for my hair desperately.

My regards to your dear sister and father.

I haven't forgotten Josefa, you know, I managed to have her engaged for small roles. Oh, I love opera with all its gossip and scandals, its lovers and mistresses and promises and betrayals.

Aloysia hesitated, the letter unfinished in her lap.

Why didn't he come? She wanted to go to masked balls and dance until the dawn, when the stars have left the sky and only the pale ghost of the moon remained, and she must, she should. She had been given a new role, and the audience had called her name: Aloysia, Aloysia.

"Dearest come quickly," she ended the letter to him, but then forgot to mail it. Weeks later she found it under the garden bench, illegible from the spring rains.

Hot summer lingered through September; dust lay over all the streets of the city, and, roused by carriage wheels or feet or a rug beater, it even drifted through the windows onto the strings of the clavier, which stood in the parlor of the second story.

Constanze had sat there almost all day copying music; now she stretched her aching back, rubbed her neck, and looked about her. She had the room to dust. After putting away her ink, she was taking the dust rag from her apron pocket when she heard the door open below and someone running up the steps.

Sophie flew through the door, her light, flowery summer dress reaching to her ankles, and threw off her bonnet. Her face was streaked with tears. "She's gone; she's gone. She left a letter on the hall table addressed to you, Josefa, and me. She's gone!"

"Who? What?"

Sophie waved the letter in the air as if to shake the words from it. "Aloysia has run away with Lange, the painter."

"Dear God," cried Constanze.

They almost fell over each other rushing up the stairs. Lange's room was stripped bare. The quiet portraitist had left nothing but his sheets neatly stripped from the bed, the smell of linseed oil, and, on the floor, a little splat of deep red paint, like blood of seduced virgins. They stared at it, holding hands. "Dearest mice," the letter said when they unfolded it and held it between them. "You might as well know because I can't hide it anymore. He came into the garden, and we went into the little shed. I don't know what came over me. Oh, my loves, he worships the ground I walk on. I can't live without him; I hardly know myself. And now I'm five months' gone with child, which I didn't plan, but what can be done? Be virtuous. I love you all with all my heart."

Five months with child. They had teased her that she was gaining weight. Only Josefa, they now recalled, had looked down at her flustered sister wryly, a slight smile on the corners of her lips. Too many dumplings, too much bread and butter, Aloysia. Then the young singer had demanded her own room, where she could struggle to lace her corset away from curious eyes. Now they understood.

The three sisters and their mother barricaded themselves in the kitchen under the hanging pots, sitting around the bowl of rising dough and the onion skins left from making the stew. "Oh Aloysia, Aloysia," Maria Caecilia said, rocking back and forth. "My darling, my sweet. First Josefa throws away the good name of Weber, and then our precious Aloysia follows. The slut, the whore! What will we do? What reputation can our family have left? And what of us, what of us? She'll lose her work and be laughed off the stage. How will I pay for this house? What can we do?"

Constanze said quietly, "Perhaps she could marry him." She spread the letter out again and read the whole of it, moving her lips quietly. "Here on the second page at the very bottom she's written that they'll marry. There, you see, Mama! We needn't grieve. It's perfectly respectable for a married woman to be with child."

Caecilia Weber swept the onion skins aside. "Marry a portrait painter? Is that what I hoped when she once had a chance to be a Swedish baroness? I never truly intended her for Mozart. Oh, you don't know what I have hoped for all of you, but mostly for her: my beauty, my enchantress, my darling girl. She looks just like I did in my youth, but I was good, I was dutiful. Why did God send me such daughters? Yes, he'll marry her; there's no hope for it. He must marry her and give me a settlement as well for the loss of her income. All the years to have supported her and bought her every pretty thing I could, and to be rewarded like this and find myself in poverty."

Josefa walked back and forth before the simmering stew, arms crossed over her chest. "Mama, why are you always thinking of yourself? You never think of anything else; even when you thought of her, it was really only for you. All these months, it's been, 'Aloysia must have,' 'Aloysia must wear!' Sew for your sister, do this and that for your sister; all of you, but Mother's the worst. Aloysia'll come back for her contract; she loves how people admire her when she sings." Josefa stared at all of them, hands on the table near the blue beer pitcher. "I suppose you'll expect me to support you all, even I, who was so condemned for my lover and may never have another, who will die a spinster, which would suit you *for certain*, Mama—keeping us all here with your dreams of finding men worthy of us."

"Girl, be still or you'll have a beating," cried the mother.

Josefa rose to her full height; she had played a girl dressed as a soldier recently, and it had suited her. "And who's to beat me, you weak, stupid, fat woman?" she cried. "Oh, I'm so very tired of all of you! You've always mocked me. You always favored her, all of you. Only Father understood me, and I thank God he has not lived to see this." Fiercely, she seized the spoon and stirred the stew.

The presence of the boarders forced them to keep their voices down, but Josefa fled from the room, letting the door bang behind her. Constanze and Sophie slipped into the garden with vegetable peels for the compost heap; then, arms about each other, they fell exhausted to the bench. There Constanze raised her hands to her mouth and drew in her breath hard.

"But how can we have forgotten Mozart?" she said. "Oh Sophie, what will he say?"

*O*n a table in their rooms in Salzburg, warm afternoon sun shone on the music for a new wind sextet for oboes, horns, and bassoons, a divertimento to be played during the palace dinners. Near it Mozart had laid the letter that had come by post an hour before, the page with its few creases open before him. He picked it up, turned it over to where he had broken the seal, and then turned it back to read once more. The writing was not even hers, but Sophie's; she wrote that Aloysia and Lange had returned to Vienna as man and wife, and were now living away from the family.

His father and sister found him sitting there.

"Let us at least eat," said his father.

Slowly, after grace was given, the story came out. Mozart's words were brief. He could almost not bear the compassionate looks of his sister, Nannerl, and his dry, spare father, and how their hands had reached out to hold his.

"Will you pass the pork? And the salt dish?"

"I'm afraid the radishes are very sharp, Father."

"Nannerl, I'll have them anyway."

They ate in silence for a time.

"Those Webers," Leopold Mozart said. "I'm not surprised. The father was a good man, but the girls run wild. A boarding-house, a mother with pretensions. We must thank God on our knees that He didn't let you become entrapped in that family." He helped himself to bread, and did not look up from the buttering as he spoke. "I hope you now agree with me that you shouldn't marry for a long time. Well, you were young, but you have been spared from a tragedy. Make your reputation; go slowly. I was nearly thirty when I married and knew more about the world than you, but then a woman like your good mother does not come along often. When the Archbishop takes you to Vienna next week on his state visit there, I hope you will not darken the door of those Webers. These radishes are sharp indeed."

Much of the day's journey to Vienna, Mozart sat with his fingers to his lips, staring from the coach window at the mountains and fields. The creaking conveyance that they had boarded before dawn was too full, and his fellow musicians pressed uncomfortably close, while someone's leather bassoon case wobbled back and forth until it found a place leaning against his thigh.

In the midafternoon the horses stopped before St. Stephan's Cathedral, called Stephansdom, and the nearby Palace of the Teutonic Knights, an old religious order where the Archbishop kept his Viennese residence. A footman showed Mozart to a narrow room with whitewashed walls and two hard beds, where the young man kicked his trunks into the corner. The only consolation was that he would see his old horn player friend Leutgeb, who was now settled over his grandfather's cheese shop with his very pregnant wife and took part in the concert life of the city.

"We're playing for a mass with the Archbishop tonight," the cellist with whom he roomed said, unpacking his trunks and pulling forth his evening shirt. "I always enjoy when state business brings him here, but I must say, you don't look very jolly. Aren't you glad to be in Vienna, Mozart? Where are you going?"

"To the devil."

In the halls he passed several servants and Count Arco, who bowed to him with a slight smirk. The Archbishop was in residence; the very walls with their somber portraits of long-dead knights and clerics should also bow discreetly in the direction of his large suite of rooms and innumerable lackeys, his private chapel, and, undoubtedly, gilded and heavily draped sleeping chamber. He would make his calls of protocol about the city, followed by his entourage of musicians, who would raise flutes to their lips and bows to their violins at his almost imperceptible nod.

Mozart walked the city for an hour, circling near and about Petersplatz, where the Webers lived under the shadow of the green-domed church. Every girl he saw he thought was her, every small woman who turned around to smile at him. He was coming down the walk under the trees in the public gardens when he saw Sophie Weber, sun glinting on her spectacles, eating a coffee ice near an ice stand. It took a moment for him to understand that the woman with her—so swollen with child that she looked like a stalk bending for the weight of its pod—was Aloysia.

He came forward, bowing stiffly. Curtseys were returned, eyes lowered. Aloysia's pretty mouth was like a slit, and she had the exhausted, sallow look women have at times when their growing unborn child is consuming their very bones. Six months now, he thought, calculating back to the time in late spring when her letters had become scant and then faded away altogether with excuses of her busyness and little time.

He said coldly, "God's greetings; you're well?"

"I'm well enough, as you can see," replied Aloysia languidly.

I'm withholding my feelings, he thought with some pride, yet the next moment he could not be silent. His small hands twitched at his side. "How could you; how could you? I loved you more than any man has ever loved. Don't you know that you have broken my heart forever?"

"What did you want of me?" she whispered, stamping her foot. A group of families with children turned around to stare at her, making her lower her voice even more. "Waiting and waiting for you to do better. I do quite well enough myself now. Once my baby is born, I'll sing again, and earn more money than before, while you're only one of many composers. You can blame only yourself. How long did you expect me to live on your letters?"

He nodded grimly, thinking how two years before Leutgeb had warned him about any involvement with the Webers. Now Leutgeb was married, whereas he, Mozart . . . what had he made of himself? And to think the child might have been his! He could hardly make his last bow.

After walking swiftly away, he paused on a small bridge and looked down. Why not simply leap? Cold water choking his lungs. Death comes, death comes. But is not death the best friend of man?

He did not know how long he stood there before he heard his name called, and looked about to see Sophie rushing toward him, freckles all the way down her neck to her bodice top. "You walked so fast, and I was following behind," she panted, "but there was a horse parade and a marching band that divided us."

Coldly, he asked, "Why did you come after me?" Vaguely, he recalled how much they had had together during their time in Munich, crawling around the floor in games, sitting side by side at the clavier playing together (she with two fingers), making up nonsense words.

"Because," she said, shaking his limp hand, "you're our friend. She's sorry, you know, but she'll never say it. I can see your heart's broken. Aloysia doesn't have a heart as you do. Many people go about the world without hearts as we know them, and we never realize until too late. She has a different sort of heart, which, of course, we love her for. Grandmother understood her, but grandmother's gone to heaven with Papa. Of course she's beautiful. Angels are beautiful and filled with love, though it must be a different sort of beauty; but then you wouldn't fall in love with an angel, would you, since they're not corporeal? And do we have the sense and wisdom of angels? Can we, while in this mortal place . . ." She went on and on in one of her long speeches, her words not entirely comprehensible. He stared at her.

A wind band some distance from them burst out with popular tunes.

She said, "I'm praying to God to give you courage. I swear, I know, that your life will be happy. No one's life here is always happy, but you will have some. I am sure you have read *The Sorrows of Young Werther*. Goethe. Josefa knows it by heart, as did our father. Lost love. But what can we expect? It's a fallen world." Then she took off her spectacles, rubbed them with her sleeve, and said, "At least come pray and then have a lemonade. It's October, and they won't keep the stands open much longer."

His eyes filled with tears, and he waited a while until he was able to control himself. Then he followed her back toward Stephansdom, where they entered the great ornate Gothic edifice, which was one of the musical centers of the city as well as the repository of some remains from hundreds of years of Habsburg emperors. They genuflected, then knelt and prayed together as he had done when in thanksgiving for a composition well received. Opening his eyes, he saw her beside him with her hands clasped.

Then she said, "Come on," and they went out into the square in the still warm autumn day to the lemonade stand, and each had two glassfuls. After that Sophie went home, and Mozart walked across the square once more to the Palace of the Teutonic Knights, which was flying the Archbishop's flag to signal his residence. Climbing to his bleak room, he brushed off his coat for the Archbishop's concert that night, which was to be held at the house of Prince Galitzen. That he had missed the rehearsal was remarked upon by a few colleagues.

*C*arnival time came to Vienna just before Lent, as it did each year, with its glittery masks, wild costumes, extravagant feasts, the parading whores, who revealed as much of their bodies as they dared to by law, the banging of drums, the playing of horns, and much dancing until dawn—all to frighten winter away. It was an old custom that he recalled from Venice and Rome as well; the city flaunted gaiety before the austerities that would come.

Mozart had dragged himself through Christmas, and the cold months which followed, seeing his lost love in every petite woman, feeling that the whole thing must have been a mistake and that any day Aloysia would appear at his door, eyes cast down, modestly dressed. He saw her dressed like his mother, in a gray-flocked gown as plain as a nun's. He saw how he would take her to his bed, losing at last his wretched and unwanted sexual innocence. He went to sleep in the room he shared with the cellist thinking of it, and woke to find it was not so. Here he was in Vienna, where Haydn had sung as a chorister, where Gluck had the performance of his radiant *Orfeo and Euridice,* where the Emperor walked daily in the parks, but he made little of the music he wished to make and seldom performed where he wished to perform.

He saw none of the Webers. Sophie had sent him a handkerchief that had been her father's, with the initials FFW embroidered on it. He looked at it from time to time with distant tenderness, but he had no desire to see her, even to thank her for her kindness. He was too ashamed, and he was in no mood for Carnival.

One day as he was drinking coffee and reading the news journal at a coffee and pastry house, Leutgeb, with his round, youthful face, slipped into the empty chair beside him. "We never see you," he said. "My wife hardly believes you exist; my baby is sure you do not."

"I do exist."

"But not well?"

"Not very well. How are you, my friend?"

"Why, married life suits me! I sell a great deal of cheese, and play my horn wherever I can. Sometimes I wonder where are the concerti my friend Wolfgang promised me. Then when I find I am covered with cobwebs from standing so long contemplating this question, I look him up in a Viennese pastry and coffee house to find out. Where are the concerti, my friend?"

Mozart shrugged and looked down into the coffee grounds.

"Never mind, I'll wait a bit longer. Look! Some old friends are here, and we're going to the puppet show at Madame Godl's *krippenspiel*. If you can get away, come with us. They're longing to go. It's crowded, but the puppets are a marvel. Come on."

The theater was long, with an intricate puppet stage at one end. The four friends crammed into the narrow, hard benches like schoolboys. Mozart gazed at the three-dimensional backdrop of Jerusalem. The harpsichordist who banged away in a corner was a poor musician Mozart had met as a boy. He heard one of his own divertimento tunes and sat straight up. "That's yours, you ass," Leutgeb said. "Don't you know how much of your music is played? They steal it before you sneeze."

They spoke loudly above the noise of housewives, a few ladies in masks to conceal their identity at such a low form of entertainment, and many stomping schoolboys waiting for the performance. "What have you been doing here besides playing His Grace's church music and mourning, Mozart? Are you writing music of any sort, since you are not doing so for me?"

"Yes I am!" he burst out. "But what good does it do? I wanted to perform something of mine at Countess Thun's the other evening (the Emperor was there), but my Archbishop needed me to play for his convalescing father, so I gave a piano/violin sonata for the dismal old man, and that was that. And I dare not even let him see my anger."

"And so you shut yourself up."

Mozart did not reply; he gazed at the marionettes that he could make out from his seat, so large and lifelike, but wooden. How odd the way they jerked and danced when their strings were pulled! Could they feel in their own way? I am one of them, he thought suddenly. Slowly, beginning with the fingertips, I am turning to wood.

Then the play began, and they saw the capture of Jerusalem. The walls fell. Cannons sparked real sparks and smoke filled the theater; in the haze marionette citizens jerked to their deaths, and marionette Romans jerked to their victory. He had seen puppets as a boy, and not particularly liked them, but the banging on the floor and the shouting and everyone choking on the smoke and weeping over the fall of Jerusalem was infectious, and he leapt up, shouting with the rest, suddenly flooded with happiness. *To write theater pieces, to write operas,* he thought. To write the sort of music he wanted to write, to be free.

The schoolboys trod on his toes going out, and the harpsichordist ran after him, and cried, "Give my regards to your dear sister." Jerusalem had fallen, and the assistants were cleaning up for the next performance, for which a line was already forming.

The four young men stood in the street. From every direction came the sound of Carnival. "Let's have a beer and supper," Leutgeb said.

In the beer cellar a flautist was trying in vain to play above the talking. Now Mozart felt his sadness return, drank a great deal of beer, and was silent. "Idiot," Leutgeb said to him. "Arsehole. I've spoken to you twice, and you don't reply. We've been here for two hours; now it's time to go, and you've never been such tedious company."

Mozart replied, "Sorry, I'm turning to wood. My heart's gone already. There you have it. At the next performance of the *krippenspiel,* look, and you'll find me hanging with the other marionettes." He stood up in a sudden fury. "That's it," he cried, "that's it."

The flautist stopped for a moment to see who was shouting, then resumed. "Sit down," someone called, "are you going to make a speech? Are you going to drink the Emperor's health?"

But Mozart continued, "I am turning to wood. I must go and speak to my saintly employer. You'll excuse me. I'm going now before it's too late."

Leutgeb cried, "Tonight, on the eve before Lent? Tonight, past the hour of nine?"

"Nevertheless." He pulled his friends to their feet, and Leutgeb ran back to pay the bill, then hurried up the steps two at a time to join the others. They stood a street away from Michaelerkirche, with its sandstone fallen angels, and turned toward the palace by the cathedral. The winds from the river and woodlands rose, blowing through the town. "Madman, madman . . ." the others cried to Mozart. A guard looked at them carefully, then motioned them on with disgust. The gaslights shone on the stone work of the elegant houses.

Two sentries stood before the palace. "Wait here," Mozart

said unsteadily to his friends. "I'll be a short while. You wait." He walked forward, looking over his shoulder at them as they stood with folded arms, shaking their heads.

Inside the palace the chamberlain motioned him on up the great stairway and then down the hall. Count Arco was walking toward him, carrying a lamp and a goblet of wine in blue molded glass. "Where are you going, Mozart?"

"His Princely Grace wishes to see me."

"He mentioned no such thing to me. Well, go on. He'll be at his prayers."

The house was dark, for most of the candles had been extinguished. "No one comes now," said the chamberlain, opening the bedchamber door and announcing the composer. There was a grunt and a muffled response, and Mozart was waved inside.

The room was papered in red damask, with bed hangings of the same weighty material. The enormous dark wood canopy bed could have slept a workman's family. The ceiling was high and parqueted with angels, who seemed ready to fall down to the carpet at any moment. His Holiness was already in his dressing gown and nightcap for the evening, drinking wine before a great roaring fire. His face seemed like a withered apple, his eyes even smaller. "Mozart, it's you," he said. "What's so important that you must see me at this late hour?"

"I wish to thank you for your kindness to me, and to say that, with much regret, I have decided to leave your service."

The Archbishop threw up his hands. "What," he cried. "You interrupt my preparation for rest with such nonsense when you have eaten my bread this past year? You brat, you idiot! I have borne with you too long. One can see you're not grateful to serve me. Where is your gratitude? Why did I let your father persuade me to hire you?"

"Well then, Your Grace is not satisfied with me?"

"Idiot, there is the door. Go."

"For Jesus sake, do not leave his service," Mozart's father had written weeks before when Mozart had confided to him his unhappiness. "The Archbishop has borne with your wanderings and mine own and took you back again only at my pleading. If you go once more, it will be the last time; I fear it. Where shall you go away from him? One cannot make a meal and roof of dreams, my son. . . ."

The words spilled from him over the crackling of the fire and into the seeping cold corners of the room. "Very good, my lord, the conditions suit us both, for as much as you want nothing to do with me, I want nothing to do with you either. If I never have to see your face again, it will be too soon."

At that the Archbishop rose, knocking over the wine by his side, and screamed, "Out, out." The dark red liquid spilled down his robe and spread across the floor. The veins in the older man's forehead stood out as he seized the bell and rang it violently. Several footmen came running; another door burst open, and Count Arco, also in his dressing gown, rushed in.

"Remove this brat," said the churchman.

Count Arco cried, "What have you done now, you impudent puppy, you knave? What disturbance have you made?" He seized

Mozart by the arm and shoved him from the ornate bedchamber. Followed by the pale footmen, composer and Count half-dragged each other down the stairs to the great palace doors. Mozart felt the Count's kick from behind and tumbled into the street. He stumbled to his feet again with a cry of outrage and rushed back toward the footmen who stood between him and the figure of the retreating assailant, the nobleman's pale satin dressing gown glimmering as he faded into the recesses of the round receiving hall. "What? Will you run off, you coward?" Mozart shouted into the echoing hall.

Someone grabbed his arms from behind. Astonished, he turned to face his musician friends. "Leutgeb, you ass, let me go!" he shouted. "I'm going to kill him."

"No, you idiot!" Leutgeb cried, shaking his head. "Come away while you have a whole skin. We shouldn't have let you go there. What did you say to your august employer? What could you have said?"

"I told him to kiss my arse, in so many words."

"What? Actually said it, came near it? Don't you know how dangerous that is? Why did you do it?"

"I am Mozart," he said hoarsely.

"And you'll be Mozart in a prison getting a good beating, believe me! Didn't you hear what happened to that fellow who struck a nobleman? Nobility has all the privileges to behave badly; we have none. Disgusting, and this with a reforming Emperor on the throne."

Mozart shook them off, his voice gruff and ashamed. "Well then, go home, fool, idiot, ass. I'll do as I like." The three wind players had half-dragged him around the corner, where they slapped some cold fountain water at him and then dipped his face in it. "That's it," Leutgeb said. "I've got a horn lesson to give at dawn, and so do the rest of us. Keep your temper, Wolfgang. Don't you know now's not the time to let it out? Go to sleep and think about mending your bridges; you're meant to walk across them, not burn them down. Will you now?"

"Yes, good night," he said, for the water had sobered him, and he walked, dripping, back toward the cathedral square by the light of the still-burning lamps. But when he returned to the palace door, he saw that his trunks had been brought down and set on the street. All his clothing and his music lay in a heap, the symphony he had written in Paris folded up into his wind band music. Out of curiosity, a few people from houses nearby had opened their windows, only to see a servant fling down onto the pile a single shoe and two books. Impudent puppy and knave, the Count had called him. He would have liked to go back and beat him. "My God, the bastard, the bastard," he muttered again and again. "To set me loose like this, as if I were some felon . . . my God, my God. So this is what it comes to. . . ."

"Do not leave his service for God's sake," his father had concluded the letter. "What security have you? You don't know how to scrape; you don't know how to bow. I have never doubted your gifts, but without these other attributes you are lost."

"Dearest Father," he thought now, composing his reply. "You've made me what I am, and I must be what I am. If I starve, sell what music I've written, but I must try, I must try. I can't believe that God has created me to be a second-rate church

Sophie Weber, May 1842

ON SPRING DAYS LIKE THIS I FEEL A PALPABLE SENSE OF all the old keepsakes in my room, as if they want somehow to shake off their dust and rise from their boxes. People say the aged are inclined to live in their memories. Why shouldn't that be? There is an irreplaceable world within me.

And then Monsieur Vincent Novello comes, carrying his walking stick or umbrella, always deferential, always hopeful. Sometimes I'm not feeling well and send him away, but today I pinned on my false curls and welcomed him, eager to tell him the things I once thought to withhold so that they will not fade away.

"I found something I thought was lost, monsieur!" I said. "Constanze's letters, journals, and keepsakes, dating from her childhood until about the time Aloysia married. She kept the box under our bed, away from Mama's prying eyes. Mama was too stout to look under there by then, as stout as I am now."

We pushed aside the sweets, and opened the small box, with real flowers preserved forever under the lacquered top. "I feel as if I'm prying," he said. "Is there anything as secret or personal as a young girl's dreams and thoughts? I am so sorry to have waited these years to come, and not to have known your sisters."

"They're always present for me."

"They are here indeed," he said after a time, respectfully putting his hand over mine. "May I?" At my nod of permission, he began to remove the contents of the box. There were folded letters, some dried flowers, some words written on the back of a piece of music, the announcement for a concert. "Who are the letters from?"

"Some from someone she loved; others are hers to someone she loved in spite of herself, most unsent."

"You didn't tell me she had such a love."

"Constanze was secretive. She was the most secretive of us, though I knew her best. Sometimes I didn't know which thoughts were hers and which were mine. We had to join together, with the older two gone their own ways, and perhaps we always had. We were the two young girls waiting for the others. I dreamed of her last night, the way we slept with arms and legs all entwined, the way I sometimes mistook my breathing for hers, her heartbeat for mine. Will you ring for coffee? I feel the need of it."

He took up the bell to ring.

"I'm going to tell you about the things in this box," I said to him. "But I want to get things in order so as not to confuse you. Let me tell you what happened to our Mozart when he found himself with his trunks in Stephansplatz before the palace of the knights."

"Ah yes, tell me," my visitor said, sitting back so that his coat opened and his vest with its watch chain seemed to expand in anticipation. I could see from the amusement in his eyes that he already knew where the proud, strong-headed composer went to lay his head.

PART FOUR

Vienna and Maria Sophia,
1781

*D*earest Father,

My "Paris" symphony was played at the benefit concert
and well received. Meanwhile, I have money from the publisher of the quartets, and I am giving another recital at
the house of the Baroness von Waldstätten, who is very
good to me, and who has an excellent new fortepiano. I am
sending on some money so you see I have begun to do a little better. For the love of God, buy yourself some undergar-
ments and good food and a new dress for my sister. It breaks
my heart that you should stint yourselves. I have two new
suits (one red with silver lace), which I bought only from
necessity, for you know I have no vanity, but one cannot appear looking shabby, and the tailor will wait for the balance
of the money. I dine at others' expense as much as possible.
My heart is steadfast, this I swear before God; I want nothing but work. (I send six, no twenty, no ninety-three kisses
to my sister's nose.)

But dearest Father, now I must explain how I managed
since that dreadful night. Leutgeb had gone home to his
rooms above his cheese shop before he knew what had

happened, and the drunken man whom I sent took two hours to bang on his door, and my exhausted friend came at once and took me with him, but there was no room there to remain, of course. His wife's family is there, and there was no place for me. On my life, I did not know what I would do, for I am but a poor wretch left in lodgings alone. You know I can write a movement of a symphony easier than arranging for a laundress to wash my things, and last night for the concert I could find only white hose already splattered with Viennese street muck. Yes, this is a trial. (I send fifty-nine embraces to you, and I embrace faster than I shit, which is fast enough I assure you.)

Now my story. Can you imagine my fortune? I met the widow of that excellent musician Weber while buying bread and ink, and she said she had an empty room for rent, and would welcome me. This is truly all I need to continue to make my success in Vienna. I am sure you will not mind. The two younger sisters, Constanze and Sophie, are sweet; they copy music, keep the household accounts, and cook. They could sew on my coat buttons when they come loose and mend my wretched hose. You know I can't manage those things myself as my music takes all my time. The older sister scowls at me; we were friendly, I thought, but she's discontent and doesn't like anyone. They say it is from a disappointment in love. Oh, if I ever found fault with the Weber sisters for the fault of the one who treated me so poorly, I beg their pardon, for they are good, chaste girls, or at least the younger two are ... what the eldest is, heaven knows. I assure you I am quite safe from romantic intrigue. The thought of marriage now repels me. I want only to work, as work I must.

I am ever your most obedient son,

W. A. Mozart

The reply came, written rapidly.

My dearest Son

I am most happy to hear of your success and have gratefully received the money you sent me, though, alas, it must go for old debts, and the underthings must wait.

One thing in your letter distressed me to my soul, and you know what it is. I do not like the idea of your living with the Webers. Did they not play about with you enough with their daughter; did you not lose your head over her? And what did she do but make herself the loose woman? But all of that family's perfidy comes from the mother, whom your own darling, sainted mother felt to be untrustworthy. I must warn you, they will cheat you or entrap you in some way. They know the softness of your heart, which you wear on your sleeve. Adieu. I am going now to settle some debts. Send me a copy of the symphony if you can. And go regularly to confession and to mass. You used to go almost every day, I recall.

Your loving old father,

Leopold Mozart

Two days later he moved into a third-story room in the house, his windows looking out on the green dome of *Peterskirche*. Frau Weber welcomed him warmly. "That hussy, that treasonous girl!" she exclaimed as she unlocked his door with a large brass key. "That she behaved so poorly to me, to you, poor, dear Mozart. Well, you never know what treachery can lie in the hearts of the children we suckle." She stood there with her jangling keys at her waist, smelling of baking. Her skirt hem was dusted with flour. His heart melted with gratitude as he unpacked his clothing and possessions, laying out on the table a small stack of paper to rule for music staves. It was a light room, with a bed, a washstand, and a pitcher for hot water, on which were painted alpine flowers and the words FROM OUR WANDERINGS, DEAR LORD, BRING US HOME.

Thus began his life in that house, a boarder among a handful of others. Constanze and Sophie looked at him, sometimes smiling as if they hoped some friendship between them might resume, yet he did little more than smile distantly in return. There were no more songs or games. He had neither the inclination nor the time for them.

He heard them whisper their sister's name, though the rash young soprano herself never set foot within the doors. He knew when, a few months later, she gave birth, and that she had sent the little girl child to the country to be raised by a wet nurse, then returned to her singing with much success. He hurried through the rooms of the house as if rushing from her ghost, which he felt standing here and there, looking at him, mocking him. For a time he felt he could not remain, but to leave the house meant to leave the sound of her name, which he still craved; and so he stayed.

*C*onstanze and Sophie could smell linseed oil and paint as they climbed the steps to their sister's marital apartment, several streets from their own. It was a few months later, a bright June day. Aloysia's husband, Joseph Lange, opened the door swiftly, as if he had been waiting behind it. He was a tall man in his middle twenties, with small teeth and a strong jaw, who now and then also acted in the theaters.

Shyly, the girls looked around the room. There was an air of sensuality about the carelessly squashed sofa pillows; a book thrown facedown on the floor; the easel, with its half-finished portrait of their sister in some operatic role, head tilted to the side, great eyes gazing intensely at the viewer. Behind a slightly ajar door, they could see the rumpled unmade bed; emerging from that door came Aloysia, also rumpled, wearing her husband's dressing gown, which she had to hold up, for it was so long it seemed like the regal train of a monarch. Her hair was down about her shoulders, as if she had just risen from that bed, where the sheets still held the warm scent of man and wife. She smelled of it as she leaned forward to kiss them, her tangled hair brushing their cheeks.

Constanze and Sophie embraced her. How odd to have her apart from them; it was a crack in their lives that did not mend.

Aloysia stretched out on the sofa pillows. On her feet dangled Sophie's slippers, which she had taken months ago when she had rushed home for her possessions, her face flushed with anger and tears, throwing randomly in her portmanteau someone's chemise, someone's hairbrush, her broken rosary, and many other things. Now, lying on the sofa in her own rooms, all rushing was gone. She yawned, and said idly, "How are things at home?"

"The same," said Sophie with a sigh. "Five boarders, including Steiner, who studies theology and never pays on time. How's the baby? Oh I wish she were here to hold; I love babies."

"You've always loved little things, but you mightn't if you knew what trouble she gave me being born; I thought I was dying. I suppose she's well; her wet nurse in the country seems like an honest woman. We're going to drive out tomorrow to see her; someone who likes my singing is lending his carriage. You can come if you like. She's an odd little thing. My husband says she looks like me, but I can't see it."

Aloysia stretched and glanced at Joseph Lange, who had again taken up his paintbrush. He felt it and returned the look. The two younger sisters reached for each other's hands. Come back, they wanted to cry. When would she be coming home? Would she ever now?

Aloysia reached for the pitcher to pour some beer; at that moment something silver glittered at her throat. Sophie squinted and leaned forward. "Why, that's Josefa's locket," she cried, instantly proprietary on behalf of her older sister. She could see Josefa on her knees, feeling under the bed, crying, "Where's my locket? Where's my locket?"

The beer was poured, a few drops making their way down the outside of the glass. "What, do you think I took it without asking?" Aloysia said. "I did borrow your slippers, Sophie, I admit that. I'll return them soon, I promise. As for the locket, Josefa said I could have it. Last month when I came for my things she thrust it at me, saying, 'I don't want it anymore.' She's more and more odd, you know. Her deportment's dreadful, even onstage. Never mind. I guess she's done with her mourning for her lover in Munich."

Aloysia sat up a little, and looked around the room as if momentarily surprised to find herself here. *"Mon Dieu,"* she murmured. "How we are all turning out differently than we thought . . . but enough of that. Come see my new dresses. I'm singing in private houses as well as the opera, and it does pay very nicely."

In the bedroom she spread out a new pink dress, a dark green one, and a petticoat that would be displayed through the front dress panels, layers and layers of white eyelet embroidered with little pink flowers. Aloysia looked carefully at her sisters. She kissed Sophie, and said, "I can't believe you're fifteen. Your birthday was months ago, and I'm sorry I missed it. I'll buy you a present; you know I always do, though it's often late. But look at you both—before we know it, you'll both be in love and married as well. By that time Josefa might actually be less abrasive and find someone to marry her. I'll be the most famous singer in Europe by then, and we'll visit one another and be civil. Yes, it will happen; I know it."

Sophie stood with her toes turned in a little, rubbing the

bridge of her nose to ease the place where the spectacles rested. "I'm not going to marry," she said. "I want to be a nun and dedicate myself to charitable works."

"Oh, that again, you tiresome child. All girls want that for a time—the perpetuation of virginity, the dedication to the sorrowful mysteries, and all those things we were taught when Papa took us to church. But tell me . . ." Her fingers caressed the eyelet of the petticoat, and she blinked a little faster. "How is . . . *Mother?*"

Constanze sighed. "Mama's much the same. Her back aches; her legs ache; the boarders tire her. I do what I can. Speaking of marriage, she has plans again. I heard her talking with Uncle Thorwart the other day from behind closed doors, something about the cousin of a count who has a small estate. She doesn't give up; she doesn't understand. When *I* marry it will be for love." She raised her face, and, in that moment, there was an unusual radiance in her heart-shaped face.

She flung herself down on the bed, pushing aside the dresses. "The last time Mama tried was in the autumn, and he was old enough to be my grandfather. He had to help himself up from the chair with his cane, though Mama said he owned four houses." Through her now loosening hair, Constanze gazed at her younger sister, beginning to laugh all over again. "And we laughed so hard, Sophie and I, we had to excuse ourselves. We collapsed on the stairs outside the sewing room, laughing. I know he heard us, but we couldn't help it! Sophie said, 'If he can't stand by himself, what will he do in *bed?*' and that made me laugh so hard I nearly fell over. It's true; the child did say it. Don't deny it, Sophie! Oh, heavens—"

"Oh, how ridiculous," Aloysia cried. "Sophie, how *do* you know such things? What use will they be in a convent? What a waste! Darlings, poor mice! Move over; don't squash my dresses."

The three sisters tumbled over one another on the bed, lying on their sides amid the pillows, hearing Joseph Lange's humming as he painted in the next room. Aloysia said, "You know, our Josefa never comes to see me, or at least hasn't in this last month. She can't make up her mind if she loves me or resents me. But she does have a lover. I know people who sing with her. It's one of the tenors, the one from Prague. The city's small; you can't blow your nose without someone noticing it, and gossip's the very bread and butter of life. Some people say two lovers. She's doing it to get back at Mother, to show others she can, to show me."

Lying on her side, Aloysia hesitated, her face taking on an unusual severity. "And if she doesn't watch it, she'll find herself where I was, with a bun in the oven, and she'll have to marry. Not that I didn't want to; I wouldn't trade Lange for the world. But there I was, so swollen with child, so distorted I hardly knew myself, and I kept saying, really, is this creature me?" Now she was laughing again, flinging back her hair. "Can you imagine our proud Josefa in that state? Children are lovely, but with the bickering and quarreling Mother and Father engaged in over us, and their concerns about how to cut the slices of meat small enough to go around. Oh mice, do you remember the hours and hours we hid on the stairs while they raged and shouted? With all that, should we be hasty to get ourselves with child?" Her voice trailed off, and she caressed the bodice of the pink dress.

Sophie lay silent in thought. Josefa did not come home often. She was singing in another opera house, where her rich voice with its deep low notes fascinated some even though her roles were small. She had made close friends with two women who lived together, one a rather mannish portraitist and the other a young composer; she was often at their house, and stayed away for days without explanation. Their mother looked at her angrily with a furrowed brow, daring to challenge her only in short barbs, then looking away, gnawing her lip, afraid of losing her. But could Aloysia's words be true? Two lovers? What did a woman do with two lovers? I am losing her; I am losing her, Sophie thought. Josefa will go just like Aly, and leave us.

Vaguely Aloysia's words floated over her, and Sophie turned to look at the young singer who now leaned back dreamily, pillow in her arms. "She'll come back, Sophie," she murmured. Aloysia knelt for a moment and touched the younger girl's freckled cheek as she had years before when Sophie was ill and she had sung her lullabies. Then she said, with slow tenderness, "Oh mice, do you ever wonder what life is for? In the end what it's really for, what's the reason for it, and how are we to behave?"

Aloysia opened her hands palms up and then reached for an ostrich feather that lay on the table near the bed. "Never mind, I'll make myself melancholy talking like that. Look, this feather's going on my blue hat . . . everyone in Paris wears them! No, wait, this is important! Tell me about you, Stanzi. There's something different about you. What is it? Do you have a secret? Are you in love? Yes, you are, look how you blush. Now I'm going to tickle your belly until you tell me."

They fell together into a heap, Constanze laughing, her dress pulling up over her dark hose as she tried to get away from her sister's tickling fingers. "Oh stop, stop, Aloysia; there's no one, I swear."

Holding her down, Aloysia whispered into her ear, "I know something about you that you don't. You could be a great flirt if you let yourself, Constanze Weber, and you could, too, Sophie, with all your talk of nunneries. You silly girls, when will you learn? Flirting's delicious, it's delicious; you have so much power. Oh, it's one of the most delicious things."

A knock sounded at the door, discreet, then sounded once more. "Beloved," came Lange's low and reasonable voice, "you have a rehearsal with the musicians in an hour. The clock just struck, and you ought to have a little food before you go."

Aloysia sat up suddenly. She stood frowning, glancing severely toward her few more common dresses, wondering which one she should wear. The two younger sisters slipped down from the bed, straightening their own dresses and refastening their hair with the pins that had come loose.

"My darling," came the call again.

"Yes, yes, I'm coming." Aloysia flung off the dressing gown and stood in her smock; she sat down on the chair to pull on her hose and fasten them to her garter. From the other room came the sound of things being moved. Smoothing her hose, Aloysia said offhandedly, "And how's Mama's boarder, Herr Mozart? I hear he writes and gives lessons and some concerts, yet still can barely make enough to feed himself. A pity. Some people say he's brilliant, and others that he's just too proud, that he wants life just as he wants it and won't have it any other way."

Sophie nodded, the corners of her mouth drawn down. "He never speaks to us except when he must," she said uncomfortably. "I wish we were still good friends! Do you ever sing the songs he wrote for you?"

"Yes, I do; they're beautiful songs. The whole tour he planned! He has a kind heart but little sense. Sophie Weber, are you going to ask me if I regret what I did? Never, not for a moment. Joseph and I are much in love, and we may travel to other countries. Perhaps to Paris for my singing, and he could paint there. His work's in demand. Did you see the lovely one he's making of me in the role of Zémire, with the feathers in my hair? Oh girls, did you see it? It's against the wall."

She was dressed now, slipping the last of the ivory pins into her hair. They followed her into the small sunny room where her clavier stood and watched as she gathered up her music, trying a scale or two. Her beautiful little voice rang out to the china figurines on the windowsill. When she turned, both younger sisters sensed that she had now entirely left them, that the laughter and tickling might have occurred years ago and not just a few minutes before.

"Don't let Mama spoil your lives," she said severely. Then she kissed them on their cheeks, for a moment letting her little hand linger on their arms. "Good-bye, my very dears," she murmured.

"I miss Papa, don't you? Sometimes I miss him so much I can't bear it."

The shop sign dripped water down its painted wood over the words JOHANN AND WENZEL SCHANTZ, MAKERS OF FORTEPIANOS AND CLAVIERS, PURVEYORS OF MUSIC FROM FRANCE, AUSTRIA, AND ITALY. Peering through the rainy windows, Constanze gazed past the instruments to the blurred, well-built man in his leather apron. Then she opened the shop door to the tinkle of the bell, and went inside, shaking off her cloak as best she could.

His voice resonated warm and deep. "*Bonjour,* Mademoiselle Weber."

She made the smallest curtsey. "*Bonjour,* Herr Schantz."

"You come in the rain! I hope all's well with your family."

"Oh, all quite well! I've come to find the music for the song we spoke of."

"Yes, of course! I was concerned for a moment that my man didn't mend your father's old clavier satisfactorily. I'm afraid he confided in me that it's seen its time." And he smiled at her. "I'll look for the music, mademoiselle," he said, and went through a door into a small room where she could hear him humming and vigorously moving boxes. Even though he left the room, she could feel his presence.

Johann Schantz's dark, muscular arms under his rolled sleeves were dusted with hair; his chest was broad, his voice deep. He smelled of the insides of fortepianos and claviers, that hidden woody smell of her childhood. He reminded her of a painting she had once seen of a gypsy. For some months now she had been making excuses to see him, spending the day before thinking of what she could say, and the days following wishing that her words had been more clever or that something about her had been more noticeable.

Aloysia always said you could define affection, relegating it to either flirtation or deep feeling, but that was so reductionary, that was so unsubtle. When Constanze was twelve there had been the schoolboy who had lived downstairs in their Mannheim house and had left her short notes slipped under a crack in one of the steps. When she was not quite fourteen there had been the lawyer's clerk. He had died young, and for months she had grieved for him.

And now she was seventeen, living in the ever-changing world of transient boarders, circumventing her mother's explosions, one of which some months ago had sent a mild boarder she had favored, a bespectacled student of ancient Eastern languages, rushing from the door, leaving behind books of very strange writing. A duller man had taken his room, and once more she had turned her back on the lot of them. They were merely meals to serve, shaving water to heat, beds to change—Aloysia's abandoned fiancé among them. They would mean nothing to her, and she would allow them to see nothing of her true self.

Constanze had decided many years before that the best way

to slip through her chaotic world was to be as quiet as possible, and to let no one know what she was feeling. When in the old days quarrels became too much between her mother and father, she had hidden on the steps, blocking her ears with her hands; then she and Sophie would quietly pick up the bits of broken plates. Yet under her full breasts, which she was always trying to lace down to obscurity, her heart was very soft. She cried for dead birds, she mourned for lonely old people—and she kept it all inside of herself. It would emerge in bursts of temper or grief, if she let it emerge at all. There was no room for her in the house, not in the early days. There were her brilliant older sisters, and her utterly charming and devout younger one, for whom she would give her life: they were gregarious and individualistic and, in the case of Aloysia, extraordinarily beautiful. There had never been any place for Constanze but in the corners, so in the corners she made her world.

Now she stood in the fortepiano shop in the midst of the instruments; she stood stiffly, for this place to which she was so drawn was a place of danger. Music opened her entirely. To some people it was pleasant; to others it brought the hope of happiness and peace; but to her it was reckless and deep. Once she had stumbled into a church when the boy's choir was rehearsing a Bach chorale; alone, huddled in the farthest pew, she had found herself sobbing with emotion. And the truth was she had wanted to sing. She had wanted to sing deeply, richly, fully, but she had not dared. She was not as good as her sisters; she had never been as good as them, so she had chosen silence. Now she could not find her way through it.

She ran her hand over the fall board of one of the instruments; still hearing the sound of boxes being moved, she sat down on the bench and softly played a scale. From the other room came Johann Schantz's jovial voice, "I do advise your family, Mademoiselle Weber, to consider buying a fortepiano. I would give it to you under generous terms. You see how much superior it is even to the harpsichord, in which the level of the tone can't vary." Then he was closer; he had come from the room. He stood just behind her. "Play something and you'll see," he said. "Play something."

The first chords filled her, and tears pricked at her eyes. She withdrew her hands after playing only a page of a piece from memory, and clasped them tightly in her lap among the folds of her gray skirt.

"Come!" he said, seating himself beside her and beginning to play. His large hands were slightly hairy, and here and there were small cuts from his work. "Now you see what the pedal can do," he said. "Is it not a remarkable instrument? But perhaps not today for you."

The shop bell tinkled, and another customer came in, shaking out his umbrella. Constanze stood up at once and walked to the window, where piles of music lay; she began to look through them. Trios; music for wind band, clavier, and fortepiano music. Outside the window, the rain streaked down, and people hurrying past were blurred. Some time passed.

Then he was at her side. "Here's the music, mademoiselle; I found it for you. You lost your copy when moving? Keep this one safe."

Johann Schantz touched her arm, but she did not turn. She knew at that moment there was another young woman inside her, and if she allowed her to burst free, then who would she be, what would she do, where would she belong? Who was she if not the dutiful daughter, her hands clasped over her apron; the one who picked up broken plates and brought scraps out for the refuse man? She knew who she was: good, sweet, obscure Constanze, who had not quite been able to keep her family together.

Then his youngest child ran into the shop and leapt into his father's arms. She walked a few streets in the rain, protecting the music under her cloak. The fortepiano maker was a married man. How could she dream of him? What would her own beloved father have said?

Still, during the next days, she reviewed every moment that had passed between them since she had first seen Johann Schantz, of the times she had visited his shop to purchase music or to present another difficulty with the aging clavier. She thought of how when he himself had come to their house to mend the clavier, she could not go into the parlor when she heard his voice.

Two days after her visit to the shop she was standing by the table just inside the boardinghouse door, looking through the post, which contained its customary weekly letter from her maternal aunts, when she saw the letter addressed to the Weber sisters. At once her heart began to pound, and she took the letters with her to the kitchen.

"What do you have there?" Sophie asked as she rolled out dough. "I know. One of Mama's schemes has worked out, and the Count's Russian cousin has asked to marry you. You're moving to Moscow."

"No, it's an invitation to a supper and dance with the Schantz family, in their rooms above the music shop. Alfonso's going as well, and he can chaperone us."

Sophie looked about for the bowl of preserved fruit to spread on the dough. "What are you hiding from me, Stanzi?" she said ruefully. "Never mind. You'll tell me when I'm on my deathbed, dying of curiosity. Let me see. Josefa won't go with us; she never does anymore. I suppose Mama will say we can go if cousin Alfonso's there."

They arrived late to the party after helping to serve supper at home. The upper room was quite full already, with more than a few dozen people, mostly musicians, some of whom the girls had known half their lives. A sideboard groaned with dark bottles of wine from Johann and Wenzel Schantz's country vineyard, for the brothers' family made fine Viennese wines in addition to fortepianos. There were also cheeses, sliced sausages, and bread.

Constanze kept her eyes on the floor or the table. She could sense the presence of the fortepiano maker, and hear his resonant, rich bass voice. This night she knew that his eyes followed her; she could feel them.

Sophie hurried off to speak to an old friend of their father's, and Constanze found Alfonso and his handsome Italian peasant wife sitting on chairs in one of the bedrooms, which had been cleared as much as possible for the party. She could estimate by Alfonso's ebullient voice and his flushed face how many glasses of wine he had already consumed. By his side, rocking back and forth shyly in his chair, was a young man. "My prodigy," Alfonso cried expansively. "I found him work in the orchestra at Stephansdom playing in the masses when he'd just come from France, and I think I may be able to find him a place with the musicians of Prince Esterházy when they travel here this winter. My dear friend, my dear Henri, I have known Constanze and her sisters since they could barely totter across the room. Their father was a good soul and my closest friend."

"Yes," replied Constanze, but she was aware only of Herr Schantz's hearty laughter from the other room.

Some minutes later Sophie appeared at the door. "They're beginning to play a game," she cried impatiently. "Come on."

In the large room the chairs had been pushed to one side but for a red velvet one in the center. Sophie held her arm and spoke in her ear in a ticklish whisper. "They're going to measure the women's calves with a ribbon and see which one's the plumpest. They guess beforehand, and make wagers; they cast lots to see who does the measuring." It was an old game Constanze had seen played once years before in her own house; her father had done the measuring, and her mother had stood by frowning. It will be Johann, she thought, who will measure. He will touch my leg. Her breasts, laced not quite so flat this evening, seemed to rise and grow warmer.

The dice were rolled, and the winner cried out. She closed her eyes. It is Johann, she thought, but when she opened her eyes, it was Alfonso's prodigy, Henri, who stood with the scarlet ribbon dangling in his hand, swinging it to and fro before the many guests who crowded around.

One by one the women were pulled laughing to the chair, crossing their legs at the knee, lifting their skirts, their petticoats, and, last of all, their plain white shifts. The men jostled and whistled. Sophie went directly and, pulling up her garments, exposed her white light wool hose; Henri knelt before her and wound the ribbon around the fullest part of her calf. With a pen he marked her initials on the silk and dangled it high.

Lastly, Constanze was pulled forward to the chair. She glanced up at all the interested faces, then gathered up her various layers until her white hose were bared. She felt Henri's hand on her calf, and gazed down at his golden hair indifferently. Everyone in the room was looking at her. Then he held up the dangling ribbon in triumph, and people broke into applause. She had won, and she stood, her skirts fallen again into place. She smiled at everyone, and yet saw only the fortepiano maker. Then he was at her side, holding out a glass of wine. "For the pretty leg," Johann Schantz said with a wink. He was slightly drunk, and the few white strands in his dark hair glittered in the candlelight. "For the pretty little girl."

Now the red velvet chair was moved to the side of the room as well and a flautist began playing a country dance. She flung herself into the steps, moving quickly around the room, as all the women did, from partner to partner, but he did not dance with her. He never seemed to reach her; he was always on another side. There was Sophie, oblivious, shrieking with laughter, but he was so far away.

And then he was quite near her. "I've brought you a little lemonade," Johann said, as Constanze rested for a moment with her hand on a chair back. "You dance well. I never knew you had such gifts, Mademoiselle Weber." Then, bending down, he murmured in a voice that stirred the soft curls above her ears, "Come, my dear, I have something to show you."

Walking softly down to the shop below, with its dark shapes of unfinished instruments, he held her hand. By the tall cabinet for strings and parts, he drew her closer. He bent down to her, and his mouth was terribly warm and smelled of wine. She had never been kissed on the lips by a man before. Her whole body grew warm as his fingers and then his mouth moved beneath her bodice to one nipple. So this was what had swept Aloysia away; this was the thing that made women throw off all resolution. It was the end of feeling such loneliness, of being the one not chosen, of living in silence.

He was panting and rubbing himself against her. His groin was hard. He pushed up her skirt and petticoats, and explored high above her knee under her drawers. "Yes," she stammered. "So it's 'yes' then?" he replied. His fingers touched the soft hair between her legs, and she gasped; he put his free hand over her mouth. "Ah, you wild kitten," he whispered. "I have wanted you since you first walked into my shop."

He pushed her back onto the table, and some materials fell to the floor. Vaguely she felt something sharp under her back, and heard the pounding of dancing on the floor above them. He was pressing against her; as she lay in shock and joy, feeling his weight, she managed to murmur, "But what does this mean, Johann? Will you leave your wife and run away with me?"

"What I wouldn't do for you!"

The street door opened abruptly, and a few men came in, dragging a great bass in its case. She rolled to the side, pulling down her skirts. Without his warmth above her she felt naked and alone. He had stridden forward to greet his new guests, his voice hearty, hand extended; in her confusion she backed up, began to pick up some bits of ivory from the floor, and then dropped them. Quickly she ran up the steps to the room with the half-empty plates and the wine bottles. And where was he? Half of her had been torn away. And then there he was, coming up the stairs with his friends.

From a corner his wife stared at her, and Constanze stood between the woman's hard eyes and the man's broad laughter. It was as if he were a different person than the one who had almost taken her virginity downstairs on the table with the instrument parts pushing into her back. Her virginity—dear Lord! She moved among the others, wondering if everyone could see on her face what had happened. Except for Frau Schantz's bitter look, no one seemed to notice her at all.

Sophie was shaking her. "It's time to go," her little sister whispered. Sophie's breath was also full of wine and cakes, and she swayed a little and burst into embarrassed giggles. "I've made a fool of myself! Someone twice my age tried to feel my breasts. I think I'm drunk. We promised we'd be home by ten. Alfonso is also drunk; I don't know how his wife will get him home. I find these evenings confusing; convent life must be easier. May I hold on to your arm. Dearest Stanzi, I am quite . . ."

They supported each other down the stairs, past the many instruments in the shadows and out into the spring evening. Sophie put her hand over her mouth. "I'm going to be sick," she gasped.

"Rest here awhile."

"We've got to be home. Blessed Saint Anne, Stanzi, *someone's coming.*"

They turned as best they could and made out Alfonso's golden-haired prodigy hurrying after them. He approached them in a nice trot, his face openly good-natured, and said, "Let me walk with you! What were the others thinking! You should not walk home alone." His glance took in Sophie, but he was discreet and said nothing, only looked a little amused.

Constanze let him take her arm, glancing worriedly at her sister on the other side of him. Whatever he said, she heard little. She thought only of the dark instrument workshop, the smell of unfinished wood, the glimmering black and ivory keys, the oddly coiled strings, the feel of the fortepiano maker as he pressed close, the sound of dancing above. What could she make of the kiss, and the hand groping above her garter? What wouldn't I do for you, he had said. And now there was Sophie, cautiously putting one flat shoe before the other, babbling about the evening. The sooner she goes to a convent, the better, Constanze thought. I ought to join her. I'll have to confess this.

Sophie's chatter grew indistinct, and they walked in silence for a while until they saw the green dome of Peterskirche rising stolidly above the tall houses. Constanze slipped her arm from Henri's and curtseyed. "We can go from here," she said.

"May I come to call on you, mademoiselle?"

"You may," she said, distracted, taking her sister's arm.

He walked away, looking back every now and then to smile at them.

For a moment, both girls leaned slightly against the dark window of a shoemaker's shop, and Constanze slowly became aware that Sophie was staring at her. "Constanze Weber," Sophie said, as if she had been asleep and just awoken. "How could I speak of myself! I had forgotten before I felt so sick. I saw you go downstairs with Johann Schantz, and your face when you came up again. Your lip looked odd, your upper lip. It still does. Did he bite it? Tell me, tell me."

"Oh God, do you think others saw it, too?" Constanze whispered, fingers to her lip. "No one will notice at home, will they? I'll tell you, but you must swear on your hope of salvation that you'll tell no one. He kissed me; he touched me. There was another me suddenly, wanting to get out, and he knew it. It was there when we arrived; it's been there for months. I felt as if I wanted to fling off everything, abandon the way I've been all my life and be something else. But I've known for a time that I love him." The last was spoken with sudden, solemn dignity as she gazed indifferently at a carriage and its horses trotting neatly through the streets. "Yes, for a long time."

Sophie cried, "I knew there was something! But Stanzi, he's married."

"Yes, he is, but don't you understand that I didn't care? I didn't care about anything, except when I ran upstairs I was suddenly afraid of ending like Aloysia, and having to marry. And yet what does it matter if we have love?"

They were walking, and stopping, and Sophie stumbled and

clutched her. As they came down the street that opened into Petersplatz, a priest out walking his little dog nodded at them. Sophie took several deep breaths, looking ahead of her, her narrow face gaining that sudden maturity that always amazed Constanze. "I think," Sophie murmured, "that we should go upstairs as quietly as possible, and talk about all this in the morning. Don't cry; I can see you're about to. I'll try not to be sick on the stairs. Oh, my head spins so!"

In the darkness, they slipped off their shoes, mounted the stairs inside the boardinghouse by touch, and slept soundly until the middle of the next morning.

They had hardly risen when they heard their mother's voice from below. She was likely shouting at a boarder for letting a candle overturn and drop wax on the carpet, but dimly they heard their own names. Josefa was gone already. They ran out onto the landing and looked down the stairs at their mother's red face.

"I met Frau Alfonso at the market early this morning," she cried. "You allowed a strange man to measure your legs? And drank so much wine that Frau Alfonso said you both behaved very loosely, that you plied her husband with more of it. Bad girls, bad, like your sisters. It is your father's blood, not mine— your rash father who gave you no sense, only music!"

Sophie leaned over the banister and called down, "It was only a game."

"Both of you will land where your sisters are and never marry, especially you, Mademoiselle Constanze. Your name will be as black as theirs."

Constanze stood speechless. What did her mother know? It seemed she was always trying to scoop her hand into Constanze's heart, trying to pull out private thoughts, crumble them, throw them away. "We never . . . ," she murmured at last, but more words would not come.

The girls ran back to their room, closing the door against the furious voice that rose up the stairs and likely carried under the door to any boarder who had not yet left for his work. Sophie barricaded the door with her own thin body, her normally placid face distorted with feeling. "Don't give in to Mother," she cried. "Don't retreat; don't let her take your laughter away. She will if she can, you know." Yet Constanze felt all the passion and longing of last night close up within her and then wilt and blow away. She felt her face turn as plain and severe as those of her spinster aunts.

"Be still, Sophie," she whispered.

But Sophie ran around the bed after her, shouting, "We had such a lovely evening. Why must she object to happiness? What does it matter what you did? Henri will come for you. He's meant to; that's why he ran after us. He'll take you away from this place." For the first time they stared at each other, each admitting how unhappy she was. They saw it in each other's eyes from across the room.

"And I need my slippers; where are my slippers?" the youngest Weber sister continued. "Aloysia never returned them. Why must she take everything? She already *has* everything. One of these days Josefa will go as well, and then there will be just us. I can't bear to be here anymore, I can't. I'm truly going to join a convent."

Constanze rushed to her, knocking over the dresses that had been flung on a chair and tripping on the shoes that were scattered on the floor, crying, "Sophie, don't, don't! What will I do without you? If you go, I'll go, too. Love leads only to unhappiness." They sat down on the floor amid the fallen dresses and sobbed, holding each other. Then Constanze broke away and sat down at the table. "I'm going to write to Johann Schantz," she said, pressing her lips together hard between her words. "I like him best. I'm going to ask him to take me away."

"Do you want to do that, Stanzi?"

"Yes, I know he loves me."

"Did he say that?"

"Wait, I think he did, or he was about to. I'd go anyplace to get away from here! You can come, too." Constanze was already writing.

"But this is madness. Would you? Would he? What about his wife? Where would you go?"

"Anywhere." The pen scratched furiously, and then Constanze signed the letter and threw it down. They looked at each other and listened.

Below came the sound of Maria Caecilia climbing the steps, stopping once to catch her breath. They knew their mother stood outside their door for a moment without knocking, and then came the very soft scratch and the old low, tender voice, "Come, my chicks, my little fleas, there's coffee and cake in the kitchen; everyone's gone out and the house is quiet. Don't you know, my loves, that I have seen life, that I want only the best for you whom I suckled and nursed and protected from this terrible world?"

The girls stood and dried their eyes. Then, holding hands, they opened the door and joined arms with their mother. The three of them went down for coffee, talking of more ordinary things: gossip of the street, the price of veal, the concerts in the public gardens this summer, the dark moods of the kitchen girl who had recently come to help them. No further word was said about the gathering at the fortepiano maker's house.

*J*anuary snow was falling heavily all over the city one evening some six months later as Mozart walked into the central hall of Prince Nicholas Esterházy's winter mansion, and stood for a moment listening to the sound of the Prince's orchestra in the allegro of a symphony. Many candles glittered in the crystal chandeliers. About him beautiful women, grease holding their curls in place, glanced at him and then looked away, barely nodding to his bow. Brushing the snow from his hat brim before giving it to the lackey, he did not enter the ballroom where the orchestra played but made his way through a few other large and beautiful rooms with their many guests, the invitation he had received dry in his vest pocket.

In a small library, head bent over a book, was the elderly Franciscan monk Giovanni Battista Martini, maestro di capella from Bologna. Mozart bounded toward him. He remembered running down the rectory halls in Italy, music under his arm, when he was fourteen years old. Padre Martini had aged since then, and Mozart had heard the monk's health was not good. "Padre Martini," he cried. "I was overjoyed to hear you were in the city."

"Wolferl Amadé," said the monk, his words light and a little breathy. "Let me look at you; it's been many years since I've seen you. The distances that separate people are untenable to me. In heaven there will be no such distances."

He made room on the blue silk sofa by a tray of wine and glasses. "I looked with the greatest pleasure the other day at the offertory that you send me some years back. But tonight you have just missed your own wind sextet; the men were here, and have now gone on to play it elsewhere and make a florin or two. A gentle piece—bassoons, horns, and clarinets—you at your most tender. A friend of yours was among them, a towering young man, laughs loudly, big teeth. His name was Leutgeb, I think."

"The boor, the oaf! I know him from Salzburg," Mozart said joyfully. "So the piece was well received? I gave it my best."

"As you always do. Your father writes me that he's worried about you, but isn't that the way of fathers? He told me you left the Archbishop's service last spring, broke your chains and flew free. You're eating decently, I hope? And where do you live?"

The sounds of the orchestra and the noise of people speaking came through the door. Mozart dropped to the sofa. "I can't tell you how glad I am to see you! Where do I live? I have a room in a boardinghouse, but am there as little as I can. I need my own rooms; within a few months I expect I'll manage it."

"Very good. So you have a decent amount of pupils? I met the Aurnhammer family before, whose daughter takes fortepiano lessons from you. They told me you gave an academy concert with her at their house, playing your new sonata for two pianos. They were looking for you."

Mozart shrugged wryly, taking a glass of red wine and studying the reflection of the candle within it, then stretching his legs and glancing toward the door. Then he felt so happy he could not keep still. "Ah yes, Mademoiselle Aurnhammer!" he cried. The side rolls of his pale brown, unpowdered hair glistened in the candlelight. "Mademoiselle Barbara Aurnhammer . . . ," he repeated, his mouth rosy and mischievous.

The monk's wrinkled face regarded him with interest. "The way she speaks your name makes me think she's in love with you. Your father wrote there was a young woman; was it this mademoiselle?"

"No, someone else."

"I will be discreet and ask no more. What a gathering tonight! Half good Viennese society is here, yes? You let yourself be known and make your way. With enough concerts, lessons to those who can afford them, commissions, and music published you will do well. That is the only way if you're not willing to wear someone's livery. You are on the brink of doing very well; I feel it. Yes, of course, here's my blessing. I have always loved you, as many do, Amadé." He glanced down at Mozart's moving fingers and smiled. "And even now you can't remain still."

"I can't, it's true!" Mozart laughed happily.

The symphony had ended, and the sound of applause carried through the rooms. Mozart listened for a moment, his face brightening more. "That's Joseph Haydn's work," he said. "I know his style."

"Yes, Joseph Haydn, an extraordinary composer. But you don't know that when he asked the Prince if I might come this evening, he asked for you as well. He is our host Prince Esterházy's kapellmeister, and knows your work very well. You've written how much you admire his quartets. Why even now—"

"He's here and asked for me?" Mozart leapt to his feet.

At that moment, Joseph Haydn appeared at the door. Mozart knew him at once from a portrait he had seen, though he was older now, perhaps fifty years. "But it is you who were conducting!" Mozart said, hurrying forward, almost stammering. "Herr Kapellmeister, had I recalled that surely it was you conducting, I would have gone into the ballroom to hear you. I know your work. I have been longing to meet you for many years, Herr Kapellmeister."

Bowing, Haydn took the young composer's hand in both of his, and looked curiously into his face. "So you are Salzburg's Wolfgang Mozart. I know your music as well; I borrow scores of it when I can't hear it played."

Closing the door slightly so that they could retreat a little from the noise of the other guests, the three men sat down under the shelves of books and a portrait of Emperor Joseph. In his excitement Mozart could hardly remain still; he rocked back and forth slightly with a great smile on his face.

Haydn was more quiet; his arm lay across the curved sofa back. "So you now live here in Vienna," he said. "You know, as a little boy, I was a chorister here at Stephansdom. I sang like an angel, but when my voice broke, they turned me into the street. I cannot say if being a musician is more difficult than other professions; it's the only one I have known."

"Are you here for long, sir?"

"For the winter, as I sometimes am with my patron. But I've been wanting to say this for a time, to write you. I've studied a score of your *Idomeneo,* so rich and deep, too much perhaps for those who wished to be amused. That quartet, and the prince's line: *'Andrò ramingo, e solo'*—I'll wander forth and alone. I wept. I am sorry it was not successful, and yet I feel it's with an opera that you will finally come to notice. Perhaps one not entirely so *seria,* eh? Not so very tragic in tone, but one that expresses the joy and the sadness of life, so entwined. Neither just one or the other."

"Herr Kapellmeister, yes! That's what an opera could be, and I could write one if I knew it would have a production, if such a commission came to me. I long for such a commission."

Haydn opened his eyes wider. "But here's good fortune, you see! I was just speaking before with the court opera's director, Count Orsini-Rosenberg, and he told me he's looking for a new work. The Grand Duke of Russia is planning a state visit to Vienna in the autumn, and they want something to appeal to him."

Mozart leapt up, began to move quickly about the room, then came back to Haydn, his face a little flushed. His fingers drummed on the scarlet fabric of his coat. "Can this be true? I've tried for an introduction and have written twice, but he's not answered my letter."

"Then you're fortunate to be here tonight to present yourself in person. He's in the ballroom still. You know his face? Good. We'll remain here a time. My orchestra played before, and my work is done for the night, praise God."

Mozart could hear a flute and piano sonata beginning as he hurried toward the ballroom. Passing a smaller chamber lit with candles, he saw the Baroness von Waldstätten, at whose house he had given a few concerts on her enviable fortepiano. This handsome woman of about fifty years arose from the curved-back sofa and sailed coquettishly toward him, her great wide dress over its panniers brushing against the few young men fawning about her; one followed her, another carried her shawl. There were faint flecks of hair powder on her shapely shoulders, and she carried her head leaning slightly to one side so that a white curl drooped prettily. No doubt one of the young men was her current lover. Mozart gazed for just a moment at her slightly chapped, rouged lips, then he told her where he was going.

"Oh the Count!" she said. "The Count. I know his wife, a dull woman. But, more important, he knows the Emperor well, and that makes him even more valuable. In the end, pleasing the Emperor means far more than pleasing silly me! When are you coming to play for me again? Come, I'll take you to him."

In the large ballroom the many white-and-gold chairs had been pushed back carelessly by those who had left after the symphony ended. At one end of the room stood the music stands, with their extinguished candles and instrument parts; a violinist's bow had been left on the floor. Before these stood Orsini-Rosenberg, a man of medium height wearing a silky white wig and a bit of rouge on his lips. His frontal lace spilled forth profusely.

"Ah Mozart, I do know your name," he said when he turned to the composer at last. "And Haydn can't cease to praise you, nor can our beautiful Baroness here. I think highly of your work, but you must understand there are so many composers and the Emperor's devoted to the ones whose work he knows. He is very fond of Maestro Antonio Salieri, whose Italian operas are not unknown to you, I am certain."

"I am familiar with Kapellmeister Salieri, of course. He is a fine teacher."

"Still, there may be a possibility. It all depends on many things, one being the appealing subject of your work. Leave word where I can send for you. Do you know my secretary, Thorwart? He has said you are acquainted."

Thorwart stood near the Count, his chest stiff, chin raised, English waistcoat buttoned tightly over his belly. Mozart had seen him about the boardinghouse now and then. What is he doing here? Mozart thought. Will this help or harm my effort?

He bowed and the secretary nodded curtly in return. But by now others had pushed close into the circle, so that there was no more opportunity at present to speak with the Count.

Bowing here and there, Mozart passed the empty music stands and made his way rapidly back to the small room with the many books to share his good news. He found it empty. Instead, Haydn was waiting for him at the bottom of the curving double set of stairs that was lined with portraits.

Haydn took his arm. "You've spoken to Orsini-Rosenberg? I will do what I can to keep your name in his ear."

"With what can I repay you, sir?"

"You will repay me when I hear your opera," said the older man.

Mozart walked around excitedly for some time, bowing to those people he knew. Orsini-Rosenberg had gone off to the dining room for supper, and the Baroness had swept away in her carriage, pressing his hand and winking at him as she left. Padre Martini had also departed, but he had left a small folded letter for him, saying he would be staying at the Stephansdom rectory.

In a small room lit by a little chandelier whose candles were sloping in the draft from one of the room's large curtained windows, someone was playing a clavier. As Mozart listened, a pure soprano voice began to sing an arrangement of a traditional song in English. Someone spoke the soprano's name, Nancy Storace, and said she was from London and was beginning to make a reputation in Vienna. He had heard of her. Now he stood leaning against the door, watching her pretty mouth form the words.

When the song ended, he turned away. I've enough on my mind without some new romance, he thought. They easily link my name with one or another and gossip. Everyone already assumes I am in love with the Aurnhammer girl, who has no charm and wears such low-cut dresses that one is forced to look even if one doesn't wish to . . . and to my embarrassment I do look, and I feel what I would not. But I must go away now and think of what subject I can take for my opera. I want nothing but that.

He retrieved his cloak and hat and made his way through the great double front doors. The carriage of another departing guest creaked by, a footman walking before it holding a torch high. The wheels left new tracks in the snowy court. He walked past waiting horses, their breaths smoky, and the smell of dung. He was almost to the gate when he heard from behind him the first E flat chord of his own wind serenade.

Looking back through the swirling snow, he could just make out the six players with their horns, clarinets, and bassoons huddled closely together under the shelter of the portico. He was drawn forward and stopped a few feet away, watching them as snow fell around him. There was Leutgeb indeed! Mozart's smile grew broader and more delighted as the six men repeated the first movement of his serenade. At the last notes, he ran forward, clapping.

"Bravo, bravo, maestro!" They grinned, clapping back. "We've made a great success this evening. We have played at three houses."

He stood among them, out of the snow. "And I'm likely to make a greater success. Johann, bravo! Very good, all! Listen, I may have a chance at an opera. I'll try to find a story written in German; the Emperor prefers that. But will you play elsewhere?"

"Ah no, the hour's too late."

The six wind players wrapped up their instruments, and they and the young composer walked a time in the snow, their voices rising among the still houses until they came to Petersplatz, where they wished him good night.

He let himself in with a large iron house key and was mounting the steps as softly as he could when he heard the sound of a woman weeping from the second-floor parlor. He turned back quietly and creaked open the door. It was perfectly dark but for the light reflected from the whirling of snow through the open window. "Who's there?" he murmured, but at his voice the sobbing ceased.

He walked cautiously past the clavier and shut the window. Whoever had been weeping was kneeling by the sofa. He came closer, and saw the long rich hair drifting down almost to the floor. Josefa glanced at him, and looked away.

"Ah, what is it?" he cried.

"Aloysia's baby has died at her wet nurse's cottage."

He raised his face to the now-closed window, watching for a moment as the snow beat against it, then dropped into a chair by Josefa. Ah, he thought, what shall I do about this? What can I do? The indifference and cruelty of the world when we hardly dare stop to pity one another.

"I'm so very sorry," he said at last.

Her words were muffled. "Are you truly, Mozart? Or are you still too angry?"

"A child is dead. How can I not be sorry? Her child. It wasn't mine. I can't begin to understand what I feel."

"I found out this afternoon. When my papa died, I sang, but I can't do that now. I can't do anything but cry; I can't stop, and I hate it. Since I was small I have never wanted to cry."

Her long face was streaked with tears, and he felt for his handkerchief in his coat, but she shook her head, refusing it. "And why should it hurt so?" she said, beginning to sob again. "Children die of so many things. Papa and Mama had two who died before I was born. But it doesn't matter if much of the world has the same suffering."

"I also never want to cry again," he said. "And yet I know I will. My priest friend told me when I was a boy that if I felt deeply in one area, I must in all."

She bent down again, her head almost to the floor. She murmured, "Why do we love the people we can't have? When Aloysia was a baby, she was my own, my own. I was jealous but for a time, she was my very own. She's nobody's now. She wouldn't understand my sorrow. And her child, her Maria, was to me . . . not much to her, but all to me . . . and that's gone."

"You'll have children of your own."

"Will I? Don't you know, Mozart? No one will love me that way, and you're cold to all of us now."

"I must be to go on. Don't you know that?"

His hand came from his knee, hesitated, and then rested on her hair. For a moment she was still. Then she sat up entirely, shaking him off, staring ahead of her. "Don't touch me; I would much prefer that you didn't touch me."

"Josefa, do you dislike me so?"

"No, it's just that I can't bear it. Will you go away now, please, and leave me alone? Oh, my little child, my little love."

He went heavily up the stairs and into his room, where a bit of snow had blown under the window and onto the sill. On the table was his music for the sonata for two pianos and the horn serenade in E flat. He stood without moving for some time in the dark room; then he covered his face with both his small, supple hands.

Sophie Weber, June 1842

M ONSIEUR NOVELLO AND I HAD BEEN TALKING ALL
afternoon, and now evening had come and the light was
fading. I rambled a great deal because remembering the death of
my little niece brought those few weeks back to me. We sat together, and he took my hand; together we mourned for the
dead.

He asked, "Did the grief bring your family closer?" He had
not taken out his writing implements that day, but only listened.

"Yes, Aloysia and Mother had a tearful reconciliation. It
didn't last very long; within two weeks they were shouting at
each other again. It broke my heart, but I should have expected
it. Josefa had gone on her own several times to see the child. It
was as if she were the mother. She could not speak for tears; we
hadn't expected this of her. But you never knew what she would
say or do about anything."

"Where did she go that night after Mozart left her alone? I
think you said she later ran out into the snow."

"We never knew where she went; perhaps to those strange
friends of hers, those mannish women. She had no luck rising in
music in Vienna at that time; that pretty English soprano rose

before her. But what did any of this matter next to the child who was gone? And then a few days after we heard of the baby's death, she left us. My little heart was truly broken."

"Who left you?"

"Josefa."

PART FIVE

Vienna and Constanze

y most beloved Sophie and Constanze,

This is my tenth day in Prague, and I have already sung twice at the opera. Alfonso and his wife, who traveled with me (you know he was engaged to play here), have found me a good place to live. I am miserable to be away from both of you, but I had to go. Oh sisters, will you visit our niece's grave and bring flowers as soon as they bloom? For now, some evergreen berries.

Stanzi, you must promise me to be steadfast and do nothing rash. Your new suitor, Henri, seems a blessing, and I wouldn't be surprised if you did run off with him to Paris, and leave Mama with her fine scheming plans. But do you know him very well? Have you fallen in love with him—as men often do with women—simply because he is so handsome? That's why Papa married Mama, because he was sick with love for her; she was such a beauty. Be careful; there's more to life than that. And don't think you have no beauty. You do have it, but you're still afraid to look at it because it's not the kind you want.

I hardly dare ask how Mother does. Frau Alfonso feels

she is a little out of her mind and is drinking too much, and that her reliance on Father's old friend Johann Franz Thorwart will lead her into more delusions and terrible plans, in which you cannot help but be involved. You know "Uncle" Thorwart insisted Mama invest her small savings in one of his ventures, and she lost all of it; Alfonso has ended his friendship with Thorwart over that. Now we're afraid the unscrupulous T is likely to want to make it up to her with far wilder schemes. Pah! I despise him.

How bad of me not to stay and help you both, but what could I do? I was drowning in that house, so very unhappy, and I am happiest when I can sing good parts. I feel so much emotion in me that it pours out in music. If I can't persuade you both to come here, I'll return eventually and we'll all live together.

My heart is with you, and I will come back for you.

In all love and always,

J. Weber

On Easter Sunday, sitting in the parlor with the stacks of music pushed to one side of the table, Constanze wrote her reply, her head resting on her hand.

Josefa,

I miss you so much. Sophie and I simply rattle around together in this house. Aloysia avoids us; she is always singing at private concerts when not at the opera and makes great sums of money. And as for Mother, her moods are so bad that yesterday the boarder in our best room took his bags and went away. The other day I came into the parlor and saw Father's ghost at the clavier. He raised his eyes and looked at me. Where are my daughters, where are my daughters? he seemed to say. Then he was gone.

I send with this letter two that have come for you from Munich, and carefully hid them so they would not be opened. Are they from him whom you loved? Alas, what is the love of a sister compared to the great pull of the world? I don't feel it so I can't understand. I have no great gifts. I would like to be happy, to make those few people dear to me happy. I wanted to keep us all together. I'm still determined to do so in the end.

Yes, Henri tells me he loves me. I didn't think anyone would love me; I have always felt myself unlovable. And then I was on the edge of loving a very wrong person, but now I never walk down his street anymore. Henri has bought me a little ring, though the engagement is not yet known. My only problem is that I'm not in love with him. I like him, but I gave my love away stupidly, and now I don't have it anymore. Do you think it comes back? So he loves me, and I pretend I love him. (I could wish he were not so vain.)

Outside of this and the fact that my temper is much worse, I am fine. I don't know why I burst out with things now; I didn't used to do it, and now I can't stop myself. I shouted at Henri the other day when he stopped by to ask me out for a coffee. He walked away from me and then I had to run after him.

Sophie says to tell you that she has taken in another cat that she found freezing in the snow. She also saw saints and cherubim in church on Good Friday, just walking down the nave as if out for a stroll. She mentioned it offhandedly, wondering if I saw them, too. But if I could see Father, I suppose she can see Blessed Saint Anne and Saint Bridget. What other news? Boarders come and go here, but we hardly see Mozart; he's so withdrawn and distant he hardly notices any of us. Letters from his father come weekly or more, and he reads them carefully. I hear him walking up and down in his room. He hardly laughs anymore. I think he's going to go away. Oh, if it weren't for Sophie, I'd run off with Henri, but one of us must stay with Mama. Perhaps when you return we can all live here so that she never has to worry about money and then she'll be a kinder person.

The Easter bells are ringing outside, but the weather is still cold. I miss you so. Sophie sends all her love. Don't let your throat get chilled after you sing; wear the warm scarf Mama knit you last year around your mouth and throat. It is very dangerous to chill the voice after singing. Papa always warned you.

With a thousand kisses, your sister in life and death,

Constanze

"You're called Constanze," her father had said. "It means constancy. In the worst of times, you hold us together." But had she? Could she? Two of her sisters were gone now, and the house was angry and scattered, her mother weeping over the breaded meat in the kitchen, declaring that life was against her and nothing was her fault. Sometimes when Constanze encountered her, the older woman would stare at her bleakly, as if to say, You see how unhappy I am? You see that you have entirely failed to make me happy?

Constanze sealed her letter and went downstairs and out into the snow, her heavy flannel underpetticoats and smock hardly keeping her warm. She posted the letter and then slipped into the church, where she sat for a long time, her head leaning forward on the seat before her.

The coffee and pastry café on the Graben was the most beautiful one in Vienna: tiers of marble shelves held cakes on silver dishes; a chandelier reflected many times in the gilded mirrors; and a trio of harpsichord, violin, and violoncello played popular tunes in one corner. The rich scent of coffee and cinnamon greeted patrons at the door. And Thorwart was expansive, generous, pouring out the steaming coffee in a neat arc with his heavy hand, into which his rings pressed deeply. He ordered a three-tiered dish of little cakes with chocolate, sweetened nuts, and a few frosted pink with sugar roses.

Maria Caecilia Weber, from her side of the small round table, brought her handkerchief to her slightly rouged mouth.

Even with the mistake he had made regarding her small investment, Maria Caecilia still insisted to her family and friends that Johann Thorwart was one of the most clever men she knew. Now he had risen to a position of general factotum of Viennese opera under Count Orsini-Rosenberg, and as Orsini-Rosenberg knew the Emperor well, Thorwart now also regarded himself as an intimate of the imperial court. These things made Maria Caecilia regard him even more highly than she had before.

"You need to get away from your cares," Thorwart had said, descending on her suddenly when she was in the midst of her housekeeping. He made her fetch her hat, then swept her away here.

Now he sat back, coat open to reveal his waistcoat and his silver watch chain, and said, "And how are your girls? How beautiful they all were when I used to come to your Thursdays in Mannheim, though the music did go on and on. I envied them, compared to my one daughter, who speaks to me almost as little as my wife."

"Johann, you've been treated unfairly!" she said. She could see the hurt in his full mouth even after he had spoken. He leaned one arm on the table and looked about the room as if to say, Has any man here been treated so ill?

"After all you've given them!" she continued. "And you're such a good man! I'm sorry that any thought has made you sad."

Turning back to her, he once more thrust out his wide chest. "Not in the least!" he cried. "A moment's reverie, that's all. I didn't ask you here today to speak of my small misfortunes but of you." He turned the tiered plate around, offering her the pink cakes with the sugar roses. "You know, I promised Fridolin I'd look after you, and more's needed than procuring your wretched pension."

"Yes, it's wretched," she said. "It barely pays for wood. For all the years my husband served the Elector, should I have only this to show for it? My boarders barely pay for the house rental with all the food they eat—the veal, the bread! The assistance from my Aloysia is often late and less than promised, and there's not so much as a letter from Josefa, much less any money. My heart breaks that I should have to depend on these heartless girls when I have always wanted only the best for them."

Thorwart nodded solemnly. "We've both tried our best. Still, my dear Maria Caecilia, I have only one child. God has given you two more daughters."

"Yes, and I need to have them married and provided for. I wouldn't want them to have to earn their bread, but I have no idea how to proceed with Sophie."

Thorwart poured more coffee—hot, creamy, and smelling of cinnamon. They leaned their heads closer together to hear each other over the chattering from other tables and the soaring of the chamber trio. "Our little Sophie," he mused, his wide finger near his lips. "Yes, how do we proceed with that girl? She has no fortune, no dowry, and, most unfortunately, no figure. (I can't quite understand how a daughter of yours can have no figure, Caecilia!) You can't encourage her to wear padding for hips and bosom as many do these days? Then what can be done for her?"

He cleared a little space before him, his wide face taking on the serious expression she had seen him wear in his office in the opera house. "But the problem of Constanze must be managed as well. She may not marry this French cellist, or he may not marry her. I know from his banker, who receives his letters of credit from Paris, that the young man's family expects him to marry a French girl."

"Then theirs is just a playful romance, even though she wears his ring! What a cruel world, my friend! Is there no justice?" Maria Caecilia cried. She thought of the little book with the tooled-leather cover decorated with flowers that she now kept in her bedroom drawer and into which she continued to write names of possible suitors for her younger girls. She had actually crossed out all the other names on Constanze's list but for this Frenchman.

Thorwart laid his hand over hers. "Still, I understand he will not be leaving for a time, so that leaves us some leisure to consider the problem. We will find someone truly splendid for our sweet Constanze, but it is Sophie whom we must manage at once, for I fear she's near danger."

"Sophie near danger?" came Maria Caecilia's whisper. "Can it be?"

"I am very much afraid of it. Recall: wasn't your closest friend in Zell years ago much like her, plain and flat as a board? And yet, did that stop her from a loss of virtue? I remember the sorrow around the courtyard, for when her mother looked the other way, the girl was on her back with her skirts up! There was wailing at the common pump. The thought's heavy with me: it will be the butcher's boy, or one of the boarders, or even one of the priests for your little one; yes, they're not above those things. It might even be, the saints forbid it, a family friend."

Now he pushed aside his empty plate and leaned forward in a

businesslike way. He gazed at the tabletop, as if studying some important papers before him. Looking up at Maria Caecilia, he said, "You've asked my advice, and I'll give it. We can find a good marriage for Constanze, if you give me time to do it. I know many more people now in my new position at the opera, but Sophie you must marry at once to an honorable man, one who will support you in your older years. I know of one such man."

"Who could you mean, my friend?"

"The answer's under your nose." He sat back expansively, fingers in his waistcoat pockets. "Your lodger, young Mozart."

Maria Caecilia was speechless for a moment. "But he has no money."

"He has little now, but I have it on good authority that his fortunes may soon change. Allow me," and he poured more coffee, adding extra cinnamon from a small silver container, and some small coarsely ground bits of sugar, stirring and stirring the silver spoon in the cup. He stirred more slowly and suddenly drew in his breath. He frowned and looked away, his eyes focusing on one of the gilded mirrors across the room.

She looked as well, and saw them both reflected. For a moment she, too, caught her breath, her fingers moving to her throat. What she saw in the mirror was not the Johann Franz Thorwart of today, a man in his late forties, but the man he had been: the round-faced university boy, the one she felt rather than saw in the dark of the courtyard so many years ago. She had been seventeen. After all these years, she could still hear the sound of her petticoats as she hurried toward him in the dark. She remembered how a shiver had rushed down her back when she took his hand and how he drew her into that dark doorway.

Now, as they both gazed into the mirror, above the heads of the other patrons, she felt his hand move across the table and take hers, rubbing her fingertips slightly as if trying to read them. And she heard his husky voice as he leaned forward. "That month in Zell when you were seventeen."

She looked at their hands together on the table and didn't pull it away. "Please don't, Johann."

"You asked me if I was melancholy today, and yes, I am. I work so hard I don't allow myself to feel it, then I go home, where I must bear silence. Only your happy household has made it possible for me—that and my work. Caecilia, my dearest. You were seventeen when I came back from university because my father was ill. You were going to be married in two months. That evening you came across the courtyard singing, and I went out to you. Do you remember? I heard your petticoats and your footsteps; you were lighter than the breeze. I begged you that day not to marry my friend Fridolin. I told you you'd be poor. I told you, Caecilia! That most beautiful evening when you came across the yard under the hanging wash to me! Did Fridolin ever suspect, ever ask you . . . the uncertainty about—"

"Enough, enough," she whispered. "Johann, you agreed never to mention that night. I'm a respectable widow; I was a respectable married woman. No scandal can be uttered about me. I spoke foolish words to my Josefa once when in grief, and I've always regretted it. I would never speak further about it. She wouldn't forgive me if she knew the truth. Keep your agreement;

you're a gentleman. I have valued you for that above everything. You are a gentleman."

Thorwart gazed at her from under his heavy eyebrows, then looked away, flustered, trying to bring back the man of business. From her reticule she took a tiny mirror and patted her face with some powder. He edged the tier of cakes toward her. "Have another."

"I couldn't." Her eyes had filled with angry tears. "What has life made of me? I do my best under the circumstances."

"One day she'll have to know, Caecilia."

"And when that day is right, I'll tell her. Now, let's pretend we didn't think of those old things. Tell me about Mozart's prospects. That is the least you can do."

He bowed his head and cleared his throat. "Within several months, perhaps sooner, I'm told on good authority, the Emperor Francis Joseph is likely to award him some sinecure, kapellmeister of this or that, and with that everyone will want his music. In addition, there's still a chance he may be given the commission for the opera in the autumn to celebrate the visit of the Russian Prince. If both of those events occur, he will at once be in demand everywhere. Every mother in Vienna will be sitting her unmarried beautiful daughter in the front row of his concerts to smile at him during the interval; he'll be brought down by the first pretty face. And you, old friend, will have lost your opportunity."

Sitting very straight with noticeable dignity, her back no longer touching the chair, Maria Caecilia said, "Then here's my plan. I'll settle on this before my poor little one gets in great trouble in her innocence, and hold out for someone finer for Constanze when she tires of her cellist. I need, I ought, to separate those two girls, you know. They're too close. One puts silly ideas in the other's head, and the other gives it back again until it passes for truth. There, my mind's settled. Sophie will marry Mozart."

She leaned forward. "But how to persuade her? Tell me!"

Thorwart blotted the table crumbs with his napkin as carefully as he might blot the damp ink of a contract. "Throw them together; make it occur. Young people are too foolish to see what is good for them. Make him feel as a young man does when an innocent girl crosses a dark yard to meet him. (I allude only to the feeling.) *Throw* them into each other's arms." His mouth was angry, and he compressed it. He folded the napkin carefully, and then, on second thought, dropped it with disdain to the tablecloth. He stood abruptly. "Good day, dear Maria Caecilia. I'll do my best to see that Mozart has the opera, and can marry Sophie."

Maria Caecilia almost felt her way home, touching the doors of buildings and the edges of lemonade stalls for support. She saw herself in the glass of a bookshop window and raised her fingers to her still soft cheeks. She was so languid with sensuality that she could hardly walk; she was caught between the memory of running across the dark yard so lithe and young, and the reality of her present heavy body. How did life change us and why? It was unfair. She could have walked to the park and sat there weeping, but what good did it do? She had her plans.

Without plans life blew away, and Thorwart was right. There were still Constanze and Sophie.

She found Sophie at home reading a book at the kitchen table. Yes, her mother thought, suddenly unhappy again, the girl's plain as bread. How on earth shall I make something of her? She'll do nothing for herself; she doesn't even notice if her dress is stained or if her hair is standing on end. Now likely she's reading a book by some saint or peculiar French philosopher. Is this truly what I have to make my plans come true?

Sophie looked up dreamily, not a bit of rouge on her pale cheeks. "Come to me, my dearest," Maria Caecilia said, opening her arms. She sat down in the one large chair by the fire, and when Sophie approached with her spectacles in her hand, her mother suddenly pulled her into her lap. "Tell me, precious child, do you truly want my happiness?"

"You're squeezing me. I was reading a book; why are you squeezing me? Why wouldn't I want your happiness?"

"Of course you do, more than the others."

"Mama, let me up. I always try to make sure you are happy. You know it." The girl's eyes looked longingly at the book, whose place she had marked with her thumb.

"My love, today I drank coffee with your good uncle Thorwart, and with his auspicious guidance and heaven watching us, I understood how God has made a path for you and for me."

Sophie had managed to stand and was looking with bewilderment at her mother. "Yes, of course, God makes paths. But what do you mean? I was wanting to go out soon, Mama. Father

Paul is giving a talk at the church on science and enlightenment and I want to go."

"Ah, what am I to do with you?" her mother cried, slamming her hands on her knees. "It's always priests and philosophy with you, when you aren't making plans to enter a convent. Don't you want to marry and have children? You loved your sister's poor infant more than she did. The answer's clear. You'll be happiest married, and I have just the man. You must marry Mozart."

"What, what?" cried the girl. "But we're friends, or at least we were friends before everything happened with Aloysia and he stopped speaking to me, and stopped telling me funny stories. Marrying has never entered my mind, you know that. I want only to be a nun. You won't ruin my happiness the way you have —"

"What are you saying? Can you speak this way to me? Don't play such an innocent! I have heard you laughing with the boarders."

"It's nothing more than laughter; why do you make more of it?" cried Sophie, staring nearsightedly at her mother. "I was having a nice afternoon. And how do you expect me to make him want such a thing when neither of us wants it?"

"How do you know he doesn't want it? He obviously doesn't know what he wants. And what of my happiness? What of my future? When my mother ordered me to marry, did I resist her? No, I had respect for her, and bowed to her wishes."

"But there are so many versions of how you and Father came together I don't know which is the truth," cried Sophie, who was now red and stammering. "You've told me half a dozen and so did he, and now I'll miss my lecture, for they'll see I've been crying and Father Paul will ask me why. He's already written to the convent on my behalf. He knows how unhappy I am with you, how unhappy we all are with your pushing and pulling us this way and that."

"So you'd go to a cloister and desert me," cried Maria Caecilia, rising to her feet. "And one day they'll come to you and say, your mother was found starved to death on the streets of Vienna. Then you can say your prayers with a quiet heart, knowing you have honored your father and mother as scripture tells you."

By this time Sophie was weeping in rage and confusion, her voice becoming childlike. She ran to her mother, who shook her off; Maria Caecilia was weeping terribly and felt blindly for her apron on its hook. "Do you think I don't know what's best for you? God had spoken to me. The young man doesn't know himself; you'll teach him. I can see now what a good son-in-law he'd be to me. Now I must cook dinner for the wretches who live here. No, I wouldn't dream of asking you to clean so much as one turnip! Go to your lecture and ask your priest if you can abandon your mother selfishly for God, and if God will be pleased when they find me dead in an almshouse from want and from your willfulness."

Sophie's best quality and her most perplexing was her honesty. She had to have everything said exactly, and in a household that was seldom exact, where the same story was told ten different ways, she fled to the church where things did not waver.

A sin could be erased by confession and so many hours of mumbled rosary prayers; in fact, she so enjoyed the stillness of the church that she long ago had taken on the penance of all her sisters. She thought logically, though her logic was small of scope, for she was very young and had known little more than her family circle and those handful of warm artists who came within it.

Still her mother had accused her of ingratitude, which seemed the worse sin. She had believed all her life in self-sacrifice, which made her freely lend slippers, petticoats, books. She wanted to stand outside the circle of immediate attention, but be loved. She had tried to be kind to Mozart from time to time, was hurt and resentful by his coolness, and was sorry he was sad; that was all.

Would the sensual part be so bad? She couldn't imagine it. What she understood of it seemed so ridiculous that the hardest part would be not to laugh when it was undertaken. Now she was astonished at the attention from her mother and the demands and plans. She had always escaped from them. In the household of girls, where each one had her own place and role, Sophie had always simply been herself—irritating when she wandered off only to return an hour late with the cheese, but placidly loved. She was not prepared to bend this way and that under the storm that blew over her neat life of house and church, and that blew harder over the next two weeks when no money came from Aloysia and not one word was heard from Josefa in Prague. She felt too ashamed to confide in Constanze, who was blissfully happy with her French cellist, and from whom every day Sophie dreaded to find a note on her pillow saying, "I have run off; feed the bird. I love you, C."

No, she must manage this herself.

It was true her mother had always had strange and sudden ideas that no one in her right mind would follow, but of how this one had developed she was uncertain. She vaguely under- stood that this change had come about after a meeting with Thorwart, whom they all disliked more intensely every day.

"Seduce Mozart," Maria Caecilia hissed when she cornered her youngest daughter in the kitchen, or under her breath as they carried in the platters for the lodgers to dine. "Once he's compromised you, he'll have to marry you. He needs taking by the hand. Hush, hush, listen to me. I know about these things. Men don't know what they want until it's plainly shown to them."

After midday dinner, Sophie mounted the stairs to the door of the young composer and cautiously opened it. Strips of sun- light lay across the table full of music. She stood there, breathing quietly. There was something sacred to her about this room. Often she would wake in her room above and hear the click of his heels in the hall when he came home from a concert. She would hear him humming softly, catching only snatches of the melody. Sometimes if she passed him on the stair he had that withdrawn, bewildered look, which meant that only his body was here, and his soul was elsewhere. His little neat body rushed, as if he could not reach his destination fast enough.

But what of Mother? What of her mother, who sat in the

kitchen after dinner surrounded by piles of greasy dishes and with her apron over her face? Didn't love mean giving your life for others, and didn't her mother want the best for her? All day the silence continued. When bedtime came, Sophie could not sleep but lay on her white sheets, her rosary entwined between her fingers, while all the shadows of the room seemed to say, You are nothing but a selfish girl, Sophie. Was her life her own? she wondered. Was anyone's life their own? To sacrifice her life for her mother's needs: yes, God would approve of that.

Sophie thought, At least I can talk to him.

She was alone that night; Constanze was staying with Aloysia.

Wrapped in her dressing gown, she went down to wait for him, but the hour chimed past twelve and he still hadn't come. Determined not to miss him, she sat on the stairs for a time longer; at last she thought she would go up and rest for a while and come down later, but she was so tired she did not wake until two in the morning. Then she tiptoed down the one flight of stairs and stood outside his door. From inside she heard his breathing. He had come home and was asleep.

Gently she rapped and whispered his name, but there was no response. Finally, she creaked open the door. As softly as possible she tiptoed across the room and stood looking down at him. There was some light from the moon. She bent over him a little, and as she did her spectacles tumbled from her nose and fell across his chest. He woke, blinking, rather astonished. He gazed up at her, his hand half in front of his eyes. He moved to sit up, and the spectacles slipped off the bed to the floor. "What is it?" he said, not awake enough to speak clearly.

"I've lost my spectacles, that's all."

She dropped to her knees and felt around the side of the bed as well. "The problem with dropping my spectacles," she said, "is that I can't find them unless I'm wearing them."

"Let me help you." He rolled groggily to his side and felt down along the side of the bed. "I think I've got them," he said. "Here, they're too loose on you. I thought that last week when I saw you. You could lose them and someone could step on them. What time is it? What are you doing here? Are you sleepwalking? Is something wrong?"

"I must . . . speak with you."

"Very well then, but keep your voice low. It wouldn't do for anyone to know you were here. They'd think the worst. You're shivering; take my extra cover. Give me your hands; they're so cold. What on earth are you doing here? What do you need to speak to me about now? What time is it?"

"Some time past two."

"It couldn't wait until the morning?"

She shook her head.

"Then tell me, dear Sophie," he said with his old affection.

She sat down in the chair, wrapped in the blanket. Pushing her glasses up, she sniffled a little. In the near darkness she could feel her face redden, and now he looked at her in a kindly, steady way. He had large eyes. Sometimes they were suspicious, but tonight they were tender. She didn't care if Aloysia said his nose was much too big for any woman to take him seriously. She found his a good, comforting face, and he was strong enough, even though he was small for a man.

"My mother wants me to marry you," she said simply. "She wants to make sure that no one seduces me and that she's taken care of in the future. I suppose she doesn't know anyone else she can marry me to. Everyone in Vienna is so lovely, and I'm plain, but I don't mind that. I have always liked you. In fact, I love you with all my heart, but not that way. I want to renounce the world for God. I'm sure I'm not suitable for marriage. Still, she says we *must* marry, and I don't particularly want to. I wanted to know what *you* felt about it. We could go to Father Paul together and ask him."

He said nothing for a time. Some anger passed his face, and she cringed a little, for she knew from some musicians who had lived with them that Mozart could be touchy as gunpowder. Then he passed his hands over his lips, and his shoulders shook; she could see he was laughing. "It's not so funny," she cried, leaping up. "I'm not so bad that it's funny."

"Bad? Not at all; you're a darling. Oh, my sweet Lord, do you really—"

"Hush, hush! Mozart, someone's coming."

They knew the singing, the slipping, the muttering, the cursing. It was Steiner, the theology student, who was coming home drunk again. His room was opposite Mozart's, but he did not go into it. He seemed to have stumbled on the stairs and sat there muttering and singing to himself, blocking her possible escape from the room.

Mozart put his finger to his lips. "Be very still, you darling," he whispered. "Let me see if I can get him to bed, and then you can slip upstairs; we'll meet somewhere tomorrow in the daylight and speak about this." At the thought he began laughing so hard he could hardly stand straight, but he took a deep breath, walked across the room and through the doorway. His thick light brown hair stood almost perfectly upward from his sleep, giving him some several more inches in height. He looked ready to take flight. She sat down again on the chair with her hands in her lap.

She heard his stern whisper. "Steiner! Up now, man, to bed."

"Can't stand . . . stay here . . . stairs . . ."

"Come, Steiner, you can do it." Sophie held her breath. It sounded like Mozart was trying to help the drunken student stand, which would have had its difficulties, for Steiner was a hundred pounds heavier and half a foot taller. "Help me, Steiner," she heard him say.

"Leave me alone, you bastard composer, you organ grinder . . . sleep here."

"Get up, Steiner."

The noise had awoken another lodger, a traveling financier from Seville, who opened his door and called down in his Spanish accent, "Damn you, you drunken lout, get up and into bed." Sophie sank deeper into the chair. She held her breath again. The other lodger had pounded down the steps and was also trying to lift the drunken man. Between them, they got Steiner into his room. After several minutes Mozart returned. He closed and locked the door behind him, then began laughing so hard he could scarcely contain himself. He threw the pillows across the bed and buried his face in them. Sophie was laughing, too.

He caught her in his arms and laughed with her. Tears ran down his face.

They sat down finally on opposite chairs, listening to Steiner snoring from the room across the way. "Now," Mozart gasped, wiping his eyes, "tell me again. We've got to marry. Can it wait until the morning? They don't make marriages at this hour, for all the witnesses are asleep. You dear, lovely child, your family's quite mad, except you and Constanze, of course. But there's a problem. We don't love each other. Let's both stay single, and now you should go back to bed."

"I ought to wait until the Spaniard upstairs is asleep again. If he finds me he'll leer at me. I hate him."

"Yes, you would of course. You saved my life once; you're the dearest girl. Please forgive me if I was ever cold to you."

"Forgiven then. But . . . Mozart."

"Sophie."

"Do you believe we are meant to find happiness with each other in this life? Constanze and I aren't sure of it. People are either very lonely, or are unhappy together. Do you think it's easier to find it just with God?"

"Perhaps, but I have no inclination to that. I have a very dear friend, an Italian monk, visiting here from Bologna. He says that contentment's as hard to find within religious orders as without, that we humans take our natures with us wherever we go. I'm going to meet with him tomorrow. He would like you, but he'd want you to become a holy sister, and I prefer you remain in the world to save me when I'm in despair."

"Are you in despair now?"

"I was, a little, but you've made me laugh. You know, we might have a happy marriage when you're a little older, but perhaps we're better friends. I do believe in falling in love. Perhaps it's like believing in angels; you hope they'll come. I think perhaps you can go upstairs now to your room. Your sister must miss you."

"She's not home. She's gone to visit Aloy—"

"Never mind, I should be able to bear to hear that name now. Good night, dear Sophie. Once more you stumbled upon me in a bad time and cheered me. Now go up before your reputation's compromised." He kissed her cheek and hands, then opened the door for her, and she slipped up the stairs.

Her disappearance was discovered the next morning. Maria Caecilia and Constanze, back from Aloysia's, hurried through the rooms calling her name, reading and rereading her note in astonishment. They never really believed Sophie would return to Mannheim to join the beloved convent of sisters there, as she always said she would. Later they learned that Father Paul had been departing to that city; Sophie had confided everything to him that morning before daylight, and he had taken her with him.

he Franciscan monk was waiting for Mozart in a priest's study in the rectory of Stephansdom. A forlorn Christ of old German wood hung from its cracking though polished Cross, and shelves held antique books, some handwritten, in worn, plain, thick vellum bindings. It had snowed six days after Easter; heaps of it lay piled on the cold windowsills, and in the cathedral yard.

Mozart stood by the window looking at a dog that barked below, then whined as an old bent woman shuffled toward it with a bowl of scraps. He heard the soft slippered feet of a servant closing the heavy, creaking door.

"But is there truly no chance for an opera of yours to be presented here?" asked Padre Martini. "It's difficult to believe what Haydn told me before he left the city with the Prince, that someone else's will be given for certain. He said it's a loss to music. He thought this Thorwart might have spoken for you, and now Haydn tells me Thorwart stopped by Prince Esterházy's mansion and said there was nothing he could do for you."

Mozart sank into one of the high-backed, leather-upholstered chairs. "What can we do?" he murmured, his hands to his lips. "No libretto I found was good enough, and while I tried somehow, in the past few days, my chance eroded. I still live from hand to mouth. I can't remain in Vienna; I'm going to London. The soprano Nancy Storace and her brother said they'd write me introductions to musical circles there, and some people they know recall my name. I speak enough English to do it, and I learn quickly. Georg Händel did well there. Perhaps I would have been better to wear some prince's livery like that great and kind Joseph Haydn instead of insisting on my freedom."

He looked up, biting his lip, left hand drumming some melody fragment on his knee. "You will not ever tell him I have said this? My thanks. I'm not sorry I left the Archbishop, but I'm sorry my father and sister, who depend on me, have been made to suffer. I must do better for them. I must put all my own hopes aside until that's done."

"When do you leave Austria?"

"I'll stay here a few weeks more, and then be off."

"Amadé, is there no way to persuade Orsini-Rosenberg to give you the opera commission?"

"He hasn't answered my letter, and when I went there this morning they said he was out, but I heard his voice. What more can I say? My hopes were too high for an opportunity that was not meant to be mine. You're returning to Bologna soon? Then I would have been without your company even if I had remained. Give me your blessing, Father."

The cathedral loomed above him when he left sometime later, and a few men were clearing the snow from the courtyard with large, scraping brooms. There was no sign of the empty bowl or the dog in that white afternoon, only a small river of yellow piss around the area where it had prowled, and some pawprints in the snow.

Climbing to his room later he passed near the kitchen, and heard the murmur of voices. With a friend Frau Weber sat near the fire, her swollen legs on a stool. She was eating thick slices of bread and cheese. Dinner was done and supper not begun.

"I shall be going away soon to England, madame," he said coldly.

The reply was a curt nod as she stared at him, her mouth full of bread. He turned and continued up the stairs.

ozart was on his way out the boardinghouse door three days later, off to give one of the final lessons of his tenure in Vienna, when he noticed a letter on the crooked round table by the door under the leaves of the potted plant. Opening it, he stepped out into Petersplatz, the sun shining on all the surrounding houses; he recalled the man whose signature was scrawled at the letter's end. He was the actor and playwright Gottlieb Stephanie, with whom Mozart had had an intense evening of conversation (he did not recall about what) in a wine cellar. The letter described a libretto the actor was writing about Englishwomen abducted into a Turkish harem, which Gottlieb Stephanie thought might be turned into an opera. Several pages of the libretto in draft were enclosed.

Mozart pondered it that day in the odd way he had of doing one thing while thinking of several others. He had a meal in an eating house rather than return to the boardinghouse, then walked over to the Burgtheater. A rehearsal was in progress. He had been turned away here the other day, but now with Stephanie's letter in his pocket, he walked up the steps again to the offices. The door to the director's room was open, and he knocked.

Orsini-Rosenberg looked up warily. On the wall behind him was a portrait of the Emperor and, arranged in shelves, several dozen opera scores.

Mozart bowed. "I came to see you yesterday, sir, but you were out."

"Yes, most unfortunately. I do believe someone said you were here."

"I came at an inopportune moment."

"Yes, I had just been called away."

"I ventured to return, you see, concerning the opera commission."

Orsini-Rosenberg rubbed the bridge of his nose and flung back his head. He had a way of speaking directly to someone with his face absolutely open, yet you never knew whether he spoke the truth or not. "Most unfortunately, I had spoken to Thorwart about you. I told him we had some interest, but he came to me yesterday and said you couldn't have an opera for us, that you had no good ideas. Your music is, of course, quite extraordinary. I've told Haydn, who has all my respect, that I am aware of your talents, but *Idomeneo* was a very serious opera, dear Mozart, for all its beauty."

"I have found a libretto you will like on a Turkish theme set in a harem."

"That's most interesting. Things Turkish are very appealing. Women sometimes have themselves painted in harem garb, though where they actually wear such things I can't know. A harem, you say? That might please the Grand Duke. A good libretto's hard to come by though. Who's the writer?"

"The actor Gottlieb Stephanie; he described the piece to me. It's comical with many serious moments. It's about faithful love and an enlightened ruler."

"That would please both our Emperor and our visitor. But I know Stephanie, and he makes more promises than he can keep.

If I was able to pave the way for this opera, Mozart, how do I know he'll keep his part of the bargain?"

Mozart gazed at him steadily.

"Very well then, let me propose a plan." The Count folded his arms over his chest, returning Mozart's gaze. "If you can show me a fair-sized portion of this opera, I might arrange for the commission to be yours. Shall we say within a few months? I will then arrange for the design of the production and costumes and the engagement of the singers. How fortunate you found me here this time, Mozart. The opera I planned to commission had nothing so exciting as a plot in a harem."

The young composer rushed back to his room and began to work at once; the next morning he took his several pages of new music down to the parlor near Fridolin Weber's beloved clavier to continue working at the music table there. A small fire barely licked the scant wood. He was writing so intently, tongue pushed against his lower teeth, that he did not notice for some time someone standing in the doorway; when he looked up, he saw Constanze Weber with some wood in her arms.

"It's too cold in here," she said. He was so much under the spell of his work that he only smiled vaguely at her.

Since Sophie's departure, this quietest of the sisters had seemed to meld into the halls of the boardinghouse. She carried sheets and kneaded bread until the young woman she had been was slowly turning into nothing but a dull servant—a pity, because she was not much more than eighteen. Wasn't she in love with a cellist, that pale fellow he had seen on the steps now and then? Hadn't Sophie said that? Then why didn't the man take her away from this wretched place? As soon as he had an advance on the opera commission he would go himself, as soon as he had a little of it done.

"You'll want more wood," she said.

"I added a bit before, and expect to bow my head before your mother. I don't blame her: not wood, candles, wine, nor pork is free."

She knelt and coaxed the flames to recognize the new log. He gazed without much thought at the delicate back of her neck and the few strands of hair that had escaped her cap. Her name was the same as the heroine of his opera, Constanze.

She stood up, dusting her hands. She said, "I interrupted your work."

"It doesn't matter."

"Mama says you aren't leaving us quite yet."

"No, I have a possible opera commission. Right now it is possible, probably, likely, yet I believe it will be, it will be. I slept only a few hours since I began it; the music won't leave my mind. Let me play the first chorus for you."

She sat down by the music table as he moved to the clavier. The bright music sprang out with its evocation of a Turkish march and seemed to shake the curtains and the new log, which rolled slightly and fell. "There'll be triangles and drums," he said. He heard the march coming closer in his head, the sound of the pasha and his worshipful court approaching. "It's harem music," he added. "That's where it's set."

She said, "Do you remember the first time you came to visit us on a Thursday?"

"I do. . . . I loved your father."

She brushed the bits of bark off her apron into her hand, and closed her fingers on it, standing suddenly as her name was called from the kitchen below. Her eyes were dark in her serious face. "I have to begin dinner," she murmured. "I'm glad about the commission; I'm very glad you aren't going to England just yet."

*M*uch later he would recall that gesture of the closed hand, her sudden standing in her great apron. Something stirred in him, but it melted away before he could recognize it.

The trees blossomed. One day he saw the dog he had seen previously in the street, nosing hopefully in some garbage. He whistled and put out his hand, but the animal, having understood the young man had no food for it, trotted away with dignity.

Mozart seldom saw Constanze in the house to speak more than a few words to her. She moved past him like a shadow, then was gone as if she had never been there at all. She's lonely, he thought suddenly. Poor girl, when I first saw her amid all the others, I didn't think it would come to this. And where the devil is this French cellist of hers? He never heard the man's voice in the hall anymore.

One day as he was coming from his music publisher, he saw her walking before him, weaving between the carts and people of the crowded and elegant market, with a leather portfolio under her arm. The sky was heavy white, and it looked as though rain would come soon. "Mademoiselle Weber," he called, catching up with her. "Where do you go?"

"I've delivered some music I copied," she said. She stood very still, though people pushed about her. Just then a woman with two small, yapping dogs passed them, and her mouth opened with delight. "Oh, the darlings," she cried. "Oh look, oh I wish I had one of my own."

"I recall you love them, and having one's an easy enough wish to grant."

She had bent over to let their wet tongues lick her outstretched hands, and didn't answer him until she had straightened and the dogs had scampered away, following their mistress about a corner. "No," she said. "Mama doesn't like them. We had one when we were very young. It piddled under our beds and made her furious. Once it piddled on our shoes, and we couldn't get the scent out when we walked to church."

"When you live away from her you'll have one."

"But I'll never live away from her." Constanze looked down the street past all the shops and stalls as if someone had called to her. "I thought I would for a time," she said hesitantly. "I thought I'd move to Paris, but I can't leave her alone, not with Sophie gone. I wanted to, and I couldn't do it. You only see how bad-tempered she is, but I see another side of her. I do see more than one side of people. That's a strength and a failing, isn't it? So I'm not going away."

So that was it. Her cellist has gone without her. Mozart suddenly offered her his arm. "Let me walk with you," he said. "I was going for a walk in the Augarten. Come with me," and they turned toward the public gardens, which had groves of linden trees and concert gazebos and stalls for ice and lemonade. He said, "I think we can walk a time and still get back to Petersplatz before the rain comes."

They walked in silence, and then gradually he began to whistle. Glancing at her, he saw her smiling slightly.

"You like that melody?"

"I do."

"It's the second aria for the maid from the opera. You're always working, running here and there. I think sometimes how much you must miss your sisters."

"Yes, I do. I didn't think Sophie would go. I can't imagine why she did it so quickly."

"When I am away from my sister, Nannerl, I miss her so. My family is very close, perhaps because there aren't many of us."

Now that they had entered the Augarten the sky was darkening even more, and people were hurrying past them into the streets. He thought to offer her a coffee and wondered if she would refuse. She withholds herself from me, he thought, concerned. Why should she? Have I ever offended her? I used to hear her laughing with others, but she only smiled a little before. I wish I could make her laugh.

He felt the first warm drops of rain. People about them scurried for cover; suddenly the heavens opened, and the rain poured down. In moments the ground was soaked. He seized her hand, and they ran together under the trees, huddling there with several other people. Above them the rain poured off the leaves and down to the dirt path. He said, "I'm sorry. I didn't think it would come so soon."

"When we were girls we would play in puddles in the rain and after. Did you ever do that with your sister?"

"No, I don't remember anything like that. I only remember friends and music. My mother and father lost several babies before my sister and I were born. They were very careful with us."

Now she was silent, nodding, arms across her chest, the portfolio wet. Under the noise of the rain, she murmured, "Herr Mozart, you once said something unkind about me and my sisters to another boarder. You said there was only one beautiful Weber girl. You never thought me pretty at all. I'm not beautiful like Aloysia, but I think I have some beauty. When I heard you say that, I wasn't in the least sorry she broke your heart. I felt you deserved it."

He nodded. "It was a stupid thing to say," he muttered. "I'm a boor, an ass, and if I said such a thing, I did deserve it." He felt for her cold fingers, and moved his hand away again. "If only we weren't so stupid, if only I knew better . . ." Then he gave up. "Ah, this rain," he said sheepishly. "We'll be soaked." He slipped his arm around her to shelter her. At first she pulled away, but when he tried once more, pulling her nearer to him inch by inch, she did not move.

They stood listening to the rain, which drummed more quietly now. Her brown shoes and the hem of her skirt were soaked. When the rain ended, they walked home through the wet streets; once she stamped her foot in a puddle, and the water splattered all about. Then she was serious and quiet again. As they approached Petersplatz she became even more silent and walked a little ahead of him, briskly, becoming once more the boardinghouse keeper's daughter. Above them from the house hung the neat little sign: FINE ROOMS TO LET BY MONTH. Both the drunken theology student and the Spaniard had left. Pigeons were shaking the wetness off their wings, and the large puddles reflected the slate-hued sky.

*S*trange that she had been in this house so long and he had barely noticed her. Now he was aware of her often. She's in the kitchen, he would say to himself, and now she's gone out. Where has she gone? he would wonder. He looked from his window to see her walking off with her basket. Outside the sun shone; there were no puddles. He smiled to himself. Otherwise he was terribly busy trying to make ends meet as the libretto arrived in disorganized pieces; he composed when he could, and still had no approval from the Count. He played at the Countess Thun's, and gave more lessons to Mademoiselle Aurnhammer, who flirted with him. He arrived home and found Constanze had become a shadow once more.

"Puddles," he'd whisper as they passed on the stairs, and sometimes, "Puppies, little darling ones with wet noses who piss in little pots. Oh no, it won't rain; it never rains in Vienna." Though he made her smile, each time she then withdrew again. She recalled what he had said about her lack of beauty and could not forgive him. She was silent and severe. How could he persuade her he meant better? Life had sobered him, and she did have her own beauty, but he had no words to express it. They met just inside the street door, by the potted plant, where she was reading a letter from one of her sisters. He leaned against the wall, by the hatrack, and read one from Padre Martini, who had returned to Italy, then another from his father, who complained of Salzburg and told him to keep his feet dry. His sister, quiet and patient Nannerl, had also written.

"Come, play this with me," he cried from the parlor the next day. "I'm setting some of my dances for fortepiano. What do you think? I know you play well." She put down her sewing, came across the room, and sat beside him. Then, as in the old days, the parlor filled with music. Her left hand brushed his, but it was all right, for they were safe in music.

"What will be your future?" he asked when they stopped.

"None. I stay here."

"Not just only that," he cried. "Not only that for you."

She stood up suddenly. Then they were laughing over something. He had not heard her laugh like that in a long time, or perhaps never, because before he had not paid attention. "Stop," she said. "I must go back to my work."

"Don't go," he said.

It was a whole world in those minutes from parlor to kitchen. She had never considered how long it was between those rooms, down a flight of stairs, through a hall past the sour faces of her ancestors' portraits, and into the kitchen and the smell of the burning fire and chopped food. It was not merely the tinkle of the bright dances she regretted leaving, but something in herself she had not experienced in a long time. She rubbed her flushed face and then slipped into the kitchen where her mother and the maid were preparing dinner.

Her mother's words came like a slap. "Look at you, Maria Constanze Weber, and God forgive you . . . laughing with him instead of helping me. You're the same as the others. I thought you were better. I have given everything to you girls, and you have cared only what happened to each other, never me, never me. Why are you with him so much these days? A poor musician just like your father. The opera will never happen. I have it on excellent knowledge."

Constanze stood stunned. "What are these mad stories?" she said, when she found her voice. "What are you speaking about? Does laughter lead to anything bad? Are you worried I'm going to fall in love with him? Yes, of course. He's not good enough for me because you are once more searching for an imaginary prince to give me a title and money, which will reflect well on you. The Grand Duke of Russia's coming here in some months; have you written him of me? Here's your answer; here's what I think of it." She snatched up the blue pitcher and hurled it against the brick oven, where it shattered into a hundred pieces.

They both turned then to see Mozart on the stairs, looking from one to the other. Constanze dropped to her knees and began to sweep up the pieces. Their lovely pitcher. She had bought it one sunny day years before while out with her father, and they had packed it in straw on their moves from city to city. Now it seemed she had lost him again in the shattered blue pieces.

Frau Weber began to slice a large onion. "Perhaps you can enlighten me on some matter, Herr Mozart," she called to him.

"I would try to do so, madame," he replied, approaching the kitchen door.

"I don't understand sons and daughters these days. I nursed my parents, and it was not until they were in heaven that I accepted Fridolin Weber's offer of marriage. Nor do I understand a young man, quick to assume that the girl who cooks his meal is also to warm his sheets."

"What do you speak of?"

"My daughter, who gathers up the broken pieces of my pitcher as if she knows nothing, my daughter and you. Do you think I've seen nothing over the past few weeks? You walk with her in the park; you whisper on the stairs. Haven't I been through this tragedy once already with my older girl, who foolishly waited for you and, in her waiting, grew tempted and fell? Yes, if you had not made her wait, this wouldn't have occurred. Now they're gone, they're all gone but this one, and I have plans for her. I have plans for her."

"It seems to me that you have plans to sell her," he said quietly. "And that she objects to being sold. There is a problem there."

Frau Weber rushed toward him. "Have you compromised her? She's easy enough; all my daughters are. I'll make life wretched for you both if such a thing has happened. I'll blacken your name, young man, so that no good person will attend your concerts, so that the Emperor will know what a shame it is that he listens to your music. Your opera will be canceled if you see her anymore. No one will *ever* hear your name. I took you in for pity, but I was wrong. Play about with the daughter of a good widow indeed, and see how the law comes down upon you!"

"But madame, this is madness. Do you threaten me?"

"I do, and I'll carry it through. You are not to see her anymore, do you understand me? Leave," she cried imperiously. "Leave!"

He turned in confusion to Constanze, her apron full of broken bits. "Yes, do go," the girl cried. "This is no place for you, Mozart. You see how we are. There's no help for us here since Papa died. Go, I'll send word. I'll be fine. Truly, I'll send word."

He went at once through the streets to Leutgeb's rooms above his cheese shop, and later they sent the delivery boy for his things. He did not look at them but walked up and down in his little room. Constanze, he thought. What on earth has occurred? If she did not come to him by the morning, he would go to her.

ut she came early the next day. He had slept badly, waking to rain pelting his window. When he heard her voice below, he ran down the stairs three at a time and found her standing in the shop, her cloak and skirt still dripping. Leutgeb walked toward him between the wedges of odorous soft cheeses, which were veined with mold like the delicate hand of an elderly person. "This is a bad thing," he muttered, straightening his shop apron. "Frau Weber seems to have gone quite from her mind."

Constanze stood between the crates, tears running down her face. "What is it. What is it?" Mozart cried, taking her hands.

"I'm never going back there. She's berated me without ceasing since you took your things, first accusing me of being your mistress, then crying that I should have seduced you so you'd have to marry me and take me off her hands. And then, worst of all, the whole truth about Sophie's leaving came out. Yes, she's gone mad. I won't go back, and I won't love her anymore. It's all over between us."

"But what of poor little Sophie?" he asked. He wondered if she would ever find out about the young girl being in his room, or if she would believe they had merely laughed, found her spectacles, and talked about God and happiness.

"My mother said you tried to seduce her."

"I never . . . but this is madness also."

"Of course I don't believe such a thing; I never could. But I didn't know where to go, and I felt terrible for the things she said. Oh what does she want of me? How can I go back there? And then suggesting that we . . ." She put down the cup of coffee Leutgeb's wife had brought her and turned to the small stove in the corner, continuing as though Mozart were not there. "Does she think I have no pride? I wore enough of my sisters' cast-off dresses, and I won't have her cast-off love. The beauteous Aloysia—you chose her and may have the memory of her!"

"What?" he murmured, astonished. "Are you angry with me now?"

"Yes, I am. I have been for a time because you said—"

"But I beg your forgiveness, dear Constanze. We discussed this when we walked home that day in the rain. You told me you'd forgotten it. I did love her; it was true. I did pay for it. My heart was broken."

They became suddenly aware that customers had entered the shop and were staring at them. Constanze covered her face and then flung her hands down again. She paced up and down between the shelves, crying, "Where can I stay? What will happen to me? I can't go back. The things of which she accused me, of which she accused you. Of course everyone has run away but me. I will never never go back there again; I'll go to Sophie's convent and ask the good nuns to shelter me."

"No, dearest," Mozart said. "No, Constanze, I'll take you to my friend, the Baroness von Waldstätten. She'll give you shelter. I'm afraid this terrible thing has made you ill; look how you shiver. Your father would wish me to take care of you. I will take you to my friend."

"Well," said the Baroness von Waldstätten, gazing with a majestic smile at the shivering girl when Mozart helped Constanze down from the carriage before the mansion some small distance from central Vienna. "What is needed is a dry dressing gown, a place close to the fire, hot wine, and a little rationality. I place great stock in rationality. Young women are not to be bartered and battered with words, are they?"

Walking so rapidly before them into the great house that they had to hurry to keep up with her, the Baroness waved her hand as if to indicate the agreement of the naked marble muses that stood in separate niches in the round entrance hall. "Especially," she added archly, "not young Viennese women in these modern times, no indeed. Have not young women hearts and minds of their own? Is this not God's gift? Come now, come!"

Settled in a large guest room and dressed in a borrowed velvet dressing gown, the coughing Constanze was brought dinner on a beautiful tray, while Mozart and the Baroness gazed at her with concern. When they wished her good night and left her, she buttoned on a nightdress of soft, rich wool trimmed with pink lace, and slid between the sheets of the great bed.

By the light of several burning candles, she looked across the room to the dressing table, then rose to examine the crystal bottles of eau de cologne and the many silver boxes. On one lid were engraved the words: NO GREATER GOOD THAN MAN AND WIFE. Near it a silver frame held a small portrait of the Baron, a rather old man, who gazed back at her with a paternal expression. Whether he had gone to another country and died, or separated from his wife for her rumored infidelities, no one was sure.

Oh, why was she here? Driven, of course, by her mother.

Dear Saints Elizabeth and Anne! How could her mother descend to such behavior after all the years Constanze had defended her and felt she alone understood her, after she vowed to stay with her? And, oh Sophie, would she ever see her again but from behind a convent grille? We'll always be together, Stanzi.

Constanze stumbled back to the large bed, wound her arms about the huge, cold pillow, and buried her nose in it. She began her evening prayers; in the middle of them her thoughts wandered to Mozart and then to the large, echoing halls of the boardinghouse, and the sound of her mother's humming rising from the kitchen. Then she wept, shoulders shaking under the feather quilt. She recalled herself stricken by diphtheria at five years old, trying to swim to consciousness, gasping for air, how the room bent and rocked, how the pictures on the wall and the windows seemed to be all crooked, how the sheer white curtains of the bed seemed to sway. . . . There was her mother by her bedside with her prayer book or her knitting. There she was, leaning over Constanze, her hand on her daughter's hot forehead, murmuring, "Stanzi, Stanzi," with the greatest love in the world.

Then again healthy and fed full of meat and dumplings, cradled in that great lap, stories whispered in her ears. Old tales of hidden princesses in a tower deep in the woods, stories of the way the world was, of how to make apple cake, of what it meant to grow up, warnings to beware of men, beware of lying, beware of trusting too much. This warm, bakery-smelling presence, this source of lullabies, cuddling her in their oldest quilt, which they kept on the kitchen chair, its floral cover long faded, a feather or two escaping. Sweet, darling Mother . . . What do you do with someone who is everything to you and yet has so angered you? Caecilia Weber was not crazed. She always distorted things when agitated; she told wild untruths and later repented them, especially when she drank too much, which she did these days.

Constanze recalled her mother's voice as she had summoned

them from their beds on Sunday mornings for so many years: Maria Aloysia, Maria Josefa, Maria Constanze, Maria Sophia . . . where are you? Later on Sundays the four sisters might build in the kitchen tents from torn sheets, hiding beneath them near the fire. They were princesses, they were queens, they were virgins in peril and righteous warriors; in whispers those holy late afternoons between dinner and their late small supper, the girls were everything to one another, while from behind their parents' closed bedchamber door sometimes came sighs. Why had it gone away? Aloysia married; Josefa off in a strange city; Sophie swallowed up by God too soon, before half the conversations were done. Constanze had been unable to hold them together, even with her great love.

She hid her face in the pillows. She wanted her Thursday evenings again, to make it all right for all of them. Now her mother, with her furious, distorted words, had driven her staggering into this great, commodious house as a refugee. Yes, it was the truth. They had all staggered away; her mother had driven them away one by one. Then why did Constanze love her still? Why did she sometimes feel as if she *were* her mother, heavy body groaning as she walked from room to room, made too old too soon by life? Constanze alone could run to her and kiss her hands and cry, "It's all right, truly," and make her laugh again. Somehow the two of them must make up for all the rest who had been lost. The two of them must fill the empty rooms, hold within them the shadows of those who had gone. Her name was Constanze, faithful to the end. They would be two old fat women together, groaning, barring the door against life's sorrows.

Then she slept, dreaming she was a sickly child again with her mother and father sitting on her bed, kissing her cheeks. She felt her father's stubble, his sharp chin against her cheek as he fell asleep beside her, holding her hand.

Stanzi?

She sat up in bed. Was her mother calling?

But it was only the rain.

She woke aching all over; even the soft wool nightdress felt hot. She did not know where she was at first, and then looked about the room, now bathed in sunlight. Someone had come and opened the curtains, just as someone must have pinched out the candles last night. On the table next to the bed was a tray containing a pot of fragrant coffee and a plate of newly baked rolls, and from below came the sound of the fortepiano, pouring out the most astonishing variations.

The Baroness swept across the room. "Mozart has been below for some time, and has eaten several rolls with cheese and coffee. He won't sit still for wanting to see you. Here's the dressing gown you wore last night; we can draw it up when we belt it so you won't trip on it."

Constanze gazed from the rich gown to the pale, powdered face. "And my mother?" she croaked. "Has there been word from my mother, madame?"

"Sadly, she sent the police to fetch you, but I turned them away."

"Oh God," the girl murmured, sliding down in the sheets

and biting the edge of her hand. "What shall I do? And what is he playing?"

"Variations on one of the themes from his opera. He says his mind is too confused to do more."

"For heaven's sake, do send him off. I can't see him. Look at me. Tell him to come again tomorrow . . . yes, and thank him for bringing me here. He's the great kind spirit of our wretched family. Ask him to forgive me."

From below the variations continued briefly, and then stopped suddenly mid passage. She tiptoed to the door to listen, then heard his footsteps. She wanted to rush down the steps and through the receiving hall, crying, Don't go! But how could she show herself to him when she was so ugly, when Aloysia was always so beautiful? Aloysia would take time to adjust a cap, or rub on a little rouge. Then she heard the sound of a carriage and knew Mozart had gone away.

"I'm going from the city but will come again in three days and hope you're better by then, dearest," read the note he sent up to her.

He returned on a day so beautiful and warm that the doors of the conservatory were thrown open to the terrace that overlooked the garden. She saw him coming through the garden, up the formal path past the rose bushes. He wore his blue linen coat to his knees and a pair of blue breeches; as usual he seemed absorbed by something within him. She stood in the velvet dressing gown, pulled up at the waist, still a little weak from her fever. Her legs felt unsteady.

His face changed when he saw her. He blinked several times and came closer. Then he kissed both her hands. "I had a concert to give and some lessons," he said. "And I've been working on the opera, but I've thought of you all the while, Constanze. I thought of you safe here and wanted to see you. I know you're likely to go back because your mother's worried about you and says she's sorry. I went to see her, you know, and she said she *was* sorry. She was in tears, and I think she won't stand against my coming to see you, Constanze, when you return."

"But will you come?"

"I will, of course, every day."

They walked out onto the terrace and stood by an enormous stone urn full of flowers; then he took her arm and together they walked up and down through the garden for a time. Looking at the long formal walks between the trees and an arbor, she repeated shyly, "You'll come every day? But Wolfgang, I don't even know what's between us . . . we haven't said. I must ask you, though perhaps I shouldn't. Are you in love with that English soprano who sings in the opera now? I know you were at an evening gathering with her where you all sang and played for hours. Someone told Mama you were in love with her."

"No, not at all," he exclaimed.

"Are you quite certain?"

"I know what I feel and what I don't," he said. "And if you ask me also about Mademoiselle Aurnhammer, I'll laugh. Dearest,

I'm glad your mother has apologized. I think I could charm her if I tried, but to tell the truth, I don't care what or how she is as long as she's good to you. Come tell me once and for all. Have you forgiven me for that stupid comment I made so long ago?" He laid his hat down on a stone bench, and drew her down to sit next to him. "I want to marry you," he said. "I want to make you my wife. I'm twenty-five, and I have wanted a wife for a long time. I think I was waiting for you, my Stanzi. I know I was waiting."

"You're asking me to marry you?"

"With all my heart. Would you, Constanze?"

"I would, yes, I would. I think I love you, even though I didn't know if I could love again. But," she said with a sigh, "how can I trust you utterly?"

"Have you any reason not to trust me?"

"You've seen so much of the world, and I've mostly been at home. But where would we live? How? We haven't any money. And besides, what will your father say? I know he doesn't want you to marry for a long time; he'll find some fault with me." She looked straight ahead, her chin raised. "Yes, and then you'll see it, too, and go away. I'm not greatly talented like Aloysia and Josefa, and I haven't got Sophie's wit and faith. I'm in the middle. I've made a shadow of myself, and now I don't want to be a shadow anymore, and it frightens me. No one expects anything of a shadow, no one notices anything much . . . my dreams are my own."

"What are your dreams? Would you trust me with one or two?"

"Oh, ordinary girls' dreams: being greatly loved, being swept away." She looked down at her fingers. "Being here I've thought of so many things, most of which I don't understand. I want to be the young woman I was and yet someone new as well. I want to escape my dull place at home, and yet I want to remain there. That's the problem. I want to go back to be with my sisters just the way we were when you first came up the stairs that Thursday night. Sometimes because I knew you then, I think I can be that way again . . . the difficulty is sorting out all the things I want. Oh, if you could simply make this clear to me."

They held each other, and kissed again and again. "But how will we get your father's blessing?" she finally gasped.

His hair stood up on end, his lace was askew, and every time he tried to make a sentence, he laughed instead, as if everything was pure pleasure to him. "My father . . ." Still laughing a little to himself, drumming some rhythm on her upper arm, he said, "Dearest, look there in the garden . . . there's a small bent gardener, and the wheelbarrow he pushes is bigger than he is."

Then he took a deep breath, blew out his cheeks in expelling it, and turned back to her, rubbing his hands. "My father, yes," he said more solemnly. "He's coming to visit me soon. I'll put it before him then. I want his blessing, of course. Once he sees you, you sweet girl, there will be no question."

He took her hands and kissed each one several times. "As for me, I'll be all good things to your family. Your mama will be like my own, and I'll be a good brother-in-law to your sisters. My father will be entirely happy, believe me. I can manage everything. Now I must leave to give some lessons and see if more of the opera libretto is written. Constanze, trust me as I trust you. No one will ever be as happy as we'll be together."

After he left her, running back several times to kiss her, she returned to her room and began to pack her things. It was time to go home. She knew the Baroness was spending the afternoon with a man who used magnets and hypnotism to free the soul to travel to earlier lives, and Constanze didn't wish to disturb her.

However, when she had just completed a letter of gratitude and laid the dressing gown she'd been using on the bed, she saw the Baroness standing, distracted and transformed, by the door. "Oh, my dear," the Baroness whispered. "I have voyaged to the tombs of the pharaohs and found I was a princess then. . . . Are you going home? Dear child, come again—now Mozart must take very good care of you, and I will come to your wedding."

In the boardinghouse her mother stumbled toward her weeping, arms open in reconciliation. Upstairs on her bed she found a letter from Sophie.

Dearest darling Constanze,

I have a small confession to make, which is weighing on my conscience. When I ran away so very quickly that early morning, I did something impulsively, which perhaps was not the wisest thing but it was done from a loving heart, and Father Paul says that if things are done lovingly, then much can be forgiven and overlooked. I don't even have the courage to tell you now what I did, and likely it will blow over and nothing ever come of it. I couldn't go away without some attempt at your happiness. Since a few months have passed and you have not said you've heard word of it, I suppose you never will, which may be a good thing under the present circumstances.

Now write me quickly and tell me if Mozart has told you yet that he loves you. I've prayed so hard over it, I have the strongest sense it's come to pass. I have a sense you'll both be married soon. I have faith in my visions, which are almost always right.

Your sister in all affection,

Sophie

P.S. Father Paul has promised he'll find a home for the cat, and until he does, don't let anything happen to her. They are giving me my novice's robe next week. Pray for me.

Sophie, she thought, what on earth have you done? And for heaven's sake, don't take vows. Come back to us. Constanze found her rosary under many petticoats and pairs of hose, and she sat on the bed in prayer, the beads slipping through her fingers. Let my meeting with his father go well, she prayed, and let Mother stay calm.

She saw him every day. They walked, he played her the newer parts of the opera, and she copied sections of it to send to his father. It was odd that his father would not know the identity of the copyist when he read the music. In the privacy of his new rooms, for Mozart had found a place just a short walk from Petersplatz, he touched her breasts and her thighs, and kissed every bit of her flesh he could manage that lay outside her corsets, lace drawers, and chemise. He took her hose off and kissed her feet. She kissed his arms to the shoulder, rolling up his shirt, and down his chest as far as his shirt would open. They stopped always at certain boundaries. She gazed at the swelling in his breeches and threw her hands over her face, rocking with delight. He seized her hand to place it there and she touched him, then flung herself away. She ran down the streets with the sensation of that place—warm, full, and yet hidden by light wool fabric—still in her slightly closed palm.

he clavier as an instrument had been outmoded for over a decade, as had the harpsichord, and yet Mozart did not yet own one of the enviable new fortepianos, though the Baroness lent him hers when he needed it. He had not considered buying one in Vienna for reasons other than simply lack of money; he felt there was none so good as Stein's in Augsburg, though Stein, he had heard, was considering opening a shop in Vienna. Still that day he thought he would look at Johann Schantz's stock, which was also reputed to be good.

He was happy on entering the shop; any instrument maker's shop was heaven to him. He felt at home, and he would always run into a friend who knew of another friend whom he had not seen in some time. All the news of the world he loved found its way in and out of such shops. This one also sold music, and he was pleased to see his six violin sonatas for sale. He had made a reasonable amount of money publishing them.

In the back room, which was stocked with parts of instruments in process, Johann's brother Wenzel Schantz was fitting a sound board, but the principal room was crowded with customers. Mozart had lifted the cabinet lid of a fortepiano to examine the hammers and the triple strings when Johann approached him.

"Herr Mozart, good day. I'm happy to hear your name is getting around more these days. Do you wish to purchase an instrument? I could set you some good terms and find one just to your liking. Allow me to show you the pedal mechanism for this particular one. My father knows yours from some thirty years back. Your father's book on playing the violin remains the best. I hope the great Leopold Mozart is well."

They stood by the fortepiano, peering inside, discussing the hammers and the string tension while an assistant spoke to other customers. Then Johann said convivially, "I understand you won't be a bachelor much longer. Word does get around the city, you know. I imagine the whole city knows about the romance between you and Mademoiselle Weber."

The fortepiano maker hesitated, running his hand soundlessly along the black keys. "Man to man, Herr Mozart, may I say a few words to you? Our fathers have long been friends!" He began to smile in a twisted way, looking very much the gypsy. "Oh, those Weber girls! Many men about the town know things of them. I'm speaking of the two younger ones. Yes, there's more to them than meets the eye."

"I doubt that. I know them well."

"You don't know, then? I recall a certain gathering my wife and I had some months ago. The two girls, of course, made no objection to joining in the game of forfeit. Well, who would? There were enough married women here to chaperone, though I was surprised to see the alacrity with which Mademoiselle Constanze lifted her skirt to have her calf measured by that young cellist. Later she drew me down to the shop, and I must tell you, I could have mounted that girl had I had five more minutes. 'I love you!' she told me. 'And I must have you!' She was all over me. Then several weeks later she sent me a letter; thank God my wife didn't see it. It said she wanted to run away with me. But this can't be important to you. It's Mademoiselle Sophie you intend to marry, isn't it?"

"No, it's not Sophie."

"Ah, then, I do beg your pardon. I spoke indiscreetly. Now I'm very sorry indeed. It was only the night and some wine. I wish you all happiness, Herr Mozart. I'll send the order around to your rooms for you to sign if you wish to purchase one of our instruments."

"I would sooner play on a piece of lumber than take one of your instruments, Schantz."

He hardly knew which way he went, and when he came to Petersplatz, he circled round and round like an angry dog. He would have left right away had he not seen Constanze waving at him from a window. Then he had to go up. She was in the parlor mending sheets, and she put them down at once to rush over to him.

He turned his face.

"Good heavens, what is it?" she murmured. Her warm smile faded away.

He told her in a few sharp words what he had learned. "So this is how you behave?" he said. "I have to learn such a thing from a man who is a stranger to me, who must be mocking me." He began to stride rapidly up and down the room. "You let a man unknown to you measure your leg before others; you went in the darkness with a married man and almost—my God, I'm so sick I can hardly think. My father's coming in a week. How can I introduce you to him? Have you no respect for your honor and mine? I myself would not have touched your leg in front of others."

"Of what do you accuse me?" she cried. She was suddenly trembling. "It's true I let him measure my leg, but my leg didn't belong to you then; you had no call on my leg or on any other part of me. As far as I knew, you didn't think of it and hadn't a right to it anyway. And yes, I went down to the shop with him in the dark."

"Alone in the dark? Alone in the dark?" Mozart's voice seemed ready to crack.

"Yes, alone in the dark, and he drew me there himself because he knew I was lonely, and if he says differently, he's a liar. No, I didn't confess it; I had no cause to confess it. Why are you fussing so much?"

"Because I must know what part of you he touched."

Her beautiful dark eyes flashed, and she clenched her small fist. "What does it matter? I was indiscreet . . . but why must you question me like this? What haven't you done? You're surrounded by pretty singers; my own sister was one. Susceptible to women, that's what our guardian said about you. How can I know what you do, what you try to cover up by accusing me?" By now Constanze was shouting. He stared at her in horror. In her anger she swept the music to the floor, and the inkwell tipped and spilled its dark rich blue liquid over the carpet. She clasped her hand to her mouth and cried, "Oh, look what you have made me—"

"The letter you sent him asking to run away with him?"

"I never sent any letter, but I wrote one when I was very wretched, before you ever deigned to look at me. Oh God, then Sophie must have sent it! I understand now; she sent it for me. She wanted my happiness."

"Sophie would do such a thing?"

"You don't understand what happened."

"I understand that I won't be laughed at," he cried. "And his father knows mine . . . perhaps they'll drink a glass together somewhere, and talk. It's bad enough that the woman I will marry lives in a boardinghouse, with all manner of men coming and going, walking through the halls with their shirts not fully buttoned, seeing your garments hanging to dry, your precious small things. . . ."

"Where else should I hang my things? Why are you so jealous? I haven't given you cause, have I? I am waiting, just as my sister waited. I'm sick to think I'll meet your father. To please him, I'll have to behave in some peculiar way unlike myself."

"I was going to tell him you're not like the other Webers."

"But I am a Weber, and I'm proud to be a Weber. Our hearts are open; we're hospitable. It was our hospitality that brought you to us. Johann Schantz says bad things of me, and you believe him. Suppose he took advantage of me—"

"I know your passionate nature."

"You've never objected to it before."

They stood glaring at each other. She would have slapped him if he had not caught her hand. "Stop, stop . . . dearest Stanzi," he said. "I didn't mean for things to get out of hand like this. I'm jealous, but I've never doubted you. It's just what Schantz said. What you did before shouldn't matter, but it does if it's common talk. I will never buy one of his instruments. I'd rather use it for firewood. Come here; stop walking up and down like a soldier on guard." He caught her in his arms, where she remained stiff and furious, eyes cast down, ready to shout again and say other things he could not imagine.

He whispered to her, "Listen, all will be well. I'm jealous because I want you so, and the thought of any other man touching your hand drives me from my mind. I'm sick with wanting you. I won't wait longer than autumn. We must be married in the autumn. I'll count the days and the hours. Listen, just think how happy we'll be! We'll have a little dog, yes, and a house full of beautiful chairs and mirrors and things. Several beautiful elegant rooms quite near Stephansplatz. Perhaps the old cathedral organist will die and I'll take his place. Yes, many things may happen to me once the opera is done and a success, and it will be a success, I swear it. And at night we'll draw the curtains and send the maid away."

Though she did not break from him, Constanze stood stiffly, eyes downcast, responding to nothing, as if she had heard none of his words. She said, "I'll be as rude as I like to your father if he's rude to me. My family is as good as yours, even if we never played before the courts of Europe. I don't care if your father comes. Your name may be known throughout Europe, but it's little enough to me." She said a great deal more until he grew pale and seemed to shrink.

"Very well then," he said, "I'll write. I can't speak with you to-day." As he left the boardinghouse, he muttered, "The girl has her mother in her. How will I ever manage that?"

he beauty, the sweetness of the warm months was gone between them. Three days passed without meeting, though Mozart sent her small hopeful notes of reconciliation. All the whispered conversations they had had, the pleasant arguments of what sort of furnishings they would have, in what part of the city they would live, even the names of their future children, stopped abruptly. When he received no answer to his last letter, he threw up his hands. He was too busy to placate her. He resented it, and sent a quick letter off to Salzburg asking his father to postpone his trip.

Unbeknownst to Mozart, it arrived two hours after the

Salzburg coach left for Vienna. Mozart was writing one morning, huddled in his shirtsleeves over the paper, when his door opened to reveal his father standing there, gray hair pulled back in wound ribbons, gazing critically about the room at the clothes thrown here and there, the unmade bed, the dirty plates pushed to the side of the table.

Mozart leapt up at once, passing his hand over his mouth to conceal his agitation. "You've come."

"You were expecting me, were you not? Surely you were expecting me. We planned—"

"Yes, of course. Come in, come in. The journey was . . ."

"Difficult. My bones ache."

Mozart kissed the older man, rang for the landlady to remove the dirty dishes, and paced the room anxiously. He hardly heard the stories of Salzburg, of work difficulties, as he hurled the covers hastily on the bed and picked up his dirty hose. He wanted to throw open his arms at the mess and cry, You see, this is why I must marry, Father. Can't you see I need a wife? But with the events of the past week, it was not the time to do it. He did not know what Constanze was feeling. He could not break through her anger, her little hard profile when he tried to see her.

He spoke about music with his father, who then said dryly, "And so? Where's the girl?" He looked about the little room as if he expected his son had hidden Constanze Weber in a closet. "I'm hungry for my midday meal; ask her to join us."

Mozart hurried from his rooms and went running down the street, dodging between horses and carts and shoppers, slipping past the stalls of goods for sale, and to the house in Petersplatz, but Constanze was not home; a neighbor said he had seen her go to market. He turned and headed that way, the dust of the warm streets now covering his shoes, and saw her emerging from the fishmonger's, a large piece of fish wrapped in old paper in her basket. He felt his hair stand on end as he approached her.

"My father's come," he said into her ear. "We'll all have a fine dinner together. He's hungry and wants to meet you. I couldn't stop him from coming; I asked him to postpone his trip. Come right now, please, and I beg you, Stanzi, my beloved, my only darling, my wife to be, don't let him see any differences between us. They'll all be gone soon, once you stop sulking and realize how much I love you, so there's no need for him to know about them now."

"I'll make up our differences when my hurt stops," she said. "It just doesn't go away that quickly. But I'll meet your father and be very nice, as I was taught to be. Oh, why couldn't he have come next week? I'm just almost over being angry; I needed only a little time more, Wolfgang." She slipped her hand in his, and he took her basket of fish. They walked together toward his rooms, past his concierge, who stood in front of the building eating an ice, and climbed the stairs.

Constanze saw a small man with gray hair and a sour face, but his hands, with their callused fingertips from his lifetime of playing the violin, were rather beautiful.

She curtseyed, suddenly aware that she was wearing a mended dress, discolored along the hem with street muck and floor sweepings.

He returned a small bow. "Ah," said Leopold. "So you are Constanze. Yes, it is a pleasure to meet you, Constanze. . . ."

"I hope your journey was well, sir."

"Coach journeys tire me. . . ."

The conversation went on in this stiff way until they were interrupted by a knock from below and the nasal voice of the old concierge. "It's my librettist," Mozart said. "He likely has more of the words for me to set; I've been waiting for them. Sit down, sit down and be comfortable. Father, show her some Salzburg hospitality. There's a little wine in the decanter. Then we'll go for supper."

Mozart's father and Constanze both took chairs. Constanze folded her hands in her lap. She realized that they were not very clean. For a few moments they listened to the agitated voices below.

Leopold muttered of wine, of church music, of childhoods. Then he cleared his throat. "You seem like an honest girl, Mademoiselle Weber," he said. "And I think I see a pleasing innocence in your face, yes, just as he has described you. You think you know my son, but that's difficult to do; he doesn't know himself, never has."

She pressed her hands together. "I believe I know him well, sir. What do you mean?"

"He thinks he loves people, but it's music he loves. I formed him for music and he belongs to music, but it won't give him a life. He can't make his way in the world, and for any woman to marry a man like that would be a disaster. Haven't you waited for him often, only to have him come late? Has he never looked up from his writing and not even realize who you are? There, you see. And what would occur if you married him? You would be waiting, waiting. You would be by a window waiting for someone often out in society, often in the presence of many beautiful women. And then you would be sorry you didn't listen to the sad words of an old man who loves him. For I have waited, mademoiselle; I have waited many years for my son to truly come home. And if he does marry . . . take this nothing against yourself, mademoiselle . . . I think perhaps your family is not the best to marry into. He will have to make his way in the world. Do not be offended by my words, but he can't succeed with you at his side. He would not be wise to choose to marry the daughter of a boardinghouse keeper."

The voices below grew louder, and a door slammed. Mozart came up the steps and back into the room, running his hand through his wild hair. "Well," he said a little breathlessly, looking from one to the other, "you've had a chance to talk. That's good. We should perhaps go and have something to eat. There's nothing here."

Constanze stood at once. "I can't come; I'm expected home."

"Tomorrow then?"

"Yes, tomorrow."

"Let me walk with you a bit."

The day was very hot, and the lemonade stand on the corner, with its gay blue-striped awning, was crowded. She let him take her arm but did not move close to him, and he said with all tenderness, "Has he said something that upset you? Beloved, beloved, tell me what he said."

The words stumbled out, and when he heard, he seemed to swell with anger. "How dare he speak to you like that?" he said, his voice rising in spite of the crowds about them. "Where's his respect for my wishes? I respect him. I'll always provide for him no matter how many wretched lessons to deaf pupils I must teach. And what of all the money I earned as a child? He invested in me; he's not poor. By God, he must let me go! If I rise or fall, I must do it on my own."

He was shaking her hands now. "He will come round and give his blessing to our marriage. He will. Nothing matters but that we make up and be the dearest friends again, my Stanzi."

Her face had become very plain. "But don't you see, I couldn't. I couldn't marry anyone with a father like him. He'd be pulling you one way, and I'd be pulling you another. I want him to like me, and he doesn't. He won't. I wouldn't ask you to choose between us. Listen, Wolferl: we were both lonely and we fell in love, but perhaps it wasn't meant to be. Perhaps we can find a way to be friends as we once were. Isn't that possible?"

"No, it isn't," he said quietly, and leaned against the side of a church where they had stopped. "But I know you've felt this way since we quarreled. Everything's going badly for me today. One day you think all's within your grasp, and the next it's swept away. That's true of life, but I always want it differently. Gottlieb Stephanie's too busy to complete the libretto, and it's likely the commission will be offered to another composer. My writing is too original for some people; I'm not handsome; and no one will forgive me for growing up, not even my own family. Today I may have lost my chance at the opera and my hopes of marriage to you. We perhaps shouldn't speak anymore of it. We'll see each other in the street now and then, Constanze. I'll always be glad to hear of you. Send my greetings to little Sophie when you write her."

He walked away with his head lowered, and she stood for a time with the basket of fish on her arm, and then walked home. Two neighbors were sitting with her mother in the kitchen drinking coffee; Constanze climbed the stairs to her room, and lay silently across her bed with her arm over her face.

The doors of the opera house were closed when he reached them, but he found a side door unlocked and hurried up the stairs. From the offices he heard movement; he knocked, and entered at once, expecting to see Orsini-Rosenberg's unrevealing face, but only Thorwart sat behind the desk, with the accounting books spread out before him as if he were the director. He pushed the books away and folded his hands on his heavy stomach to gaze at the composer.

Mozart cried passionately, "What opera competes with mine? I heard it from my librettist. I was assured mine would be given when I played parts of it last week for the Count."

"Yours might have a chance if you had it ready," Thorwart said dryly. "But you don't. We must have an opera in place, and there are others to choose from; thus, we've done so."

"But I'll have mine done in a few weeks; the librettist swears there will be only a very short delay."

Thorwart frowned and wagged his heavy finger. "Ah, young man, young man, you think too highly of yourself. Remember that you are but one of many composers in Vienna. I'll tell you what your downfall is, Mozart: your pride. You're a musician, which makes you a servant. Servants aren't nobility. I'm not nobility, but I come closer to it than you because I act like a gentleman. You had a chance to make a decent living as a church musician and turned away from it."

"You have stood against me."

"What cause have I to stand for you?"

Mozart clutched the edge of the table hard. "Sir," he said, "it would be easier for me to get all the positions you could ever obtain than for you to become what I am, even if you had three lifetimes to do it."

With the greatest dignity he bowed himself out of the room. Then he darted down many streets, between carriages and wagons, to the door of his librettist, and was let in by Stephanie's startled wife. He pushed past her into the bedroom, shook the rotund, snoring man from his sleep, crying, "Where is the libretto? Give me the libretto!"

The sections came on time as promised, and he did nothing but write. After three days his father went home, and Mozart continued in his cluttered rooms alone, composing piece after piece of his opera.

In her bedroom some days later Constanze sat to write to her younger sister, now and then nibbling the end of her pen. There was a spot of ink on her apron front.

18 July 1782

Dearest dearest Sophie,

It's all over between Mozart and me. Just this morning his friend Leutgeb was here for an hour trying to persuade me to go back. He stood with his head to one side, listing all the true attributes of his friend ("Honest Wolfgang, good Wolfgang!"). "But I don't think I want to marry at all," I said. "And not with a father like his, not with that wretched cold man! I'll stay home and help my mother. I'm the last sister, what can I do? I won't marry at all." And he came very close to me and said, "What a waste," rather warmly, and I felt that old flush of heat that so frightens me because then I don't know what I'll do. I really don't. My heart breaks for M., but after saying I wasn't pretty, and attributing the worst to all of us, besides his wretched father, I feel it's against my pride to go back. And he does nothing, nothing, but send me music. No words, just music. He sent me a rather astonishing serenade for thirteen wind instruments, and Leutgeb ran around singing the parts and shouting, "Listen to this—what music!" until I wanted to cry or cover my ears.

I have almost forgiven you sending my letter to Herr Schantz, though it is the silliest thing you ever did. Perhaps it's a good thing to do the silliest thing so young; then you can have the rest of your life to be wise. I must recall you're only fifteen and a half.

But why do I write any such things? I cry a lot. Tell me what to do. Even after that letter, I still trust you.

Constanze

The reply, sealed with the convent's seal (a blurred impression of the Holy Ghost in blue wax), came rapidly.

Dearest Constanze,

After receiving your letter I couldn't sleep, and went down to our chapel in the middle of the night. There was only one candle burning before the statue of Our Lady, and I knelt before it a long time and then perhaps I fell asleep and dreamed this, or perhaps it was a real vision sent to me. An angel came and sat beside me, his great soft wings almost pushing me out of my place. He smelled of lemonade. He was naked to the waist and rather beautiful, and I tried not to look at him, because I felt rather too moved. He sat there for a while talking of this and that, and then he said, "You must go home and make the marriage between your sister and Amadeus." I couldn't recall who Amadeus was at first, because we have never called him that, but it's his middle name, right? The "A" he puts when he signs his music (and he prefers Amadé, he told me once). So it seems if you are being so silly, I must come home.

I am rather glad to do so, to tell you the truth, because I find after testing my vocation that I prefer to love God in the world and not behind cloister walls, and besides, I don't mind flirting. I like conversation on the true meaning of life with friends and wine and people playing music in a comfortable room, and my ideal is just what I had as a little girl, and I can't have it here. I don't ever intend to marry because I am more virtuous when chaste, but I intend you to marry him, so I can have what I want for you and we can have our Thursdays

again. So I am packing my things. Two of our nuns are traveling to Vienna, and I am coming with them.

Please don't tell me that anything has happened to my cat.

Constanze wrote back eagerly, using one of her father's pens.

Dearest Sophie,

You are welcome, welcome, welcome. I read your letter
with tears of joy. I want you to come here, and we'll always
be together, but I can't marry Mozart. I'll be thirty and old
before we get his father's consent. You must stop trying to
arrange all our lives, but do come back.

The cat is well and has six new kittens, which, as Josefa
would say, must mean that she has been very well indeed,
and enjoying the life of Vienna.

Love always,

Your sister C.

ophie swept home dragging her one modest leather
portmanteau, pins falling from her untidy hair, and rushed up
the stairs on her thin legs. She kissed the cat, was pleased that
Constanze had watered the plants in the garden and in the hall,
and went at once to see Father Paul, who confirmed her decision
that her vocation was in the world and not behind convent
walls. She found her favorite old straw hat and pinned flowers

on it, wearing it over her pale freckled face with her spectacles. "I'll dedicate myself to good works," she said. She made a list that first night of the most pressing of them: find more boarders, persuade Mother to eat less noodles and cake, and burn that ridiculous book of suitors.

The next morning, after she had lain in bed talking until ten with her sister, she got up and began to tie on her petticoat. "Come on," she said. "You're not marrying Mozart's father, and Mozart's jealous of anyone you've ever smiled at only because he loves you. Go and tell him that you're at least friends again with him. I'll walk with you. Wear your straw hat . . . wait, I'll pin flowers on yours as well. "

They walked over in their flower-printed dresses and large straw hats. "Now, go up," Sophie said when they arrived at his rooms; they saw the concierge out front eating dark bread and sausage. "I'll wait here. When you come down, we can all have a lemonade."

Constanze walked up the stairs, her hand lingering on the banister. She could hear the fortepiano that Mozart had ordered on credit from Stein, Johann Schantz's competitor in the instrument business, and she stood for a moment in the open doorway watching him play, gazing at his fingers, which seemed hardly to touch the keys.

"Constanze," he said, looking up; then, after a long moment, he added, as if nothing difficult had ever passed between them, "Come look at this aria for the maid Blondchen from my opera. Will you sing it for me?"

"I don't sing very well. And I didn't know there will still be an opera."

"There will be," he said grimly. "And I'll give all the fortune that I'll ever have if you'll sing this aria for me." She came closer, and he caught her fingers and pulled her down to the bench beside him. "Listen to me," he said. "Beloved, listen to me. I think of you all the time. There can't be anyone for me but you. Let's pretend we've just met. I know nothing about your family, nor you of mine. We introduce ourselves just so. Now I must tell you I have a present for you."

"But you didn't know I was coming."

"Sophie sent word last night."

"Oh, that child—I'll be forced to send her back to the convent. Well, show me the present but . . . stop, we've just met. Remember that. We've just met, and we're beginning again."

He took her hand and led her down to the concierge's dark room by the main door, where in the corner there was a basket containing a dog and four pups. He knelt, pulling her down. "I already told her I'd take the brown one off her hands. Look, I said to myself, they'll be taken and drowned, but not if there are homes for them. I said, this one's for Stanzi. You can't take her yet, she's too young; but you can visit daily, or twice daily, or hourly, and when you do now and then, you will remember the lonely composer upstairs." He hesitated. "When we have our own rooms, when we're married, she'll be ours."

"I hope that will be soon," she said, her face hidden under the brim of her hat.

"It must be very soon, Constanze, for I'm suffering for want of you."

"And I'm suffering wanting you," she murmured, her words muffled by her drooping hat brim and the soft puppy noises. "I suppose I should tell my mother and you'll have to tell—"

"I've already written him."

They were all already assembled as he came into the boardinghouse parlor with Leutgeb at his side, though the hour had not yet struck. Caecilia Weber wore her darkest and most formal dress, buttoned to the neck, and her white cap with the faintly yellowing lace at the edge. At her throat was fastened a brooch he recognized; he had always wondered if the piece contained a holy relic or some memento of her late husband.

He bowed, and she inclined her head.

To her right was Thorwart with a rolled piece of paper on his knee, which Mozart assumed to be the marriage contract. Behind him was Constanze, her small hands clasped in her lap and her head lowered. Mozart could see her only a little through the bulk of the others, but he thought she looked anxious. He would have liked to kiss her hands. Beside her, on the chair with a crooked leg, Sophie also sat with hands clasped in her lap. Whenever she moved a little, the chair tilted. He wondered which would last longer, the meeting or the chair.

He took a seat and placed his hat on his knee. Leutgeb sat by his side, rocking back and forth slightly, his mouth twitching hard now and then. Mozart kept his eyes firmly focused on the bald spot of the rug around the clavier leg. If he dared look directly at Leutgeb or Sophie, he would not have been able to contain himself. He might have rolled across the worn rug, seizing one of the old red sofa cushions to stuff in his mouth. "You will behave?" he had pleaded to Leutgeb as they walked over. "The seriousness will be a bit higher than if the Archbishop of Salzburg had tried me for assault, but then, this is more important. After all, she owns the girl, or thinks she does."

"The wind bag, the moldy cheese."

"She's not quite that bad."

But Mozart, raising his eyes to his future mother-in-law, thought, She's worse.

Thorwart cleared his throat. "We are gathered here—"

Maria Caecilia put up her hand to silence him, inclined her head. "Herr Mozart," she said. "My dear Herr Mozart, I believe I understand that you wish the hand of my daughter Constanze."

"I wish to marry her, yes, hand and all. Both hands and all other limbs, dear Frau Weber."

"You must understand certain things. We are not now quite as you found us some time ago in Mannheim, when my poor dear husband yet blessed us with his wisdom. I'm a widow now, with only two remaining daughters. You wish to marry my Maria Constanze, but how do we know you'll do it? I am asking you as a mark of good faith to sign this contract that you will pay a certain sum of money if you haven't married her within three years. You understand we are aware of the slowness between your words of love and your finalizing them in the blessed church, Herr Mozart. We should not wish a repetition of what occurred in my family between you and another."

Thorwart nodded gravely. His jaw was so stiff with purpose that it looked as if it might shatter, loosing his teeth all over the carpet. Mozart took a deep breath. He raised his eyes, and there saw Sophie looking at him, deliberately cross-eyed, nose wiggling, looking all the world like a drunken rabbit. He felt his laughter rising, and then Leutgeb's hand on his knee to restrain him.

"Your answer, Herr Mozart?"

"You know I've agreed. I'll agree to anything to have her. Give me a pen; you'll have my signature." He put out his arms impulsively. "I'll marry her within three months. Madame, if I could, it would be within three days. Where's the ink and pen? Where's the notary?"

"I am notary," Thorwart said. "Maria Sophia is witness. Come."

At once all in the room except Maria Caecilia stood and walked to the table. Outside they heard the kitchen maid screaming at someone, and a crash of crockery. Maria Caecilia ignored it, watching as the young composer signed, and then she stood up, sweating faintly.

Suddenly, Constanze pushed in among all of them and snatched the contract. "I need no contract from you," she cried. "I believe your word. I believe it." Turning to her mother, she cried, "Mama, it has nothing to do with you; it has only to do with Wolfgang and me." The contract, now in many pieces, drifted down and settled under the clavier legs.

They escaped outside the house to the back of the church, where they held each other without speaking. Then Sophie came trotting toward them with a large umbrella. "It will rain, I think," she said. Her eyes crossed, her nose wriggled, and there was the rabbit in spectacles again.

Later Constanze and Sophie locked themselves in the parlor while the boarders hurried up and down the stairs; outside the rain fell persistently over Vienna, over the linden walk and the opera houses and the imperial palace, streaming down the stone saints and angels of the churches, dampening organs and forte-pianos, wetting the windows of the great shops of the market-place with all their gorgeous apparel. The rain fell on the posters in front of the opera announcing the first performance of Wolf-gang Amadeus Mozart's *Die Entführung aus dem Serail—The Abduction from the Seraglio.*

One week later, Josefa returned from Prague.

She dropped her canvas bag by the front door of the board-inghouse, and took the steps two at a time to the room she had shared with her sisters. No one was there. She gazed at the hats, dresses, stockings, and books scattered about, then stooped to pick up one of Sophie's flat, worn shoes, and held it against her heart. Her face contorted, and she shut her eyes hard. She would not cry now, not until it was over, and then maybe never again.

Why weren't Constanze and Sophie here? She had thought of them all the carriage ride to Vienna, of the games they had played as children. She had often been the hero; she had slain dragons, led her sisters from burning castles, removed evil spells with the wave of a crooked stick that seemed to glitter as it cut the air like a sword. Now she needed her sisters more than she ever had in her life, but of course she had not told them she was coming. No one knew at all.

Josefa pulled the pins out of her hair, which fell halfway down her back, and with the pins clutched in her fingers, she descended the steps, slowing as she approached the parlor. "Papa," she whispered. She opened the door, leaning against the frame. Maybe he would be there . . . maybe! But he was not. There was his clavier, the fall board open, the overcast light from the window playing on the discolored and worn ivory keys. Hanging above it on the wall was his portrait, his slightly crooked and sweet smile. Fridolin Weber, second tenor in the chapel, violinist, generous host, throwing open the door as his guests mounted the Mannheim stairs. *Come up, I long to embrace you!* Playing scales as she stood before him learning to sing.

"What, are you leaving so suddenly?" the bass Hofer had asked after her last performance in the Prague Opera when she had come into his dressing room to say good-bye. He stood, still in the robes of the king he had played in the opera that day. "I've been watching you since you've come, you know. You have a magnificent voice, but the feeling within you is what makes it so rare. People come to hear you. Why are you going away?"

"I have to go."

He had crossed the room, and taken her hand; he was not a

handsome man, but he listened to people, and she had always felt him listening to her.

She said, "You are very kind, Monsieur Hofer."

"But you will return to Prague?"

It all began in a parlor much like this, she thought; it began with my father. He gave me music and love. He always protected me; I was his girl. She turned abruptly, and descended to the kitchen.

Maria Caecilia Weber was asleep in the old armchair they had brought in their travels from city to city, her hips spread out under her vast skirts, her head with its heavy chins drooped on her chest, which rose and fell with her breathing. Rain beat on the kitchen window, a little seeping under the casement, while the upper floors of the boardinghouse were still and quiet, the way they sometimes were in the morning. Josefa listened. Not even the cellist played; he must be at rehearsal or moved away. The kitchen table was full of cold chicken, which would later be smothered in warm sauce and piles of vegetables and onions.

She took a deep breath. "Mama," she said sternly.

Maria Caecilia sighed and stirred. She seemed to start a little as her eyes opened and focused on her eldest daughter. For a moment something soft crossed the heavy face with its still youthful skin, and Josefa remembered years before when she had rushed into her mother's capacious lap and her mother had said, "Whose little girl are you? And who loves you best?"

Her mother sat forward now, rearranging her expression, straightening her puckered white cap. "You stand there like a loose woman with your hair all down," she said, her voice husky from sleep. "Well, Josefa, you might have sent word you were coming. Have you come trailing your lovers? What on earth do you want? Away for months and months and no letter to me, not a coin for me when I might need one. In and out of our lives, isn't it?"

"Oh, how nicely you welcome me!" Josefa muttered.

But tears had formed in her mother's wide, plain face, obscuring her eyes; she stood up, her hand bracing her back for a moment, and began to stir the soup that had been simmering over the fire. "Yes," she said, her broad back to her daughter. "You come home likely boasting, after the reputation you left here from which we've just begun to recover. I suppose you know the news. Your sisters write, I'm told. Stanzi's betrothed, though without a contract, foolish girl; he'll leave her with her belly swelled, mark my word. Aloysia seems content with her portraitist when she could have done so much better. Now I suppose you come back to bring me shame. You could at least help with the dinner instead of being useless. Sophie's off doing good works for the poor."

"Don't you want to know where I've been?"

"No, I don't, but you'll tell me anyway."

"I left Prague a month ago. I've been traveling. I went to Zell, where you were born and where you met Papa."

Maria Caecilia's back stiffened slightly, and then she rubbed the small of it and resumed stirring the soup. Turning to the table, she began to cut the cooked chicken with a knife. She never raised her face. "You went to Zell? Why? You never showed much interest in my sisters, your aunts. Poor Gretchen, poor Elizabeth!"

Josefa watched the adept hands cutting up the chicken, deboning it, arranging it in neat piles. She said, "I wanted to find out what I could about you and Papa. Do you remember what you said in the carriage coming back from Papa's funeral? I never forgot it. There were many people who remembered you quite well in Zell. Your family didn't have very much money at all; I found that out. I badgered my aunts until they confessed. Your family was never wealthy; there was never much silver. None of it was true, ever."

Her mother did not look up. "How long did you say you'd be staying with us, Josefa?" she said coldly.

"Not long! I have friends in this city; I can stay with them, but before I go, I want you to tell me who my real father is. I want to hear the truth from you."

Maria Caecilia began to untie her apron, and then flung down her hands. "How dare you ask that question!" she cried. "What a ridiculous question! Because of a remark I made in my grief after burying my saintly Fridolin? How dare you question my respectability? Yes, you'd like to drag me down to the dirt, wouldn't you?" Covering her face with her arm, she began to weep, her large bosom heaving.

Then, throwing her arm down, Maria Caecilia cried, "All I've struggled to maintain all these years, negotiating with bill collectors, managing the scorn of your father's brother, and his whole family who thought I wasn't good enough. Always making fun of me for my lack of education, because I didn't understand music. 'She can hardly read,' they said, 'much less understand music.' How can you know what was between me and your father? How can you know what I suffered?" Her beautiful skin was now splotchy.

The kitchen door creaked open, and Thorwart came in, smelling of that familiar perfume he wore, which always preceded him into a room. "Why, what's happening?" he said sternly. "I could hear your voices all the way down at the street door. I see the prodigal has returned, and at once begins to shout at her mother. Haven't you had enough bad behavior from this young woman, Maria Caecilia? I would have the police send her away. She does no one any good here. Girl, why do you look at me?"

Josefa clutched the back of a chair. "It's him, isn't it, Mama? I found it out in Zell. Oh dear Lord, it's him, this horrible man we have to call 'uncle,' the one we're made to respect, who is my real father. He never could keep his hands to himself with all of us, though you wouldn't believe us if we told you. He tried to catch me on the stair and rub himself against me, though I'm his own daughter."

"What, what?" cried Thorwart; the kitchen was hot, and he had begun to sweat.

"I went to Zell! I spoke to your sisters, Mama. I spoke to lots of people. There was nothing respectable about you, Mama; you were wild. You hated your home; you wanted to escape. I know what happened. This disgusting man saw you coming across the courtyard at dark, and he came out and asked you to a tavern with his friends. It was two months before your marriage to Papa, who was working hard to earn money. You didn't come home until dawn. You stayed with him that night."

"How dare you!" cried Maria Caecilia. She tried to rush forward, but Thorwart grabbed her arm to restrain her.

"You went to your wedding with a baby inside of you, with me inside of you. It's him, isn't it? When I look at him I see my face; when I look into the mirror, I see his expressions. I think I would rather die than know this."

Thorwart shook his head, releasing his hold on Maria Caecilia. He gazed coldly at Josefa's wild hair and dirty traveling dress. "My dear girl," he said, drawing out his handkerchief and wiping his forehead. "You have never known truth from fantasy, and as a child you made up such things no one knew what to think of you. The stage is where you belong, where you may live out your wild dreams. However, I am sorry to disillusion you about your paternity. I'm not your father. And I'm very glad I'm not, for you're not meek and gentle the way a young woman should be, as any daughter of mine *would* be."

He cleared his throat in the silent room, looked at her sternly, head to one side, and then, in a voice that touched the words only lightly, as if they were dirty, he said, "I never went to bed with your mother, though I was sorely tempted, as were my friends, for she was a flirt then. Oh yes, standing by the window in her chemise. She didn't stay with us that night, but went off with someone else from the tavern. Excuse me for revealing it, Madame Weber, but I can't have my name dirtied when I'm innocent. You came to me weeks later in tears because you were carrying a child. I beg you both, Madame Weber and Mademoiselle Josefa, do not impute me in this. All other allegations are spurious as well." He raised his heavy chin defiantly and straightened his coat with a firm tug. "I am, and will always be, a gentleman."

The sound of two boarders laughing in the hall reached them; Josefa still clutched the back of a chair as if she would keel over without it. "Then who *is* my father?" she cried. "Who did you go with that night, Mother?"

Maria Caecilia sank down into a chair, covering her face with her hands. When she looked up, she seemed to have aged several years. Looking over at the bowl of onions, she said bleakly, "I was just seventeen, and I knew nothing. You must understand this. Your father was a soldier in the service of the empire. It didn't happen that night but a few nights following. I was not myself since the first time I saw him; he was so strong, so handsome with his mustache, like the stories my sister and I would tell one another. His coat buttons shone. Like you, he was tall." She reached out for an onion and cradled it in her hands. "I gave myself to him, and I would have married him, but he was sent away with his regiment. My letters went unanswered; my heart broke. I returned to Fridolin Weber, who was a good man. He knew; I confessed it to him. He was more forgiving than you, my girl, more so than you have ever been."

Maria Caecilia began to peel away the first fragile onion skins, a tear running down her cheek. "Yes, he knew you weren't his, Josefa, but he loved you the same as if you were, maybe more. And he married me anyway because he loved me so."

Josefa closed her eyes. If she could have left the room she would have, but she knew she did not have the strength to go. Her mother's voice came broken and accusing across the table that stood between them. "You girls!" Maria Caecilia said. "Do any of you know what it's like to lose your beauty forever, to be fat and old and ridiculous, to go to sleep each night alone, to be no one's love, no one's little cabbage? To struggle to keep food on the table and yet be the butt of jokes to your daughters, to be nothing but stupid? I was once as young and beautiful as any of you. As beautiful as Aloysia or you—"

"I can't bear it," Josefa cried. For one brief moment, she had wanted to go to her mother and console her but was so horrified she fled. She ran stumbling, weeping, pushing past the astonished boarders who were talking in the hallway. Her hair streamed loose down her back as she rushed into the streets of Vienna. She ran past the shops and wagons, not knowing where she was going.

After some minutes she turned and hurried blindly to Petersplatz. Father Paul, just coming from confession, was taking off his stole. "Josefa Weber," he said, smiling at her so that his beaked nose wrinkled. "We heard you were in Prague. Sophie tells me all about your letters. Has the opera season ended? Why have you come home? Why, you've been weeping! What on earth is the matter? You're not in trouble are you, dear girl?"

"Where's my sister?"

"Sophie is working with some of the nuns in the orphanage two houses down. I'm so glad she returned; we don't know what we would do without her! But what can be the trouble?"

Without answering, Josefa ran to the large building down the street, where she was met at once with the sound of infants and little children tumbling around in the hall. She ran into a room where she saw a few wet nurses feeding babies, then rushed up the steps to a schoolroom, where there was hanging a portrait of Christ and the children.

Sophie had been teaching the alphabet to a group of children sitting at one long table. At the sight of her sister, she stood up and almost fell over a chair to reach her, crying, "Oh darling, what are you doing here?"

"I need to speak with you."

"When did you arrive? Why did you leave Prague? Oh, I'm so glad! Wait, I'll send the little ones across the way to Sister Maria Elisa. There, pets . . . my sister's come!" The five children looked back curiously as Sophie shepherded them out. Then, closing the door, she hurried back to Josefa. They held each other amid the long low table of books containing the letters of the alphabet, small drawings of animals or flowers illustrating each one.

Then they sat down on two low chairs, knee to knee, hands clasped.

Sophie said, "You're trembling and you're crying."

"I've had such words with Mother. . . ." Josefa began to tell the story. She kept looking away, as if trying to find a way to escape the truth.

"Oh Josy, how terrible," murmured Sophie. Her lips parted, and she grew so pale that her freckles seemed to darken. "Oh, my love."

"It means that nothing is real anymore," Josefa said hoarsely.

"Nothing's real. Whatever I did, right or wrong, I could return to that one thing: I was Papa's girl. My father taught me singing, I tell people. My father always stood up for me, rode me on his shoulders; now he's not my father at all. A stranger was my father. I can't bear that loss; I can't. I don't know where in the world to go with a loss like this."

Sophie began to kiss Josefa's fingers one by one. "Come, don't cry," she whispered. "I'm crying, too, and I can't even give you a handkerchief because I always lose mine. Wait, wait! I think I can make something of it. Now I'll explain it to you. Yes, it's clear to me."

She wiped her nose on her apron and said in the clear voice in which she always made her proclamations, only now the words stumbled a little, "The soldier doesn't matter at all."

"How could he not matter? What are you saying?"

Sophie took several deep breaths. "He doesn't matter one bit. You were Papa's most precious girl; you were his own Josefa. He *chose* you; he could have put you in a basket and delivered you to an orphanage like a heap of old clothes, but he didn't. Well, did he?"

"I can never forgive Mama."

"Oh . . . Mama!" Sophie took a few more breaths, and laid her hand flat on her knees to steady them. "Why she is the way she is . . . this is part of it, of course, but there's another bit. Remember when we first looked at that book of suitors in secret in Mannheim, and I noticed the first pages were cut away? I eventually found them under the paper lining in the drawer where Mama keeps her hose. Listen, I'm telling you to distract you."

Sophie leapt up and began to rush about picking up fallen toys, stammering a little, glancing back at her sister. "Are you listening, Josy love? Mama bought the book when she was young and began to plan for her own sisters' marriages. Someone fantastical, of course. Those pages were full of the names of pashas and princes and sons of the city fathers. Only poor Aunt Gretchen believed her and refused every other offer, and so she never married at all. Mama has always felt bad about that, but she couldn't stop herself. She had to keep planning fantastical lives for all of *us* to make up for it, and to make up for her own fall. She couldn't see the happiness she had all along. She saw it only sometimes. And after Papa died, she knew."

"She should have known before!" came Josefa's savage cry.

"I think she did sometimes. Josy, people do just bumble along. We have to forgive one another. What else can we do? I tell you this now because it's all part of the piece, you see, of understanding why Mama is the way she is."

"I don't want to understand her!" Josefa yelled, clenching her fists. "I don't want to understand anything about her; I hope never to see her again! I will never, never get over this." She wrapped her arms about her chest and rocked back and forth.

Sophie dropped to her knees before Josefa, the rag dolls she had just gathered up spilling back onto the floor, their little button eyes staring up at the two sisters. "But Papa loved you best! I was always a little jealous; we all were. You had a part of him that no one else did, not even Mama. And she misses him so."

Josefa twisted her head away. "I hate it when I cry!" she

gasped. "I've just been holding it in for so long." After several minutes, she managed to calm down a little. "Well," she said with a bit of grim laughter as she picked up one of the rag dolls, "perhaps with what I told Mama about Thorwart's wandering hands he won't be round anymore, and that's a mercy! But Sophie," she said, looking up at her sister, "I haven't asked a word about you and your good works."

"Heavens, what's that compared to your news?"

"Tell me to distract me and keep me from crying again. I'll buy you six crescent rolls and six coffees if you distract me."

Sophie turned over her hands, a little chapped from washing, but they had always looked that way, even when she was a child. On the back of one was a deep scratch from a stray cat. "Nothing to tell." She shrugged. "I'm teaching the little ones to keep myself from trouble. Oh, I'm also starting a shelter for homeless sick animals in an unused yard here. You could help me with it, particularly the larger dogs."

"I might . . . I will. Tell me more. No, not about Aloysia; she wrote me of her triumphs herself. Tiresome girl! How's our Stanzi? Is she really going to marry Mozart?"

"Yes, I hope quite soon. Don't you want to talk about Papa now?"

"No, anything but that. Tell me of all of you." Josefa tidied a doll's dress, her face lowered so that her expression could not be read. "Mozart is a very good man, Sophie," she said, "and you know that, and Stanzi knows that. I suppose when you marry that's the most important thing to know. But I've thought a lot about it when I was away. The woman who marries him marries as well the part of him that creates such extraordinary music. It's *all* part of him, and always will be."

She laid the doll aside and, reaching inside her dress, drew out her silver locket. "I wrote and asked Aloysia to send it to me while I was in Prague," she said, rubbing her thumb over the worn initials. "I wanted it with me for good luck. She never knew what was in it. I'd like to tell you. It's strange how you keep secrets for a long time, and then they just spill out. Maybe tears bring them, but this is going to spill out also now. Are you ready, mouse? The strands of hair tucked inside my locket are mine and Mozart's."

Sophie sank down to the floor, pulling off her cap. "Mozart's?" she whispered.

"Yes."

"But Josefa, what do you mean? Why on earth would you wear his hair in a locket? We thought your lover gave it to you, your first lover, and the hair was his."

Josefa rose and walked to the window. Sophie began to rise as well. "Josy?" she whispered, staring at her sister's tense shoulders. She could not see Josefa's face, for it was turned to the window. "What is it? Tell me!"

"I've never had any lovers, mouse; I made it all up. I wanted you all to think someone loved me that much. I found the locket in a secondhand jewelry shop and bought it myself, and I took the hair from some he gave Aloysia."

"Josy, are you serious? Not a single lover?"

"Not a single one."

"You're still a virgin?"

"I am." Josefa hesitated, leaning her head on the window overlooking the busy Petersplatz with the bookstore and lemonade stand, and children walking home from school arm in arm. The voice was lonely now. "Are you disappointed?"

"No but . . . but we were so certain that you . . ." Sophie now managed to stand, thrusting her hands deep into her apron pockets and walking close to her sister. She rubbed her nose against Josefa's shoulder, then reached for one of Josefa's large, nail-bitten hands again. She glanced up at her sister's stern profile, and moved her mouth a few times as if to find the right words.

She said, "Did you love Mozart, Josy? Did you?"

"I did," Josefa replied. "I did with all my heart. I think I still do, though I'd never say it. You have all my secrets now, and you must swear as my sister never to tell them to anyone as long as I live. I wish Mozart and Constanze every good thing. Hug me . . . how I've missed you! Did Papa truly love me? I'm going to cry again. I am unforgiving. I'll try not to be. If he forgave her, why can't I? Oh, Sophie, when will I find where I belong?"

Sophie Weber, June 1842

MONSIEUR NOVELLO LEANED FORWARD, THE BOOK IN which he had been writing held carefully on his knee.

It was a long time before he spoke. "And did Josefa always keep the locket, madame?"

"But for that brief period when she lent it to Aloysia, she wore it all her life, and, as I promised, I kept her secrets as long as she lived."

"And she never had any lovers at all?"

"She did marry eventually; you know that. She married the bass Hofer, whom she had met in Prague. He moved to Vienna with her, where they both sang. They had a music shop for a time, a very nice one, and they were very close to Mozart. She and Mama made up, but they never did like each other very much. Did Hofer know about what was in the locket? I don't know. She did love her husband with all her heart."

"And you married as well. Your name is Haibel."

Using my cane, I rose slowly. "I did marry, though the others thought I wouldn't. I didn't marry Johann Haibel until I was in my middle forties. Before then I stayed home, trying to keep

Mama from madness and manipulation; I succeeded at the first but not the second. That was beyond me."

I began to make my way across the room past my table and to the trunk near the bed. "I know your visit to Austria is coming to a close soon, my English friend, and I must say, I will miss you. I will miss telling you my stories, but to tell the truth, you did not need to come such a very long way to know the Weber sisters."

My back ached unmercifully, and I put my hand on the small of it before bending over the trunk. I pulled away the shawl, which covered it, then had to use both hands to open the top. The smells of dust and old paper and wood rose to my nose.

Monsieur Novello joined me beside the trunk, holding up a lamp. "What is all this music?" he asked, looking down at the contents of the trunk, and then his voice grew softer. "I know. They're his operas; they're his operas in his own hand, the original scores. I know his handwriting from some of his other works, but I had no idea where the opera scores were. Forgive me, but I'm overcome. I can't help it."

He dropped to his knees and began to take out the heavy bundles, laying one after another on his knees. "All here," he murmured. "*Le Nozze di Figaro, Idomeneo* . . . and here, *Abduction*. Here's the second aria for little Blondchen! And *Zaide*, which sadly he never finished."

My English biographer sat with the scores all around him and wiped his eyes, turning his face so that no tears would fall to the pages. I lowered myself to a chair, and he reached out and grasped my hand hard. I felt his gold ring on my palm and the cuff of his English shirt as it brushed my wrist.

He murmured, "Here are all the operas. . . ."

"Here are all of them, monsieur. Constanze had them, and then they came to me."

He loosed my hand but held his in the air so that I would understand he couldn't speak for emotion; in that moment I was so glad he had traveled from England to find me. For some time there was no sound but that of his uneven breathing and the creaking of a carriage passing in the street. Then he wiped his face once more and began to turn the pages.

I said, "Monsieur Novello, when you first came to speak with me, you told me how real you found the women in Mozart's operas, and asked if I and my sisters were any influence on their creation. With all modesty, I think I may reply that we were a fair influence indeed. Indeed we were, monsieur."

This congenial biographer moved the lamp closer, and continued to turn the pages of the scores with their many lines for instrumentation. "Yes, we're all there," I said. "All of us, you see—Aloysia, Constanze, Josefa, and me—all our moods, our sensuality, our youth. Whatever score you take up—*Giovanni, Così Fan Tutte*—you'll find something of us. We're the playful girls, the lonely countesses, the abandoned women. I see myself in the chambermaid disguised as a notary, though alas! I never did sing, never could sing at all."

I shook my head. "I wish I had. Constanze sang some of his roles in concert later in her life; her voice was good, but she lacked the boldness needed. Josefa, as I told you, was the fiery, brilliant Queen of the Night. When I saw her, she seemed to glitter from within. It brought back to me how she appeared in our sleeping chamber when she was not yet ten years old, waving her stick over us, releasing us from all sadness and harm."

He managed a half smile. "And did she?"

"Yes, often as children, and then many times through our later years."

I leaned over as best I could, and he held up the score. "This little aria from *Figaro* when the young Susanna sings in the garden for her husband to come to her quickly on this their wedding night . . . *'Come, my beloved, come without delay.'* There's no music more simple and sweet, or that Mozart felt more deeply."

Monsieur Novello let his fingers touch the scoring for strings that accompany that aria, and after a time he raised his face to me. "Will you tell me then of the marriage, his marriage," he asked quietly, "and how it truly happened at last?"

"Yes, how it truly happened," I said. "It almost didn't happen, you know. Or perhaps you didn't know that after all."

PART SIX

The Abduction from
the Boardinghouse

Aloysia Weber Lange stood, late in the morning, before the hand-lettered poster that hung outside the Burg-theater. The words announced Mozart's new opera. Instrumentalists were hurrying inside, carrying their violin or cello cases, greeting one another, talking about their upcoming engagements. "No, there's not a ticket left for this performance," one of them was saying. "My wife was hoping to come. She'll have to hear the work tomorrow night."

A group of workmen were carrying out a red carpet, which would be rolled from the carriage to the door so that Emperor Joseph and the Russian Grand Duke might not dirty their feet. Two servants hurried by discussing the supper that would follow the five o'clock performance.

Aloysia followed them into the theater.

It was now lit only by a few high windows, with a standing set for a Turkish harem on the stage. "Where is Mozart?" she asked one man.

"Where is he? Likely in the musician's gathering room. He's still correcting orchestral parts."

Aloysia walked back through the door, turning past the rolled canvas backdrops. There was all around the bustle that signaled something extraordinary was going to take place within several hours. From behind a closed door came the high scales of a soprano. She knew a few people recognized her face, even under her enormous straw hat with its great dipping feathers. She wore a white muslin dress with a slashed silk band tied about her waist. "It is Madame Lange," she heard someone whisper. "It's the soprano from the other opera house."

"Your sisters have a ticket for you for the opera premiere tonight," Lange had told her over his shoulder after she woke; he was, as usual, engrossed in his painting. "It was the last one; I'll go tomorrow. It seems half the city's talking about your old friend Mozart!" But she hadn't replied; she'd been so intent on studying herself in the mirror.

Something had happened the day before that had disturbed her. A soprano who had been well known some years before had applied to sing again at the opera and been turned away by the directors. "She was once beautiful," they said, with a smile in their voices. "But she's now past forty, too old for what's wanted." Aloysia's hands had fumbled when she overheard their words, sitting in her dressing room meticulously removing the feathers and false jewels she had worn in her hair during the performance. It had not just disturbed her; it had *terrified* her. She thought, One day I will also be old, and people will talk through my arias, if they come to hear me at all. And is this all there is to life? Lange won me, and now he says, Yes, my dear; no, my dear. He sighs when I disturb him, looking at me with little wrinkles near his eyes. Have some soup, he says, and returns placidly to his painting.

There were only the sounds of a pen scratching rapidly and paper shifting as she opened the door of the gathering room. Mozart was bending over a long table marking changes in instrumental parts, an older man beside him. The man nudged Mozart, and the young composer looked up impatiently, frowning at the interruption.

She said, "I wanted to wish you well, Mozart."

"You're very kind to come to say it!"

"I've seldom seen such a fuss. Everyone hopes for a great success."

"The production's expensive. I've done my best, and it will do as it will. I sent over a number of tickets to your mother's house, but I suppose you'll be singing at the other theater."

"We don't sing tonight; I'll come."

He came closer, a look of concern on his face. "Is everything well with your family? Is Constanze well?"

"She's well enough," Aloysia said, lowering her voice. "But you don't ask of me anymore. You've never come to hear me sing. Don't you care if I'm happy or well? I was the center of your life, or so you told me, and now I'm a stranger because you court my sister. I wonder how she can bear to let you court her. But that's not important; only this evening can have any importance." Her words poured forth in an angry whisper, though she never lost her pure silver tone in speaking. "I was fortunate to fall out of love with you, knowing how inconstant you are. I feel sorry for Constanze; she'll find out."

He took her arm, opened the door to a costume room, pulled her inside, and closed the door behind them, not noticing that the doorknob had caught on the bow of her sash and pulled it. "What's the matter with you?" he said impatiently, his voice also low. "Why do you ask me if I've forgotten you? It took me years to do so, and I have at last. No one will ever know what pain you caused me. You can see I'm very busy today. You could have come another time, Aloysia."

"Well then," she said, "will you become simply another dull married man? Will you be just like Lange then, faithful, stupid, asking your wife about the soup?" She bit her rouged lip hard. "No," she said, shaking her head. "That's not what I wanted to say. I didn't come here to argue with you or berate you, but to make a proposition. It's this, dear Wolfgang! Yesterday I recalled again the tour you wanted to make with me. Now is truly a good time to go forth with it. Why not? Your reputation's greater, mine's very good. I'm wanting to leave this city; I'm tired of everything here. We have much in common, our very natures. There's a restlessness in you, too."

At that moment he heard his name called; anger passed his face, and he stood against the door, blocking it almost as if to prevent her leaving.

She said, "How can you be so cold to me?"

"I'm sorry for your misery. I don't just say that," he said, seeing her expression. "I didn't expect you today; I was working. But you know I did expect you for a long time. Every time I lay sleepless in bed I'd hear your footsteps coming up the steps to me. Every soprano who sang was you. Then I would have to say, 'It's not her.' I thought even after you were with child that you'd come to me, and I knew if you did I would have taken you back. I loved you that much."

"Do you ever think of me now?"

Again came a voice calling his name, and he replied sharply; then he turned to Aloysia, his face stiff, muttering, "I think of you, Aloysia."

"What do you think?" She reached out gently, laying her hand on his chest.

He flinched. "I think of how recklessly I loved you and how much pain it caused me, and I think *never* to experience such pain again. Life hurts so much in so many ways, I wonder how I can go forward with it."

He looked over her head at the racks of costumes. "Then I begin to think more plainly, and I wondered what there is to all this, what remedy? What recourse? And I concluded somewhere in my grief that the only recourse is to love simply, faithfully. To go home at night to someone who loves me alone and to think what I can do for her comfort and happiness. I can have that; I *will* have that. Perhaps I'll have children one day and love them the same. I was unable to give you anything that you wanted, Aloysia, except my songs. But I can assure you of this: I've stopped waiting for you at last."

"Why did you stop?"

"Because I want to be as happy as I can be; I want to love and be loved in return."

"Do you hate me?"

"I did for a time, but no more. I want your happiness."

"You want what I can't have."

"Why, my dear?"

"I don't know. What have I done? Is what we had over truly? I thought, If I wanted to enough, I could go back. And today I said, 'I want to go back; I want to begin again, and he'll be waiting for me.' Time's such an odd thing, an unreasonable thing. How can you say, 'Be happy, Aloysia!' when you withhold happiness from me? Tell me this one thing, let me smile today: Will you meet with me when you are married?"

"I'll try to be your friend. More I can't do, *won't* do. I saw your husband last week, and he said he'd like to paint me. Aloysia, do you know what you seek? You couldn't have found it with me." He reached for the door. "Look, I must go now." Pushing open the door to the gathering room, he was greeted with the smell of paint and wood, and the perfume of dozens of long white chandelier candles. Then he returned to his orchestral parts.

It was Johann Schantz, coming to replace a string in the theater fortepiano, who glimpsed Aloysia running from the theater in tears, her silk sash in her hand; she stopped and looked at him haughtily. He mentioned the scene to Thorwart, who told it to his wife; she, in turn, walked over to the boardinghouse near Peterskirche and reported that Aloysia Lange had been to see Mozart privately, that they had been closeted together for some time, and that no banging on the door could bring them out. Constanze came up from the kitchen as Maria Caecilia and Madame Thorwart were speaking. She, too, had been to the theater late that morning looking for Mozart, only to be told that he had gone away to speak privately with the beautiful singer and would not come out when they called.

To Constanze the coming of autumn was the most beautiful time of the year, with the stone buildings glowing in the late afternoon sun and the green trees drooping toward the washed cobbles. Sometimes when you turned a street corner you felt the faintest tinge of cooler weather, or saw a single tree whose leaf edges were drying. Everything was rich, heavy, and warm. The lemonade stands were crowded. Yet, she thought as she walked between Josefa and Sophie toward the theater for the performance, all my life from now on there will also be a terrible sadness for me in this time.

She understood that even with all the tenderness between her and the young composer, in his mind she had been and always would be a mere substitute for Aloysia. She had spent much of the last hours grieving alone in the sewing room and had decided that she would bid him good-bye with as much dignity as possible. She would hear the opera with whose composing she would always feel deeply connected, and she would send him word tomorrow. She would not make any kind of scene. She respected him for his hard work; she loved him for it. She was her father's daughter.

Dozens of horses and carriages were gathered before the theater, though the royal parties had not yet arrived. Constanze walked up the steps with her two sisters, and they found their places on the gilt and red-velvet-covered chairs to the left of the stage. The house was half full already with perfumed men and women, their hair powdered and jewels glistening, who came to see the first performance of the new work in the presence of the Russian Grand Duke and the Emperor himself. They could hear musicians tuning.

Constanze closed her eyes.

With the rustling of fabric and the scraping of chairs, the entire audience stood and bowed deeply toward the imperial box. The Emperor and his guests seated themselves and turned to the stage. Mozart entered in his white wig to take his place at the fortepiano. Constanze leaned forward. He's tired, she thought, but in a moment anger consumed her sympathy. The overture began, and the singers came onstage.

She had heard a great deal of *Die Entführung aus dem Serail* before, but only in pieces: arias, duets, choruses accompanied passionately on the fortepiano, the sound flowing down the steps from his rooms and pouring from his open window, accompanied by his light tenor. Now the full glory of orchestra with horns and timpani and rich singers swept over her. She clutched her fan and leaned forward still more.

The heroine and her maid had fallen to pirates and been sold to the Pasha, and their faithful lovers, a nobleman and his amusing servant, came to rescue them. Not far into the opera, the tenor began his poignant aria, whose lyrics poured through the theater with their aching repetition of the heroine's name: *Constanze, Constanze.* She could feel her sisters turn to her, and Sophie took her hand. In front of all the people in the theater, he was calling to her, and it was as if there were no one in the theater but the two of them as he declared his love.

> *"Constanze, dich wiederzusehen, dich!"*
> (Constanze, when will I see you again?)

She put her head down; had she not been seated in the middle of a row, she would have run out, weeping. *"Immer noch traurig, geliebte Constanze?"* (Are you still sad, dear Constanze?) spoke the bass voice of the Pasha. She could feel Sophie squeeze her hand hard. Each aria, duet, or chorus passed in sequence, until the great quartet when the two pairs of lovers have been reunited.

> *"Wohl, es sei nun abgetan, es lebe die Liebe!"*
> (Now let all our doubts be gone; our love will be lasting!)

The lovers are caught, and forgiven by the benevolent Pasha, then sent on their way to the joyful singing of soloists and chorus over the bright orchestra. Then it was over, and the audience broke into cheers and applause. Through her tears, Constanze saw the neat little figure with the white silky wig bowing to the audience.

"You'll wait to see him," Josefa said.

"No, I must go home."

Darkness was beginning to fall as they approached their street; looking up, they saw one of the new boarders in his shirtsleeves, gazing out over the church and smoking his pipe. They walked into the entrance of the boardinghouse. As they began to mount the long dusty carpeted stairs, they saw their mother waddle from the kitchen. "Home at last," she crowed. "Come, tell me about it; it's bound to fail. Frau Thorwart says it's too florid; I knew it."

Constanze gazed at her carefully. She frowned, and then turned to look back through the still open door toward the carriages rolling past the church. "I've been mistaken," she said quietly. "I know it in my heart; I know it. I heard it in the music. It's all wrong what people have said. I'm going to him."

"What!" her mother cried. "Are you mad? What of your reputation? Can I at least hope that you're going to tell him good-bye?"

"Mama," shouted Sophie. "It's not your concern."

Constanze ran through the streets. The lamplighters were now moving their ladders from lamp to lamp, and the beautiful stone houses glowed in the soft golden yellow light. Coming toward her were members of the opera's audience, chatting about the music and the dresses, the jewels and the hair, about the Emperor and his party, who had all gone off to a great supper where there would be woodcock and fish and wine from the vineyards that surrounded the city. Would Mozart be home yet? It was less than an hour since the opera ended, and he likely was still receiving congratulations.

The concierge was standing idly before the house in which Mozart's rooms were located. The two women nodded to each other, and Constanze creaked open the heavy door and mounted the two flights of stairs.

Mozart had just come in; his door was still ajar. He stood there in his red coat trimmed with silver lace, faint splotches of rouge still visible on his cheeks. He gazed at her, his expression blank for a moment, as if he didn't recognize her. "Come in," he said at last. "I didn't think you'd be coming. I heard what you were told. Stanzi, it isn't true. I never looked at your sister after I understood how much I loved you. You know that, don't you? You believe me?"

"Yes, I believe you."

"Thank God. I'm so tired I don't know if I have words to defend myself, not tonight anyway. I've done it; I've done it. God was with me, and I've done it. But I saw—you were there."

He moved to her side and kissed her gently several times. Leaning against him, she murmured, "The concierge knows I'm here alone with you."

"And if she does? Do we care? Do we care what anyone thinks?"

"No, not really. Not anymore. So many people were cheering for you tonight."

"I heard some of it. As I was leaving, the Archbishop's man, Count Arco, came up to me. He said he hoped Salzburg would have the pleasure of hearing my opera soon. At first I didn't even turn to him, and then I said simply, 'You were speaking to me, monsieur?'"

"I hope you *kicked* him. He's owed it."

"I would have liked to, but he is, after all, a nobleman, and I'm as common as angels, as Sophie would say. Verbally I kicked him; that must suffice."

"I'm glad I came; I'm very glad. I couldn't be happier, but now I must go."

"Don't," he said.

They stood in the room holding hands, and kissing by the light from the street. He unfastened her dress buttons and kissed her neck and shoulders, and together they moved toward the rumpled bed. His ordinary clothes were thrown on it, and she felt the buttons of his day coat when she lay down. His mouth pressed against hers, and his hands untied her bodice. The lacing snagged. Her leg was entwined with his. They felt for each other, their hands exploring more secret places than they had before. He was clumsy, and she was shy. He entered her, and she cried out when he poured himself into her.

Afterward, they lay gazing at each other in the near darkness. "You know," he whispered, "after we're married, we'll take bigger rooms on the Graben itself, the best rooms. And musicians and actors will come. It will be like your old Thursdays, but at the end of the evening I won't kiss your hand and go away but lead you to the bedroom."

Then he said seriously, "I never was with a woman before this. I hope I did well."

"I've never been with a man, but I don't think it could have been better."

"We won't wait for anyone's permission," he said. "We'll marry."

Dawn woke her, and she dressed rapidly, finding her hose curled under the bed, tying her petticoat over her shift, slipping on her bodice, lacing her skirt. She moved as softly as possible so as not to wake him. Mozart lay on his back with his arms above his head, his breath coming softly through his lips. She touched his lips and whispered in his ear. He sighed, moved to kiss her, and fell asleep again before doing so. The still gray light fell on the table containing his closed, bound opera score. She ran down the steps past the concierge, who was eating soup with a tin spoon as she surveyed the newly washed cobbles in front of the church and the faithful as they slipped inside for morning prayer.

At home Constanze could hear the clatter of breakfast dishes. She was about to rush up the steps when her mother came from the kitchen, her face pale and angry. "You come here like a whore. You've been out all night with him, haven't you? You know what he is, what all men are! I doubt he'll marry you after having gotten what he was after, but if he does, even then I won't come to your wedding."

"Then don't come," said Constanze simply, as she climbed up to her room, flung her arms around her younger sister, and told her everything.

*N*early a month had passed since the premiere of the Turkish opera, which had been performed many times; on the strength of the opera's success, several lucrative commissions, and a public concert that was already almost sold out, Mozart had taken rooms for himself and Constanze in the elegant Graben, where the world, or at least the most beautiful part of it, would pass daily beneath their windows. After predictions of hunger and infidelity, their mother came forward suddenly to help with the planning.

Josefa and Sophie sat for hours in the sewing room embroidering flowers on the yellow satin wedding dress. The wedding was to take place at Stephansdom at three o'clock on a Thursday at the end of October.

Then it was half an hour before the ceremony. Constanze, in her bedchamber and still wearing only her smock and petticoat, pulled away from Sophie and Josefa who were helping her dress and burst into tears. She had suddenly recalled being lost in the Mannheim market when she was about four years old, and wandering for what seemed like hours before her father found her sitting under the sausage vendor's stall. And then she remembered the year everyone forgot her birthday. She sobbed, "I want Papa! How do I know what marriage will be like? Sharing everything with him the way I did with you, and besides, how do I know that he'll still love me in a year or two?" She stared at both of them, tears streaming down her cheeks. "And now I've cried myself into ugliness; he won't want me when he sees me."

Sophie held the wedding dress carefully folded over her arms like an offering. "Let me bathe your eyes," she said. "All women feel this way just before they marry; everyone says it, not that I have any personal knowledge. Of course you want to marry him. Stop crying, for heaven's sake."

"But if it's horrible and wretched, I still have both of you. We could come back here as we once were, couldn't we? Couldn't we?"

"Yes, my love," Josefa replied. "We could, but do we want to? I don't think you'll want to come back anymore. Now, will you fasten your hose? Do you intend to be married in your bare feet? Blessed saints, look at the time! We'll have to run all the way."

Constanze allowed her sisters to lace up the bodice and tie on the wide yellow satin skirt that opened over the petticoat. The embroidered flowers had been sewn with varying skill by the three of them. Finally, Sophie lifted a white, broad-brimmed velvet hat from a box. "It's Aloysia's gift," she said, turning it around admiringly. "It's from Paris, truly made there. She's the only one of us who could afford it. I pinned on the flowers. Oh come, wear it! I think she wanted you to be pretty today. Yes, she'll be at the church. Just a little rouge: there! You're the loveliest woman in Vienna. Now let's go. Mother's waiting as well, and if we don't hurry she'll be back here looking for that book of suitors, which I burned weeks ago. If I ever marry, it will just have to be for love."

Constanze's hands were so cold she could hardly feel them. "Good-bye, room," she murmured. "Good-bye, childhood," and they went down the steps into the late October day.

At the cathedral she saw everything through a lace veil worked with flowers. The man wavering at the door, red faced and smiling, was Alfonso, who was to lead her to the altar. As her sisters released her and she walked forward with him, she saw through the lace the interior of the huge Gothic church, and the faces of family and friends, including her father's wretched brother, Joseph. Constanze saw her mother weeping, murmuring to those about her, "Well, all has turned out as I wished." She thought an older man smiled at her, and wondered if it were Mozart's friend Haydn. There was the violinist Heinemann, Father's old friend, come from Munich to see the marriage, but where were Mozart's father and sister? The blessing had come by mail the day before, but the father had not.

By the altar she saw Leutgeb, grinning, hands clasped before him, but Mozart was nowhere to be seen. It was only when a burst of music came from the great pipes of the organ, and Leutgeb raised his eyes to the organ loft, that Constanze understood her husband was playing for her. When the music ceased, she heard his footsteps racing down the stairs from the organ loft.

They both wept through the ceremony, particularly when they knelt for the first time as man and wife to receive holy communion. Everyone around disappeared then, so focused they were on each other. At the end he took her arm and together they walked through the group of friends and family.

"And now, my Constanze," he whispered, pressing her close, "we'll be happy forever."

They held each other, laughing and wiping away their tears, waiting at the entrance of Stephansdom for the others to come sweep them away to the marriage supper.

Sophie Weber, July 1842

MONSIEUR NOVELLO SAID ADIEU TODAY FOR THE LAST time, and I sat awhile in the dim light of my room before calling for candles. In truth, I thought at times over the past year to tell him the few things I withheld, but in the end did not. I have burned the letters from Mozart to Aloysia, which I denied having. I looked at them only once, for they were too painful. In them he asked Aloysia many times why she couldn't love him as he loved her. Constanze never saw them; there was no need for it. They would only have troubled her.

"But were they happy always and forever?" Monsieur Novello asked me a few times that afternoon as he stood with his folded writing desk in his arms, taking leave of me. I had tried to explain it to him during some of our many afternoons together. There was passion, oh yes, that. There was a lot of gaiety, and then other times there were troubles because our beloved Mozart was not quite suited to this world. There were times when Constanze was furious at him and then forgave him. It was enough to see his little shoulders under his coat, his unshaven face, his hair, in performance concealed under a white wig, brown and rumpled. His hair smelled of candlewax. She told me this. There were several children. He died young; he was thirty-five and she merely twenty-nine when she lost him.

Still I thought about Monsieur Novello's question for a long time before going to bed. Ah, sir, with all your pages of notes and inky fingers! Who can truly know all that is between man and wife? Even they sometimes do not know, but it was sweet much of the time, and more than that one cannot ask on this earth.

HISTORICAL NOTES

This novel is based on events in the life of the young Mozart.

He was closely involved with the four Weber sisters, among them Aloysia, who broke his heart, and Constanze, whom he married. We know that he and his wife were close to Sophie (he always sent kisses in his letters to her) and that he wrote some of his greatest music for Josefa.

Mozart had a hard time making a living in Vienna; acclaim for his opera *The Abduction from the Seraglio* began the short period during which he saw some prosperity. He indeed hid Constanze at the Baroness's house to protect her from her unstable mother and was horrified that she allowed a young man to measure her leg. Though some of the dates of personal and musical events have been slightly rearranged for the novel, he really was physically kicked from the palace of his Archbishop. His close friend, the horn player Leutgeb, for whom Mozart wrote much of his horn music, also had a Viennese cheese shop. After his marriage, Mozart was quite kind and generous to his difficult mother-in-law.

The Englishman Vincent Novello came to Constanze (who by then had lost her second husband) in her old age in Salzburg to gather what he could from her of Mozart's life. Sophie, also a resident of Salzburg, lived until eighty-three and was the last surviving sister.

Stephanie Cowell